THE END OF ALL THINGS

John Scalzi is one of the most popular and acclaimed SF authors to emerge in the last decade. His debut, *Old Man's War*, won him science fiction's John W. Campbell Award for Best New Writer. His *New York Times* bestsellers include *The Last Colony*, *Fuzzy Nation*, *Lock In*, and *Redshirts*, which won the 2013 Hugo Award for Best Novel. Material from his widely read blog *Whatever* (*whatever.scalzi.com*) has also earned him two other Hugo Awards. He lives in Ohio with his wife and daughter.

BY JOHN SCALZI

The Old Man's War Series

Old Man's War
The Ghost Brigades
The Last Colony
Zoe's Tale
The Human Division
The End of All Things

Other Novels

Agent to the Stars
The Android's Dream
The God Engines
Fuzzy Nation
Redshirts
Lock In

Praise for The End of All Things

ɔlished and powerful . . . Scalzi knows just how to satisfy ɪs fans, providing tense, thrilling action scenes while turning critical eye on the interstellar equivalents of the military-ɪdustrial complex'   *Publishers Weekly* (starred review)

's classic crowd-pleasing Scalzi, offering thrilling adventure ɔnes (space battles, daring military actions, parachute jumps ɪrough a planet's atmosphere), high-stakes politics, snarky ɔmmentary, and food for thought. Delightful, compulsively ɪadable, and even somewhat nutritious brain candy'
Kirkus Reviews (starred review)

ʰis is fascinating, uncharted territory for military science ɔtion . . . I can't wait to see what happens next'   *Io9*

loved returning to this universe so much. John Scalzi is a ɔad set genius and I can't wait for there to be more from this ries wherever and whenever that may be'   *PagesAndPages*

ɪnchy and cleverly executed'   *Bibliosanctum*

ɪighly enjoyable book, and a must for all Scalzi fans'
Space and Sorcery

ɔ *End of all Things* will satisfy not only those genre fans but vone looking for an entertaining and thrilling read'
Last Bookstore

'Written in Scalzi's customary breezy style with plenty of sarcasm and verbal jousting, Scalzi delivers another fun, interesting book that explores the implications of intergalactic space relations'   *EMissourian*

THE END
OF ALL THINGS

John Scalzi

TOR

First published 2015 by Tom Doherty Associates, LLC

First published in the UK 2015 by Tor

This paperback edition published 2016 by Tor
an imprint of Pan Macmillan
20 New Wharf Road, London N1 9RR
Associated companies throughout the world
www.panmacmillan.com

ISBN 978-1-4472-9050-6

1 3 5 7 9 8 6 4 2

A CIP catalogue record for this book is available from the British Library.

Printed and bound by CPI Group (UK) Ltd, Croydon, CR0 4YY

Visit **www.panmacmillan.com** to read more about all our books
and to buy them. You will also find features, author interviews and
news of any author events, and you can sign up for e-newsletters
so that you're always first to hear about our new releases.

To Jay and Mary Vernau, of Jay and Mary's Book Center of Troy, Ohio;

To Alan Beatts and Jude Feldman of Borderlands Books of San Francisco, California;

To Duane Wilkins and Olivia Ahl of University Bookstore, University of Washington;

And to all the booksellers who have shared my work with the readers in their stores.

You are the best. This one is for you, with thanks.

Contents

THE LIFE OF THE MIND

To my friend John Anderson, dearly departed, and to all who were friends with him.

Let the music play.

PART ONE

So, I'm supposed to tell you how I became a brain in a box.

Huh. Well, that starts off a little *dark*, doesn't it.

Also, I don't really know, technically, how they did it to me. It's not like once I woke up as a disembodied brain they showed me an informational video about how they did it, just in case I was curious. *Here's the part where we snipped off all the blood vessels and peripheral nerves,* the video would say. *Here's how we removed the skull and spinal column, and here's how we stuffed your brain full of nifty little sensors to track your thoughts. Pay attention, there's a test later.*

Jesus, I'm really bad at this.

I'm not a writer or an orator. I'm not a storyteller. I'm a spaceship pilot, so let me just get that right out there. The Colonial Union asked me to tell what happened to me because they think that information will be useful to them. Fine, I'll do it, happy to help. But it's not going to be, you know, classic literature. It's going to skip around. I'm going to get lost telling the story and come back to points and then get lost again. I'm doing this off the top of my head.

Well, metaphorically. I don't have a head anymore. Pretty sure they tossed my head into an incinerator or something.

See what I mean?

Someone's going to have to edit this if it's going to make any sense at all. So to you poor anonymous Colonial Union editor: I salute you and I apologize to you. I'm not trying to make your life difficult, I swear. I just don't know what they really want, or how they want me to do it.

Just tell us everything, I was told. Get it all down. Don't worry. We'll sort it out. Which I guess is where you come in, anonymous editor. Happy sorting.

And if you're reading this: I'm sure the editor did an excellent job.

Where to start this damn thing? I don't think any of you will give a crap about my childhood; it was standard-issue pretty happy, mostly noneventful, with decent parents and friends. Schooling likewise unremarkable with all the usual bits of stupidity and libidinousness with occasional moments of cramming for tests. Honestly, no one will want to hear about any of that. I hardly do and I lived it.

So, I think I'll start at the job interview.

Yes, that's a good place to start. The interview that gave me the job that turned me into a headless wonder.

In retrospect, I kind of wish I hadn't of gotten the gig.

Oh, and maybe I should say what my name is. Just for the record.

It's Rafe. Rafe Daquin.

I'm Rafe Daquin, and I'm a brain in a box.

Hi.

The reason I got the interview at all was because of a university friend of mine, Hart Schmidt. He works as a Colonial Union diplomat, which I always thought was the very definition of a thankless job, and in some recent downtime was in a bar on Phoenix Station and talking to the executive officer of the *Chandler*, a cargo hauler doing a standard triangle run between Phoenix, Huckleberry, and Erie. Not exactly a prestige job, but a gig is a gig. They can't all be glamour postings.

Anyway, in conversation the XO was griping about how when they got to Phoenix Station the *Chandler* was met by a bunch of law enforcement types. Seems one of the *Chandler*'s pilots had a little side thing going, down on the actual planet of Phoenix, the details of which I'm still a little hazy on but which involved blackmail, intimidation, graft, and bigamy, the last of these being one not so much like the others. The point was the *Chandler* was now down a pilot and needed one, fast.

Which was nice, because I was a pilot, and I needed a job. Also fast.

"This tells me you were a programmer before you were a pilot," the XO said, as he looked at my work history. We were in a burger joint on Phoenix Station; I had hauled my ass up from the planet as soon as Hart told me about the gig. The burgers were legend, but I wasn't really there for the culinary thrills. The XO's name was Lee Han and he had the look of someone who was going through the motions. I had a feeling that as long as I didn't admit to murdering adorable kittens in front of children, I was going to get the gig.

"I went to school for computer engineering," I said. "Graduated and did that and programming for a couple of years. Worked for Eyre Systems, mostly on starship navigation and maintenance software. You might have one of our setups on the *Chandler*."

"We do," Han said.

"I can throw in some technical support," I said. It was a joke.

I'm not entirely sure Han got that. "It's not the usual move from programming to piloting," he said.

"It's the programming that got me interested in piloting," I said. "I was one of the programmers who had some semblance of social skills, so eventually I was assigned to go up to Phoenix Station and work on ships to customize the software. So I spent a lot of time in ships and talking to crew and listening to them talk about where they've been in the universe. You do that long enough and just sitting at a desk pushing code seems like a way to spend a lot of time wasting your life. I wanted to see what was out there. So I hustled my way into an apprentice piloting gig. That was seven years ago."

"Not exactly an upward move, paywise," Han said.

I shrugged. I figured that the shrug would come across as a casual and cool *Hey, some things are more important than money* rather than *Hey, I'm living with my parents who are beginning to resent that fact so I will take what I can get.* Anyway both were true. Lots of things can be more important than money when you lacked other options.

Not to paint my parents as the bad people here. It's just that they had made it clear that it was one thing to support me while I was working my way up a ladder, and another thing to support a thirty-two-year-old human while I was sitting on my ass at home between gigs. Maybe they wouldn't let me starve, but they weren't going to make me comfortable.

Which was fine. I wasn't out of work because I was lazy.

"Says here you've been out of work for the last nine months," Han said.

"I've been between ships, yes," I said.

"Want to explain that?" Han asked.

Well, there was no way around that one. "I'm being blackballed," I said.

"By whom?"

"By Captain Werner Ostrander of the *Lastan Falls.*"

I thought I saw a faint smile on Han's lips when I said this. "Go on," he said.

"There's not much to say," I said. "I was second pilot on the *Baikal* and the first pilot wasn't going anywhere anytime soon, so when I heard there was an opportunity to move up to first pilot on the *Lastan,* I took it. What I didn't know was that there was a reason why the *Lastan* had gone through six pilots in two years, and by the time I found out it was too late. I ended up breaking my contract."

"That must have been expensive."

"It was worth every penny," I said. "Also, as I was leaving the ship I dropped my mother's name to the chief steward. My mother's a labor lawyer. The class action suit against Ostrander that followed was, shall we say, *very* satisfying."

Han definitely smiled at that.

"But it also meant that Ostrander now goes out of his way to warn off anyone I try to get a pilot's job with," I said. "No one likes a troublemaker."

"No, no one does," Han agreed, and inside I groaned, because I figured this was where I just blew the gig. "But then, I crewed on the *Lastan Falls* for a year, early in my career."

I blinked. "You did?" I said.

"Yes," Han said. "Let's just say I can understand wanting to break your contract. And also that at some point I want to hear the details of that suit."

I grinned. "You got it, sir," I said.

"I'm going to be blunt, Mr. Daquin, this position is a step back for you," Han said. "It's third pilot, and it's a straight bread-and-butter trade run. We go here, we go to Huckleberry, we go to Erie, we repeat. It's not exciting, and just like the *Baikal,* there's little chance for advancement."

"Let me be equally blunt, sir," I said. "I've spent nine months at the bottom of a gravity well. You know as well as I do that if I spend too much more time there, I'm going to get stuck. You need another pilot right now so you don't lose time and money on your trade run. I get that. I need to get off the rock so I can have another shot at first pilot somewhere else without Ostrander's blackball over my head. I figure we're both in a spot and can help each other out."

"I just wanted to be sure everyone's expectations were in order," Han said.

"I have no illusions, sir."

"Good. Then I can give you a day to close out your business here."

I reached down and patted the crew bag at my feet. "Business closed. The only thing I have to do is find my friend Hart and buy him a drink for setting up this interview."

"If you can do that quickly there'll be a shuttle to the *Chandler* at gate thirty-six in a couple of hours."

"I'll be on it, sir," I said.

"Well, then," Han said, stood up, and extended his hand. "Welcome to the *Chandler*, pilot."

I took the hand. "Thank you, sir. Glad to be aboard."

I found Hart a half hour later, on the other side of Phoenix Station, in a reception for his boss, Ambassador Abumwe.

"She got the Meritorious Service Award," Hart said. He was on his second glass of spiked punch and he was never one who held his alcohol very well, so he was on his way to being a little tipsy. He was also dressed in a formal diplomatic uniform. I thought it made him look like a doorman. But then I had just spent the better part of the year in sweatpants, so who the hell was I to say.

"What did she do that was meritorious?" I asked.

"She kept her entire staff alive while Earth Station was being attacked, for starters," Hart said. "You heard about Earth Station?"

I nodded. The Colonial Union was pretty good at keeping bad news from reaching the civilians of the colonies, but some pieces of news are harder to hide than others. For example, the news that the Earth's sole space station was destroyed by unknown terrorists, killing thousands including the cream of the Earth's diplomatic corps, and that the Earth blamed the Colonial Union for the attack and severed all diplomatic and economic ties.

Yeah, that one was a little hard to hide.

The Colonial Union's official story about it, said only that it had been a terrorist attack; the rest of it I had filled in from former shipmates and friends like Hart. When you live at the bottom of a gravity well, you only tend to hear the official story. The people who actually move between the stars, on the other hand, hear a lot more. It's hard to sell the official story to people who can see things for themselves.

"Some people saved themselves," said Harry Wilson, a friend of Hart's who he'd just introduced to me. Wilson was a member of the Colonial Defense Forces; his green skin gave him away. That and the fact that he looked the same age as my kid brother, but was probably something like 120 years old. Having a genetically modified, not-quite-human body had certain advantages, as long as you didn't mind being the same color as guacamole. "Your friend Hart here, for example. He got himself to an escape pod and ditched from Earth Station as it was literally blowing up around him."

"A slight exaggeration," Hart said.

"No, it actually was literally blowing up around you," Wilson said.

Hart waved him off and looked back over to me. "Harry's making it sound more dramatic than it was."

"It sounds pretty dramatic," I admitted.

"Space station *blowing up around him*," Wilson said again, emphasizing the last part.

"I was unconscious for most of the trip down to Earth," Hart said. "I think that's probably a good thing."

I nodded toward Ambassador Abumwe, who I recognized from pictures, and who was on the other side of the reception hall, shaking hands with well-wishers in a receiving line. "How was the ceremony?"

"Painful," Wilson said.

"It was all right," Hart said.

"*Painful*," Wilson repeated. "The guy who gave out the medal—"

"Assistant Secretary of State Tyson Ocampo," Hart said.

"—was a fatuous gasbag," Wilson continued. "I've met a lot of people in the diplomatic corps who were in love with the sound of their own voice, but this guy. He and his voice should just get a room."

"It wasn't that bad," Hart said to me.

"You saw Abumwe's face while that dude was going on," Wilson said, to Hart.

"Ocampo," Hart said, clearly pained that the assistant secretary of state was being referred to as "that dude." "The number two man in the department. And there was nothing going on with her face," Hart said.

"She was definitely wearing her 'please shut the hell up,' face," Wilson said, to me. "Trust me, I have seen it many times."

I looked over to Hart. "It's true," he said. "Harry has seen the ambassador's 'shut up' face more than most."

"Speak of the devil," Wilson said, and motioned slightly with his head. "Look who's coming this way." I glanced over and saw a middle-aged man in a resplendent Colonial Union diplomatic uniform, followed by a young woman, heading our direction.

"The fatuous gasbag?" I asked.

"Secretary *Ocampo*," Hart said, emphatically.

"Same thing," Wilson said.

"Gentlemen," Ocampo said, coming up to us.

"Hello, Secretary Ocampo," Wilson said, very smoothly, and I thought I saw Hart relax maybe a tiny bit. "What may we do for you, sir?"

"Well, since you're standing between me and the punch, perhaps you would be so kind as to get me a cup," he said.

"Let me get that for you," Hart said, and nearly dropped his own glass in the process.

"Thank you," Ocampo said. "Schmidt, yes? One of Abumwe's people." He then turned to Wilson. "And you are?"

"Lieutenant Harry Wilson."

"Really," Ocampo said, and sounded impressed. "You're the

one who saved the daughter of the secretary of state of the United States when Earth Station was destroyed."

"Danielle Lowen," Wilson said. "And yes. She's a diplomat in her own right, of course."

"Of course," Ocampo said. "But the fact that she's Secretary Lowen's daughter didn't hurt. It's one reason why the U.S. is one of the few countries on Earth that will speak to the Colonial Union in any capacity."

"I'm happy to be useful, sir," Wilson said. Hart handed him his punch.

"Thank you," Ocampo said, to Hart, and then turned his attention back to Wilson. "I understand you also skydived from Earth Station all the way down to Earth with Miss Lowen."

"That's correct, sir," Wilson said.

"That must have been some experience."

"I mostly remember trying not to go 'splat' at the end of it."

"Of course," Ocampo said. He turned to me next, registering my lack of dress uniform and the crew bag at my feet, and waited for me to identify myself.

"Rafe Daquin," I said, taking the hint. "I'm crashing the party, sir."

"He's a friend of mine who happened to be on station," Hart said. "He's a pilot on a trade ship."

"Oh," Ocampo said. "Which one?"

"The *Chandler*," I said.

"Isn't that interesting," Ocampo said. "I've booked passage on the *Chandler*."

"You have?" I asked.

"Yes. It's been a few years since I've taken a vacation and I decided to take a month to hike the Connecticut mountains on Huckleberry. That's the *Chandler*'s next destination, unless I'm mistaken," Ocampo said.

"You could just take a department ship, I would think," I said.

Ocampo smiled. "It would look bad to commandeer a State Department ship as a personal taxi, I'm afraid. As I understand it the *Chandler* lets out a couple of staterooms for passengers. I and Vera here," he nodded toward his assistant, "have taken them. How are they?"

"The staterooms?" I asked. Ocampo nodded. "I'm not sure."

"Rafe has just been hired as of about an hour ago," Hart said. "He hasn't even been on the ship yet. He's taking a shuttle over in about an hour."

"That's the same shuttle you'll be on, sir," Vera said to Ocampo.

"So we'll experience it for the first time together," the secretary said, to me.

"I suppose that's true," I said. "If you would like I would be happy to escort you and your assistant to the shuttle gate, when you're ready to depart."

"Thank you, I'd appreciate that," Ocampo said. "I'll have Vera tell you when we're ready. Until then, gentlemen." He nodded and wandered off with his punch, Vera following behind.

"Very diplomatic," Wilson said to me, once he was gone.

"You jumped out of an exploding space station?" I said to him, changing the subject.

"It wasn't exploding that much when I jumped," Wilson said.

"And you got out in an escape pod just in time," I said to Hart. "I'm clearly in the wrong line of space travel for excitement."

"Trust me," Wilson said. "You don't want that much excitement."

The *Chandler,* as advertised, was not exciting.

But it's not supposed to be. I said before that the *Chandler* had blocked out a triangle run. That means that you have three destinations, all of which want something that's made and exported on the previous planet. So, for example, Huckleberry is a colony that's largely agrarian—a large percentage of the land mass there is in a temperate zone that's great for human crops. We take things like wheat, corn, and gaalfruit and a few other crops and take them to Erie. Erie colonists pay a premium for Huckleberry agricultural products, because, I don't know, I think they think they're healthier or something. Whatever reason, they want 'em so we take them there. In return we load up on all sorts of rare earth metals, which Erie has lots of.

We take those to Phoenix, which is the center of high-technology manufacturing for the Colonial Union. And from there, we get things like medical scanners and PDAs and everything else it's cheaper to mass produce and ship than try to put together yourselves in a home printer, and take those to Huckleberry, whose technology manufacturing base is pretty small. Wash, rinse, repeat. As long as you're working the triangle in the right direction, you'll get rich.

But it's not exciting, for whatever definition of "exciting" you want to have. These three colonies are well established and protected; Huckleberry's the youngest and it's nearly a century old at this point, and Phoenix is the oldest and best defended of any of the Colonial Union planets. So you're not exploring new worlds by trading there. You're unlikely to run into pirates or other bad people. You're not meeting strange new aliens, or really any aliens at all. You're shipping food, ore, and gadgets. This isn't the romance of space. This is you and space in a nice, comfortable rut.

But again, I didn't give a crap about any of that. I'd seen enough of space and had the occasional bit of excitement; when I was on the *Baikal*, we were pursued for four days by pirates and eventually had to ditch our cargo. They don't chase you anymore when you do that because then you have nothing they want. Usually. Sometimes when you ditch your cargo they get pissed off and then try to send a missile into your engines to register their displeasure.

So, yeah. As Harry Wilson suggested, excitement can be overrated.

Anyway, right now I didn't want exciting. What I wanted was to work. If that meant babysitting the *Chandler*'s navigational system while it crunched data for a run that it had done a thousand times before, that was fine by me. At the end of the stint I'd have the blackball off my career. That was also fine by me.

The *Chandler* itself was your basic cargo hauler, which is to say a former Colonial Defense Forces frigate, repurposed for cargo and trade. There were purpose-built cargo haulers, of course, but they were expensive and tended to be built and used by large shipping lines. The *Chandler* was the sole ship owned by its small consortium of owners. They got the obsolete frigate that became the *Chandler* at an auction.

When I did my research of the *Chandler* before the interview (always do your research; I didn't with the *Lastan Falls* and it cost me), I saw pictures of the frigate at the auction, where it was sold "as-is." Somewhere along the way it had gotten the living crap beat out of it. But refurbished, it had been doing its run for almost two decades. I figured it wouldn't accidentally spill me into space.

I took the shuttle ride with Secretary Ocampo and his aide (whose last name I finally learned was Briggs; that came from the crew and passenger manifest, not from the secretary), and said good-bye to them at the ship. Then I reported to Han and my immediate boss, First Pilot Clarine Bolduc, and then to Quartermaster Seidel, who assigned me quarters. "You're in luck," she said. "You get private quarters. At least until we hit Erie, when we take on some new crew. Then you'll get two roommates. Enjoy your privacy while you can."

I went to my quarters and they were the size of a broom closet. Technically you could fit three people in it. But you wouldn't want to close the door or you'd run out of oxygen. I got to pick my bunk, though, so I had that going for me.

At evening mess Bolduc introduced me around to the other officers and department heads.

"You're not going to be running any scams in your spare time?" asked Chieko Tellez, who was assistant cargo chief, as I sat down with my tray.

"I did a thorough background check," Han said, to her. "He's clean."

"I'm joking," Tellez said, to Han. She turned back to me. "You know about the guy you're replacing, right?"

"I heard a little about it," I said.

"A shame," Tellez said. "He was a nice guy."

"As long as you're willing to overlook corruption, graft, and bigamy," Bolduc said.

"He never did any of that to me, and that's what really counts," Tellez said, and then glanced over at me, smiling.

"I can't tell whether you're joking or not," I admitted.

"Chieko is never not joking," Bolduc said. "And now you know."

"Some of us like a little humor," Tellez said, to Bolduc.

"Joking is not the same thing as humor," Bolduc said.

"Hmph," Tellez said. It didn't look like she was particularly put out by the comment. I figured she and Bolduc ribbed each other on a frequent basis, which was not a bad thing. Officers who got on okay were a sign of a happy ship.

Tellez turned her attention back to me. "You came over on the shuttle with those State Department mucky-mucks, right?"

"I did," I said.

"Did they say why they were on the ship?"

"Secretary Ocampo is going on vacation on Huckleberry," I said. "We're headed that way so he and his aide rented a couple of spare staterooms."

"If I were him I would have just taken a department ship," Bolduc said.

"He said it wouldn't look very good if he did," I said.

"I'm sure he's actually worried about that," Bolduc said.

"Seidel said that Ocampo told her that he wanted to travel inconspicuously and without having to feel like he was dragging his title around," Han said.

"Do you believe that?" Bolduc asked. Han shrugged. Bolduc then turned to me. "You talked to him, yeah?"

"Sure," I said.

"That sound reasonable to you?"

I thought back on what Wilson said about Ocampo being in love with the sound of his own voice, and thought about the shuttle ride, after the polite conversation was over, listening to Ocampo dictating notes to Vera Briggs. "He doesn't strike me as the kind who prefers to be inconspicuous, no," I said.

"Maybe he's just screwing his aide and wants to be inconspicuous about *that*," Tellez said.

"No, that's not it," I said.

"Explain," Tellez said.

I shrugged. "I didn't get that vibe from either of them."

"And how is your vibe sense in general, Daquin?"

"It's all right."

"What's your *vibe* about me?" Tellez asked.

"You have a quirky sense of humor," I said.

"His vibe sense works just fine," Bolduc said.

Tellez shot a look at Bolduc, who ignored it. "Why would anyone vacation on Huckleberry anyway?" she said. "We've been to Huckleberry. A lot. There's nothing there worth a vacation."

"He said he wanted to hike the Connecticut mountains," I said. "Whatever those are."

"I hope he packed a jacket," Han said. "The Connecticuts are a polar range, and it's winter for Huckleberry's northern hemisphere."

"He had several trunks," I said. "His aide Vera complained that he brought three times the clothing he'd need. There's probably a jacket or two in there."

"Let's hope so," Han said. "Otherwise, he's in for a disappointing vacation."

But as it turned out there was no vacation at all.

I looked up from my chair and saw Captain Thao and Lee Han looking down at me, Thao with a severely pissed-off look on her face, and my first thought was, *Shit, I don't even know what I did wrong this time.*

My second thought was to be confused as to why I was seeing her at all. I was third pilot, which meant I got the shifts where the captain was usually not on deck; she was usually sleeping or tending to other ship duties when I was in the pilot's chair. For the three days I'd been piloting, XO Han sat in the command chair while I sat in mine, and we did a whole lot of nothing—the course from Phoenix Station to our skip point was plotted for us by Phoenix Station and all I had to do was make sure we didn't drift for one reason or another.

We hadn't. I could have napped through all of my shifts and it would have had the same effect.

We were twelve hours out from skip. At that time the captain would be in the chair, Bolduc would be piloting with Second Pilot Schreiber assisting, and with any luck I would be asleep in my bunk. Having the captain on deck now meant something was out of whack; that she was standing over my chair said maybe what was out of whack had to do with me. What it was I had no idea. Like I said, we were exactly where we needed to be for the skip. There was literally nothing I could have been doing wrong.

"Yes, ma'am?" I said. When in doubt, be ready to take an order.

Captain Thao held out a memory card. I looked at it, stupidly. "It's a memory card," I said.

"I know what it is," Captain Thao said. "I need you to help me with it."

"All right," I said. "How?"

"You worked on the piloting systems as a programmer, yes? Lee tells me you did."

"I did several years ago," I said, glancing over at Han, whose expression was blank.

"So you know how it works."

"I haven't worked on the code for the most recent versions of the software, but it's built using the same language and compilers," I said. "I wouldn't have a problem catching up on it."

"The piloting system has the ability to accept encoded commands, yes? Destinations can be plugged in without openly revealing what they are."

"Sure," I said. "That's a standard feature. It was put into military piloting software so if a ship or drone is captured, it'd be harder for whoever captured it to find out its destination. We don't usually use the secure mode on trade ships because there's no point. We have to file courses with the Colonial Union anyway. They know where we're going."

"I have an encrypted destination on this memory card," Thao said. "Can you tell me where it is?"

"No," I said. "It's encrypted." And then I realized that it was entirely possible that last comment came out in my "condescending nerd" voice, so I quickly added to it. "What I mean is that I would need the encryption key for it. I don't have it."

"The system has it," Thao said.

"Right, but the system doesn't tell *us* what it is," I said. "The point of the secure mode is to let the navigation computer and only the navigation computer know where the ship is going."

"Could you crack it without a key?"

"The encryption?" I asked. Thao nodded. "How much time do I have?"

"How long until skip?"

I checked my monitor. "Twelve hours, twenty-three minutes."

"That long."

"No," I said. "If you gave me a month I could maybe do it. Or if I had passwords or biometrics or whatever it was that let whoever gave you that memory card into the encryption system in the first place." I motioned to the card. "Was that encrypted on the *Chandler*?"

"No."

"I would need more time than we have, then, ma'am."

Captain Thao nodded, moody, and looked over to Han.

"May I ask what's going on, ma'am?" I said.

"No," Captain Thao said. She reached out to me with the memory card. "I need you to put this new destination into the navigation system. Let Han know when you've done it and the new destination is confirmed."

I took the card. "It'll take about a minute and a half," I said.

"Fine," Thao said. "Tell Han anyway." She left without saying anything else. I looked over at Han. He was still working on his utterly neutral face.

"Mr. Daquin," Secretary Ocampo said, as he opened the door to his stateroom and saw me standing on the other side of it. "This is unexpected. Come inside, please." He stood aside to let me in.

I entered the stateroom, which was roughly twice the size of my own, which is to say, the size of two broom closets. A lot of the space was taken up by Ocampo's luggage, which was, as Vera Briggs hinted, a lot for a month-long trip. But Ocampo struck me as a likely candidate for being a clotheshorse, so maybe that volume of luggage wasn't unusual for him.

"I apologize for it being cramped," Ocampo said.

"It's bigger than my quarters," I said.

"I would hope so!" Ocampo said, and then laughed. "No offense," he said, afterwards.

"None taken," I said.

"We're fortunate Vera isn't in here as well, we might not be able to move," Ocampo said, and sat in the chair next to his very small table. "Now, let me guess why you're here, Mr. Daquin. I'm guessing that sometime in the last few hours, your captain came to you with a new destination, is that correct?"

"It might be," I said.

"Might be indeed," Ocampo replied. "And this new destination is secret, and now I strongly suspect that you and the rest of the *Chandler* crew are having a merry little time speculating about where this destination is, why we might be going there, and why your captain is following an order that no one should have been able to give her. Is that about right?"

"That's about the size of it, yes."

"And I bet you were volunteered by the rest of the crew to come see me about it, because you and I shared a boat ride over to the *Chandler*."

"No, sir," I said. "You're right that the crew is talking about it. But none of them put me up to this. I came on my own."

"That's either initiative or stupidity, Mr. Daquin."

"Yes, sir."

"Maybe a little of both."

"That's equally possible, sir."

Ocampo laughed. "You understand that if I can't tell your captain where we're going, I'm not going to be able to tell you."

"I understand that," I said. "I'm not here about the 'what,' sir. I'm here about the 'why.' "

"The why," Ocampo said.

"Yes," I said. "As in why the number two person in all of the Colonial Union State Department is pretending to go on vacation to an arctic mountain range and using a cargo ship to get there, instead of just taking a State Department ship with a formal diplomatic mission on it to wherever and whomever he is meeting and negotiating with."

"Well," Ocampo said, after a moment. "And here I thought I was being clever about it."

"You were, sir," I said. "But it looks different inside the ship than out of it."

"Fair enough. Have a seat, Daquin," Ocampo said, motioning to his bunk. I sat. "Let's talk theoretical scenarios for a moment. Are you okay with that?"

"Sure," I said.

"What do you know about how the Colonial Union is doing these days?"

"I know we're not on very good terms with the Earth anymore."

Ocampo snorted. "You've unintentionally made the understatement of the year. It's more accurate to say the Earth hates the Colonial Union's guts, thinks we are evil, and wants us all to die. They blame us for the destruction of Earth Station, which was their major egress into space. They think we did it."

"And we didn't."

"No, of course not. But many of the ships used in the attack were pirated from the Colonial Union. You've heard about that, at least? Cargo ships like this one being captured and turned into attack vehicles?"

I nodded. This was one of the more wild rumors out there—that pirates, or someone posing as pirates, would take and board ships, but instead of the cargo, they were after the ships themselves. They would use the ships to attack targets in the Colonial Union and in the Conclave, a big political union of alien races.

I thought it was wild because it didn't make much sense. Not that the ships were taken; I knew that was true. Everyone in space knows someone whose ship was lost. But it didn't make sense to use cargo ships as attack platforms. There were easier ways to strike both the Colonial Union and the Conclave.

But now Ocampo was telling me that part wasn't just a rumor. That these things were happening. One more reason, I guess, to be glad to be doing a trade run safely inside the Colonial Union's borders.

Except now we weren't doing that safe trade run anymore.

"Because the ships were originally from the Colonial Union, it looks like the Colonial Union attacked," Ocampo said. "And so our diplomatic relations with nearly every nation on Earth are entirely shut off. Even those we're not entirely shunned by we still have to be very careful approaching. Understand me so far?"

I nodded again.

Ocampo nodded in response. "In which case, Mr. Daquin, ask yourself: If the number two man of the Colonial Union State Department wanted to pry open diplomatic relations with the Earth, even just a crack, in a way that didn't immediately require everyone involved to strike a political pose, how might he do it?"

"By pretending to go on vacation but actually commandeering a trade ship to take him to an unofficial meeting at a secret destination, perhaps," I said.

"That might be one way, yes," Ocampo agreed.

"But he would still need to convince that ship's captain."

"Convincing takes on many forms," Ocampo said. "One form might be an official request from the Colonial Union itself, the refusal of which would cause the ship in question to be refused dock at any space station the Colonial Union controls. Which would be all of them, in Colonial Union space."

"And the refusal would happen because the captain didn't play ball."

"Well, officially there would be all sorts of reasons given,"

Ocampo said. "It would vary from station to station and from circumstance to circumstance. But in reality, it would be the Colonial Union expressing its displeasure at the lack of cooperation, yes."

"I don't imagine the captain would be happy about that."

"No, probably not," Ocampo agreed.

"There's also the problem that the ship, and its owners and crew, would take a loss because their trade route was messed with."

"If something like that were to happen, in theory, the ship, and its owners and crew, would be fully compensated by the Colonial Union for any losses, with additional compensation for time and other incurred expenses."

"Really."

"Oh, yes," Ocampo said. "And now you know why it doesn't happen very often. It's expensive as hell."

"And you told the captain all this."

"I might have," Ocampo said. "But if I did, I don't imagine it made her any happier. No captain likes being ordered about on her own ship. But at this point there's nothing to be done for it. How do *you* feel about it, Mr. Daquin?"

"I don't know. Better, I suppose, because I have some idea what's going on. At least, if what you're telling me is accurate, sir."

"I haven't told you anything, Mr. Daquin," Ocampo said. "We're just having a conversation about possibilities. And this seems like a reasonable possibility to me. Does it seem like a reasonable possibility to you?"

I thought it did.

The next day, I got shot in the head.

Before that happened, though, I fell out of my bunk.

The falling out of the bunk was not the important part. The important part was how I fell out of it. I was shoved—or more accurately, the *Chandler* was shoved, and I pretty much stayed where I was. Which meant one second I had a bunk under me and the next second I didn't, and then I was tumbling through the air, toward a bulkhead.

When this was happening I had two thoughts. The first thought, which if I'm truthful about it took up most of my brain, was *Whaaaaaa*, because first I was airborne, and then I smacked into the wall.

The second thought, in the part of my brain that wasn't freaking out, was that something serious had happened to the ship. The artificial gravity field on the *Chandler* and nearly all space ships is incredibly robust—it has to be, or even simple acceleration would turn human bodies into jelly. It also acts to dampen skew and yaw inside a ship. It takes a lot of energy, basically, to shove a ship so hard that people fall out of their bunks.

There was also the fact that while I was shoved out of my bunk, I wasn't falling. Which meant the artificial gravity wasn't working. Something happened to knock it out.

Conclusion: We either hit something or were hit by something.

Which meant that the part of my brain that was previously going *Whaaaaaa* was now going, *Oh shit we're all gonna die, we're dead we're dead we're so fucking dead.*

And then the lights went out.

All of this took maybe a second.

The good news is I peed before going to sleep.

Then the emergency lights clicked on, as did the emergency gravity, rated at .2 standard G. It wasn't a lot, and it wouldn't be on for long. The whole point of it was to give the crew enough time to strap things down and lock them away. Everything that had been previously flying around in my quarters—toothpaste tubes, unhampered clothes, me—began to settle to the floor. I touched down, quickly put on some pants, and opened the door to my room.

And immediately saw Chieko Tellez running down the hall.

"What happened?" I asked.

"Power's out," she said as she passed me. "We skipped and then the power went bye-bye."

"Yeah, but how?"

"Hey, man, I'm just a cargo monkey," she said. "You're bridge crew. *You* tell *me*." And then she was gone.

She had a point. I started on my way to the bridge.

Along the way I saw Secretary Ocampo, who looked mussed and like he hadn't gotten much sleep. "What's going on?" he asked.

"Power's out."

"How'd that happen?"

I just had this conversation, on the other side. "I'm heading to the bridge to find out."

Ocampo nodded. "I'll come with you." I didn't think this was a particularly great idea, but I just nodded and kept going, assuming that Ocampo was following me.

The bridge was busy but controlled. The first-shift bridge crew were at their stations, offering up status reports to Thao, who took them in and asked questions. I nodded to Ocampo, who had indeed followed me in, and then went over to Han.

"You're not on duty," he said to me as I came up.

"Thought you might want some help."

"We already have a pilot." Han nodded to Bolduc.

"Available for other things."

"Fine," Han said. "See if Womack needs help with the sensors." I headed over to Sherita Womack, handling the sensors. Han then turned his attention to Ocampo. "You're not part of this crew, Secretary Ocampo. You're officially in the way."

"Thought I might be useful," Ocampo said.

"You're not," Han said. "Go back to your stateroom."

"Belay that," Thao said, turning to the conversation. "I want him here. I've got questions for him, and he damn well better have answers for me. Don't you move, Secretary."

"I'm at your service, Captain," Ocampo said.

Thao said nothing to this, and switched her attention to Womack. "Sensors. Report. Tell me if we hit anything coming out of skip."

"Doesn't appear so, ma'am," Womack said. "If we hit anything, we'd probably be dead."

"Depends on the size of what we hit," I said. "We get peppered with tiny bits of dust all the time."

"Those aren't going to knock out our power," Womack said. "They're not going to shift us off course, either."

"How far have we shifted?" Thao asked.

Womack shrugged. "Can't give you a precise reading because our inertial sensors are screwed up. So are our outside sensors. I can't tell you what's out there, ma'am."

"Anything before the sensors went out?"

"Nothing pinged," Womack said. "One second there's nothing but vacuum and the next we're jolted and our power is screwed." Womack stopped talking and frowned at something in her diagnostics screen. I craned my head in to look.

"What is it?" Thao asked.

"The diagnostics say the outside sensors should be working fine," I said, going off the readings on the screen.

"But we're not getting anything from them," Womack said. "Communications should also be working but I'm getting nothing."

"We're being jammed, maybe," I said.

"I think so," Womack said, and looked over to Thao.

The bridge went silent at this. Thao nodded at the report and then turned her attention back to Ocampo. "You want to explain this?" she said.

"I can't," Ocampo said.

"You said that you were meeting diplomats from Earth."

"Earth and the Conclave both, yes," Ocampo said. This was slightly different than what he told me, but then he said he wasn't actually telling me anything, so.

"Why would *diplomats* want to jam our sensors?" Thao asked.

"They wouldn't," Ocampo said. "This is where we're supposed to meet. They knew I was coming and they knew I was coming on this ship. They know we're not a threat."

"And yet our sensors are jammed and we're sitting here blind," Thao said.

"It could be pirates," Han said.

"No," Thao said. "Pirates follow trade routes. This isn't a trade route. We followed a route to a secret location only Secretary Ocampo's diplomat friends would know we'd be at. Isn't that right, Ocampo? Isn't this trip supposed to be *top secret*?" The sarcasm of those last two words coming out of the captain's mouth was unmistakable.

Ocampo looked uncomfortable with this line of questioning. "Information about the Colonial Union's diplomatic missions has been leaky in the last year," he said, finally.

"What does that mean?" asked Thao.

"It means that the State Department might have a problem with spies," Ocampo said. "I made every precaution so this information would be secure. Apparently it wasn't enough."

"You have spies?" Thao said. "Spies for whom? The Conclave? Earth?"

"Either," Ocampo said. "Or spies for someone else."

"Who else?"

Ocampo shrugged at this. Thao shot him a look that was a textbook example of disgust. Then she turned back to Womack and me. "There was nothing on the sensors before the power went out."

"No, ma'am," Womack said. "Nothing but clear space to the skip point."

"Outside sensors still down."

"Yes, ma'am," Womack said. "They should be working fine. They're just not. I can't tell you why."

Thao turned to Han. "Tell someone to go to an airlock and look out the goddamned portal, please," she said.

Han nodded and spoke briefly into a headset; presumably somewhere belowdecks a crew member was heading to an airlock. "We should start forming security details, Captain," he said, after he was done.

"You think whoever it is out there is going to board us," Thao said.

"I do," Han said. "You said it yourself, whoever this is, they're not your typical pirates. I think the only thing of value on the *Chandler* to whoever they are is the *Chandler.*"

"No," Thao said, looking back at Ocampo. "There's something else here, too."

A ping came up from Womack's console. We both turned to look at it.

"What is it?" Thao asked.

"An outside signal," I said.

Womack picked up her headset. "It's addressing you specifically, Captain," she said to Thao a moment later.

"Put it on speaker," Thao said. Womack switched it over and nodded to the captain. "This is Captain Eliza Thao," she said.

"Captain Thao, you have three Melierax Series Seven missiles locked onto your ship," a voice said. It had that metallic, grating tone that made it clear it was artificially generated. "The first will impact and detonate midships, at a point where the structural integrity of the *Chandler* is the weakest. This will not destroy your ship but will kill many of your crew, and open a direct path to your engines, where the second missile will strike. That will vaporize two-thirds of your ship instantly, killing nearly every one of your crew. The third missile is for mop up.

"As a trade ship, you have no significant defenses. Even if you had, we have jammed your external sensors. Your communications are also jammed and you are light-years away from any civilian or CDF station in any event. Your skip drone launchers are already targeted by particle beams. Your power is down and you will discover, if you have not already, that you will be unable to get it back online before your emergency battery power exhausts itself. If you were not already targeted for destruction by our missiles, you and your crew would freeze, and those who did not would asphyxiate."

"Listen to me—" Thao began.

"If you interrupt again we will launch our missiles," the voice said.

Thao shut up.

"This is not a negotiation or a parley," the voice continued. "We are telling you what you will have to do in order for you and your crew to survive the next few hours.

"And it is this. You will open your airlocks for external entry. You will assemble your entire crew in your ship's cargo hold. We will enter your ship and take control of it. If any of your crew is found outside of the cargo hold when we board, we will destroy the ship and everyone on it. If any of your crew attempts to attack us or thwart us in taking control of your ship, we will destroy the ship and everyone on it. If you attempt to abandon ship, we will target and destroy the lifepods and destroy the ship and anyone remaining on it. If you and your crew do anything other than assemble in the cargo hold and await further instruction, we will destroy the ship and everyone on it.

"You will have five minutes from right now to signal your understanding of these directions. You will then have one hour to signal that these directions have been fulfilled. If we do not receive both, then your ship and everyone on it will be destroyed.

"That is all."

"Is that channel still clear?" Thao asked Womack.

Womack looked at her panel. "Yes," she said. "Everything else is still jammed up."

Thao turned to Ocampo. "These aren't your *friends*, I assume."

"No," Ocampo said. "This is definitely not how they would have greeted us."

"And what do you think has happened to your friends?"

"I don't know," Ocampo said. "It's entirely possible they were attacked, too."

"Options," Thao said, turning to Han.

"Assuming they are telling us the truth about the missiles, none," Han said. "Whoever that was is right. We have no real defenses. We can't outrun them. And even if we direct all emergency power to life support, we don't have much time."

"And if they're not telling us the truth about the missiles?"

"Then we launch lifepods, fight them when they arrive on the ship, and destroy the ship ourselves if necessary," Han said. "To Hell with these guys."

"We'll fight, Captain," I said. I don't know why I said it. I wasn't thinking about fighting at any point before. It just came up in my brain at that moment. It was like Lee Han said: To Hell with these guys, whoever they were. And if that meant fighting them with sticks, that was better than nothing.

I looked around the bridge and saw people nodding. We were all ready for a fight.

Thao smiled at me and then nodded, as a way of letting me know my comment had been registered and appreciated. Then she turned back to Han, who was not smiling. "But," she said to him.

"But they already have knocked out our power in a way we couldn't and didn't track," Han said. "They're jamming our communications and external sensors. That says to me they have more up their sleeves. Even if they don't, if we fight them and repel them we'll likely take losses and additional damage to the ship. We'll all end up on lifepods just to survive. In which case whoever *they* are"—Han motioned outward, signifying our attackers—"can still take the ship without any of us on it. In which case, we've risked everything for nothing."

Thao turned to Bolduc, who was the pilot on duty. "Any chance we could skip out of this?"

"No," Bolduc said. "We entered this system near a planet. Under the best of circumstances we'd need three days to get to skip distance."

"We can't skip without engines anyway," Han said.

"When can we get them back?" Thao asked.

"Eller estimated twenty hours," Han said, speaking of the chief engineer. "Our emergency power is going to last six. We'd still have to get the crew to lifepods. Whoever stayed would find breathing difficult until the power's completely back."

"No matter what, we lose the ship," Thao said.

Han paused an almost infinitesimally small amount of time before replying. "Realistically, yes," he said. "Even if whoever is attacking us did *nothing*, we'd still have to get nearly all the crew to lifepods. And I don't think it's realistic to assume that whoever is attacking us will do nothing. They've already done enough."

Thao sat for a moment, silent. Ocampo and everyone else on the bridge waited, conscious of the timeline for a response.

"Fuck," Thao said. She nodded to Womack. "Tell them we understand their terms. The airlocks will be open within the hour. We'll signal when the crew is in the cargo hold."

Womack blinked, swallowed, and nodded. She turned to her console.

Thao turned to Han. "Tell the crew. We're under a deadline here." Han moved.

Then Thao looked over to Ocampo. "Well, Mr. Ocampo. I'm beginning to think I should have refused your request."

Ocampo opened his mouth to reply, but Thao was already ignoring him.

The three creatures approaching Captain Thao wore black, were armed, and had knees that went the wrong way. One had something resembling a handgun, and the two others had longer weapons I assumed were automatic rifles of some sort. A larger squad of the alien creatures held back and fanned out through the cargo hold, getting good vantages to fire into us, the *Chandler* crew. There were about sixty of us, totally unarmed. It wouldn't take them long to go through us, if they wanted to.

"What the hell are they?" Chieko Tellez whispered to me. She was standing next to me in the group.

"They're Rraey," I said.

"Not friendly," she said. "Not counting these ones, I mean."

"No," I said. The Colonial Union didn't spend a lot of time advertising specific battles, but I knew enough to know we'd kicked the Rraey's asses pretty seriously more than once in the last decade or so. There was no reason to believe any of this was going to end well for us.

The three Rraey reached Captain Thao. "Identify your pilots," the center Rraey said to her. It spoke in its own language, which was translated by a small object clipped to its clothes.

"Tell me why," Thao said.

The Rraey raised its weapon and shot Lee Han, standing with the captain, in the face. Han lifted in the low gravity and took a long time to fall to the deck.

"Identify your pilots," the Rraey said again, after most of the shouting from the crew had subsided.

Thao remained silent. The creature raised its weapon again, this time at her head. I considered stepping forward. Tellez suddenly grabbed my arm, guessing what I was thinking of doing. "Don't you fucking *dare*," she whispered.

"Stop it," someone said. I followed the sound of the voice to Secretary Ocampo. He stepped forward, away from the *Chandler* crew. "There's no need for that, Commander Tvann."

The Rraey turned its head to look at Ocampo. So did Thao. I think she realized, like I just did, that Ocampo had called the creature by name and rank.

"Secretary Ocampo," Tvann said, nodding its head in salute. "Perhaps you would be so kind as to identify a pilot for me."

"Of course," Ocampo said. Then he pointed into crew members, directly at me. "He's one. Take him."

Two Rraey peeled off and came at me. Tellez put herself in front of me. One of the two advancing Rraey raised its weapon at her. "You son of a bitch," Thao shouted at Ocampo, and the crew of the *Chandler* began to agitate.

"Quiet," Ocampo said. He said it in a loud voice that he was clearly proud of, the sort of speaking voice that had been polished by years of diplomatic speeches and the assumption that people would naturally listen to what he had to say.

And it worked; even the Rraey coming to get me stopped and looked at him.

He held up a hand to further the call for silence. The crew hushed to a low murmur.

"You will survive this," Ocampo said, loudly. "Let me say this again: You *will* survive this. But only if you listen to me right now and do as I say. So listen. Quietly."

The *Chandler* crew was dead silent now.

"I regret the death of Lee Han," Ocampo said. "Rraey commanders are not accustomed to having orders questioned or refused. There will be no more killings unless you resist or disobey. I also recognize that from your point of view this looks very much like both piracy and treason. I assure you that nothing could be further from the truth. I am sorry I don't have time to explain it to you further.

"Now. I require the *Chandler* and I require a pilot. I am taking the ship and I am taking Mr. Daquin here. As for the rest of you, very shortly you will be escorted to the *Chandler*'s lifepods. The lifepods will be launched and immediately after the *Chandler* has skipped away—three days from now—an emergency drone will be sent to Phoenix Station and the Colonial Union with the precise coordinates to this system and your lifepods. You know that the Colonial Union keeps ships at skip distance specifically for rescue missions of this type.

"So you will be rescued in four days, five days at the outside. The lifepods are rated for seven days under a full load. You will be rescued with time to spare.

"I repeat: *You will survive this.* But in order to do that you must now offer no resistance. You must not fight. You must not argue. If you do, the Rraey here will show no hesitation in putting you down. I want you to see your family and friends again. I want you to make it back safely to Colonial Union space. Help me help you get there. Let's get to it."

"I don't believe you," Thao said, loudly, to Ocampo.

"That's fair," Ocampo said. He nodded to Tvann.

The Rraey shot the captain in the forehead. She collapsed, dead.

Ocampo waited for the screams to die down. "As I said, you must not argue. Now follow the Rraey's orders, please." He turned away from the *Chandler* crew and motioned to Commander Tvann to follow him.

The two Rraey continued toward me, and I saw Tellez tense up to fight.

"No," I said to her.

"They're going to kill you," she said.

"They're going to kill you if you try to stop them," I pointed out.

"We're dead anyway," she said.

"I'd rather you take your chances with a lifepod," I said. I put my hand on her shoulder as the Rraey arrived. "Thank you,

Chieko. I appreciate that you're willing to fight for me. I really do."

"Well, you would for me, right?" Tellez asked.

"Yes," I said. "It's what I'm doing now." I nodded to the Rraey, letting them know I was ready to go. One of them grabbed me by the shoulder, and we marched away from Tellez and the crew of the *Chandler*.

I barely knew any of them.

I was already feeling guilty that I knew I was going to survive.

I heard Secretary Ocampo talking to Tvann as I was marched up to him. "How much damage did you do to the ship?" he asked the Rraey.

"Very little and none that would threaten the ship structurally," Tvann said. "We only needed to disrupt and disable certain systems."

"Good," Ocampo said. "The *Chandler*'s chief engineer said he could get the power back online in twenty hours. Can you do it in the same timeframe?"

"We will take less time than that," Tvann said. "We have experience with this, Secretary. As you know."

"Indeed I do."

"It will be good to have you with us full-time now."

"Thank you, Commander Tvann," Ocampo said. "I agree."

"What do you want to do with the rest of the crew?" Tvann said.

"I told them we'd put them on the lifepods. Let's do that."

"It will be a shame to lose the lifepods."

Ocampo shrugged. "They're really not going to be needed, are they?"

"No," Tvann said.

"Then no real loss. One thing, though. One of the lifepods needs to be destroyed. It has to be plausible that my body isn't recoverable. Having a lifepod torn up will help with that."

"Of course," Tvann asked. "You have an assistant, yes? Will she be going into the lifepods?"

"Offer her the choice of the lifepods or coming with us," Ocampo said. "How much you want to hint to her that the lifepods are a bad idea is up to you."

"She did not know?"

"About this? No. This was a secret, remember?"

"I believe I will simply order her to come with us. Less complicated that way."

"It's your show," Ocampo said, and clapped the Rraey on the shoulder, dismissing it. Tvann went to direct the herding of the *Chandler* crew. Then Ocampo turned his attention to me.

"Well, Mr. Daquin," Ocampo said. "Today is your lucky day. You will survive this day, after a fashion."

"There's no emergency drone, is there?" I asked.

"You mean, to let the Colonial Union know about the *Chandler*'s crew," Ocampo said.

"Yeah," I said.

Ocampo shook his head. "No. No, there is not."

"So you're going to let everyone on the *Chandler* suffocate in their lifepods."

"That's the most likely scenario, yes," Ocampo said. "This isn't a populated system. No one else is likely to come by in the next week. Or year."

"Why?" I asked. "Why are you doing this?"

"You're asking why I've apparently become a traitor?"

"For starters," I said.

"The full answer is too long for the time we have now," Ocampo said. "So I'll just say that the real question is where one's loyalties should be: with the Colonial Union, or with humanity. The two are not the same thing, you know. And I've come to realize that my loyalties are with humanity first. The Colonial Union's time is coming to an end, Mr. Daquin. I'm just trying to make sure that when it ends, it doesn't take the human race with it."

"If your loyalty is to humanity, then prove it," I said. I gestured back to the crew of the *Chandler*. "They're humans, Secretary Ocampo. Save these people. Send a skip drone back to Phoenix Station letting them know where they are. Don't let them die in the lifepods."

"It's noble of you to try to save them," Ocampo said. "I wish I could grant your wish, Mr. Daquin. I truly and sincerely wish I could. But for now the Colonial Union can't know that I've abandoned them. They need to think I'm dead. That only happens if there's no one to report otherwise. I'm sorry."

"You said you needed me as a pilot," I said. "I won't help you unless you save them."

"I think you'll change your mind," Ocampo said, and nodded to one of the Rraey.

My feet were knocked out from under me and I was pushed down hard to the floor of the cargo hold.

Something was pressed to the back of my head. It felt like a gun.

I felt the vibration of the gun firing at the same time I felt something hit the back of my skull.

I don't remember anything after that.

PART TWO

So now we're at the part where I actually become a brain in a box.

I don't remember the first part of it at all. I was shot in the back of the head point-blank with some sort of electrical stun gun; I was out. After I got zapped, I was taken to the Rraey's ship, where a doctor of some sort (at least I hope it was a doctor) put me into a medically induced coma; the first step of the process. I was unconscious through the skip, three days later. I was unconscious when we arrived at our destination.

I was, thankfully, unconscious for the part that came next.

And then there was the recovery period, which is substantial, because, and I think this may be obvious when you think about it, removing someone's brain from their head and keeping the brain alive in a box creates a considerable amount of trauma for the brain.

All told, I was out for eighteen days.

And when I say I was out, I mean that I was *out*. I didn't dream. I didn't dream because I don't think that technically I was sleeping. There's a difference between sleeping and what was happening to me. Sleep is an actual thing your brain does to rest itself and tidy up after a day of stimulation. What was going on with me was something else entirely. If sleep was going for an easy swim in a calm pond, what I was doing was fighting to surface in the middle of an ocean storm, far from any land at all.

I didn't dream. I think it's probably better that I didn't.

During all this time I surfaced only once—well, once that I remember. I remember feeling like my consciousness was being dragged hard through sludge, and thinking, *I can't feel my legs.*

And then: *I can't feel my anything.* And then falling back down into the sludge.

I did feel something the next time I regained consciousness.

I had, bluntly, the worst fucking headache I had ever had in my life.

I'm trying to think of the best way to describe it. Try this. Imagine a migraine, on top of a hangover, while sitting in a kindergarten of thirty screaming children, who are all taking turns stabbing you in the eye with an ice pick.

Times *six.*

That was the good part of my headache.

It was the sort of headache where the best possible course of action is to lie there motionless and quiet, eyes closed, and pray for death. Which is why I think it took me longer than it should have to figure out a few things.

The first thing was that it was dark in the sort of way that shouldn't be possible.

Go ahead and close your eyes. Do it right now. Is it totally dark?

I just realized you wouldn't have read that last question if in fact you'd just closed your eyes when I asked you to. Look, I told you I wasn't a writer.

Let me try this again: Close your eyes for a minute. Then when you've opened them up again, ask yourself if it was totally dark when you had them closed.

And the answer was, no, it wasn't. If you were in a room or place that had any light in it, some of that light found its way through your eyelids. If you were in a dark room, reading this on a screen, then you had afterimages of the screen on your retina. And even if you were in a dark room, maybe listening to this being read to you, eventually the very physical fact of your eyes would eventually make something happen. If you rubbed your eyes, you'd press on your optic nerve and ghost images and colors would appear in your brain.

The darkness is never totally and inescapably dark.

But this darkness was.

It wasn't the absence of light. It was the absence of *anything*.

And once I realized that about the darkness, I also realized it about the silence. There's no such thing as perfect silence, either. There's always some noise, even if it's just a phantom hum from the hairs in your cochlea moving around in your head.

There was nothing but the perfect clarity of nothing.

Then I realized I couldn't taste my mouth.

Don't look at me like that, because even though I can't see you I know you're looking at me like that.

Listen. I don't care if you ever *think* about the fact that you can always taste your mouth. You are *always* tasting your mouth. It's where you keep your tongue. Your tongue doesn't have an off switch. You are tasting your mouth *right now*, and now that I've brought it to your attention, you're probably realizing that you should probably brush or chew some gum or something. Because your mouth, by default, is a kind of a little *off*, taste-wise.

You can taste your mouth. Even when you're not thinking about it.

I was thinking *very hard* about it. And I couldn't taste a god-damned thing.

And *this* is where I started to lose it. Because you know about blindness. It's a thing that happens to people. They lose their sight and maybe even their eyes, and while it's possible to re-grow eyes or to create artificial ones, you still accept that blindness is real, and maybe it's happened to you. The same with deafness.

But who the *actual fuck* can't taste their own mouth?

So, yeah. This is where my brain well and truly started saying *oh shit oh shit oh shit* on a more or less infinite loop.

Because after that *everything* I wasn't sensing hit me head on: No feeling in my hands or feet or arms or legs or penis or lips. No smells coming in through my nose. No sensation of air going past my nostrils and into my nose. No sense of balance. No sense of heat or cold.

No nervous swallow. No feeling of fear sweat in my pits and on my brow. No racing heart. No heartbeat.

No anything.

I would have positively shit myself in fear, except I had no sense of losing sphincter control, either.

The only thing I could feel was pain, because my headache decided that this was a fantastic time to get a dozen times worse.

And I focused on that headache like a starving dog focuses on a steak *because it was the only thing in the world I could feel.*

And then I passed out. Because I think my brain decided I was feeling too much about not feeling anything.

I can't say that I disagreed with it.

When I came to again I did not freak out, and I felt a little bit proud about that. Instead, I tried to calmly and rationally figure out what was going on.

First hypothesis: I was dead.

Discarded because that seemed kind of stupid. If I were dead, then yes, I wouldn't be feeling anything. But I also probably wouldn't be aware that I wasn't feeling anything. I just . . . wouldn't *be.*

Unless this was the afterlife. But I doubted it was. I'm not much of a religious person, but most afterlives that I'd heard of were something more than a blank nothingness. If God or gods existed, and this was all they put together for eternal life, I wasn't very impressed with their user experience.

So: probably alive.

Which was a start!

Second hypothesis: was in some sort of coma.

This seemed more reasonable, although I didn't really know anything about the medical facts of a coma. I didn't know if people in comas could actually think about things while they were in them. From the outside they didn't seem like they were doing much. Tabled this idea for later thought.

Third hypothesis: not in a coma but for some reason trapped in my body without any sensation.

This seemed like the most reasonable explanation on the surface, but two questions arose that I didn't have answers for. One, how I got into this predicament in the first place. I was conscious and knew who I was, but otherwise my memory of recent events was shaky. I remembered falling out of my bunk and then going to the bridge, but anything after that was a blur.

This suggested to me that I had some sort of event; I knew people's memories of accidents or injury were sometimes wiped out by the trauma of the event itself. That seemed likely here. Whatever it was, I was in a bad way.

Well, that wasn't news. I was a consciousness floating around in nothing. I had gotten the "you're not doing so well" memo.

But that was the second thing: Even if I were in terrible shape, which I assumed I was, I should be able to feel something, or to sense something other than my own thoughts. I couldn't.

Hell, I didn't even have a headache anymore.

"You're awake."

A voice, perfectly audible, indeterminate in terms of any identifying quality, coming from everywhere. I was shocked into immobility, or would have been, if I had any way to be mobile.

"Hello?" I said, or would have, if I had been able to speak, which I wasn't, so nothing happened. I started to go into panic mode, because I was reminded so clearly that there was something wrong with me, and because I was desperate that the voice, whoever it was, would not leave me alone again in the nothing.

"You're trying to talk," the voice said, again from everywhere. "Your brain is trying to send signals to your mouth and tongue. It's not going to work. Think the words instead."

Like this, I thought.

"Yes," the voice said, and I would have cried with relief, if I could cry. A jumble of thoughts and emotions rose up in a panicky need to be expressed. I had to take a minute to calm down and focus on a single coherent thought.

What happened to me? I asked. *Why can't I speak?*

"You can't speak because you don't have a mouth or tongue," the voice said.

Why?

"Because we took them from you."

I don't understand, I thought, after a long minute.

"We took them from you," the voice repeated.

Did something happen to them? Was I in an accident?

"No, they were perfectly fine, and no, you weren't."

I don't understand, I thought again.

"We removed your brain from your body."

It's hard, looking back, to accurately convey the amount of utter incomprehension I was experiencing at this moment. I tried very hard to express my level of confusion and incredulity at the statement I just heard. What came out was:

What

"We removed your brain from your body," the voice repeated.

Why would you do that?

"You don't need them for what we need you to do."

I was still not comprehending well, and absent anything else was numbly carrying on with the conversation, waiting for the whole thing to make the slightest bit of sense to me.

What do you need me to do? I thought.

"Pilot your ship."

I need my mouth for that.

"No you don't."

How will I talk to the rest of the crew?

"There is no other crew."

At this, something surged in my brain—something like a memory, but not an actual memory. A thought that I used to know what had happened to the crew of the *Chandler,* but now I didn't, and that whatever had happened wasn't good.

Where is the rest of the crew, I thought.

"They are dead. All of them."

How?

"We killed them."

My sense of panic was back. I knew this was right, that the voice was telling me the truth. But I couldn't picture how it had happened. I knew I used to know. I desperately *wanted* to know. But there was nothing in my mind that could tell me, nothing but an approaching wall of dread.

Why did you kill them? I thought.

"Because they weren't needed."

You need a crew to run a ship.

"No we don't."

Why not?

"Because we have you."

I can't operate an entire ship by myself.

"You will or you'll die."

I can't even fucking move, I thought, exasperated.

"This will not be a problem."

How do you expect me to pilot and operate an entire ship when I can't even move?

"You are the ship now."

And then suddenly the complete incomprehension was back. *Excuse me?* I finally thought.

"You are the ship now," the voice repeated.

I am the ship.

"Yes."

I am the Chandler.

"Yes."

What the fuck does that even mean?

"We have removed your brain from your body," the voice said. "We've integrated your brain with the *Chandler*. The ship is now your body. You will learn how to control your body."

I tried to process what I was being told and failed miserably. I could not imagine a single element of what I was being hit with. I could not imagine being a ship. I couldn't imagine trying to control such a complex machine all on my own.

And if I don't? I thought. *What happens if I can't learn how to control it?*

"Then you will die," the voice said.

I don't understand, I thought, again, and I imagined that the complete helplessness I felt was entirely obvious. Maybe that was the point.

"It's not important for you to understand," the voice said.

To which some part of my brain immediately said, *Fuck you, asshole.* But it didn't appear to have been sent—or at least the voice didn't respond to it. So I said something else to the voice instead.

Why would you do this to me?

"This ship needs a pilot. You are a pilot. You know this ship."

That doesn't require taking my brain out of my goddamned skull, I thought.

"It does."

Why?

"It's not important for you to know."

I disagree!

"It doesn't matter that you disagree."

It matters that I won't pilot the ship. I won't.

"You will or you will die."

I'm already a brain in box, I thought. *I don't care if I die.*

I thought this was an excellent point, until a spasm of pain started.

Remember that headache? That was a twinge compared to this. It felt like my entire body was turned in a seizing electrical cramp, and not even the wonder of feeling like I had a body again distracted me from just how much I hurt.

Objectively, it can't have gone on for more than a few seconds. Subjectively I think I aged a year through it.

It stopped.

"You do not have a body, but your brain does not know that," the voice said. "All the pathways are still there. All the ways that your brain can still make you experience pain are ours to control. It's very simple to do. All the settings are already programmed. If we were so inclined we could run them on a loop. Or we could simply leave you in the dark, deprived of every possible sensation, forever. So, yes. If you will not pilot and operate this ship, then you will die. But before you die you will learn just how far and how long your death can be delayed, and how much pain you can feel between now and then. And I assure you that you will care."

Who are you? I thought.

"We are the only voice you will hear for the rest of your life, unless you do what we tell you."

Is that the royal we? I thought, not to the voice but to myself. I don't know why the hell I thought that. I think being made to feel like I had a power station's worth of electricity run through my nonexistent body might have made me a little loopy.

The voice didn't respond.

Which was the second time that happened, when I didn't think directly to the voice.

Which was interesting.

What happens if I do what you tell me? I asked, to the voice.

"Then at the end of it you will get your body back. It's a simple exchange. Do what you're told, and you will be you again. Refuse and you will die, in pain."

What is it you want me to do?

"Pilot and operate this ship. We have already told you this."

Where and for what purpose?

"That comes later," the voice said.

What do I do now? I asked.

"Now, you think," the voice said. "You will think about what your choices are, and what the consequences of those choices will be. I will give you a day to think about it, here in the dark. It will be a long day. Good-bye."

Wait, I thought, but the voice was already gone.

So for the next day I thought.

First thought: Definitely not dead. No need for a religious crisis. One small thing off the list of things to worry about. It was the only one, but anything would do at this point.

Second thought: Whoever it was who had me had captured my ship, killed my crew, taken my brain out of my body, and now expected me to run the ship entirely on my own, for their own purposes, and would kill me if I didn't.

Third thought: To Hell with these people. There was no way I was going to do anything for them.

In which case they would be more than happy to torture me just for the fun of it. As I knew from experience. Which was an actual consideration I had to take into account.

Fourth thought: Why me?

As in, why did they take me and not someone else? I was

third pilot of the *Chandler*. I was literally the newest crew member. They could have picked anyone else from that ship and they would have made a better choice, in terms of knowing the ship, how it works, and what its capabilities were. I was not the obvious choice.

Identify your pilots.

The sentence barreled out of my subconscious and stood in front of me, daring me to give it some sort of context. My memory was still spotty; I knew it had been spoken, but not by whom, or when. I would need to rack my brain to figure it out.

The thing was, I had time.

And in time an image popped into my head: a creature dressed in black, knees going the wrong way, giving the order to Captain Thao and shooting Lee Han when she questioned the order.

A Rraey. The Rraey had taken me. That answered the question of who these people were. But it didn't answer the question of why me. The captain hadn't identified me as a pilot. She hadn't identified anyone as anything. Someone else did that.

Secretary Ocampo.

Suddenly the image of that bastard pointing me out blazed into my consciousness, clear as if I were reliving the moment.

And then all the rest of it came back too—every blank spot in the memory suddenly filled with hard force, almost painfully jammed in.

I had to stop.

I had to stop to grieve for the crew of the *Chandler*. To grieve for the few friends I had made there, and for everyone else who I did not know but who did not deserve to die, just as I did not deserve to live instead of them.

It took some time. But as I said before, I had the time.

I took it.

And then when I was done I started fiddling with the problem again.

Why was I taken? Because Secretary Ocampo knew me. He'd been introduced to me even before we'd gotten to the *Chandler,* we took the shuttle ride over, and I came to him when I had questions about our change of destination.

He knew I was a pilot, but he also knew me as a person— probably the only person he knew on the *Chandler* other than Captain Thao and Vera Briggs.

It's possible he picked me simply because he knew I was a pilot. He knew there were other pilots on the ship—he'd probably seen Bolduc on the bridge—but I was the first that came to mind. Because he'd met me. He knew me. Or thought he did.

So maybe he didn't *just* pick me because I was a pilot. Maybe he picked me because he knew me as more than a random crew member. Maybe he saved me because there was a personal connection there.

And wasn't there? Didn't I feel like I could go to his stateroom and ask him about the orders he'd given the captain? Wasn't he at least a little impressed that I had figured it out?

So, yes. Maybe he picked me because he knew me. Maybe because he liked me. Maybe he even thought he was *saving* me. Maybe he thought he was doing me a favor.

Picking you to have your brain plucked out of your body is not my idea of a favor, some part of my brain said.

Good point, brain, I thought, ignoring that I was now speaking to myself. But the point is not what *I* thought of it, it was what Ocampo thought of it, and me. I wasn't flattering myself that I was important to Ocampo—I thought back to him telling Commander Tvann it was up to him whether or not to tell Vera Briggs to stay out of the lifepods. If Ocampo was like that with his own assistant, who he'd worked with for years, he wasn't going to care much if I got uppity and troublesome.

But until then, there might be something there to work with.

What? And for what purpose?

I didn't know yet.

That wasn't the point. The point was that I was now listing my potential assets. And one of those assets was that Ocampo, for whatever reason, picked me to pilot the *Chandler*—to *become* the *Chandler*.

So that was one thing.

Another possible asset: what Ocampo *didn't* know about me.

He knew my name. He knew my face. He knew I was a pilot.

And . . . that was it.

Which meant what?

It could mean nothing. Or it could mean that when they hooked me up to the *Chandler*'s systems, they wouldn't know how much I already knew about the systems. Or how to use them.

Don't get too excited, that other part of my brain said. *You're a brain in a box now. And they can see everything you do. They're probably looking at you thinking all this right now.*

You're depressing, I said to that other part of my brain.

At least I'm not talking to myself, it said back. *And anyway you know I'm right.*

It was a fair point. I had to accept that leaving me alone with my thoughts could be part of a test that I was being given, to see how I would respond. If they were able to follow my thoughts right now, I had to accept that they would use that information to decide what to do with me—kill me or torture me or whatever.

But I had a feeling they weren't. I had a feeling that the day alone with my thoughts was for another purpose entirely. It was to dominate me. To terrify me. To remind me how alone I was and how helpless I was. How utterly dependent I was on them now for my survival.

And you know what? They would be right about that. I *was* alone. I *was* dependent on them for survival. I *was* terrified.

But I wasn't going to be dominated.

Yes, I was isolated. Yes, I was scared.

But I was also really, really *pissed off*.

And that was the thing I decided I was going to work with.

If they were listening to me when I was thinking this, they could kill me at any time. In which case they could get on with it, because otherwise they were just wasting my time and theirs.

But I didn't think they were.

I don't think they thought they *had* to.

Which was another possible asset. They assumed they had the upper hand in dealing with me.

Again, fair enough. I was a brain in a box and they could kill me or torture me any time they wanted. That's a pretty good definition of having the upper hand.

But the fact was, they needed me.

They needed a pilot for the *Chandler*. They had me.

And they had *only* me. Everyone else in the crew they had killed off, suffocating them in those lifepods. They were so sure they had the upper hand with me that they didn't bother with a spare.

Which said to me either they had never done this before, and had no idea what they were doing, or they had done this a lot, and the response by their pilot victims was always the same.

I thought about the Rraey saying that their engineers could repair the ship and get it going again because this was something they were used to. I thought of their efficient way of dealing with the crew, to cow them and get what they wanted.

It was clear this wasn't something they were new to.

They had done this before. And maybe were right now doing it with pilots other than me. They expected the pilots to be desperate and to be willing to do anything to get their bodies back. They were so used to the response they didn't really think any other response was possible.

So no, I didn't think they were listening in on me right then.

I didn't think they thought they had to. I could be wrong, but it was an assumption I was willing to go on.

That gave me free time to think. And plan. Another asset that I had. For now, anyway.

Then there was the final asset I had:

I knew I was already dead.

By which I mean I knew that their promise to return me to my body was almost 100 percent certain to be complete bullshit. There was no way that was going to happen.

I knew that because they killed the crew of the *Chandler*. I knew it because of what Ocampo said when I pleaded with him to send the skip drone back to Phoenix Station to save the crew. I knew it because of how they lied to the crew to lead them willingly to their deaths.

They had no intention of putting me back into my body. I was as close to certain as I could be that my body was already gone—incinerated or tossed into space or put into a stew because the Rraey had a reputation for eating humans when they had the chance.

I thought about my body in a very large pot, simmering.

I actually found it blackly amusing.

Whatever was done with it, my body was history. I was sure of it.

I was also sure that whatever it was that Ocampo and the Rraey—or whatever it was they were working for—wanted me to do, when I was done with it they would flip whatever switch they had and simply murder me then.

That is, if whatever mission they were going to have me do wasn't already a suicide mission. Which I suspected it probably would be. Or at least, they wouldn't lose a lot of sleep if I didn't come back.

I was under no illusion that my fate wasn't the same as that of the rest of the *Chandler*'s crew. It was just a question of when.

And the answer of "when" was: when they were done using me for whatever it was they had planned.

Which meant that I had whatever time existed between now and then to, in no particular order, find out who they were (besides Ocampo and a bunch of Rraey soldiers), discover what they had planned, learn how to stop them, and kill the hell out of all of them.

All of them, that is, except Ocampo. If there was some way to bring him back to Colonial Union space, I was going to do it. Because no matter what else, I think they were going to be very interested in whatever it was he was wrapped up in.

And because he didn't deserve to get off as easy as him dying would let him.

You're pretty ambitious for a disembodied brain, that other part of my brain said again.

I've got nothing else to do, I replied. Because it was true. All I had right now were my thoughts, and time. Lots of time.

So I took it.

At some point I think I slept. It's hard to tell when you have no outside frame of reference to let you know if you're actually asleep.

I do know I didn't dream. I was okay with that.

And at some point the voice came back.

"You have had time to think on your situation," the voice said. "Now it is time to make your decision."

The voice was right: it was time to make my decision.

Not whether or not I would decide to stay alive. I'd already decided that one early on.

What I was deciding now was how to act in front of the voice.

Should I be cowed and afraid? Should I be defiant and rebellious, but still willing to do what they wanted? Should I just remain silent and do only what the voice told me to?

This was an important decision because how I responded to the voice now would establish what our relationship was and possibly what would be allowed me in the future—and what I might be able to get away with.

If I picked the wrong attitude, that would have negative consequences. If I was too complacent maybe they would simply treat me as the machine they made me into. Too rebellious and I'd spend all my spare time getting zapped. Neither was what I wanted, especially getting zapped. Once was enough.

"What is your decision?" the voice asked.

I have questions, I thought, suddenly. Which wasn't how I was expecting to go, but, okay, let's see what happens next.

"Your questions are not relevant," the voice said.

Let me rephrase that, I said. *I'm going to do what you want. I've decided that. But it would help me if I knew a few things as well. I understand I can't force you to answer any questions. But it would help me be helpful to you if you would consider answering them.*

There was an actual pause here. "What are your questions?"

I have three, I said. Which again, was news to me, but I could come up with three questions, right?

And in fact one popped up in my head. *First, do you have a name?*

"Why would that matter?"

Because I feel awkward just thinking of you as "that voice in my head," I thought. *If we are going to be working together it would be nice to have a name for you.*

"You may call me Control," the voice said.

Okay, good, I thought. *Hello, Control.*

Control waited, silent. Well, fine.

Second, would it be possible for me to speak to Secretary Ocampo at some point?

"Why would you need to speak to him?"

I don't need to speak to him, I thought. *I have already agreed to help you. But when I was taken off the* Chandler *he told me that he was doing this, whatever this is, to help humanity. I want to talk to him more about that, to understand what he meant.*

"It doesn't matter if you understand," Control said.

I know this, I thought, *and though I know you're under no obligation to care, I disagree. You have my help. But if you had my understanding I might be even more useful. Secretary Ocampo is an admirable man. I respect him. If he's doing this, he must have a reason. I think that reason could make sense to me. I would like to know more about it.*

"We will not let you speak to Secretary Ocampo now," Control said. "But if in your work you do well, we may consider it for the future."

Fair enough, I thought.

"Do not ask us about it again."

Of course not. You've already said you'd think about it. That's enough.

"Your final question."

Will you give me your word that I will get my body back?

"My word," Control said.

Yes, your word, I thought. *Your promise. I already said I would help you. I will. I will do everything you ask me to. You said that if I did I would get my body back. That was the deal. But there are deals, and there are promises. A deal you can make with anyone. A promise is something you make with someone you trust. If you make a promise with me, that means I can trust you. And that means I can stop worrying about whether I can believe you or not. And that means I can do what you ask me to, better.*

And once more there was a pause.

I had a point in asking these questions, even if I didn't know I was doing it when I started.

Information. Trust. Creating intimacy and a relationship.

I'd asked for a name, and while Control wasn't much of a name, it was something. A personalization. Something that made that royal we into an "I." Asking to speak to Ocampo further extended our deal, and turned it from something general—something they probably forced on every pilot whose brain they put into a box—into something specific to me.

And asking for Control's word? More intimacy—making the deal between me and it. Something with reciprocity. Something with trust.

It was also a test.

"You have my word," Control said.

Now I knew everything I needed to know about Control.

And Control had no idea that I knew.

That's all I need, I said. *I'm ready to get started when you are.*

"Then let's begin," Control said.

The *Chandler's* bridge appeared all around me.

Or, more accurately, a computerized visual representation of the *Chandler's* bridge; cleaner, plainer, and with all extraneous detail stripped from view.

"You recognize this," Control prompted.

Of course, I thought.

It was the standard bridge simulation program, used for training purposes, configured for the *Chandler's* bridge setup, which in itself was pretty standard.

I recognized it because like anyone else who ever did time on a bridge, I'd spent a couple hundred hours using it in addition to actual physical training at the specific bridge station.

I also recognized it because I helped to program it.

Or a slightly earlier version of it, anyway. It'd been a few years. This was probably an updated release of it.

That said, a quick glance suggested that not much had changed in the software since I had worked on it. It didn't even look like it was a new major release from what I had worked on. A point release, maybe? With some minor fixes? How does an organization clearly not hooked into the mainstream of Colonial Union commerce even get these programs? I felt vaguely annoyed on behalf of my former employer that this program had clearly been pirated.

Not that I was about to mention to Control that I had worked on the program. Control didn't know because Ocampo didn't know, and I saw no reason to let either know. Control already thought I was stupid enough to believe its word on things. I wasn't going to do anything to dissuade it of that notion.

It's the bridge simulator program, I thought, to Control.

"It used to be a bridge simulator program," Control said. "And for now, it will continue to be so. But we've adapted it to control the *Chandler*. Ultimately you will be able to control all the ship systems from inside of it."

How will I do that? I asked. *The simulator program is designed as a virtual space but tracks actual hand and body movements. I'm missing both.*

"Here," Control said, and I was in a virtual body. My view was clearly meant to be from head height; by thinking about it I could move it on a swivel, like I had an actual neck. I looked down and a stripped-down, visual representation of a human body was there. I imagined moving my hands and my hands came up from my sides, palms toward me, featureless where there should have been palm lines and fingerprints.

I nearly had a breakdown right then, I was so grateful. Even a fake body like this was better than no body at all.

Even so . . .

Some part of my brain—I think maybe the same part that argued with me earlier—was going *Really? That's it?*

I knew what it meant. It meant that these assholes had taken my brain out of my body to run the *Chandler,* and I had to run the *Chandler* all on my own, and the way they intended me to run the *Chandler* was with a simulation of a human body I no longer had.

Which seemed, I don't know. *Inefficient.* If you're going to take the time to get rid of my body, then *maybe* take the time to create a control metaphor that takes advantage of not being limited to a human body anymore.

They didn't take you out of your body for efficiency's sake, said that part of my brain. Well, yeah, I figured *that* out a while back. It was about fear and control.

But *still*. Kind of a waste of effort.

I pulled myself back together (metaphorically), and looked around the simulated bridge.

Are you coming onto the bridge with me? I asked Control.

"No," it said. "Please go to the captain's chair."

I nodded. The captain's chair had a screen where she could look at the information from all the stations, either at once or one at a time. Captain Thao, like most captains, tended to take reports from her bridge crew, who were better at boiling down the information into what she needed to know immediately. But she could get all the information from the screen if she wanted to boil it down herself. Which meant that I could, too.

Likewise, the captain could control the ship from the screen if she wanted, rather than giving orders. Very few captains did, because things got complicated fast, and besides, if you want to make your bridge crew unhappy, the best way to do it was to try to do their job for them. The fact is that no captain was competent at every bridge station. Most didn't try to be.

Except now I would have to be.

I sat in the virtual captain's chair and pulled up the captain's screen.

I'm ready, I thought to Control.

The virtual captain's screen lit up, and all the department windows opened in a grid. Tapping twice on one of the windows would cause it to expand to full screen and become fully interactive. Only one department screen could be full screen at one time but you could also chain full-size department screens together and swipe through them to access them quickly. It was all pretty basic except for the fact that I would be responsible for monitoring and dealing with all of them.

I looked further at the captain's start grid.

Some of these are blank, I said.

"Some of the ship functions you no longer need to control," Control said. "You will be the only living thing on the ship and your living area is tightly sealed and controlled by us, so you will not need life-support controls. Likewise communications. We control those and several other ship-related functions. Others, such as engineering, you need to control only on a limited basis, and the maintenance of those functions will now be handled by us. The only ship's functions you need to concern yourself with are navigation, weapons, and propulsion, including skipping."

That makes things simple, at least, I thought to Control. I made the windows for navigation, propulsion, and weapons full-sized and chained them together.

I'm ready, I sent.

"We're sending you a simulated mission now," Control said. "It is a simple one, focused primarily on navigation. Let's begin."

Ten hours of simulation that first day, at least by the simulation clock, almost all of it dead simple navigation that as a pilot I could do in my sleep. I had a suspicion that the simulations were not specifically chosen for me by Control, but might have been simply on a list of simulations to run that it was running through.

It was boring.

But it was also manageable. There was nothing that first day that I wasn't able to do. The piloting, like most piloting, was about feeding information into the computer and then dealing with anything unusual that might go wrong. Nothing went wrong with any of these initial simulations.

The most difficult thing I had to do was slide the simulated *Chandler* out of the way of a chunk of rock floating out in space. I considered using the simulated *Chandler*'s lasers to vaporize it—it was small enough—but I figured that wasn't what the simulation was about yet, and anyway vaporizing it ran the risk of creating a bunch of even tinier bits of rock, harder to track, that some other ship would then ram into. Most ships could handle a micrometeor impact, but why create a problem for someone else when you didn't have to?

So I moved the *Chandler* out of the way, logged the rock's present location and direction, and then would have simulated sending a data packet to nearby ships, except that I was not in charge of ship's communications. So instead I made a notation to have the data sent to other ships at the earliest opportunity.

If Control were noting any of this, I didn't know about it. Control was entirely silent for that entire simulation, and the other runs we ran that day. "You will be controlling the ship alone," Control said, when I asked it about the silence, between runs. "You will not have us nor any other person to communicate with once you begin your missions. You need to get used to the silence."

You're not worried about boredom? I asked. *Human minds need a little stimulation outside of monitoring navigation systems.*

"This has not been a problem before," Control said. Which is how I learned for sure that I was not the first person they had done this to.

I thought about other people in the same predicament and would have shuddered if I could.

It also suggested to me that I might not even be the only person currently in my situation. That Control, whoever it was, might also be running simulations with other people and ships, even as it was working with me. It would be something I would need to find out, eventually.

"We're done for the day," Control eventually said. "We will continue again tomorrow."

How many hours will that be? I asked. I didn't know if Control was human, and wherever we were was almost certainly not a human outpost, so I had no idea of how long a day would be.

"About twelve hours from now," Control said, after a minute. I think it may have had to look up what "hours" were to make the conversion.

What do I do now? I asked.

"Whatever you like," Control said.

I'd like to go jogging, I thought.

Control didn't say anything to that. I was getting the idea that Control, whoever it was, did not have a particularly good sense of humor.

What is there for me to do? I asked.

"If you like, you may reload today's simulations, and run them again," Control said. "In fact, I suggest it."

Is there anything else? I asked. *Anything to read? Anything to watch? Anything to listen to?*

"No," Control said.

May I request some form of entertainment? I asked. *Anything would be good. If I only have navigation simulations, I think my effectiveness will eventually decrease.*

"If it decreases too far then you'll be punished," Control said. "If it decreases after that you will be killed."

Well, that's motivation of a sort, I thought to Control.

Control didn't respond. I suspected Control had left the simulation.

You need to get used to the silence, I thought to myself, repeating Control's words from earlier in the day. Well, I was getting used to it whether I liked it or not.

I looked down at the simulated captain's chair and at the captain's screen, on which a small menu tab appeared, with the day's missions. I could reload them if I liked.

Instead I got up and ran around the simulated bridge, doing laps. Then I did some push-ups and lunges and sit-ups.

I want to be clear I was under no impression that what I was doing constituted actual exercise. I couldn't feel my simulated body; even the double taps and swipes I made during the day were numbly done. I wasn't doing it to keep my body in shape. I didn't have a body to have a shape.

I did it because it was something else to do besides what Control wanted me to do. Something I wanted to do on my own time. My way of exercising my own control. If you want to put it that way.

It even kind of worked. Eventually I got tired. I lay down on the simulated floor to go to sleep.

And discovered I didn't have simulated eyelids.

It didn't matter. I was asleep fast enough anyway.

This time I knew I had slept.

Two days later I broke the bridge simulation and escaped. Sort of.

It happened after hours, once Control had gone off for the night, or what I assumed was night, anyway. I was running one of the day's previous simulations, this one requiring me to navigate the *Chandler* into a docking position at a space station. It's the sort of maneuver that I'd done dozens if not hundreds of times, both simulated and real. There was no challenge to it whatsoever.

So I did what anyone doing a simulated run does when they're bored and there's no penalty for misbehavior:

I started wrecking things.

First I rammed the space station with the *Chandler*, because I was interested, purely for the science, how realistic the impact would be in terms of the simulation's rendering of classical physics.

Answer: not bad. I had limited control of outside sensors, so

I saw both the *Chandler* and the space station crumple nicely, with appropriate bursts of metal and glass due to explosive decompression as the *Chandler* plowed through the station. My sensors did not indicate the *Chandler*'s engines overloading, however, which would have created a nice bit of mayhem.

So I ran the simulation again, this time giving the *Chandler* enough distance to make for some impressive acceleration before I hit the space station.

This time the *Chandler* exploded. All my control windows flashed red before blanking out, never a positive sign for the structural integrity of the ship. The simulation did not detail either economic or human losses, but I doubt anyone in the station sections I hit, or the *Chandler* crew, would have survived.

The Chandler *crew didn't survive already,* that other part of my brain said.

I ignored it.

The next run-through I was curious what would happen if I attacked the station. The simulations I'd run didn't require me to operate any of the weaponry systems, so while Control was around I hadn't bothered with them.

But I had control of them anyway, and they were fully operational, so. In the next simulation I launched three missiles at the station, just to see what would happen.

A minute later my damage sensors went bright red as ten missiles from the station struck the *Chandler* at various critical spots, taking out weapons, engines, crew compartments, and outside sensors. About a second after that my screens went blank, because in this simulation the *Chandler* had just been turned into an expanding cloud of debris.

Well, that was rude, I thought, and would have smiled if I could.

Several more simulations after that, attacking the space station, then attacking other ships at the station, firing at shuttles, basically any combination of tactics that involved surprising someone with a missile. All the simulations ended pretty much the same way: the *Chandler* being turned into a missile pincushion.

All right, fine, let's try this, I thought, and ran the simulation again.

This time I didn't ram the station, or fire on it. I just slid the *Chandler* into docking position, and waited until the simulation gave me the "victory condition" signal—the signal that I had done what the simulation required of me.

Then I launched a barrage of missiles at the space station, aiming specifically for its weapon systems, the ones I could see visually, but also the ones I couldn't, going off the data I had of the space station. I timed the missiles so they would impact all the weapons systems at the same time.

Which they did. And then, while everything was blowing up nicely, I opened up the throttles on the engines and headed straight into the mess.

And as the *Chandler* made first contact with the skin of the space station, something happened.

Everything went black.

Not just the captain's screens, which would have indicated that the *Chandler* had been destroyed. No, *everything* went black. There was the simulation, and then, for several full seconds, there it wasn't.

I spent those several seconds in the complete blackness wondering what the hell had just happened.

Then the bridge simulation popped up again around me.

I knew what had just happened: I'd crashed the simulator.

And then, I'm not going to lie to you—my brain just went *off*.

Here is the thing about that bridge simulator: The bridge simulator was now my whole world. I lived in it, running simulations, and nothing else. I couldn't leave it—I was in it, but I didn't have any control over it other than being able to run the simulations Control gave me to run. I couldn't step outside of the simulation, or close it out, or mess with the code in any way. I was trapped in it. It was my prison.

But when I crashed the simulator, it booted me out. For a few seconds there, *I* was somewhere else.

Where else?

Well, what happens when a program crashes? You get booted back into the system the program runs on.

Not literally *in* the system; my consciousness hadn't been sucked into a computer or anything. That's stupid. My consciousness was in my brain, like it always was.

But before, my senses had been dropped into the bridge simulation. Everything I could see or sense was inside of it. For those few seconds when the simulator crashed, I was somewhere else. The system the simulator ran on.

I wasn't seeing anything, and then the bridge simulation popped up again, which said to me that the bridge simulator crashing wasn't entirely unheard of. Control (or whomever) had set up a restart routine to go directly back into the bridge simulator, without giving the pilot any time to figure out what was going on, or to see the computer interface he or she was working within.

But that didn't necessarily mean the pilot was completely locked out of the system.

I launched the docking simulation again.

If Control knew the program crashed, then that meant it knew where the bugs were—or knew where some of them were. So either it knew where they were and did nothing about them other than relaunching the system directly back into the simulator, or it did something about it and tried to patch the code—and in the process possibly created new bugs when the new code interacted poorly with the old code.

Control wouldn't know anything about the new bugs unless

they glitched during a run it was watching. And no one would do what I just did while Control was watching because Control would probably electrocute them for farting around.

So: Control didn't know that *this* glitch was there.

But some glitches are transient and not reproducible. Those are the hardest as a programmer to fix.

I ran the simulation exactly as I had before to see if the glitch would replicate in the same way.

It did.

So I ran it a third time.

And this time, when the program crashed, I thought about the commands that, when the system we programmed the bridge simulator on was booted up, would open the diagnostics and modification screens for the system.

I thought about them *really hard*.

And two seconds later, there they were.

The diagnostics and modifications screens. Ugly and utilitarian, just like they have been since the very beginnings of visual user interface.

They were beautiful.

They meant that I was into the system.

More specifically, I was into the *Chandler*'s system.

Well, a little, anyway.

This would be the part of the story where, if this were a video piece, the heroic hacker would spew a couple of lines of magical code and everything would open up to him.

The bad news for me was that this was very much not my personal situation. I'm not a heroic hacker with magic code. I was a brain in a box.

But I *am* a programmer. Or was. And I knew the system. I knew the software.

And I had a plan. And a little bit of time before anyone was going to bother me again.

So I got to work.

I'm not going to bore you with the details of what I did. If you're a programmer and you know the system and the hardware, and the code, then what I did would be really cool and endlessly fascinating and we could have a seminar about it, and about system security, and how any system fundamentally falls prey to the belief that all variables are accounted for, when in fact the only variables accounted for are the ones you know about, or more accurately that you *think* you know about.

The rest of you would have your eyes glaze over and pray for death.

I assume that's most of you.

So for the rest of you, what you need to know:

First, the work, the first part of it anyway, took more than a single night.

It actually took a couple of weeks. And during all that time I waited for the moment where Control, or whoever, looked at the *Chandler*'s system and found evidence of me wandering around in it, making changes and trying to get into places where I shouldn't. I waited for the moment they found it, and the moment they decided to punish me for it.

But they didn't.

I'm not going to lie. Part of me was *annoyed* that they didn't. Because that's some lax security. *All* of it was lax. When whoever it is took over the *Chandler*, they left the system wide open, with only the basic level of security that would have been outmoded right at the beginning of the computer era. Either they were so sure that they didn't need to worry about security where they were—everyone could be trusted and no one would try to screw with things—or they were just idiots.

Maybe both! The level of insecurity was actually offensive.

But it worked to my advantage, and without it I would probably be dead, so I shouldn't really complain.

Those first two weeks were the scariest for me because what I was doing was pretty much out in the open. I tried to hide what I was doing as well as I could, but someone who was looking could have found it. If Control or anyone else looked into my extracurricular sessions, they would have seen me running one particular simulation the same way over and over and could have seen what I was doing.

It meant that if during the simulations where Control was watching, if the program crashed, it might code a patch, and that patch could affect the bug I was using to exit the program. Which meant I would be trapped again.

I was very very *very* careful in the simulations Control watched. Never did anything rash, never did anything not by the book.

The irony of doing things exactly as they wanted me to, so they wouldn't find out the things they might torture or kill me for, was not lost on me.

Those two weeks were, literally, the worst two weeks of my life. I already knew that whoever it was that had me was planning to kill me after I did what they wanted of me. But even knowing that didn't ease any of the stress of messing with the code. Of knowing I was exposed if anyone decided to look, and yet doing it anyway.

It's one thing to know you're already dead. It's another to work on something that might give you a chance to stay alive, as long as no one decides to look.

They never looked. Never. Because they didn't think they had to.

I was so grateful for it.

And at the same time, so contemptuous of it.

They deserved what I was going to do to them. Whatever it was. I hadn't figured it out yet.

But when I did: no sympathy.

What I did with those two weeks: blue pill.

No, I don't know where the phrase comes from. It's been used for a long time. Look it up.

But what it means is that I created an overlay for the *Chandler*'s computer system. A just about exact replica.

I copied it, tweaked it, attached everything coming in from the outside to it, as well as the bridge simulator. It looked like, responded like, and would control things like the actual computer system for the *Chandler*.

But it wasn't.

That system, the one that actually ran the *Chandler*, was running underneath the copy. And that one, well.

That one, I was totally in control of. The reality underneath the simulation. The reality that no one but me knew existed below the simulation. The simulation that everyone thought reflected reality.

That's the blue pill.

For the next month, every day, all day, I ran more and more complex missions on the bridge simulator. More simulations where I had to juggle navigation with weapons.

It was clear to me that whatever they were training me for, it had a significant military component. They were expecting me to go to battle for them. They may or may not have expected me to survive the battle. I think "not survive" was the more likely scenario.

This was not a surprise.

Through this all, I kept up the chatter with Control. To engage it. To make it feel something for me. To make it see the person it had put into a box.

I was not notably successful.

But I wasn't expecting to be.

What I had to be was the *same* person Control thought I was. The one who had decided to help. The one who had decided to trust Control.

I didn't want to mess that up. I wanted Control and anyone else listening to get exactly what they were expecting. I wanted them to be as smug about their small-c control over me as they ever were.

They did not disappoint.

And while they were thinking that, when Control left me alone after a day of simulations, I had free run of the *Chandler*.

Which, as it turned out, was undergoing some drastic renovations. Notably, having the actual weapons systems reinstalled. Before it had been the *Chandler*, the ship had been a Colonial Defense Forces frigate. When it was decommissioned those weapons systems were removed and dismantled.

Now systems were being put back into place. The ship was crawling with workers inside and out. I hadn't been aware of them before, because why would I be? I was a brain in a box, trapped in a simulation.

But *now* I could see, and hear, everything that was going on with the ship.

The workers were not mostly human. Most of them, as far as I could tell, were Rraey, just like the soldiers who attacked the *Chandler* in the first place.

Every now and then, however, a single human would show up on the ship, and advise or direct the weapons installation. It was always the same human.

She was not Ocampo. Or Vera Briggs, his assistant. This was someone entirely new. Whatever was going on, from the human side, there was more than Ocampo involved.

Watching the workers installing the weapons systems, I realized I had gotten lucky. In a couple more weeks, they'd be done with their installation and then the weapons systems would be plugged into *Chandler*'s computer system. If the work had been done earlier, or I had started my work later, I would have been found out. There was a small window, and I had plopped into it.

Which made me feel like the luckiest guy in the universe, until I remembered I was still a brain in a box.

Which brings me to the other thing I found on the *Chandler*: Me.

I was on the bridge, in a large rectangular box that looked, for all the world, like a coffin. The top of the box was clear; from my vantage point of the bridge cameras, I could look straight down into it and see: my brain.

And the electronic elements that were attached to it, to the surface of the gray matter and, I assumed, inside of it as well. I could see the hard wires snaking out of it, toward a juncture on the side of the box.

I saw the liquid in which my brain was suspended, discolored, slightly pink. I saw tubes connected to my brain, I assume taking in and bringing out blood or something substituting for it. Something that brought in nutrients and oxygen, and took out waste. The tubes also snaked out to a juncture in the box's interior wall.

A change in camera and in perspective and I saw another box, into which the wires and tubes went. It's this box I saw two Rraey, who I assume were doctors, come to and open daily, doing diagnostic work. Inside were filtering systems, intake and sampling valves, hardwired computers to monitor my brain's well-being, and something else that I couldn't identify at first, until one of the Rraey accidentally jostled it, and the other yelled at it for doing so.

The *Chandler*'s system has within it a translation library for several hundred known species. It, like most such libraries on trade ships, almost never gets used because we're mostly dealing with humans. Nevertheless it's there and on hand for when or if you need to translate anything. It translated what the second Rraey said to the first.

"Keep that up," it said. "You'll blow up all three of us."

"Then at least our remains would get to go back home," the first Rraey said.

"I would prefer to go back home in a form that would allow me to enjoy it," the second Rraey said, and then inserted a dongle into one of the hardwired monitors, I assume to check on how my brain was doing and make adjustments.

I imagine the information showed that at that very moment I had a spike of anxious brain activity.

Because of the bomb.

On top of everything else, they had a bomb attached to me.

In case I was at all concerned that they ever had any intention of letting me get out of this alive.

In case I was thinking I was really going to escape this hell.

"You have performed well in simulation," Control said one day, more than three months after I had first woken up to find myself a disembodied brain.

Thank you, I thought. *I have been trying to live up to my end of our deal.*

"You have been," Control said. "You may find it useful to know that you have become one of our best pilots, in terms of hitting training performance goals."

Well, of course I was. It was because I was very careful to perform simulations exactly to spec, so the software wouldn't glitch and they would have to root about in the system to fix it. The blue pill system I made was pretty solid, but why tempt fate.

The other reason was that when Control wasn't paying attention I was watching videos and listening to music that had been in the *Chandler*'s entertainment library. Which helped to keep me sane instead of dwelling on my complete and utter isolation from the rest of humanity. It's not exactly surprising that staying sane is useful when trying to hit performance markers.

None of which I expressed, or even thought, while Control was around.

By now I had some understanding of why Control only "heard" what I thought directly to it—the brain-reading software recognized intentional attempts at communication and filtered that away from the constant low-grade babbling and monologuing every brain does all the time, in order to optimize communication. The software kept the thoughts I meant to myself internal—but if you remember how many times in your life you unintentionally said something out loud you meant to keep quiet, and made a mess of your life for a day because of it, then you'll know why I tried to keep my mind blank when Control was around.

I'm happy to know that, I thought. And then waited, like I always did.

"You have done well enough that we have agreed to your request," Control said.

My request?

"You asked if you could speak to Secretary Ocampo at some point," Control said. "We have arranged for you to speak."

Is he coming to visit me? I asked.

"In a manner of speaking," Control said. "We have arranged for a feed to be ported through to this simulation."

So, not on the *Chandler* itself. Well, that was just fine. *Will that be today?* I asked.

"No. We have work to do today. But soon."

Thank you, I thought. *I am grateful.* And that was certainly true, as far as it went.

"You're welcome," Control said. "Let's begin today's simulations."

When will you have an actual mission for me?

"Why do you ask?"

You have been training me all this time. I've been doing well, as you said. I'm ready for missions.

"You want to fulfill your obligations to us," Control said.

I do.

"In order to regain your body."

I would be lying if I said that wasn't a big part of it, I thought. Which was also true as far as it went.

"I don't have any information for you," Control said. "You

will get a mission when we decide the time is right. It is not the right time yet."

I understand, I thought. *I am just anxious.*

"Don't be," Control said. "You will be busy soon enough." And then it opened up a simulation in which I was fighting three Colonial Union frigates at the same time.

It was one I had done before, with some variation. The goal wasn't to destroy all the frigates. The goal was to make them expend as much of their firepower on me as possible so that when three *other* ships skipped in to attack them, they wouldn't have the defenses to survive.

Basically I was bait in the scenario.

It wasn't the only scenario that I'd been bait for, recently.

Let's just say I wasn't loving the pattern of the simulations I was seeing.

The communications window on my captain's screen, normally dead as the famous doornail, lit up. I put the feed inside of it onto the virtual bridge's largest monitor.

On the feed, as advertised, was Secretary Ocampo.

"Mr. Daquin, are you there?" he asked. He was looking into his PDA camera, inside what looked like a stateroom even smaller than the one he had on the *Chandler*.

I am, I thought.

"Okay, good," Ocampo said. "I only have an audio feed for you. They didn't give me a video feed for some—" He stopped here abruptly. He had just realized that the reason he didn't have a video feed was because there wasn't a body for him to look at, just an exposed brain in a clear box.

But *I* had a video feed, so I could see a flush rising through Ocampo's features. He had at least enough grace to be ashamed of himself for forgetting what he had gotten me into.

It's all right, I thought. *I just wanted to talk anyway. If that's all right. If you have time.*

"Today is a religious observance day for the Rraey who run this outpost," Ocampo said. "So nothing's going on today. It's why I'm able to speak to you at all."

Hooray for Rraey Christmas, I thought, to Ocampo.

He smiled at this. "So, what's on your mind?" he asked. And then I got to see another flush rise through his face as he realized just how inappropriate that particular phrase might be to me. This time, at least, he didn't try to run from it.

"Jesus, Rafe," he said. "Sorry about that."

It's all right, I assured him.

"I'm not sure why you even wanted to speak to me," Ocampo said. "If I were in your shoes—*fuck.*"

Okay, if I could laugh, I would definitely be laughing right now.

"I'm glad one of us would be," Ocampo said. "My point is I don't know why you want to speak to me. I assumed that given what has happened to you, you would never want to speak with me again. That you would be furious."

I was *furious,* I admitted, which was 100 percent true. *I can't say I'm happy even now with the situation I'm in. You know what they did to me. To my body.*

"Yes."

That's nothing to be happy about. But I remember what you said to me the last time I saw you. Do you remember?

"Not really," Ocampo said. "I, uh." He paused. "There was a lot going on that day," he said.

You said that you had to ask where your loyalties were, to the Colonial Union or to humanity. You said there was a difference between the two.

"All right. Yes. I remember that now."

I want to know what you meant by that, I thought to him. *Because while neither you nor I can change what's happened to me, maybe there's something you can tell me that makes sense of it all. So I don't think I've lost my body and my freedom for nothing.*

Ocampo was quiet at this for a moment, and I was content to let him take his time.

"You understand there is a lot that I can't tell you," he said, finally. "That much of what I'm doing now is classified. That my colleagues could be listening in to this conversation so that it wouldn't be safe to share anything confidential with you, and that even if they weren't listening in that I wouldn't share it anyway, because that's the nature of things."

I understand that, I thought. *Secretary Ocampo, I know what my role is.* "Mine is not to ask why, mine is to do or die."

Ocampo blinked, and then smiled. "You're quoting Tennyson to me," he said.

Misquoting him, more likely, but yes. What I'm saying is that I'm not asking about the tactics and strategy, sir. I'm asking about the philosophy. Surely that's something you can talk about.

"I can," Ocampo said, and then, jokingly, "but how much time do you have?"

I have all the time you want to give me, I thought, and let that just sit there, between us.

And then Ocampo started talking. Talking about humanity, and about the Colonial Union. He gave me a brief history of the Colonial Union, and about how its first encounters with intelligent alien species—all of which went badly for the Colonial Union, and almost destroyed the young political system—permanently marked it as aggressive and warlike and paranoid.

He talked about the decision to sequester away the planet Earth, to intentionally slow its political and technological progress in order to make it essentially a farm for colonists and soldiers, and how that gave the Colonial Union the raw human resources it needed to become a power among intelligent species far more quickly than any of the other species expected, or could deal with.

He explained how the Conclave, the union of hundreds of intelligent species, was formed in part *because* of the Colonial Union—how its leader, General Tarsem Gau, realized that more than any other species or government, the Colonial Union had a template that would eventually lead to domination of the local space—and to the genocide, intentional or otherwise, of other intelligent species. That creating the Conclave was the only solution: that the Colonial Union would either be absorbed into the Conclave as one voice among many, or counteracted because the Conclave would be too large for the Colonial Union to take on.

He explained how this was a great idea in theory—but in reality the Colonial Union had nearly destroyed the Conclave once, and only General Gau's personal decision to spare the Colonial Union kept all the species of the Conclave from falling on it like a train bearing down on a rodent on its track. He explained that once Gau was gone, the Colonial Union was a target—and all of humanity with it.

And he explained—only generally, only in vague terms—how he, a few trusted allies, and a few alien races who were presumed to be enemies of humanity but were in fact merely enemies of the Colonial Union thought there was a way to save humans as a species even if the Colonial Union should fall. And by "should" it was understood what was meant was "would," and that, in fact, the Colonial Union wouldn't so much fall as be pushed, and in a particular direction.

All of this Ocampo expounded, with himself in the role as a reluctant catalyst or fulcrum for history, someone who wished it were not necessary to give the Colonial Union that push, but one who, recognizing it was necessary, nevertheless stood up—regretfully, yes; heroically, *perhaps?*—to administer the push, in the service of the species.

In short: what an asshole.

Which is not what I said.

Which is not what I even came close to allowing myself to think at the time.

What I said and what I was thinking during all this were variations of one simple phrase, that phrase being *do go on*.

I wanted him to talk, and talk, and then talk some more.

Not because he was the first human I had spoken to since that day on the *Chandler*. I didn't like him that much, although of course I didn't want him to know that.

I wanted him to think I was interested and curious in what he had to say, and thought as well of him as I could under the circumstances.

I wanted him to think I thought his thoughts were golden. Pure nuggets of humble wisdom. *Do go on.*

I wanted him to think this because while he was talking to me, he was connected to the *Chandler*. His PDA, more specifically, was connected to the *Chandler*.

And while he was talking to me, I was going through and copying into the *Chandler*'s storage every single file he had on his PDA.

Because here was my problem: No matter what sort of free run I had with the *Chandler*'s system, I was trapped there.

I couldn't get into the system that Control used to connect to the *Chandler*. Someone would notice that the *Chandler* was trying to address the system. They could log every request. And they would eventually figure out who was doing that. And then I would be screwed.

Besides that, whatever system there was would be entirely alien. I had suspected and Ocampo unwittingly confirmed that wherever we were, it was someplace controlled and run by the Rraey. I knew nothing about Rraey computing systems, or their design, or their programming languages. There was likely to be a computing shell of some sort in which human-designed operating systems could run, and some software that could port documents created on either side to the other.

But full access to the system? That wasn't going to happen. I didn't have the time or resources to get up to speed if it did, and I would be found out and probably tortured and then maybe killed if I tried.

Ocampo's PDA, on the other hand. I knew *all about* that software and hardware.

Official Colonial Union PDAs were manufactured by lots of different companies but all had to run the same software. They all had to be able to talk to every other PDA, and any computers the Colonial Union used for official business. When you have that level of standardization across a government spanning trillions of miles, every *other* computer, operating system, or piece of technology is either standardized to it, or is able to communicate with it.

Oh, I *knew* Ocampo's PDA, all right. Once he opened that connection to the *Chandler*, I knew how to access it, how to look around it, and how to extract files.

And I knew how to do it without him knowing.

Not that I expected him to know; he didn't exactly have the "programmer" look to him, if you know what I mean. He'd be the programmer's boss. The one they hated. The one who made them work on holidays.

I also knew that Ocampo would have all sorts of interesting files on his PDA. Because simply put, where else would he have them? That's the computing and storage unit that he left the *Chandler* with. He would be even less familiar with Rraey technology than I would be. Makes sense that he would keep it, and that he would keep his own information on it. I remembered the exchange Ocampo had with Tvann about Vera Briggs. That poor woman was kept in the dark about a lot of things. Ocampo was used to keeping his own counsel about his business.

The longer I kept Ocampo talking, the more I could find out about his business.

Not that I was trying to sort through any of it while he was talking to me. I had to stay attentive and keep him talking. If I gave any indication he was boring me figuratively out of my skull then he'd drop the connection.

So I kept him talking and had a program make a copy of his PDA. All of it, right down to the communication program he was using to talk to me. I could sort out all of the data later, including the encrypted files.

All of which, it turned out, were keyed to the PDA, so opening them in a virtual copy of the PDA would open the files just fine.

Sloppy.

Three cheers for sloppiness.

The entire copying process took just a little under two hours. I kept Ocampo talking the whole time. It required very little prompting.

Ever heard of "monologuing"? The thing where the captured hero escapes death by getting the villain to talk just long enough to break free?

Well, this wasn't that, because I was still a brain in a box and likely to die the first time I was sent on a mission. But it was something close. And Ocampo had no problem talking and then talking some more.

I don't think it was sheer megalomania, or, if I wanted to be nice about it, him taking pity on the guy he'd caused to be turned into a naked brain. I don't know how many other humans there were where we were; I only knew of Ocampo, Vera Briggs, and whoever the woman was who helped supervise reimplanting weapons systems on the *Chandler*. Of the other two, the weapons systems supervisor looked sort of busy whenever I saw her. As for Vera Briggs, I imagine at this point she might not be feeling especially friendly toward Ocampo.

In other words, I think Ocampo just plain might have been lonely for human contact.

Which I could understand. I had been lonely too.

The difference being, of course, that one of us had made the *choice* to be lonely. The other one of us rather unexpectedly had the choice thrust upon him.

As it turns out, Ocampo's desire to monologue lasted about fifteen minutes longer than the time I needed it to. I knew he was done when he said "But I must be boring you" to me, which is narcissist-speak for "Now I'm bored."

You're not boring me, I thought at him. *But I understand how much of your time I've already taken up today. I can't really ask for more of it. Thank you, Secretary Ocampo.*

"Of course," he said, and then his face got a look. I thought it resembled what the face of someone who felt guilty about something, but didn't actually want to be troubled by doing anything to deal with that guilt, might look like.

I waited and eventually I think Ocampo's vestigial sense of moral obligation kicked in.

"Look, Daquin, I know I've put you in a bad spot," he said. "I know they've promised to return your body to you, and I know they will. They've done this before. But between now and then, if there's something I can do for you, well . . ." He trailed off here, letting me imply that he'd be willing to do something for me, without actually saying it, which I think he thought would give him an out.

This guy was a treasure, this Assistant Secretary of State Tyson Ocampo.

Thank you, sir, I thought. *I can't think of anything I need from you right now.* On the monitor, I could see Ocampo visibly relax; I had just let him off the hook. Which gave me the space to say what I really wanted to. *But there is one thing you can do for me in the future.*

"Name it," Ocampo said.

Someday soon they will give me a mission. My first real mission, not the simulated ones they've been having me running. It would mean a lot to me if, on that day, you and Vera Briggs came to see me off.

"You mean, there on the *Chandler*."

Yes, sir. I realize that to some extent, in my condition—and that was an intentional knife thrust to the guilt centers of Ocampo's brain, right there—*it wouldn't matter whether you said good-bye inside of the* Chandler *or outside of it. But it would mean a lot to me. You and Ms. Briggs are the only people I know now. I'd like someone to see me off. Just a couple of minutes here before I go. If you would.*

Ocampo thought about it for a minute, which was either him figuring out the logistics or trying to see if he could get out of it. "All right," he then said. "We'll do it."

You promise? I asked. Because this was the guy who just trailed off on "If there's something I can do for you."

"I promise," Ocampo said, and I believed him.

Thank you, Secretary Ocampo, I said. *You're a good man.*

Ocampo either smiled or winced at that.

Either way, then he waved and cut the signal.

Things I learned from Ocampo's PDA:

One, there was no doubt Ocampo had known he was going away. He stocked himself quite a library of entertainments—several thousand videos ranging from classic movies from Earth to the latest serials from Phoenix, an equal number of books and musical tracks, and a fair sampling of video games, although these were mostly a decade or more old; I guess when you're running the universe, you don't have time to keep up with everything.

Oh, and *mountains* of porn.

Look, no judgment. Like I said, it's clear he knew he was going to be away for a long time, and probably without significant human companionship. I'm not going to say I wouldn't do the same thing in his shoes. I'm just saying there was more of it than any other sort of entertainment.

And yes, I looked at some. I may be a brain in a box, but that saying that the biggest sex organ is the mind? In my case, both literally and figuratively true.

Also I was curious to see if lack of gonads meant lack of response.

The answer: definitely not. Which was more of a relief than you might think.

Anyway, I might have just gone on about porn too long.

The point was: Ocampo planned for the long term.

Also in the PDA: a truly impressive amount of confidential information from the Colonial Union.

To begin, all the information I think there might have been on the Colonial Union's military capabilities—not just the general Colonial Defense Forces but also its Special Forces and its capabilities. Information on ships, their capabilities, and their state of readiness.

Information about the manpower of the Colonial Defense Forces, its fatality rate over the years, and information about how the lack of relationship with Earth was having an impact on CDF readiness—after all, if you can't get new soldiers, every soldier you lose becomes one less soldier you can muster.

Detailed files on the civilian arm of the Colonial Union government with particular emphasis on the Department of State, which made sense considering who Ocampo was, but every aspect of the CU bureaucracy was gone over in what looked like exhausting detail (I did a lot of skimming).

Information on the Colonial Union merchant fleet—the thousands of trade and cargo ships that crossed between the planets—including which ones were purpose-built and which ones were repurposed from CDF ships, and their most recent trade routes.

Briefs on the current relationship between the Colonial Union and every known nonhuman intelligent species, as well as the Conclave as a political entity, and the Earth.

Briefs on every single Colonial Union planet, population, defensive capabilities, and a list of targets that would offer maximum damage, either to population, to infrastructure, or to industrial capacity.

Blueprints and assessments of Phoenix Station, the seat of the Colonial Union government and humanity's single largest spaceport.

In other words: just about every single bit of information you would want to have in order to plan an attack on the Colonial Union and make it stick. Or at least what *I* thought you would need. I'm not an expert. But that's what it looked like to me.

Now, not all this information was classified. Some of this information you could get just from looking at an encyclopedia or public records. Ocampo or anyone else using this information wasn't exactly going to have the ability to just access a local data network. Ocampo brought with him everything he'd need—or thought he'd need.

But then there was the rest of it.

The *new* information.

The data Ocampo was given since he got here—*here*, incidentally, being a military base hollowed out of an asteroid, made and run by the Rraey until some recent tangles with the Colonial Union and some others made them scale way, way back—and information he'd created since he'd been here.

With this group.

With the Equilibrium.

Which is what they were calling themselves, anyway.

I thought it was a stupid name. But they weren't giving me a vote. And if they did I would probably name it "The League of Assholes," so I don't think they would mind not having my input.

This new information included audio and video recordings of meetings and the automatic transcriptions of the same. Those were useful because they tagged who was saying what. This was useful because some of the people in the meetings were from species I'd never encountered before—a fact that was not especially impressive since most of my travel was within the Colonial Union, but still something to deal with.

Most of the transcriptions were of meetings about unexciting things—discussions about the maintenance of the base, for one, which apparently had a mold problem that was aggravating the respiratory systems of several of the species there, to which I thought, *Well, good.*

But then I found some interesting transcripts after all.

For example: one recorded only a couple of weeks into our stay at the base, which started off with Ku Tlea Dho, a Rraey diplomat, catching Ocampo not paying attention.

"You seem distracted, Secretary Ocampo," Dho said. The video had him down the arc of the table that dominated a tiny meeting room, which had a dozen people in it, most from different races.

"I'm still getting my bearings on the station, Ambassador Dho," Ocampo said.

"You will be here for a while, Secretary," Dho said. "You will have time."

Ocampo smiled here. "Hopefully not too much more time."

"How do you mean?" asked Ake Bae. He was an Eyr. The Eyr were members of the Conclave, or so I learned when I checked the files Ocampo brought with him. Increasingly unhappily members of the Conclave.

"The time has come to discuss the endgame," Ocampo said, to the room. "*Our* endgame."

"Has it."

"It's why I am here, Ake Bae," Ocampo said.

"Indeed," said Ake Bae. "Are you sure, Secretary Ocampo, that you're not confusing your own endgame with *our* endgame? I understand that you are now in exile from the Colonial Union for the duration of the campaign at the very least. That does not imply that Equilibrium must now change its schedule to accommodate your personal needs or inclinations."

Ocampo smiled again, but not exactly a nice smile. "I understand the concern," he said, looking around the room. "I know very well that many of you have the view that humans, individually and as a species, have an outsized opinion of our importance to events, both in general and here with our particular activity. I'm also aware that many of you are of the opinion that I've always been a pain in the ass."

There were noises in the room that I assumed equated to laughter.

"Let me remind you, however, that the roots of this rebellion of ours come from when we, the Colonial Union, struck out against the Conclave at Roanoke," Ocampo continued. He looked around the room at the assembled species. "How many of your governments watched the Conclave form, and felt helpless to do anything about it?" He looked at Ake Bae. "How many of your governments joined the Conclave rather than fight it? The Colonial Union—humanity—were the only ones to bloody the Conclave. The only ones to show they *could* be bloodied. The only ones to show that General Gau's experiment with hegemony could be toppled."

"You seem to be discounting the attempted coup of Gau after Roanoke," Ake Bae said.

"A coup given impetus by the Colonial Union's attack on the Conclave fleet," Ocampo countered. "My point, Ake Bae, is that we are here today because of what humans have done. If we have a high opinion of our importance to this cause of ours, it's because we've earned it. It's not merely ego."

"There's irony in praising the Colonial Union's actions against the Conclave when it's that very action that convinced us all that it must be destroyed along with the Conclave," said Utur Nove. Nove was from Elpri. I had no idea until that moment that a planet named Elpri even existed.

"We all agree that the return to an equilibrium of power is best for all of our species," Ocampo said. "Thus the very name of our organization. The Conclave represents the primary threat to that equilibrium. We agree about that. We also agree that the Colonial Union grew too powerful in opposition to the Conclave. But don't confuse the Colonial Union with humanity."

He nodded to Paola Gaddis, who was the other human I'd seen, the one who supervised the installation of the weapons systems. She nodded back at him.

"My colleague here represents the interests of several governments of Earth," Ocampo said. "She will be happy to tell you all the ways those governments are not even remotely concerned about the Colonial Union's interests. In the end, the Colonial Union is not humanity. It is merely a government. When the Colonial Union falls, and it will, then the Earth might finally take up the mantle of leading the former worlds of the CU. Or those worlds might form other unions. *Humanity* will survive. Humanity will continue as part of the new equilibrium."

"Humanity, perhaps," Ake Bae said. "But I was speaking of *you* in particular, Secretary Ocampo. You and your own endgame, which is different from that of the Equilibrium."

Ocampo smiled again, picked up his PDA from the table. The video feed got momentarily wavy, trying to stabilize the image while being lifted. "You know what this is, Ake Bae."

"It's a personal data assistant, I believe," Ake Bae said.

"It is," Ocampo said. "And it contains nearly all of the last decade of data from the Colonial Union State Department and the Colonial Defense Forces. Nearly every confidential file and report on the CU's doings and conflicts. Everything they don't want known, or would want swept under the carpet. Every double-cross of an ally, completed or intended. Every military action on one of its own worlds. Every assassination. Every 'disappearance.' All of it true. All of it verifiable. All of it hugely damaging to the Colonial Union."

"The data you promised us to help us plan our strategy for our next phase," Ake Bae said.

"No," Ocampo said. "Not the next phase. The *last* phase." He shook the PDA for emphasis, and the video got woozy again. "Understand that every piece of data from the Colonial Union is accurate and verifiable. It all happened. And so it will serve as cover for what I will *add* to it."

"What will you add?" asked Dho.

"All of *our* operations," Ocampo said. "Every ship we've commandeered, human and Conclave. Every agitation we've spearheaded on Colonial Union and Conclave worlds. Every attack, up to and including the destruction of Earth Station. All of it altered, to make it look as if it happened under the aegis of the Colonial Union and the Colonial Defense forces. All verified by both my security hash and the security hash of my former boss, the current secretary of state."

"And how did you get that?" asked Paola Gaddis.

"The weakest part of any security and verification scheme is the people who use it," Ocampo said.

Right then I nearly paused the video to savor the rich irony of that statement, all things considered.

"And the fact they trust the people they've known for years as friends and allies," Ocampo continued, oblivious to my scorn. "Secretary Galeano is no pushover, but she has a soft spot for loyalty. I earned her trust long ago. I've never done anything that would cause her to doubt it."

"Except this," Gaddis pointed to the PDA. "And everything else you've done for Equilibrium."

"I'm not going to suggest Galeano will ever forgive me," Ocampo said. "She won't. I like to think that in time she'll recognize the necessity."

"She won't," Gaddis said. Ocampo shrugged.

"This does not explain why this would be the *last* phase," Ake Bae said, bringing the discussion back around. "It just makes the Colonial Union culpable for our actions."

"No," Gaddis said, before Ocampo could speak. "The Earth already believes the Colonial Union made the attack on Earth Station, to cripple us and to keep us dependent. Getting confirmation would mean a state of war between us."

"Which would force the hand of the Conclave," Ocampo said.

"Right," Gaddis said. "Right now it's playing nice with Earth but still keeping us at arm's length because it doesn't want to antagonize the Colonial Union. But if the CU's verifiably responsible for the destruction of Earth Station, as shown by its own documents, it all falls by the wayside. The Conclave will invite the Earth to join."

"Which will antagonize those of us who don't want the humans in the Conclave," said Utur Nove. "No offense," he said, to Gaddis.

"None taken," she said. "And that's what we want, anyway. The division will weaken the Conclave, just as the Colonial Union decides that it's a material threat and moves to destroy it."

"A move which would fail," Nove said.

Ocampo shook his head. "The Colonial Union will fail if it goes toe-to-toe with the Conclave, yes," he said. "But it wouldn't do that. It *didn't* do it when it destroyed the Conclave fleet at Roanoke. It didn't send its ships into combat with the Conclave's. It sent *assassins*—Special Forces to sneak up and place antimatter bombs on each ship, and then detonate them all at the same time. It was a psychological blow as much as a physical loss. That's how the CU did it. That's how it would do it again. One assassin, one shot—total destruction. Which is how it will happen this time."

"You plan to assassinate General Gau!" Nove exclaimed, following Ocampo's implication.

"No," Ocampo said, and pointed to Nove. "*You* are going to plan it." He pointed at Ake Bae. "Or *you* are going to plan it. You two are both in rather better positions to make it happen. Whoever does it is not my particular concern. The point is whichever of you plans it, it will become obvious that you did it at the behest of the Colonial Union. The CU knows that humiliating Gau nearly brought the end of the Colonial Union. It knows that Gau requires loyalty to *him,* not the Colonial Union. Killing him destroys that loyalty. Killing him destroys the Conclave."

"Which leaves the Colonial Union the largest power standing," Ake Bae said.

"No," Gaddis said. "Not without the Earth. No soldiers. No colonists."

"Unless the Earth changes its mind," said Ku Tlea Dhu.

"At the right time, we will motivate them otherwise," Ocampo said. "We've done it before. We can be equally persuasive this time." He motioned away from the room, toward, I guessed, the docks in which the *Chandler* was being worked on and equipped. "Unless you've got a better use for all the ships we've been taking."

"A thing which is getting harder to do," Dhu said. "We can't trick all the ship captains as you did with the *Chandler*'s."

"All the more reason to bring things to an active conclusion," Ocampo said. "We've always been a small but potent unit. Small isn't the problem. The potency of our actions is the key."

"And all this begins by releasing the information on that," Ake Bae said, pointing to the PDA.

"Yes," Ocampo said.

"And where do you suggest we release it?"

"We release it everywhere," Ocampo said. "Everywhere, all at once."

"I think this is a good plan," Gaddis said. "I even think we have a chance of making it work as we intend to."

"It's nice the two humans are in agreement," Nove said. I noted that sarcasm was a near-universal trait of intelligent species.

"With respect, Ambassador Nove, our agreement is a good thing," Gaddis said. "Don't forget that through all of this, it's *my* planet that is the most vulnerable. We lack spaceships. We lack military power. The governments I represent believe Equilibrium offers us the best chance to build up our defenses before everyone else turns their attention to us again. This plan can make that happen." Nove shifted its weight, unhappy.

Gaddis turned her attention back to Ocampo. "Which isn't to say it doesn't have risks. Principal among them being that the Colonial Union has to believe you are dead. And died loyal. If they think you're alive and a traitor, you know they won't stop looking for you."

Ocampo nodded. "The Colonial Union knows what it means when a ship is taken," he said. "They know everyone but the pilot is killed. They won't think it will be any different for me."

"You are an undersecretary of the State Department," Nove pointed out.

"On vacation," Ocampo said. "Nothing to identify me as anything other than an unlucky civilian."

"You don't think they will suspect you," Gaddis said.

"I've been part of this for several years now," Ocampo said. "I've been funneling information to Equilibrium all this time. If they were going to catch me they would have done it before I left."

"You had people you used," Thu said.

"I had a small number of people who operated independently and subcontracted," Ocampo said. "I cleaned up before I left."

"You mean you had them killed," Thu said.

"The ones who could bring things back to me, yes."

"And *that* won't look suspicious at all," Gaddis said, archly.

"Give me a little credit for subtlety," Ocampo said.

"All this talk," Ake Bae said. "All this planning, all this strategizing, and yet we still don't know your endgame, Secretary Ocampo."

"It's the same as the endgame for Equilibrium," he said. "The end of the Conclave. The end of the Colonial Union. The end to superpowers in our little corner of space. And when it's all said and done, our group, which acts in the shadows, fades into them forever. And we go back to our worlds."

"Yes, but *you're* dead," Ake Bae said. "Or at least the Colonial Union thinks so. And it is in your—and our—interest for them to continue to believe so."

"For now," Ocampo said.

"And later?" Ake Bae asked.

"Later things will be very different," Ocampo said.

"You don't think this will be a problem."

"I don't."

"And you're sure about this."

"Nothing is ever certain," Ocampo said. "But to go back to earlier points in this conversation, after what I've done for this group of ours, and for our goals, I think I've earned some confidence for my opinions. And my opinion is: No. When all is said and done, this won't be a problem at all."

And then they started talking about the mold problem some more.

I came away from this with two thoughts.

One, and again: Ocampo was a real piece of work.

Two, that sob story he told me about humanity and the Colonial Union was a load of crap.

Scratch that—not *entirely* a load of crap. What he told me was the nice version. The version where he was a selfless martyr for humanity rather than the guy who was planting a bomb in order to profit from the chaos. I had no love for that Ake Bae character, but he or she or it was not wrong. Whatever Ocampo was up to, he was in it for himself as much as, if not more so, than he was for anyone or anything else.

And then there was the third thought: Ocampo's megalomania, or whatever it was, had already gotten thousands of people killed.

Not *only* his megalomania. He wasn't working alone. But he sure seemed to be doing some of the heavy lifting.

And soon, they would want to use me to do more of it.

And then, like that, it was time.

"We are giving you a mission," Control said, one morning, or at least during the time of day that I'd been thinking of as morning since I got to the Equilibrium base.

Okay, I thought to Control. *That's good news. What's the mission?*

"We will provide you with a mission brief once you're near the skip point."

So two or three days from now, I thought.

"Sooner than that," Control said. "More along the line of eight of your hours."

That was an interesting admission. Skip drives, which are how we travel immense distances in space, only engage when space-time is flat enough—that is to say, far away from a gravity well.

By telling me the rough amount of time it would take to get to skip distance, Control was telling me something about where we were. That the base was someplace that had a low mass, not especially close to anything more massive, like a planet or moon.

Basically Control was telling me we were at an asteroid, at a far distance from its star.

Which I *knew*, but which Control didn't know I knew. Control never told me.

By telling me now, either Control slipped, or didn't think it mattered.

Since I knew Control had done this before many times, it didn't seem likely it was a slip. So Control figured it didn't matter. And I figured it didn't matter because either they thought I was well conditioned to respond like they told me, or they didn't plan on me surviving the mission.

I thought about my armaments—a couple dozen missiles and beefed-up beam systems, perfect for blinding communication systems and incoming missiles. And then I thought about my defensive systems, which hadn't been substantially upgraded from when the *Chandler* was a trade ship.

So, yeah. I was betting on the "not coming back" scenario.

All right, I thought. *It would at least be helpful to know the general sort of mission it is, however. So I might practice some simulations on the way.*

"That won't be necessary," Control said. "We prefer you to stay focused on the mission once it starts."

Understood, I said. *Does this mean I'll have control of the ship to skip distance?*

"No," Control said. "We will control the *Chandler* for the disembarkation and for a short portion of time thereafter. After which a course will be set. You will have full control after the skip. Until then you are to monitor systems. We will keep a communication channel open so you may alert us if there are any problems."

The further I get from you the longer the lag will be in our communication, I pointed out. *The speed of light still applies.*

"We don't anticipate any problems," Control said.

You're the boss, I thought. *When do we start?*

"Secretary Ocampo has asked us to delay the start of your

mission until he can say good-bye to you," Control said. "As was your request."

Yes.

"As a courtesy to him, we will allow this. He is currently otherwise engaged. When he's done, he will travel to you. You will have ten of your minutes to say your farewells. This will happen within the next two hours."

Understood. Thank you, Control. It means a lot to me.

Control didn't say anything to this; I could see that it had broken its connection. That was fine.

I had a couple of hours to prepare for my mission.

I prepared.

"I remember the last time I was here," Ocampo said.

He was standing on the bridge of the *Chandler*. With him were Vera Briggs and an escort of two Rraey soldiers.

I imagine it looks a little different now, I thought to him. *A bit emptier.*

Ocampo visibly winced at this; I could see it happen through one of the bridge cameras. Vera Briggs was silent and staring, in a horrified fashion, at the box containing my brain. The Rraey, for their part, were unreadable to me. That's the thing about aliens, I suppose.

Thank you for coming to see me, I thought, to both Ocampo and Briggs. *I really appreciate it.*

"You're welcome," Ocampo said. "To be honest it's nice to be off that rock—"

One of the Rraey made a throat-clearing sound here, suggesting some nonverbal cues were universal; that is, if you have a throat.

"—it's nice to have a change of scenery, I should say." Ocampo fairly glared at the Rraey.

I don't want to take up too much of your time, I thought. *I know the two of you are busy. Also, Control told me that I had ten minutes with you.*

"Right," Ocampo said. "And in fact we should probably start on our way back. They were annoyed with us enough when I insisted we say good-bye."

I understand, I replied. *And I think I need to get started anyway.*

From outside the bridge came a loud clanging noise, followed by what sounded like voices. It might have been the *Chandler*'s intercom speakers acting up. Or it could have been something else.

Both Ocampo and Briggs jumped. The two Rraey said something to each other in their own language and hoisted their weapons. One of them held a hand out to Ocampo and Briggs, signaling that they were to stay on the bridge. The Rraey then exited the bridge to investigate.

The automatic, reinforced door to the bridge slammed shut, sealing Ocampo and Briggs in and the Rraey out.

"What the hell?" Ocampo asked.

There was a low thrumming sound as the *Chandler*'s engines ramped up from their resting phase to propulsion phase.

"What are you doing?" Ocampo asked me.

I'm not doing anything, I replied. *I don't have control over the ship yet.*

There was a banging on the bridge door. The Rraey were trying to get back in.

"Open the door," Ocampo said to me.

I don't have control of the door.

"Who does?"

Whoever it is that has been running my simulations. I don't know who they are. They just told me to call them Control.

Ocampo swore and pulled out his PDA. Then he swore again when he couldn't open up a line back to base. When the PDA got to the *Chandler,* it automatically connected to the ship's network. The *Chandler*'s network gave every appearance of being down.

Ocampo looked around at the bridge stations. "Which of these is for communications?"

None of them are right now, I thought at him. *The bridge stations are cut out of the command loop. Everything gets routed through a simulated bridge which I'm supposed to control.*

"So you *are* in control of this ship!"

No, I said "supposed to," I pointed out. *I'm not in control of the ship yet. I only get control once the ship has skipped. It's Control who is behind this.*

"Then talk to Control!" Ocampo yelled.

I can't. I've never been given the ability to contact them. I have to wait for them to contact me.

And lo and behold, guess who suddenly came onto the line.

"The *Chandler* is moving," Control said. "Explain how."

I don't know, I thought. *You're the one in control of this ship. You tell me.*

"I'm not in control of the ship."

Well, someone is.

"It has to be you."

How can that be? I exclaimed. *Check it yourself! I'm not doing a damn thing in the simulation!*

There was a brief pause here as Control ascertained that, indeed, inside the simulation I was doing nothing. While this was happening the banging at the bridge door became more insistent and it sounded like fists were being replaced by weapon butts.

Then Control's voice came over the bridge speakers. "Secretary Ocampo," it said.

"Yes?"

"You are controlling the *Chandler* in some way."

"The hell I am," Ocampo said.

"You've sequestered yourself in the bridge," Control said.

"We're locked in here, you asshole," Ocampo said. "And I can't help but notice that my Rraey escort is on the other side of the door. What are you up to?"

"Please cease your actions."

"I am not doing a goddamned thing!" Ocampo yelled. He motioned to the bridge stations. "These fucking things don't work! It's you who is doing this!"

There was a pause; Ocampo looked confused. It took him maybe a second or two longer to realize that the hammering on the door had stopped while he was yelling at Control.

"You have purged all the air everywhere but the bridge," Control said, after a minute. "You have just killed two Rraey."

"Jesus Christ," Ocampo said, clearly exasperated. "*It's not me!* I'm not in control of this ship! You are! You are the one who is doing this! You're the murderer, not me! Why are you doing this?"

"Enough," Control said. By this time I could see on my simulated sensors that the *Chandler* had completed its disembarkation process and was beginning to accelerate away from Equilibrium base. This would be the point where Control would have no choice but to cut its losses and try to either disable or destroy the *Chandler*. I was curious to find out what would happen next.

What happened next was that a ping hit my personal set of sensors. It was a signal that was meant for the bomb, nestled next to my brain in my box.

It was supposed to detonate the bomb, killing me.

What it did instead was launch a dozen missiles from the *Chandler*.

Let's just say I had a philosophical disagreement with the whole "blow up my brain" strategy. And this was my editorial comment on that plan.

I think I actually heard a squawk of surprise from Control as those dozen missiles popped up on its sensors.

There were three ships aside from the *Chandler* docked at Equilibrium station: one a refurbished Colonial Union frigate like the *Chandler,* one that looked like a purpose-built trade ship to me, and one of a design I didn't recognize, so probably an alien ship. I imagined that all three of them were like the *Chandler,* currently being repurposed for whatever asshole plan Equilibrium had up its sleeve for each of them.

I tasked a missile to each ship.

If those ships had crews on station, it's possible that they could have stopped the missiles. But if all they had were brains in boxes, not given control of their own ships, then they were sitting ducks.

Each of those missiles hit home, crippling but not entirely destroying the ships.

Intentional on my part. If there were other brains in boxes in those ships, they didn't deserve to die at my hand.

They didn't deserve any of the horror that happened to them.

Six missiles aimed for Equilibrium base's weapon arrays, because I didn't want them to have a chance to mess up my getaway with a well-placed missile, or two, or ten.

One missile homed in on the Equilibrium base energy generator, because I figured if they were worried about things getting dark and cold, they would have less time to worry about little old me, or the *Chandler.*

One missile went to the base communication array, to make it more difficult to get the word out. They'd undoubtedly try to launch some skip drones, but I'd already configured my beam weapons to burn those out before they got anywhere close to skip distance. Factoring in tracking lag from the speed of light would be tricky. But I'd had time to practice.

That left one missile.

That one went to my best guess as to where Control was.

Because fuck that guy.

Yes, you could say that I'd been busy, using the *Chandler*'s outside cameras to scope out the base, and double-checking the information with the data I had taken from Ocampo's PDA.

I knew I was going to have one chance to get it right. Any misses and everything suddenly became a lot more complicated.

Fortunately I still had a couple dozen missiles left.

But as it turns out I didn't need them. When I launched the missiles I was still really close in to Equilibrium base. The targets had anywhere from ten to twenty-five seconds to respond. Which might have been enough in a battle situation.

But as a surprise? When the base and ships were unprepared for attack and the only person who could have raised the alarm was being kept busy with an argument with the very confused and increasingly hostile Secretary Ocampo?

Nope. Not enough time.

Every missile hit its mark.

The resulting chaos was glorious to me.

Glorious.

"Hello?" Ocampo said, and I realized that from his point of view, nothing had happened. He was still waiting for a response from Control.

I'm sorry, Secretary Ocampo, I thought at him. *Control isn't likely to respond to you at this point.*

"Why not?"

Because I just stuffed a missile down its fucking gullet, that's why.

"What?"

I just attacked Equilibrium's base, I thought at him. *Twelve missiles, all in the right places. It's going to keep them busy while the three of us get to skip distance.*

"What?" Ocampo said again. He clearly wasn't getting it.

"You mean we're going back?" Vera Briggs said. "Back home? Back to the Colonial Union?" It was, honestly, the first time I remember her speaking a complete sentence.

Yes, I said. *That's the plan. Back to Phoenix Station. Where I think they will be very interested in what Secretary Ocampo has to say for himself.*

"You can't do that," Ocampo said.

Take you back to the Colonial Union? I asked. *Yes I can. Yes I will. In fact, that's what I was waiting to do.*

"I don't understand," Ocampo said.

I've had control of the Chandler *for weeks. I could have tried for an escape long before now. But I needed your data to take back. And I needed you to back it up. You're going home, Secretary Ocampo.*

"You don't understand what you're doing," Ocampo said.

Sure I do.

"No, you don't," Ocampo said. "Don't you understand that what we're doing here is saving humanity—"

Everything after that point was cut short by the *whoofing* sound Ocampo made as Vera Briggs walked the couple of feet separating the two of them and kneed her boss square and hard in the balls.

I don't even have balls anymore and *I* felt that.

Ocampo collapsed, groaning. Briggs kicked him several more times in the ribs and face, inexpertly but enthusiastically, until he stopped doing anything but lying there in a ball.

"Motherfucker," Briggs said, finally backing away.

You didn't kill him, did you? I asked.

"Trust me, I'm going to make *sure* he lives," Briggs said. She spat on him; he didn't even flinch. "Make me look like a fool by perpetrating treason behind my back? For *years*? Kill a ship full of people and give me the choice of death or being kidnapped? Make me an accomplice to killing even more people? No, Mr. Daquin. This asshole lives. And I'm going to make sure the Colonial Union knows everything I know, too. So you just get us back. You get us back. I promise you I'm going to take care of the rest of it. And *you*," Briggs said to Ocampo. "You so much as *move an inch* between now and then and you're going to wish I kicked you to death. You understand me, *sir*?"

Ocampo didn't move a muscle for the entire rest of the trip.

"Let's talk about the future," Harry Wilson said to me.

It had been a busy week.

I had skipped the *Chandler* into existence roughly ten klicks from Phoenix Station itself, setting off every single proximity warning the station had. Which was the point; I didn't want them to miss me.

As soon as I skipped I started broadcasting that I had Secretary Ocampo *and* critical information about an alien attack, which got everyone's attention. Less than an hour after that the *Chandler* was swarming with Colonial Defense Forces, Ocampo and Briggs were taken off the ship—Ocampo to the infirmary of Phoenix Station's detention facility and Briggs to high-level debriefing—and then the CDF tried to figure out what to do with me.

That's when Wilson showed up.

"Why you?" I asked him—*asked* him, because he connected directly to me with his BrainPal, the computer inside his head.

"Because I've done this before," he said. He explained that later, during his debriefing of me, during which I told him of my experiences and gave him all the information I had.

"The future," I said, back in the present.

"Yes," Wilson said.

"What I want for the future is to have a body."

"You're going to get that," Wilson said. "We're already working on it. The Colonial Defense Forces have already authorized growing a clone for you."

"You're going to put my brain in a clone?"

"Not exactly," Wilson said. "When the clone is grown we're

going to transfer your consciousness into it. You'll leave this brain behind and be put into a new one."

"That's . . . unsettling," I said. My brain was the only part of me left, and now they were telling me that I was going to leave it behind.

"I know," Wilson said. "If it helps, I've been through the process. You're still you after it happens. Promise."

"When can we start?" I asked.

"Well, that's up to you," Wilson said. "That's what I want to talk to you about."

"What do you mean?"

"They've already started working on your body," Wilson said. "If you wanted it—and no one would say anything against you wanting it—we can get you one in a few weeks. But for someone with an already existing consciousness that we need to port into the new brain, it's not optimal. They'd rather build your body slowly and pre-prime the new brain to accept your consciousness. That way the transfer goes off without a hitch."

"How long will that take?"

"Less time than making a body the natural way, but still a few months," Wilson said. "Honestly the longer we take prepping the body for consciousness the better it will be."

"And in the meantime I'm stuck here on the *Chandler*."

" 'Stuck' is a relative term," Wilson said.

"What does that mean?"

"It means that if you want, I might have a job for you. And the *Chandler*."

"What's the job?"

"The job is to be you. Both you, Rafe Daquin, and you, the brain running the *Chandler*. We want the various species we talk with to be aware that you're real and that your story is real."

"I already gave you all the information I have on Equilibrium," I said. "It's pretty convincing."

"*We* don't need to be convinced," Wilson said. "*We* know you're telling the truth. But you understand that us knowing about Equilibrium—us knowing that they were the ones behind the attack on Earth Station and the ones who have been setting the Conclave and the CU against each other—isn't enough. Thanks to what Equilibrium has already done, the CU has almost no credibility. With anyone. Not with independent species. Not with the Conclave, or any species within it. And certainly not with Earth."

"And having me around changes that?"

"Well, no," Wilson admitted. I would have smiled at this if I could. "It doesn't change it. But it does get our foot in the door. It offers others at least the possibility that we might be telling the truth. You can get us a hearing, at least."

"What about the Equilibrium base?" I asked. "You sent ships there?"

"I'm not supposed to tell you anything about that," Wilson said.

"Are you kidding me?"

"Relax. You didn't let me finish. I'm not supposed to tell you anything about that. Specifically, I'm not supposed to tell you that we found the base and we found a lot of fresh damage that corresponds to what you told me, but aside from that the base was deserted."

"What do you mean deserted?" I said. "When did you get there?"

"We sent probes almost as soon as we got coordinates from you, and a couple of warships right after that."

"Then you should have found *something*. They couldn't have disappeared."

"I didn't say *disappeared*," Wilson said. "I said deserted. There was a lot of evidence of someone having been there, and of the base having been used up until very recently. But whoever was there was gone. They left in a big damn hurry."

"What about the other ships?" I asked. "The ones like me, I mean."

"We found wreckage," Wilson said. "Whether they were the ships like you or some other ships we can't tell you yet."

"They wouldn't have been able to go anywhere," I said. "If you found wreckage, it was those ships."

"I'm sorry, Rafe."

"I don't understand how they could have deserted the base that quickly. I knocked out their communications."

"There's the possibility that they had drones or ships in other systems set to investigate *if* there was no communication with the base," Wilson said. "These assholes were building a fleet with hostage pilots. They probably figured one of them might try an attack or lead someone back to them sooner or later."

"But *I* got away. If they planned for it, how did *that* happen?"

Wilson grinned. "Maybe you were better at it than they expected. They had to decide between evacuating their people or going after you."

"But we still have all the evidence. You have Ocampo, for God's sake! Have *him* talk."

"He's not going to be talking to anyone other than CDF intelligence for a while," Wilson said. "More to the point, he doesn't really have the capability to talk to anyone else at the moment."

"What does that mean?"

"It means that right now, you and he have a lot in common," Wilson said.

It took me a second to figure out what *that* meant. Then I imagined Ocampo in his own little box.

"I don't know how I feel about that," I said, eventually.

"I think you should probably feel disgusted by it, but that's just me," Wilson said. "I wasn't in charge of that decision. Look, Rafe, you're right. We have all the facts. We have names. We have data. And when and if people choose to look at all that *rationally*, then they'll realize that the Colonial Union isn't to blame for a lot of the crap it's currently getting the blame for. But until that time, being able to have you around to appeal to their emotions and sense of morality doesn't hurt. We could use you."

"To evoke pity."

"Yes," Wilson said. "Among other things. Also, we kind of need a ship."

I thought about this. "For how long?" I asked.

"Hopefully not too long," Wilson said. "Things are moving fast now. We're already a week behind. We've sent back-channel messages to the Conclave and are arranging meetings now. We're trying the same with Earth. In both cases things are complicated by the fact that some of their people are involved too. And meanwhile Equilibrium is still out there. And you've probably accelerated their schedule. Everything's going to get done very soon, I expect."

"And if it all works out, then my body is waiting for me."

"Even if it doesn't work out your body will be waiting for you," Wilson said. "Although in that case you may have less time to enjoy it than you'd want."

"Let me think about it," I said.

"Of course," Wilson said. "If you can give me an answer in a couple of days that would be good."

"I will."

"Also, if you say yes, then we'll be working together," Wilson said. "You and me and Hart Schmidt. Who is worried about you and quietly furious that he's not allowed to talk to you yet and that I can't tell him anything. Let me suggest that you let him in to see you as soon as that's cleared from above."

"I will," I said again.

"You also need to tell us whether you want us to tell your parents about you yet," Wilson said, gently.

This was something I had been waffling about. I was alive.

But I didn't think my family would be comforted by how I was right now.

"They still think I was lost with the rest of the crew," I asked.

"Yes," Wilson said. "We found lifepods and are retrieving the bodies and notifying the families. There was one lifepod that was destroyed. As you know. We can always say to your parents that some bodies haven't been found. Which happens to be true, as far as it goes."

"I'll tell you what to do when I give you my other answer," I said.

"Fair enough." Wilson stood up. "One last thing. The State Department asked me to ask you if you'd do a write-up of your experience. A personal history."

"You've already debriefed me."

"I did," Wilson agreed. "I got all the facts. I think they're wanting to know everything else, too. You're not the only person they've done this to, Rafe. I know that for a fact. At the end of this we're going to have to put other people back together too. You telling us what it's been like for you might help with that."

"I'm not a writer," I said.

"You don't need to be," Wilson said. "We'll get someone to clean it up so it scans. Just talk the whole thing through. We'll figure it out from there."

"Okay," I said.

And that's what I did.

And that's what this is.

The life of the mind.

Well, my mind, anyway.

So far.

THIS HOLLOW UNION

To William Dufris and Tavia Gilbert, and any other audiobook narrator who might work in the Old Man's War universe. Thanks for giving these characters a voice.

"I have to tell you that I am deeply concerned that our union is on the verge of collapse," Ristin Lause said to me.

It's been said, and I suspect largely by people who are not terribly fond of me, that I, Hafte Sorvalh, am the second most powerful person in the known universe. It's certainly true that I am the confidant and closest advisor of General Tarsem Gau, the leader of the Conclave, the largest known political union, with over four hundred constituent member species, none of whom number less than one billion souls. It is also true that in my role as confidant and advisor to Tarsem, I have a great deal of choice in terms of which things to bring to his attention; also that Tarsem chooses to use me strategically to solve a number of problems he would prefer not to be seen involved with, and in those cases I have a wide amount of personal discretion in solving the problem, with the full resources of the Conclave at my disposal.

So yes, it would not be inaccurate to say that I am, indeed, the second most powerful person in the known universe.

Note well, however, that being the second most powerful person in the universe is very much like being the second most of anything, which is to say, not the first, and receiving none of the benefits of being the first. And as my position and status derive entirely from the grace and need of the actual most powerful person in the universe, my ability to exercise the prerogatives of my power are, shall we say, constrained. And now you know why it is said of me by the people who are not terribly fond of me.

However, this suits my personal inclinations. I don't mind having the power that is given to me, but I have only rarely grasped for it myself. My position has come largely from being usefully competent to others, each more powerful than the next. I have always been the one who stands behind, the one who counts heads, the one who offers advice.

And, also, the one who has to sit in meetings with anxious politicians, listening to them wring whatever appendages they wring about The End of All Things. In this case, Ristin Lause, the chancellor of the Grand Assembly of the Conclave, an august political body that I was always aware of having a grammatical redundancy in its title, but nevertheless not to be ignored. Ristin Lause sat in my office, staring up at me, for I am tall, even for a Lalan. She held in her hand a cup of iet, a hot drink from her planet, which was a traditional morning pick-me-up. She had it in her hand because I offered it, as was customary, and because she was, at a very early time on the clock, my first meeting for the sur, the Conclave's standard day.

"In truth, Ristin, are you ever *not* concerned that our union is on the verge of collapse?" I asked, and reached for my own cup, which was not filled with iet, which to me tasted like what might happen if you let a dead animal ferment in a jug of water in hot sunlight for an unfortunately long period of time.

Lause made a head movement which I knew corresponded to a frown. "You are mocking my concern, Councilor?" she asked.

"Not at all," I said. "I am offering tribute to your conscientiousness as chancellor. No one knows the assembly better than you, and no one is more aware of the shifts in alliances and strategies. This is why we meet every five sur, and I am grateful we do. With that said, you do proclaim concern about the collapse of the Conclave on a regular basis."

"You suspect hyperbole."

"I seek clarity."

"All right," Lause said, and set down her iet, undrunk. "Then here is clarity for you. I see the collapse of the Conclave because General Gau has been pressing for votes in the assembly that he shouldn't be. I see it because his enemies have been pushing votes to counter and undermine the general's power, and they are losing by smaller margins with each outing. For the first time there is open dissatisfaction with him, and with the direction of the Conclave."

"For the first time?" I said. "I seem to recall an attempted coup in the not ancient past, brought on by his decision not to punish the humans for the destruction of our fleet at the Roanoke Colony."

"A small group of discontents, trying to take advantage of what they saw as a moment of weakness on the part of the general."

"Which almost succeeded, if you recall. I remember the knife coming down toward his neck, and missiles immediately thereafter."

Lause waved this away. "You're missing my point," she said. "That was a coup, an attempt to wrest power from the general by extralegal means. What I see now, with every vote, is the power and influence—the moral standing—of the general being whittled away. You know that Unli Hado, among others, wants to put the general to a confidence vote. If things progress, it won't be long until he gets his wish."

I drank from my cup. Unli Hado had recently challenged General Gau's actions dealing with the human Colonial Union, and been knocked back when he asserted evidence of new human colonies that turned out not to exist—or more accurately, they had been so thoroughly removed from their planets by the Colonial Union that there was no hard evidence they had ever existed. Those colonies had been quietly removed at

General Gau's request; Hado had been fed the outdated information on their existence in order to be made to look like a fool.

And it had worked; he had looked like a fool when he attempted to call out the general. What I and the general had underestimated were the number of other assembly members who would willingly continue to follow a fool.

"The general isn't a member of the assembly," I said. "A confidence vote wouldn't be binding."

"Wouldn't it?" Lause said. "The assembly can't remove the general from the leadership of the Conclave, no. There's no mechanism for it. But you understand that a no confidence vote on the general is the fatal crack in his armor. After that General Gau is no longer the beloved, and almost mythical founder of the Conclave. He's merely another politician who has overstayed his welcome."

"You are the chancellor of the assembly," I noted. "You could keep a confidence vote on the general from reaching the floor."

"I could," Lause agreed. "But I could not then keep the confidence vote on *me* from reaching the floor. And once I was out of the way, Hado, or more likely one of his more pliable lieutenants, would ascend to my position. The general's confidence vote would not be avoided, merely delayed."

"And what if it were to happen?" I asked, setting down my cup. "The general is not under the illusion that he will be the head of the Conclave forever. The Conclave is meant to survive him. And me. And you."

Lause stared at me. In point of fact, as Lause had no eyelids, she was always staring. But in this case it was with intent.

"What is it?" I said.

"You have to be joking, Hafte," Lause said. "You have to be either joking or oblivious to the fact that it is General Gau himself who has kept the Conclave together. It's loyalty to him and his idea of the Conclave that kept it from falling apart after

Roanoke. It was loyalty to him that allowed it to survive the coup attempt that followed. The general knows this at least—he made everyone swear personal loyalty to him. You were the first to swear it."

"I also warned him of the dangers of doing it," I said.

"And you were right," Lause said. "Technically. But *he* was right that at that moment it was loyalty to him that kept the Conclave in one piece. It still does."

"We have perhaps moved on from that personal loyalty. That's what the general has worked toward. What we have all worked toward."

"We're not there," Lause said. "If General Gau is made to step down then the center of the Conclave falls away. Will this union still exist? For a while. But the union will be hollow, and the factions that already exist now will pull away. The Conclave will fracture, and then those factions will fracture again. And we'll be back to where we were before. I see it, Hafte. It's almost inevitable at this point."

"Almost," I said.

"We can avoid a fracture, for now," Lause said. "Buy some time and perhaps heal the fracture. But the general has to give up something he wants very much."

"Which is?"

"He has to give up the Earth."

I reached for my cup again. "The humans from Earth have not asked to join the Conclave," I said.

"Don't spout nonsense at me, Hafte," Lause said, sharply. "There isn't a representative in the assembly who doesn't know that the general intends to offer Earth significant trade and technological concessions, with the intent of drawing them into the Conclave sooner than later."

"The general has never said anything of the sort."

"Not publicly," Lause said. "He's been content to let his

friends in the assembly do that for him. Unless you believe that we don't know who is working Bruf Brin Gus's levers on this subject. It's not been exactly *discreet* about the favors it can pull from the general now. Or from *you*, for that matter."

I made a note to schedule a meeting with Representative Bruf at the earliest convenience; it had been warned against preening to other assembly representatives. "You think Hado would use any deal with Earth as leverage for a confidence vote," I said.

"I think Hado has a hatred of humans that borders on outright racism."

"Even though the Earth is not affiliated with the Colonial Union."

"That's a distinction too subtle for Hado," Lause said. "Or perhaps it's more accurate to say that it's a distinction that Hado will not bother to make, either for himself or to others, because it would interfere with his plans."

"Which are?"

"Do you have to ask?" Lause said. "Hado hates the humans, but he loves them too. Because they might get him to the job he really wants. At least he thinks so. The Conclave will have collapsed before he can get much use of it."

"So remove the humans, and we remove his lever."

"You remove the lever that he's grasping today," Lause said. "He has others." She reached for her cup of iet, saw that it had grown cold, and set it back down again. My assistant Umman popped his head into the room; my next meeting partner had arrived. I nodded to him and then stood. Lause stood as well.

"Thank you, Ristin," I said. "As always, our chat has been useful and enlightening."

"I hope so," Lause said. "A final piece of advice for the day, if I may. Get Hado in here the next chance you get. He's not going to tell you what he has planned, but it's everything else he says that will matter anyway. Talk to him even briefly and you'll know what I know. And you'll know why I worry the Conclave is in trouble."

"That is very good advice," I said. "I plan to take it very soon."

"How soon?"

"As soon as you leave me," I said. "Unli Hado is my next appointment."

"I'm worried that the Conclave is being pushed toward destruction," Unli Hado said to me, almost before I had time to sit down after welcoming him into my office.

"Well, this is certainly a dramatic way to begin our discussion, Representative," I said. Umman discreetly slipped back into the office and deposited two bowls on my desk, one closer to me and one closer to Hado. Hado's was filled with niti, an Elpri breakfast food that would kill me if I attempted to eat it, but which Hado was known to relish. My own bowl had tidbits on it shaped like niti, but made of Lalan vegetable matter. I did not wish to die in this particular meeting. I had other plans for the rest of the sur. I nodded thanks to Umman; Hado appeared not to notice him. Umman slipped back out of the room.

"I didn't know that coming to you with a concern would be dismissed as drama," Hado said. He reached over and fished one of the niti out of his bowl, and then started sucking on it, loudly. I did not know enough about Elpri table manners to decide whether he was being rude.

"I would in no way dismiss your concerns, as drama or anything else," I replied. "But you may understand that from my end, leading with the destruction of the Conclave doesn't leave much room for anything else."

"Does General Gau still intend to bring the humans into the Conclave?" Hado asked.

"You know as well as I do that the general never lobbies a species to join the Conclave," I said. "He merely shows them the advantages and allows them to ask, if they are interested."

"That's a nice fiction," Hado said. He swallowed his niti and reached for another.

"If the humans asked to join the Conclave—if *either* of the human governments asked to join the Conclave, because as you know there is more than one—then they would go through the same process as everyone else has."

"For which the general would heavily place his support for the humans."

"I would imagine only to the extent he has done for any of our species, including the Elpri, Representative Hado. You may recall him standing in the well of the Grand Assembly, praising your people at the time of the vote."

"For which of course I offer him many thanks."

"As you should," I said. "As should every member state of our Conclave. In point of fact, to date, the general has welcomed every species who has asked to join and was willing to accept the terms of union. I wonder why you would think—if in fact either human government wanted to join our union—that the general would do otherwise."

"It's because I know something about the humans that the general does not."

"Secret information?" I said, and reached for one of my own tidbits. "With all due respect, Representative, your track record on secret information regarding the humans is spotty."

Hado offered what to anyone else would appear to be a genial smile. "I am well aware that I have a history of falling into the traps that you've set for me, Councilor. But between ourselves let's not pretend that we don't know what really happened."

"I'm not entirely sure I catch your meaning," I said, pleasantly.

"Have it your way," Hado said, and then reached into his vest to pull out a data module. He placed it on my desk between us.

"Is this your secret information?" I asked.

"It's not secret, just not well known. Yet."

"Will you give me a précis, or should I just plug it into my computer?"

"You should look at all of it," Hado said. "But the short version is that a whistleblower from the Colonial Union has released information on all of the Colonial Union's military and intelligence operations for the last several of their decades. Including the destruction of our fleet at Roanoke, the attacks on Conclave ships and planets using pirated Conclave member trade ships, biological experimentation on Conclave citizens, and the attack on Earth Station."

I picked up the data module. "How was this whistleblower able to procure all this information?"

"He was an undersecretary of the Colonial Union's State Department."

"I don't suppose this undersecretary is available to us."

"My understanding is that the Colonial Union reacquired him," Hado said. "If the Colonials' standard practices hold, if he's not already dead, he's a brain suspended in a jar."

"I'm curious how this information came to *you*, Representative Hado."

"I got it this morning by diplomatic courier drone from Elpri," Hado said. "The information has been readily available there for an Elprian day. The information was apparently released widely. I wouldn't be surprised if you're offered the information by others, including your own planetary government, Councilor. Nor would I be surprised if it's offered to the Conclave itself by the end of the sur."

"We don't know if this information is reliable, is what you're telling me."

"What I've read of it—which has been the most recent events, primarily—seems accurate," Hado said. "It explains at the very least why we've been losing trade and cargo ships, and how the Colonial Union has been using them against us."

"It might not surprise you to know that the Colonial Union has maintained their own civilian ships have been pirated."

"I won't deny I am not fond of humanity, but that isn't to say that I think they are stupid," Hado said. "Of course they would be doing a magnificent job of obfuscating their plans."

"And what are their plans, Representative Hado?" I asked.

"The destruction of the Conclave, obviously," Hado said. "They tried and failed at Roanoke Colony. They are trying again by using our own trade ships against us."

"At that rate they should topple us at about the same time as the heat death of the universe," I said.

"It's not the physical damage. It's persisting despite the obvious strength of the Conclave."

"And attacking Earth Station?" I said. "How does that relate to the Conclave?"

"The Colonial Union has denied the attack. Who else should Earth think could orchestrate it?"

"But you don't want the humans in the Conclave in any event."

"Neither do I want Earth reconciled with the Colonial Union, offering it soldiers and colonists again."

"In which case I'm not sure why you would oppose Earth's admission into the Conclave," I said. "That would shut the door to the Colonial Union using it as a recruiting station."

"And frustrate the Colonial Union even further, making them more dangerous," Hado said. "And aside from that, how would we ever be able to trust any humans? If one group of humans were at war with us and the other our ally, how many of our so-called allies would feel obliged, by species solidarity, to act against our interests?"

"So we are damned if we admit the humans, and damned if we don't."

"There is a third option," Hado said.

I stiffened at this. "You know the general's opinion on pre-emptive war, Representative Hado," I said. "And on genocide."

"Please, Councilor," Hado said. "I am suggesting neither, obviously. I am suggesting, however, that war with the humans is inevitable. Sooner or later they will attack, out of opportunism or out of fear." He pointed to the data module. "The information here makes that much clear. And when they do, if the general does not have a response, then I fear what happens next for the Conclave."

"The Conclave is robust," I said.

"Again, it's not the physical damage to the Conclave I worry about. The Conclave exists because its members are confident in its leader. The general spared the humans once when he could have crushed them. If he does it twice, there comes the legitimate question of why, and for what purpose. And whether his judgment can be relied upon any further."

"And if the answer is 'no,' then I suppose you have an idea of who might take his place," I said. "To restore this 'confidence.'"

"You misunderstand me, Councilor," Hado said. "You always have. You think I have ambitions beyond my station. I assure you I do not. I never have. What I want is what you want, and what the general wants: the Conclave, whole and secure. He has the power to keep it that way. He has the power to destroy it. It all depends on how he deals with the humans. All of them."

Hado stood, bowed, took a final niti from his bowl, and left.

"He thinks *this* is going to be the thing that destroys the Conclave," Vnac Oi said, holding the data module Unli Hado had given me. I had traveled to its office, in part to get a change of scenery and in part because as the Conclave's head of intelligence, its office was substantially more secure than my own.

"I think it's more the thing Hado plans to use to try to oust Tarsem," I said.

"It took some nerve to drop it on your desk," Oi said. "He might as well have put a sign up over his head announcing his plans."

"Plausible deniability," I said. "It can never be said he was not the first to alert us to this information and the dangers within. He's being the perfect example of a helpful and faithful officer of the Conclave."

Oi gave a whistle of derision. "The Gods should protect us from such faithfulness," it said.

I pointed to the data module. "What do we know about this?"

"We know Hado wasn't lying about how he got it," Oi said. "This information has showed up at several dozen Conclave worlds already and more reports are coming in. The data is consistent across the various planets. It even showed up here."

"How?"

"Diplomatic courier skip drone. Credentials forged, which we determined right away, but we examined the data anyway. Same data as in every other packet we've been offered."

"Any idea where it came from?"

"No," Oi said. "The skip drone is Faniu manufacture. They make hundreds of thousands of them a year. The drone's navigational cache was clear, no skip history on it. The data itself was unencrypted and in standard Conclave format."

"Have you looked at it?"

"There's too much to just look at. Reading it manually would take more time than we'd want. We've got computers doing semantic and data analysis on it to get the important information and trends. That will still take several sur."

"I mean did *you* look at it," I said.

"Of course," Oi said. "There was a document that came with it highlighting particular bits of information whoever sent it thought might be relevant to us. I skimmed."

"What do you think?"

"Officially or personally?"

"Both."

"Officially, anonymous information that shows up randomly at one's door should be treated as suspicious until proven otherwise. That said, the documents we've done spot analysis on conform strongly to the Colonial Union's data formatting and known activity. If it's fake, it's very cleverly done, at least superficially."

"And personally?"

"You know we have sources in the Colonial Union, yes?" Oi said. "Ones I don't go out of my way to let either you or the general know too much about?"

"Of course."

"As soon as this started popping up I sent a query to one of them about this alleged whistleblower, this Undersecretary Ocampo. Just before you got here I got a ping back. He exists, or at least *did* exist. He went missing several of their months ago. He would have had access to this information. So personally I think it's very possible this is legitimate."

"Hado seemed to be under the impression that the Colonial Union had found this Ocampo."

"I have no information on that, and I'd be curious to know how he does," Oi said.

"It might be a rumor."

"This would be the time for rumors about this information," Oi agreed. "Do you want me to look into it?"

Before I could answer my handheld buzzed out the sequence that told me Umman was trying to reach me for a critical purpose. I answered. "Yes?"

"Your manicurist called and wishes to inquire about your next appointment," Umman said.

"I'm in Oi's office, Umman," I said, glancing over at Oi, whose expression was studiously neutral. "And you can be sure it already knows about my 'manicurist.'"

"I'll just send the message over, then," Umman said.

"Thank you." I terminated the call and waited for the message.

"Thank you for not being offended that I know your business," Oi said.

"Thank you for not pretending to be offended that I would suggest you know my business," I said.

The message arrived. "And what does Colonel Rigney of the Colonial Union have to say?" Oi asked.

"He says, 'By this time you've probably seen the data alleging to be from our Department of State Undersecretary Ocampo,'" I read. "'Some of it is true. Much of it is not. What is not is of concern to both the Colonial Union and the Conclave. We are sending an envoy to treat with the Conclave on this to reach an amicable resolution before things escalate. She is Ambassador Ode Abumwe, known to you, and will be in possession of information to clarify or refute what you have in your possession. I ask, with the basis of our previous association as proof of earnest intent, that you see her and hear what she has to say.' And then there's data on Ambassador Abumwe's intended arrival time and position."

"The Colonial Union's coming here without pretense," Oi said. "That's interesting."

"They want to indicate their openness," I said.

"That's one interpretation," Oi said. "Another is that they don't think they have time to do their usual sneaking about before this blows up in their faces. And another will be that this is simply a move in a long-term game to maneuver us to where they can strike us most effectively."

"That's not been my experience of Colonel Rigney or Ambassador Abumwe."

"Which doesn't matter much because *officially* you haven't had any experience with either Rigney or Abumwe, have you?" Oi said, and raised tendrils to pause my reply. "It's not about what you or I think, Hafte. It's about how Unli Hado and those around him will interpret the Colonial Union's move here."

"You think we shouldn't meet with them."

"I don't have an opinion one way or another," Oi said, lying diplomatically. "That's not my job. But I do suggest that you talk with the general about it and find out what he and you want to do. And that you do it sooner than later. 'Immediately' would be my suggestion."

"I have another meeting first," I said.

"You know that the nations of Earth would never condone or participate in any action that would bring about the destruction of the Conclave," said Regan Byrne, the envoy to the Conclave from the United Nations, a diplomatic corporation that was not actually the government of the Earth, but which pretended to be for situations like this.

I nodded, minutely, to avoid hitting my head on Byrne's ceiling. Byrne's offices were former storage units that had been hastily cleared out when it was decided that it would be beneficial to have an Earth presence of some sort at the Conclave headquarters. These storage units were amply tall for most Conclave species, but then, again, Lalans were tall and I was taller than most.

I stood because there was nowhere for me to sit; Byrne usually came to visit me, not the other way around, and her office did not have a stool that would accommodate me. Byrne had the grace to look embarrassed by this fact.

"I assure you that no one in the Conclave has suggested that this new information has cast the Earth in a suspicious light,"

I said, choosing not to mention that Unli Hado, in point of fact, had accused the planet of being full of traitors and spies. "What I am interested in knowing, prior to my meeting with General Gau, is whether the Earth has received this information, and what their response has been to it."

"I was about to call Umman when he called me to set up this meeting," Byrne said. "I received a skip drone from the UN this morning with the information, to give to you in case you did not already have it, and the denial of involvement that I just offered you. Done up much more formally, of course. I will have all of it sent to your office."

"Thank you."

"I have been also told to tell you that we're sending a formal diplomatic party to brief the Conclave on the Earth's definitive response to this new information. They will be here in less than a week. The diplomatic party is under the aegis of the UN but will consist of representatives of several Earth governments. That information is also in the data packet I am sending along."

"Yes, fine," I said. This meant that we were about to be in the rather awkward position of having diplomatic representatives from both the Earth and the Colonial Union at the Conclave's headquarters at the same time. This would have to be managed. I frowned.

"Everything all right, Councilor Sorvalh?" Byrne asked.

"Of course," I said, and smiled. Byrne offered up a weak smile in return. I remembered that my smile looked rather ghastly to humans, in no small part because it was offered by a creature who was close to twice their height. "This will all be of great use to me when I meet with the general."

"That's good to hear," Byrne said.

"And how are you, Regan?" I asked. "I'm afraid I don't see you or other members of your mission as often as I would like."

"We're good," Byrne said, and I was aware that I was once again being lied to diplomatically. "I think most of the staff are still getting our bearings and learning the map of the station. It's very large. Larger than some cities back on Earth."

"Yes it is," I said. The headquarters of the Conclave was a space station carved into a large asteroid and was one of the largest engineered objects ever made, not counting some of the more impressive bits made by the Consu, a race so technologically advanced above the rest of the species in this area of space that they should not be included in an estimation, simply out of politeness to everyone else.

"It would have to be," I continued. "We have to house representatives from four hundred worlds, all their staff, and many of their families, plus a great number of the Conclave's own government workers and their families, plus all the support workers and their families. It adds up."

"Is your family here, Councilor Sorvalh?"

I smiled, more gently this time. "Lalans don't quite have the family structure that humans and many other species do. We are more communally oriented, is the best way to put it. But there is a strong Lalan community here. It's very comforting."

"It's good to hear," Byrne said. "I miss my family and other humans. It's lovely here, but sometimes you just miss home."

"I know what you mean," I said to her.

"If the Conclave must end, at least this is a pretty place for the end to begin," General Tarsem Gau, leader of the Conclave, said to me, standing next to where I sat in the Lalan community park. The park, one of the first created on the Conclave's asteroid, was large enough for all three hundred of the Lalans stationed at Conclave headquarters to meet, relax, deposit eggs, and monitor the hatched young as they grew.

Tarsem spotted some of the Lalan young, playing on a rock on the far side of the park's small lake. "Any of yours?" he asked. Jokingly, because he knew I was too old for further egg-laying.

But I answered him seriously. "One or both of them might

be Umman's," I said. "He and one of the diplomats were in phase not too long ago and she laid her eggs here. Those young are just about the right size to be theirs."

There was a sudden squawk as an older youth emerged from behind the rock, wrapped its jaws around one of the two youth sunning themselves, and began to bite down. The trapped youth began to struggle; the other one scuttled away. We watched as the younger youth fought to survive, and lost. After a moment the larger youth stole away, younger youth still in its jaws, to eat it in privacy.

Tarsem turned to me. "That still always amazes me," he said.

"That our young prey on each other?" I asked.

"That it doesn't bother *you* that they do," he said. "Not just you. You or any Lalan adult. You understand that most intelligent species are fiercely protective of their young."

"As are we," I replied. "After a certain point. After their brains develop and their consciousness emerges. Before then they are simply animals, and there are so many of them."

"Did you feel that way when they were your own?"

"I didn't know which were mine at the age of that unfortunate youth," I said. "We lay our eggs in common, you know. We go to our local common ground, to the laying house. I'd lay my eggs into a receiving basket and take the basket to the house supervisor. The supervisor would put them in the room set up for the eggs the house received that day. Thirty or forty women would lay eggs at a house each day. Ten to fifty eggs each. Fifteen of our days to hatch and then another five days before the outside door to the room was opened to let the surviving young out into the park. We didn't see the eggs again once we left them. Even if we went back the day the outside door was opened, we wouldn't know which of the survivors were our own."

"But I've met your children."

"You met them after they grew into consciousness," I said.

"Once you're an adult, you're allowed to take a genetic test to learn who your parents are, provided they had consented to be placed in the database. The two you met are the ones who decided to find out. I may have had others who survived but they either didn't take the test or chose not to contact me. Not everyone asks to know. I didn't."

"It's so—"

"Alien?" Tarsem nodded. I laughed. "Well, Tarsem, I *am* an alien to you. And you to me. And all of us to each other. And yet, here we are, friends. As we have been for most of our lives now."

"The conscious parts of it, anyway."

I motioned back to the rock, where the youth who had run away had returned. "You think the way we cull our young is cruel."

"I wouldn't say that," Tarsem said.

"Of course you wouldn't say it," I said. "You wouldn't say it because you're diplomatic. But it doesn't mean you don't *think* it."

"All right," Tarsem admitted. "It does seem cruel."

"That's because it *is*," I said, turning again to Tarsem. "Terrible and cruel, and the fact that adult Lalans can just watch it happen and not weep in agony over it means that *we* might be terrible and cruel as well. But we know a story that other people don't."

"What's the story?"

"The story is that not too long ago in Lalan history, a philosopher named Loomt Both convinced most of Lalah that how we culled our young was wrong and immoral. He and his followers convinced us to protect all of our young, to allow them all to grow into sentience, and to reap the benefits of the knowledge and progress so many new thinking individuals would give us. I imagine you think you know where this is going."

"Overpopulation, famine, and death, I would guess," Tarsem said.

"And you would be wrong, because those are obvious things, to be planned for and dealt with," I said. "We did have a massive population boom, but we'd also developed spaceflight. It's one reason why Both suggested we stop culling our youth. We populated colony worlds quickly and grew an empire of twenty worlds almost overnight. Both's strategy gave us a foothold into the universe and for a time he was revered as the greatest Lalan."

Tarsem smiled at me. "If this is meant to be a cautionary tale, you're doing a bad job of it, Hafte," he said.

"It's not done yet," I said. "What Both missed—what we all missed—was the fact that our preconscious life is not wasted. How we survive our culling leaves its traces in our brains. In point of fact, in a very real sense, it gives us wisdom. Gives us restraint. Gives us mercy and empathy for each other and for other intelligent species. Imagine, if you will, Tarsem, billions of my people, emerging into consciousness without wisdom. Without restraint. Without mercy and empathy. Imagine the worlds they would make. Imagine what they would do to others."

"They could be monsters," Tarsem said.

"Yes they could. And yes we were. And in a very short time we tore each other apart and tore apart every other intelligent species we met. Until we had lost our empire and almost lost ourselves. We were terrible and cruel, and in time we wept in agony over it and everyone we had doomed to a conscious death." I pointed again to the youth on the rock. "What happens to our young on their way to consciousness is pitiless. But it strengthens us as a people. We take our pain and our risk early, and as a result we as a people are saved."

"Well," Tarsem said. "This is not what I was expecting when I suggested we meet here. I just thought it was a pretty place to talk."

"It is a pretty place," I said. "It's just not *nice*."

"Tell me what you think about the news today."

"About the Ocampo data?" I asked. Tarsem nodded. "I think it means very bad things for the Conclave. Ristin Lause is right, Tarsem. The Conclave is in a fragile state because you've been pushing things too hard, including bringing the humans of Earth into the Conclave. I've warned you about that."

"You have."

"And you haven't listened."

"I've listened," Tarsem said. "I have reasons not to agree."

I gave Tarsem a look that expressed my disapproval, which he took without complaint. I continued. "She's also right that if you lose a confidence vote, it could fracture the Conclave. You already have dozens of species wanting to bolt and either go it alone or form smaller alliances they think they will be able to control. If you give the Conclave an opportunity to crack, it will crack."

"That's independent of the Ocampo data."

"But the Ocampo data feeds right into that," I said. "It seemingly confirms that the humans can't be trusted and that they mean us harm, the Colonial Union portion of humanity, in any event. If you try to bring Earth into the Conclave after this, Unli Hado will use that to suggest that you're letting the enemy through the front door."

"So we hold off on admitting Earth into the Conclave."

"Then Hado hits you with leaving it available to the Colonial Union to retake. Make no mistake, Tarsem. Hado is going to use Earth against you no matter what you do. And if you take the unspeakable third option of attacking the Colonial Union without direct provocation, Hado will use your first military defeat as an opportunity for the confidence vote he's looking for. Every option leads to the assembly voting to remove you. And when that happens it all falls apart."

"This used to be easier," Tarsem said. "Running the Conclave."

"That's because you were building it," I said. "It's easier to be the aspirational leader when the thing you're building doesn't exist. But now it exists, and you're not aspirational anymore. Now you're just the chief bureaucrat. Bureaucrats don't inspire awe."

"Do we have time to finesse this?"

"We might have had, if both the Colonial Union and the Earth weren't sending full suites of diplomats for discussions," I said. "Having one set of them would be bad enough. Having them both here, posturing over the Ocampo data, means that Hado and his partisans are going to have real live targets for their ire and might use that to push a confidence vote sooner than later. If you think they're going to miss an opportunity to trim down your reputation, with real-life human diplomats, then you'll be playing right into their hands."

"Then tell me what you suggest," Tarsem said.

"That you don't see Ambassador Abumwe when she arrives. Turn her away publicly. That deprives Hado of the spectacle of the Colonial Union being received diplomatically."

"And what about the new information they promised?"

"Leave that to me. Colonel Rigney and I can set up a meeting and I can get it then. All discreetly."

"He won't be happy."

"We don't need him to be happy," I said. "We need him to understand the political landscape we're working in. I can make him do that."

"And the diplomats from Earth?"

"We'll have to meet with them," I said. "And as for Earth itself, we need to get it out of the reach of the Colonial Union without bringing it into the Conclave."

Tarsem smiled. "I'm looking forward to hearing how this is going to happen," he said.

"We have them ask for protection," I said.

"Protection," Tarsem said. "From whom?"

"From the Colonial Union, who attacked Earth Station," I said.

"If it did."

"It doesn't matter if it did. It matters that Earth believes it's a threat."

Tarsem gave me a look that suggested a complicated response to this statement, but decided not to immediately follow it up. "So they ask for protection," he said. "What does that solve?"

"It solves Unli Hado, for one," I said. "Because the Earth *doesn't* ask to join the Conclave, and it *doesn't* stay vulnerable to the Colonial Union. And when it asks for protection, we'll assign three of our member states to take up the guard."

"Which three?"

"Two of them it doesn't matter. Pick who you like. But the third—"

"The third is the Elpri," Tarsem said.

"Yes," I said. "And then Hado is trapped. His entire ploy is based on you being too soft on the humans. But now one branch of humanity is publicly rebuffed and the other is guarded by Hado's own species. He said to me today that his sole concern is the unity of the Conclave; let's hold him to his words, and let's make him do it publicly. He's trapped by his own posturing."

"And you think the Earth will go along with this."

"I think they believe we both have a common enemy, and they know they are defenseless without us," I said. "The only thing we have to do is not make it look like we're bottling them up, like they were under the Colonial Union."

"Although that's actually what you're proposing we do."

"These are the options at the moment."

"And you think this will actually work," Tarsem said.

"I think it buys us time." I turned back to the rock where the young Lalan had been a few minutes before, and noticed it wasn't there anymore. There was a splotch of blood, however. Whether it belonged to the youth or the one who had been killed before it, I didn't know. "Maybe enough time to save the Conclave from collapsing. And that's enough for now."

PART TWO

"Wake up, Hafte," someone said.

I woke up. It was Vnac Oi. I stared at it for a moment before gathering enough wit to speak.

"Why are you standing in my sleeping chamber?"

"I need you awake," it said.

"How did you get in?"

Oi gave me a look that said, *Really, now.*

"Never mind," I said. I lifted myself off my sleeping pedestal and moved to my wardrobe to get dressed. I don't usually prefer other people see me without clothing, but it's for their sake, not mine; Lalans don't have a taboo against nudity. "Tell me what's going on, at least."

"A human ship has been attacked," Oi said.

"What?" I looked out from my wardrobe at Oi. "Where? And by whom?"

"In our space," Oi said. "And we don't know. But it gets worse."

"How does it possibly get worse?" I slipped a basic robe onto my body and stepped out of the wardrobe. Other accoutrements could wait.

"The humans' ship is out of control and being dragged in by the gravity of this asteroid," Oi said. "We have four serti before it hits."

"That doesn't leave much time," I said. There are thirty serti in a sur.

"It gets worse," Oi said.

"Stop *saying* that," I said. I stood in front of Oi, now. "Just tell me what's going on."

"There are humans trapped on the ship," Oi said. "Including the diplomatic mission from Earth."

"Here is the *Odhiambo*," Loom Ghalfin said, pointing at the image of a tumbling spacecraft on the briefing room monitor. Ghalfin was the director of the Conclave's ports and facilities. In the briefing room were me, Oi, General Gau, Chancellor Lause, and Regan Byrne. Along the wall of the briefing room stood several of Ghalfin's subordinates, all of whom looked as if they were lined up to be shot. Well, and if *Odhiambo* struck the asteroid, it would be the most merciful thing that could be done to them.

"The *Odhiambo* skipped into Conclave space roughly a hundred ditu ago," Ghalfin said. Ninety ditu in a serti, so not very long ago at all. "Almost as soon as it entered Conclave space, it reported several explosions and extensive damage."

"Do we know what caused the explosions?" Gau asked, and nodded toward Oi. "Vnac here told me and Hafte it was an attack."

"We don't know what it was," Ghalfin said. "At entry the *Odhiambo* was reporting, verbally and by automated monitoring, that all systems were nominal. The next thing we know everything went haywire."

"Vnac?" Gau said.

"My analysts started looking at data as soon as the damage reports came in, cross-referencing with what we know of the *Odhiambo*," Oi said. "The *Odhiambo* is a lend-lease ship, originally an Ormu freighter. The pattern of damage it reported right after the explosions occurred isn't consistent with what might happen with a power systems failure. It is consistent with what would happen if the power systems were attacked to cause secondary damage."

"So an attack," Gau said.

"Seems likely to me." Oi motioned to Ghalfin. "Although I will bow to any additional information our colleague here can offer."

"We're combing through our own data now to see if anyone or anything else skipped in just before or close to the arrival of the *Odhiambo*," Ghalfin said. "We're back a full sur on the data now and nothing's pinged."

Tarsem nodded. "Let's get back to the current situation."

"The current situation is that the *Odhiambo* is heavily damaged and tumbling in Conclave space. The explosions have imparted a small bit of momentum on the ship toward the asteroid, and the asteroid's native gravity is doing the rest. Left unchecked it will impact in three serti, fifty-five ditu." The image Ghalfin was showing tracked out and showed the projected path of the *Odhiambo* toward the Conclave's headquarters.

"What will the impact damage here?" I asked.

"No habitats, either general or specialized," Ghalfin said. "We're not looking at any substantial death toll. But the *Odhiambo* will impact directly on one of our solar power farms, and several surface-level agricultural domes are nearby, which are at substantial risk of damage. How much damage depends on how the *Odhiambo*'s power systems fail at impact. Best-case scenario is we lose the solar farm, solely from the impact. Worst-case scenario is the ship's power systems fail spectacularly in addition to the impact."

"In which case the asteroid gains a shiny new crater, debris gets thrown far and wide, including potentially into the docking area, damaging other ships, and into other areas of the asteroid, including possibly populated areas," Oi said. "Which makes the potential death toll a bit more substantial."

"And the crew of the ship?" Tarsem asked.

"Sixty crew, ten passengers, all part of the diplomatic team from Earth," Ghalfin said. "The ship's captain reported six dead, eight seriously wounded from the explosions, most from the engineering department. The dead are still on the ship. The wounded and most of the rest of the crew evacuated the ship via lifepods. The captain, executive officer, and the chief engineer are still aboard."

"But our diplomats are trapped," said Regan Byrne.

"That's what the captain reported," Ghalfin agreed. "The passenger quarters housing your team are sound but the passageways into their quarters are heavily damaged. There's no way in or out without landing on the hull and cutting our way in."

"The problem with that is that the *Odhiambo*'s power systems are damaged," Oi said. "They could go at any time. If we send rescue crews and the ship goes up, we lose our people as well as theirs."

"You can't just leave them trapped there," Byrne said, staring at Oi.

"We have to rationally judge the risks involved," Oi said, staring back. It turned to face the room. "And we have to make a decision soon." It pointed to the image of the *Odhiambo*. "The ship is three and a half serti from impact, but *we* don't have that much time. Right now, if we destroy the ship with our defenses, it's far enough away that we can control the debris and minimize any damage to ourselves and other ships. After that serti, it becomes progressively harder to contain the possible damage. Add to that the fact the ship can go at any time, in which case its destruction is uncontrolled, which makes our risks greater."

Tarsem turned to Ghalfin. "Loom?" he said.

"Director Oi's not wrong," she said. "Controlled destruction of the *Odhiambo* is the best option and the sooner the better. We cannot allow it to impact, and the longer we wait the more chance the ship's power systems will rupture."

"That means potentially sacrificing the diplomats," I said. "Which is an unacceptable option."

"I agree," said Lause, looking at Oi. "If the Conclave doesn't at least make the *attempt* to save them, what does that say about us?"

"You're asking our rescue crews to risk their own lives," Oi said.

"Which is part of their job," Lause said.

"Yes, but not stupidly," Oi replied. It turned to Ghalfin. "Your estimate for the *Odhiambo*'s power systems to fail, please."

"In the next serti?" Ghalfin asked.

"Yes."

"Given the damage we know about, I'd say sixty percent," Ghalfin said. "Which means realistically the chance is greater, because the damage we know about is the bare minimum possible."

"We're asking our people to go to their deaths, almost certainly," Oi said.

"Ms. Byrne," Tarsem said. "I want to know your thoughts."

Byrne took a moment to collect herself. "I can't tell you I don't want you to save my people," she said. "I can't even tell you that I will entirely understand if you didn't. What I can say is that if you don't, I'll recommend to the governments of Earth that your refusal to act not be a factor in future discussions."

Tarsem looked at me after the comment. I stared back, silently, knowing that after all this time he would almost certainly know what I thought of Byrne's *realpolitik* answer.

"How long until we can have rescue crews on the way?" Tarsem asked Ghalfin.

"They've been prepping since the *Odhiambo*'s first distress call," Ghalfin said. "They're ready to go when you want them."

"I want them," Tarsem said. "Send them, please."

Ghalfin nodded, and turned to a subordinate, who handed

her a headset conforming to her species. Tarsem turned to Byrne. "We'll get them out, Regan."

"Thank you, General," Byrne said. Her relief flowed off her like a waterfall.

"General, we have a complication," Ghalfin said.

"What is it?"

"Hold on—" Ghalfin held up a hand while she listened to her headset. "A rescue attempt is already under way."

"By whom and under what authority?" I asked.

"It's being undertaken by the *Chandler*," Ghalfin said, after a moment of listening to her headset. "It's a human ship, from the Colonial Union. It skipped in right around the time we started this meeting."

I looked over to Tarsem, who was smiling at me. I knew what that meant. It meant, *Now aren't you glad I decided to meet with the Colonials despite your advice.*

"What do you want to do now?" Ghalfin asked Tarsem.

"I want you to tell the *Chandler* they have a serti to complete their rescue and after that we're vaporizing the *Odhiambo* for the safety of our headquarters," Tarsem said. "And I want you to tell them that we're sending a crew to assist if they need it and to observe if they don't." Ghalfin nodded and spoke into her headset.

Then Tarsem turned to me.

"Don't tell me, I already know," I said. I got up.

"Where are you going?" Byrne asked, looking up at me.

"I'm going with our rescue team," I said. "To observe."

"You might blow up," Oi said.

"Then the Earth knows I blew up helping to save their people." *And knows the Conclave didn't let the Colonial Union take on all the risk alone. Or sacrifice,* I thought, but chose not to say. I knew that was part of Tarsem's math. I nodded to those in the room and made my way to the exit.

"Hafte," Tarsem said, and I paused at the doorway. I looked back to him. "Come back alive, please."

I smiled and left.

"All right, this pilot is just showing off," Torm Aul, the rescue shuttle pilot, said to me, as we approached the *Odhiambo* and the *Chandler*. The rescue shuttle contained me, Aul, zis co-pilot Liam Hul, whose seat I was currently occupying while Hul loitered in the general cabin, and six fellow members of the Fflict species as the rescue team. The Fflict recognized five genders: male, female, zhial, yal, and neuter. Aul was zhial, and ze liked zis pronouns accurately stated. I would too, in zis position.

"Which pilot?" I asked.

"The pilot of the *Chandler*," Aul said, pointing at the monitor that gave zim zis external view. "The *Odhiambo* is tumbling chaotically so the *Chandler* is matching its movements."

"Why would it do that?" I asked.

"It's safer for the people running the rescue," Aul said. "Makes the two ships stable relative to each other. But it's difficult to do because the *Chandler* pilot has to track the *Odhiambo*'s movements precisely."

"Once the ship started tumbling it should continue to do so in the same manner," I said. "I think that's close to a thermodynamic law."

"Yeah, but that assumes no additional input of momentum," Aul said, and pointed to the *Odhiambo* in the monitor. "But the *Odhiambo* is damaged and venting all sorts of things. And we can't tell when those venting events will happen. No, it's a mess. So the *Chandler* pilot's tracking all of that in as close to real time as it can."

"Could you do it?"

"If I wanted to show off, sure," Aul said. I smiled at this. "But

I wouldn't do it with anything larger than this shuttle. Whoever the *Chandler*'s pilot is, it's doing it with an entire ship. If it messes up, you're going to have two ships tumbling down on headquarters, not just one."

"We need to tell them that," I said.

"Trust me, Councilor, they're way ahead of you," Aul said.

"Hail the *Chandler*, please," I said. "Tell them we've come to offer assistance if they wish it."

Aul did as ze was told, muttering into a headset in zis own language while I watched the two human ships tumble in tandem.

"The captain of the *Chandler* is named Neva Balla, it sends its compliments and says that it requires no assistance at this point," Aul said, after a moment. "It says that they are under some time pressure and incorporating us into their plans would just add to the pressure. It asks us to hold position at twenty klicks relative—that's about twenty-five chu—and to monitor the *Odhiambo* for power surges or rapidly rising temperatures."

"Can we do that?"

"Maintaining a twenty-five-chu relative distance is something we can do on autopilot. And this shuttle's packed with a good amount of sensory apparatus. We're good."

I nodded up to the monitor. "Any way we can stabilize the image of the ships so they don't look like they're tumbling? I want to be able to see what's happening without getting vertigo."

"No problem."

"If the captain of the *Odhiambo* is still on the ship, ask it to send us a real-time data feed, please," I said.

"Will do."

"Also, Captain Neva Balla is 'she,' not 'it.'"

"You sure?"

"I've met her before," I said. "Humans generally prefer to not be called 'it' whenever possible."

"The things you learn about people while you're on the job," Aul said.

"Here we go," Aul said, nodding to the monitor. On it a lone figure stood in an open airlock on the *Chandler*, directly across from the *Odhiambo*. The distance between the two ships was less than thirty plint—about fifty meters in human measurement. Aul was right: Whoever was piloting the *Chandler* had impressive control.

The figure in the airlock continued to stand, as if waiting for something.

"Not a good idea to run out the clock," Aul said, under zis breath.

A stab of light shot from the *Chandler,* striking across and at a small angle from the figure in the airlock.

"They're firing on the ship," I said.

"Interesting," Aul said.

"Why is it interesting?"

"They need to cut into the hull," Aul said. Ze pointed at the beam. "Normally for a rescue we'd send a crew over with some particle beam cutters to get through the hull. We have a couple here on the shuttle, in fact. But it takes time. Time they don't have. So instead they're just burning a big damn hole in the hull with a beam."

"It doesn't look very safe," I said, watching. A venting blast of air puffed out of the *Odhiambo*, crystalizing in the vacuum wherever the beam didn't turn it into plasma.

"It's definitely *not*," Aul said. "If there's someone in the cabin they're cutting into, they probably just died of asphyxiation. That is, if they weren't vaporized by the beam."

"If they weren't careful they could have blown up the ship."

"The ship's going to blow up anyway, Councilor," Aul said. "No reason to try to be dainty."

The beam shut off as abruptly as it began, leaving a three-plint hole in the *Odhiambo*'s hull. In the monitor, the figure in the *Chandler* airlock launched itself toward the hole, trailing a cable behind it.

"Okay, now I get it," Aul said. "They're running a cable from the *Chandler* to the *Odhiambo*. That's how they're going to get them off the ship."

"Across a vacuum," I said.

"Wait for it," Aul said. The figure disappeared into the *Odhiambo*. After a moment, the cable, which had drifted slightly, tightened up. Then a large container started moving across the cable.

"I'm guessing vacuum suits, harnesses, and automatic pulleys in that," Aul said. "Get them suited up, secure them in a harness, and let the pulleys do all the work."

"You sound like you approve."

"I do," Aul said. "This is a pretty simple rescue plan with pretty simple tools. When you're trying to save people, simpler is better. A lot fewer things to go wrong."

"As long as the *Chandler* can keep in sync with the *Odhiambo*."

"Yes," Aul agreed. "There is that. This plan has all its complications in one place, at least."

There were several moments of nothing obvious going on. I took the time to look at the co-pilot monitor set, on which we were tracking the *Odhiambo*'s power and heat signatures. No excitement there either, which was a good thing. "You might suggest to the *Odhiambo*'s captain that any remaining crew might want to disembark as soon as possible," I said to Aul.

"With all due respect, Councilor," Aul said. "I'm not going to suggest to a captain that it abandon its ship a single moment before it makes that decision on its own."

"Fair enough." I glanced back over to the monitor with the *Odhiambo* on it. "Look," I said, pointing. The first of the diplomats was making its way across the line, swaddled in a highly reflective vacuum suit, chest in a harness, trailing behind a pulley.

"That's one," Aul said. "Nine more to go."

The *Chandler* collected seven before the *Odhiambo* blew itself up.

There was almost no warning. I glanced over as the seventh diplomat disappeared into the *Chandler*'s airlock and saw the feeds on the co-pilot's monitor spike into critical territory. I yelled to Aul to warn the *Chandler* just as the external monitor showed a wrenching jerk, severing the cable between the two ships. Aul zoomed out the picture in time to catch the eruption on the *Odhiambo*, midships.

Aul yelled in zis headset and suddenly the image in the monitor began spinning wildly—or appeared so, as the monitor had stopped tracking with the two ships' movements and had reoriented itself to our perspective. The *Odhiambo* had begun tearing itself apart. The *Chandler* had begun moving away from its doomed compatriot.

"Come on, come on, come on," Aul was yelling at the monitor. "Move it, you stupid shit-for-brains, you're too close." I had no doubt ze was yelling at the *Chandler*'s pilot.

And ze was right; the *Chandler* was too close. The *Odhiambo* had now split in two and the pieces were moving independently of each other, with the fore portion now careening dangerously close to the *Chandler*.

"They're going to hit!" Aul yelled.

And yet they didn't; the *Chandler*'s pilot yawed and skewed its ship, moving it across three axes in a mad ballet to avoid collision. The separation between the ships widened, too slow for my taste: fifty plint, eighty, a hundred fifty, three hundred, one chu, three chu, five chu, and then the *Chandler* stabilized its movement relative to Conclave headquarters and began to pull away at speed from the *Odhiambo*.

"You should be dead!" Aul yelled at the monitor. "You should be dead, your ship should be dead, you should all be dead! You magnificent shit-eater!"

I looked over to Aul. "Are you all right?"

"No," ze said. "I'm pretty sure I've soiled myself." Ze looked over and on zis head was an expression that I assumed was of sheer amazement. "That *should not* have happened. Everyone on the *Chandler* should be dead. The *Chandler* should be an expanding cloud of debris. That was the single most amazing thing I've ever seen in my life, Councilor. I'd be surprised if it weren't the single most amazing thing you've ever seen, too."

"It might be in the top few," I allowed.

"I don't know who that pilot is, but I am going to buy that shit-eater all the drinks it wants."

I intended to respond but Aul held up a hand, listening into the headset. Then it looked up at the monitor. "You have got to be kidding me," ze said.

"What is it?"

"Those three other diplomats and the *Chandler* crewman," ze said. "They're still alive." Aul spoke into zis headset and zoomed in on the aft portion of the *Odhiambo*, where the *Chandler* had burned its hole through the hull.

And as we zoomed in, we saw it: a reflecting suit, launching out from the hole, tumbling into space, followed by a second, followed by a pair, holding on to each other—the final diplomat and the crewman from the *Chandler*. The *Odhiambo* spun away from them, slowly.

"How much breathable air do you think they have?" I asked Aul.

"Not a lot," ze said.

I glanced over to the co-pilot's monitor, which still erroneously showed the *Odhiambo* as a single unit. The fore of the ship was rapidly cooling; all power had shut down and heat and power were venting into space.

The aft of the ship, on the other hand, was warm and getting warmer as I watched.

"I don't think they have much time," I said.

Aul followed my gaze to the co-pilot's monitor. "I think you're right," ze said, then looked up at me. "You didn't bring a vacuum suit with you, by any chance, Councilor?"

"I did not," I said. "And the very fact of your question makes me begin to regret that very much."

"It's fine," Aul said. "It just means I have to do this without a co-pilot." Ze pressed a button on his pilot monitor. "Attention, team," ze said. "You have two ditu to get on your vacuum suits. In three ditu I'm pumping the air out of the hold and opening her up. Be ready to take on passengers at speed. Have emergency air and heat prepared. These people are going to be cold and near asphyxiated. If they die once you get them, I'm leaving you out here."

"Inspiring," I said, after ze had finished.

"It works," Aul said. "I've only had to leave them out here once. Now, slide in a little more, Councilor. I have to seal up this compartment. Unless you want to try holding your breath for a while."

"The four of them haven't drifted too far from each other," Aul said, as we were underway, two ditu later. Ze put an image on the main screen showing the positions of the diplomats. "And two of them are together so we really only have three targets." A curving line swept through all three positions. "We open the gate, bring our speed down, and literally let them drift into the hold. Three targets, three ditu, we go home, we're heroes for the sur."

"You'll curse us if you put like that," I said.

"Don't be superstitious," Aul said.

The aft portion of the *Odhiambo* erupted.

"Oh, come *on*," Aul yelled.

"Give me tracking, please," I said. Aul transferred the screen to the co-pilot monitor. The main portion of the *Odhiambo*'s aft was still spinning away from the diplomats, but a large chunk of debris was now launching itself in a different direction entirely. I watched as the shuttle's computer plotted its trajectory.

"This debris is going to hit these two," I said, pointing to the paired diplomats.

"How long?" Aul asked.

"Three ditu," I said.

Aul seemed to think about it for a moment. "All right, fine," ze said.

"All right, fine, what?" I asked.

"You might want to make your center of gravity as low as possible. The inertial and gravity systems in this thing are pretty reliable, but you never know."

I hunkered down. "What are you about to do, Aul?"

"It's probably best you wait until it happens. If it works, it will be really great."

"And if it doesn't?"

"Then it'll be over quickly."

"I'm not sure I like where this is going."

"If it's all the same, Councilor, don't talk to me until it's over. I need to concentrate."

I shut up. Aul pulled up the diplomats' positions on zis pilot screen and overlaid the trajectory of the debris. Then ze started moving the shuttle forward. Aul stared at zis pilot screen, typed furiously into it, and never looked up.

I on the other hand looked at the external view monitor and saw a distant rising mass of debris, and our shuttle moving inexorably closer to it. We appeared to be on a suicide mission straight to the heart of that debris. I glanced over to Aul but ze was in focus, all attention drawn to the screen.

At almost the last possible instant I saw on the monitor a

white starburst which I registered—too late!—as a vacuum suit we were going to hit head on, just as the debris rose like a leviathan below us. I sucked in a breath to shout, saw the images on the monitor streak, and then clenched for the violence of the debris smashing into our shuttle from below. As Aul promised, it would be over quickly.

"Huh," Aul said, and spoke into zis headset. "You get them? Yes. Yes. Right. Good." Ze looked over to me. "Well, that worked," ze said.

"What worked?" I asked.

"High-speed rotation around the target," Aul said. "It takes a tiny bit of time for the shuttle's inertial field generators to register a new entity and adjust its velocity. If I picked up our new passengers on a straight path at the speed I was going, they would have turned into jelly against the interior of the shuttle. So I rotated us very quickly, to give the field just enough time to register their presence and match them to us."

"Oh."

"That's the short version," Aul said. Ze was entering commands into zis pilot monitor, presumably to pick up the two remaining diplomats. "I also had to tell the shuttle what speed I wanted the targets to have relative to the interior of the shuttle, and burn off the momentum we suddenly had dumped into the system. And such. Point is, it worked."

"Where's the debris?"

"Behind and above us. It missed us with a couple plint to spare."

"You almost killed us."

"Almost," Aul agreed.

"Please don't do that again."

"The good news is, now I don't have to."

Picking up the other two human diplomats was the very definition of anticlimactic.

As we headed back to the Conclave's asteroid, Aul restored

air to the cabin and opened up the pilot's compartment. "One of the rescued diplomats would like to speak to you," Aul said.

"All right." I ducked and found my way to the main cabin. As I did so a Fflict nudged past me, nodding; the co-pilot, anxious to get back on duty. I ducked again and entered the cabin.

The rescue team were busily attending to the diplomats, all of whom were covered in self-heating blankets and sucking air through masks. All except one, who was covered only in what I now recognized was a Colonial Defense Forces combat unitard. The unitard's owner was kneeling, speaking to one of the diplomats, a woman with dark, curled hair. She was holding his hand with a grip that I imagined would be uncomfortable for anyone other than a genetically engineered supersoldier, which is what the unitard's owner was. His green skin gave him away.

The soldier saw me and motioned to the woman, who stood up, shakily. She removed her mask and shrugged off her blankets—a bad idea because she started shivering immediately—and walked over to me, hand extended. The soldier stood with her, slightly behind.

"Councilor Sorvalh," the diplomat said. "I'm Danielle Lowen, of the United States Department of State. Thank you so much for rescuing me and these other members of my team."

"Not at all, Ms. Lowen," I said. "Welcome to the Conclave's headquarters. I am only sorry your entrance was so . . . dramatic."

Lowen managed a shaky smile. "When you put it that way, so am I." She began shivering violently. I glanced over at the soldier, who picked up the hint, stepped away, and returned with a blanket. Lowen accepted it gratefully and slumped slightly into the solider, who bore her weight easily.

"Of course, we of the Conclave cannot take all the credit for your rescue," I said, nodding at the soldier.

"I regret to say that I was only seventy percent successful with my own rescue attempt," the soldier said.

"No, you were one hundred percent successful," I said. "You got seven safely to the *Chandler,* and you knew that if you got the other three away from the ship, we would come find you."

"I didn't know," he said. "I did hope."

"How lovely," I said. I turned to Lowen. "And you, Ms. Lowen? Did you hope as well?"

"I trusted," Lowen said, and looked at the soldier. "It's not the first time this one's tossed me out into space."

"I was with you the whole way the last time, too," the soldier said.

"You were," Lowen said. "That doesn't mean we have to keep doing it."

"I will keep that in mind," the soldier said.

"The two of you have an interesting history, clearly," I said.

"We do," Lowen said, and then motioned to the soldier. "Councilor Sorvalh, if I may introduce you to—"

"Lieutenant Harry Wilson," I said, finishing her sentence.

Lowen looked at the both of us. "You two have met before, also?"

"We have," I said.

"I'm popular," Wilson said, to Lowen.

"That's not the word I would have used," she said, and smiled.

"If memory serves, the last time we met there were also exploding starships," I said, to Wilson.

"That's odd," Lowen said. "The last time I saw Harry, there were exploding starships, too."

"It's coincidental," Wilson said, looking at Lowen and then at me.

I smiled at him. "Is it?"

"I didn't expect you to challenge me so much on my request to come back alive," Tarsem Gau said to me, as I entered his office after the rescue mission.

Tarsem's private office was, as ever, cramped; after years in spaceships and their tiny spaces Tarsem still felt most comfortable in close quarters. Fortunately I was not claustrophobic, and I agreed with the political wisdom of his personal office being smaller than that of even the most undistinguished Conclave representative. The office was even smaller than the one given to the human envoy, which I suspect might shock Ms. Byrne. Fortunately Tarsem kept a sitting pedestal for me so I did not have to crimp my neck.

"If you don't want me to almost die, you shouldn't task me to missions where dying is a real possibility," I remarked, sitting. "Or at the very least don't put me on missions where the pilot is a mad Fflict."

"I could have zim disciplined, if you would like."

"What I would like is for you to give zim a commendation for quick thinking and admirable piloting, and never put me on another of zis shuttles."

Tarsem smiled. "You have no sense of adventure."

"I do have a sense of adventure," I said. "It's overawed by my sense of self-preservation."

"I don't mind that."

"Nor do you seem to mind testing the proposition, from time to time."

"I don't want you to be bored."

"I am, alas, never that," I said. "And now with chatty preliminaries out of the way, I want to impress upon you what an utter disaster this entire event has been for us."

"I thought it went rather well," Tarsem said. "The humans were saved, the *Odhiambo* was successfully destroyed without collateral damage to headquarters or other ships, and thanks to the actions of your mad Fflict in rescuing the stragglers, we remain in the good graces of Earth, and even got a tiny bit of credit with the Colonial Union diplomats for rescuing one of their own."

"A thin skin of self-congratulation on a rather messy pudding," I countered. "Which includes the very likely fact of an enemy action against the *Odhiambo* in our own space, which we neither saw coming nor could defend against, the fact that now we are no longer able to keep separate the humans from the Colonial Union and the Earth, as we intended to do for these discussions, and the fact that all of this plays perfectly well into the plans of those who are even now gathering against you in the Grand Assembly."

"I seem to recall you arguing to save the human diplomats," Tarsem said. "And me taking that advice."

"You were going to attempt to save the diplomats regardless of what I advised," I said, and Tarsem smiled at this. "And the decision to save them was more important than mere politics. Nevertheless, saving them will be seen by your enemies as proof of your regard for the humans, not a sign of basic decency."

"I don't see why I should care how they see it. Anyone with intelligence will understand what happened."

"Anyone who isn't blinded by ambition and frustration with the Conclave will understand it. But those who are blinded will *choose* not to see it, as you well know. They will also choose to see Colonials rescuing the earthlings as hugely significant, which it is."

"You don't think any ship so close would have made the attempt to rescue those diplomats?"

"No," I said. "I think the *humans* might have made the attempt regardless. These particular humans, at the very least."

"You think well of the Colonials."

"I think well of Ambassador Abumwe and her team, including their CDF liaison," I said. "I wouldn't trust their government with a cooking fire, and I don't advise *you* do, either, no matter what comes out of Ambassador Abumwe's mouth in your meeting with her."

"Noted," Tarsem said.

"Even the two sets of humans arriving within a serti of each other will be augured as consequential," I said, returning to the topic at hand. "And this was an easily avoidable blunder, as I warned you not to meet with the Colonials."

"And if I had not agreed to, then all the humans would likely be dead because our rescue mission might have failed. And you dead with them, I might add."

"You wouldn't have sent me on the rescue mission if the Colonials hadn't been there," I pointed out. "And if the humans from Earth were dead that would indeed be tragic, but it would not then be leverage for your enemies."

"The fact their ship was destroyed in our space would be."

"That's something we could finesse with findings and if necessary with resignations. Torm Aul would not be pleased to be out of a job but that's easily dealt with."

"This line of conversation is the sort of thing that makes me smile when people who don't know you praise your gentility to me," Tarsem said.

"You don't keep me around for gentility. You keep me around because I don't lie to you about your situation. And your situation is now worse than it was when we woke up this morning. It's going to get worse from here."

"Should I send both sets of humans away?"

"It's too late for that now. Everyone will assume you've had clandestine meetings with both groups and your enemies will intimate you had that meeting with both at once, because they are functionally the same in their eyes."

"So no matter what, we're damned."

"Yes," I said. "Yes we are. Although as always I am merely providing you with information. It's what you do with it that counts."

"I could resign."

"Excuse me?"

"I said, I could resign," Tarsem said. "You said before that I was most effective when I was building the Conclave, when I was a symbol of a great idea, and not an administrator of a bureaucracy. All right, fine. I resign, stay a symbol, and let someone else be the administrator."

"Who?"

"You could take the job," Tarsem said.

"What in this benighted universe gave you the impression that I would ever *want* it?" I asked, genuinely shocked.

"You might be good at it."

"And I might be appalling at it."

"You've done pretty well so far."

"That's because I know my talents," I said. "I'm the advisor. I'm the councilor. I'm occasionally the knife you slide into someone's side. You use me well, Tarsem, but *you* use me."

"Then who might you suggest?"

"No one," I said.

"I'm not going to live forever, you know. Sooner or later it has to be someone else who is in charge."

"Yes," I said. "And until that moment I'm going to make sure it will remain you."

"That's loyalty," Tarsem said.

"I am loyal to you, yes," I replied. "But even more than that I am loyal to the Conclave. To what you've built. To what we've built, you and I and every member state has built, even the stupid ones who are now trying to tear it apart for their own gain. And right now, being loyal to the Conclave means keeping you where you are. And keeping certain people from making confidence votes in the Grand Assembly."

"You think we're that close to it," Tarsem said.

"I think a lot matters in how the next few sur play out."

"What do you suggest?"

"At this point you have to take Ambassador Abumwe's report," I said. "You have yourself locked into that action."

"Yes."

"Abumwe expects to make it to you directly."

"She does," Tarsem said. "I imagine she expects you will be there, as well as Vnac Oi, either in person or via surreptitious listening device."

"She does not expect the report to stay private for long."

"These things rarely do."

"Then I suggest getting to that point a little earlier than expected," I said.

"You still think this is a good idea," Vnac Oi said to me.

"It's a useful idea," I said. "This is a thing separate from good."

Oi and I sat in the far reaches of the Grand Assembly chamber, on a level typically reserved for observers and assistants to representatives, the latter of whom would occasionally swoop down into the inner recesses of the chamber, like comets in a long-term orbit, to do their representative's bidding. Normally when I was in the chamber I sat on the center podium as Tarsem did his regular question-and-answer period, counting heads.

This time, Tarsem was not on the podium, and I wanted a slightly different vantage for the head counting.

The Grand Assembly chamber was filled. Tarsem sat, alone, on the bench usually reserved for the chancellor and her staff; for this particular address the chancellor had been demoted to her usual representative bench and her staff milled at the level just below mine. I saw some of their expressions; they were vaguely scandalized by their demotions.

On the level below that were the humans. The Colonial Union diplomats sat on the side of the arc; the humans from Earth filled the other side. There was a substantial gap between them.

"We still don't know what's in this report," Oi said.

"A fact I find very impressive, considering who you are," I replied.

"Yes, well," Oi said, and made a gesture of annoyance. "Obviously we made an attempt."

"What did you do?"

"We tried to infiltrate the *Chandler*'s system," Oi said. "We got shunted into a sandbox with a single file on it, with the title 'For Vnac Oi.'"

"Dare I ask what was in it?"

"A video clip of a human exposing its posterior and the words 'Wait like everybody else.'"

"It's nice they thought of you."

"It's less nice that their computer systems are now firewalled too well for us to get into them."

"You have other sources in the Colonial Union, I'm sure."

"I do," Oi said. "But not for this. This is why this is not a good idea, Hafte. You have no idea what this human is about to say. You don't know what damage it can do."

"It's the general's choice to do it this way, not mine," I said, which was technically true.

"Please." Oi gave me a small look. "This has your smell all over it. Don't pretend I don't know who put this idea into his head."

"I put lots of ideas into his head," I said. "And so do you. That's our role. He decides what to do with them. That's *his* role. And look." I pointed. Ambassador Abumwe had emerged from behind the central point and was moving to the lectern that had been provided for her. "It's time."

"Not a good idea," Oi repeated.

"Maybe not," I allowed. "We're about to find out."

The sounds of hundreds of species of intelligent beings quieted as Abumwe reached the lectern and placed, unusually, several sheaves of paper on them. Usually human diplomats kept their notes on handheld computers they called PDAs. This information was apparently sensitive enough that Abumwe chose to keep it in a format difficult to replicate electronically. Next to me I heard Oi make a sound of annoyance; it had seen the paper too.

"To General Tarsem Gau, Chancellor Ristin Lause, and the representatives of the constituent nations of the Conclave, I, Ambassador Ode Abumwe of the Colonial Union, send honorable greeting and offer humble thanks for this opportunity to address you," Abumwe began. In headsets, her words were being translated into hundreds of different languages. "I wish that these circumstances were happier.

"As many of you know, very recently information has come into the possession of many of your governments. This information appears to detail both historical records relating to Colonial Union activity against many of you, and against the Conclave generally. It also purports to outline future plans against the Conclave and several of your nations generally, as well as against the Earth, the original home of humanity.

"Much of the information in this report—specifically information relating to past action—is true."

There was an eruption of noise in the chamber to this. I understood why and yet I was not impressed. Abumwe had essentially admitted that things we already knew to be true were in fact true; that the Colonial Union had warred against many of us, and against the Conclave. This was not news to anyone, or should not have been. I scanned the room for the affronted, as opposed to the unimpressed.

"However—*however*," Abumwe continued, holding up a hand for silence. "I have not come here to either justify or to apologize for past action. What I am here to do is to warn you that the other information in the report is false, and that it represents a danger to all of us. To the Colonial Union, to the Conclave, and to the nations of Earth.

"We believe, we have believed, that each of us is the other's enemy. Let me suggest today that there is another enemy out there, one that threatens human and Conclave nations alike. That this enemy, though small in numbers, has been extraordinarily adept in strategy, using dramatic action for outsized effect, terrorizing each of us while allowing us to believe we are terrorizing each other. That this enemy means to destroy both the Colonial Union and the Conclave for its own dogmatic ends."

Abumwe looked up to her staff two levels down from me and nodded. One of them, who I recognized as Hart Schmidt, tapped the PDA he was holding. Beside me Oi grunted and pulled out its own computer. "I'll be damned," it said softly, and then was entirely lost into its screen.

"I have just authorized my staff to release to Vnac Oi, your director of intelligence, a complete accounting by the Colonial Union of our knowledge of this mutual enemy, a group which calls itself Equilibrium," Abumwe said. "This group is comprised of members of species unaffiliated with either the Conclave or the Colonial Union, including, prominently, the Rraey. But it also has active in it traitors from other governments and nations, including Tyson Ocampo, former undersecretary of state for the Colonial Union, Ake Bae of the Eyr, Utur Nove of the Elpri, and Paola Gaddis of Earth. Their schemes include, among many others, a planned assassination of General Gau."

The chamber erupted in chaos.

I scanned quickly to where I knew Unli Hado sat. He was up from his seat, screaming. Around him several other representatives were screaming and gesturing at him. I scanned again, to the Eyr representative, Ohn Sca. Sca was pushing past several other representatives, trying to exit the chamber; other representatives were pushing back, trying to force Sca back into its seat. I glanced up to the humans; a couple of the ones from Earth were yelling at the ones from the Colonial Union. In the middle, three figures were leaning into each other, apparently conferring. I recognized them as Danielle Lowen, Harry Wilson, and Hart Schmidt.

"Oi," I said, over the din.

"She's not lying," Oi said, still looking at its screen. "About the file, I mean. It's huge. And it's here."

"Send it out," I said.

"What?" Oi looked up at me.

"Send it out," I repeated. "All of it."

"I haven't had time to mine it."

"You didn't have time to mine the Ocampo data either," I said.

"That's not a recommendation for sending *this* out."

"The longer you have it solely in your possession, the better position you give those who just now got accused that we are massaging the data, in collusion with the Colonial Union. Send it out. Now."

"To whom?"

"To everyone."

Oi's tendrils danced across its screen. "I don't think this is a good idea, either," it said.

I turned my attention back to Abumwe, who was waiting silently at the lectern. I was beginning to wonder if I should have assigned her a security detail. I also wondered when she was going to speak again.

That, at least, was answered momentarily. "None of us is innocent," she said, forcefully. The chaos began to settle. "*None* of us is innocent," she said again. "The Colonial Union and the Conclave, those from Earth and those outside of our governments. All of us have people who saw weaknesses, who saw pressure points, and who saw ways to use our own ways and stubbornness against us. This threat is real. This threat is both practical and existential. If it isn't met by all of us, all of us are likely to be destroyed."

"You are the enemy!" someone shouted to Abumwe.

"I may be," Abumwe said. "But right now, I'm not the enemy you should worry about." She walked off the podium, to a rising chorus of anger.

"How *dare* you," Unli Hado spat at Abumwe.

We were in the conference room adjacent to Tarsem's public office, the impressive one he used for formal events. In the room were Tarsem, me, Oi, Lause, Abumwe, Hado, Sca, Byrne, Lowen, and Harry Wilson; essentially, representatives of every group called out in Abumwe's speech. Tarsem had us all pulled into the room immediately after the speech.

"How dare you," Hado said again. "How dare you question my loyalty, or the loyalty of my nation to the Conclave. How dare you suggest that any of my people would conspire against it, or conspire with *you*."

"I didn't *dare*, Representative Hado," Abumwe said. She sat at the conference room table, impassive. "I merely told the truth."

"The truth!" Hado said. "As if the Colonial Union had ever bothered with *that* particular concept."

"Where is Utur Nove, Representative Hado?" Abumwe

asked. "Our information about him tells us that he was a diplomat of some note among the Elpri. If you doubt the information that we've provided, why not ask him?"

"I'm not obliged to stay apprised of the whereabouts of every member of the Elpri diplomatic corps," Hado said.

"That may be, but it's of interest to me," Oi said. "And I've just looked at the cached version of his information. We have Utur Nove allegedly retired for several Elpri years, and offered a sinecure at a research foundation. The foundation's contact information for Nove has him 'on sabbatical,' with no additional information."

"Are you serious, Director Oi?" Hado said. "The absence of information is not the same as the presence of information. I knew Utur Nove. There is nothing in his past that even suggests he would act against Elpri or the Conclave."

"Not against Elpri, I'm sure," Oi said. "But against the Conclave?"

"What is that supposed to mean?"

"It means that you have been immensely critical of the Conclave recently. It's not unreasonable to assume you are offering a perspective shared by your government at large."

"I have been critical of *them*!" Hado flung an arm in the direction of Abumwe, who continued to sit impassively. "These humans, who represent the single largest material threat to the Conclave in our history. Or have you forgotten Roanoke, Oi?" Hado turned to Tarsem. "Have *you*, General?"

"I don't recall the Colonial Union pretending to be an ally, Hado," Oi said.

"Do that again," Hado said, turning his attention back to Oi. "Accuse me of treason one more time, Director Oi."

"Enough, both of you," Tarsem said. Hado and Oi quieted. "No one will accuse anyone here of treason, or of faithlessness to the Conclave."

"It's too late for that, General," Sca said, speaking for the first time. It glowered at Abumwe.

"Then let me say it plainly," Tarsem said. "*I* have not accused either you or Unli Hado of treason or faithlessness, nor will I. In this particular case, this is a statement that matters."

"Thank you, General," Sca said, after a moment. Hado said nothing.

Tarsem turned to Abumwe. "You've dropped a bomb on us, haven't you?"

"I offered to share this information with you alone, General," Abumwe said.

"Yes you did, but that's not the relevant part," Tarsem said. "The relevant part is that you've accused us of having traitors in our midst."

"Yes," Abumwe said. "Traitors. And spies. And opportunists. And all of the above, in one or more combinations. Just like we have." Abumwe nodded to Byrne and Lowen. "Just like they have. But that's not the real problem, General. There have always been traitors and spies and opportunists. Our current problem is that all of our traitors and spies and opportunists have found each other and decided to work against us, for their own ends."

"And what do you propose we do about it?" Oi asked Abumwe.

"I am not proposing *we* do anything about it," Abumwe said, and turned back to Tarsem. "Allow me to be blunt, General."

"By all means," Tarsem said.

"We need to be clear why I am here," Abumwe said, turning her attention back to Oi. "I am not here because the Colonial Union feels fondly toward the Conclave or because we believe sharing this information will allow our two unions to move in a more friendly direction." Abumwe motioned to Hado, who gave every impression of being offended that a human would dare to bring attention his way. "Representative Hado may be wrong about his obvious suspicions concerning this information, but he's not wrong that the Colonial Union has been a material threat to you. We have been."

"Thank you," Hado said, and then immediately appeared to realize the inappropriateness of his comment.

"It's nothing I need to be thanked for," Abumwe said, and I admired the subtle stomp of the statement, adding to Hado's embarrassment. "I am merely stating an obvious fact. This isn't an overture or a thawing of relations. I am here because we have no other choice but to share this information with you. If we allow the Equilibrium's lies about our intentions to spread unchallenged, two things are very likely to happen. One," Abumwe motioned again to Hado, "he or someone like him would be demanding the Conclave attack and destroy the Colonial Union."

"Which it could do," Sca said.

"We do not disagree," Abumwe said. "But the cost of doing so would be high, and it would not be nearly as easy as some people would want to suggest it is, despite the Colonial Union's current situation with regard to the Earth." She looked at Tarsem directly. "Humans have a term called 'pyrrhic victory,' sir."

"'Another such victory and we are undone,'" Tarsem said.

"You're familiar with the term, then."

"It pays to know one's enemy."

"No doubt," Abumwe said. "And no doubt you are aware that we know you as well as you know us. You could destroy us. But we would take you with us."

"Not all of us," Hado said.

"We would take the Conclave," Abumwe said, looking directly at Hado again. "Which is the only enemy here that matters, Representative Hado. And that is the second thing. Once we have bloodied the Conclave, diminished its vaunted reputation of being too big to fail, and have bled the fear of it out into the vacuum of the stars, the Conclave itself will crack." She pointed rather than motioned to Hado. "This one or someone like him will do it. Especially if, during this struggle with the Colonial Union, the Conclave moves to bring the Earth into its ranks."

"We have no official interest in joining the Conclave," Lowen said.

"Of course you don't," Abumwe said, looking at her. "At this point why would you, because at the moment you're getting the benefits of an association with the Conclave without any of the obligation. But if the Conclave and the Colonial Union go to war, you will start to worry that we will come to you and take what you used to give to us: soldiers. And then you'll ask to join the Conclave. And that will be the leverage someone like Representative Hado needs."

"Again we come to my alleged treason," Hado said.

"No, not treason, Representative Hado," Abumwe said. "Allow me to give you the compliment of assuming you are too intelligent for that. No, I imagine you, or someone like you, will position yourself as the savior of the Conclave, someone to rescue it from the shadow of itself that it's become. And if you can't get enough other members to come along, then perhaps you'll break away, with a few other like-minded nations, and call yourself the New Conclave or something. And after that, it won't take long. Because while you are too intelligent to commit treason, Representative Hado, I sense that you are not nearly intelligent enough to realize how your ambitions outweigh your ability to keep four hundred species together. Once again, bluntly: You're not good enough, sir. Only one person in this room is."

I glanced over to Oi, who glanced back. I knew it was enjoying the dressing-down Hado was getting from a representative of the species he hated the most.

"How arrogant of you to assume so much about me in these few ditu, Ambassador," Hado said.

"I didn't," Abumwe said. "We have a file on you." She turned to Sca. "And on you. And on every diplomat for every nation we know has a representative in Equilibrium, including our own. It's all in the report."

"I'd like to return to this report," Tarsem said.

"Of course," Abumwe replied.

"The existence of this report implied that you have a spy in Equilibrium, and have had for some time. Which makes me curious as to why you chose now to give us this information, if this group has represented a threat to both of us."

"Again I ask permission to be blunt."

"Ambassador Abumwe, at this point I cannot imagine you being otherwise."

"If Equilibrium had never done its own data dump, we never would have shared this," Abumwe said. "We would have been happy to take the information and shape it, and Equilibrium, to our own needs. I reiterate that we are not sharing this information to be friendly, General."

"Understood."

"But as to our spy, the fact of the matter is that we didn't have a spy. Equilibrium made an error and took a hostage it couldn't control. That hostage was smarter than his captors. He stole their data and one of their ships and brought both to us."

"Out of loyalty to the Colonial Union?"

"No," Harry Wilson said. "Mostly because Equilibrium pissed him off."

"Before we commit to trusting this information, perhaps we should consider the source," Hado said. "Where is this so-called source of yours?"

"As it happens, he's the pilot of the *Chandler*," Abumwe said.

Hado turned to Tarsem. "Then I move he is brought here for questioning."

"It's not that simple," Wilson said.

"Why?" Hado said, to Wilson. "Is he somehow *incapable* of taking a shuttle ride?"

Wilson smiled at this for some reason.

"General Gau, Councilor Sorvalh, Representative Hado, and Ms. Lowen, allow me to introduce to you Rafe Daquin, pilot of the *Chandler*." Wilson motioned to the box on the bridge of the *Chandler*, in which a human brain had been placed.

"This seems familiar," I said, to Wilson, as I stared into the box.

"I thought you might think so," he said.

"Who did this to him?" Hado asked.

"Sir?" Wilson said.

"Removing brains from skulls is a thing the Colonial Union does," Hado said. "It's notorious for it."

"Are you asking me if the Colonial Union did this?"

"Yes, although honestly I wouldn't expect you to answer truthfully if it had," Hado said.

"You could ask him," Wilson said.

"Pardon?"

"You could ask Rafe," Wilson said.

"Yes, you could," a voice said, through speakers. "I'm literally right here."

"All right," Lowen said. "Mr. Daquin, who did this to you?"

"Put my brain in a box? That would be the group calling itself Equilibrium, Ms. Lowen," Daquin said.

"Why did they do it?" Tarsem asked.

"Partly to trim down the number of working parts they needed to run the ship," Daquin said. "Partly to make sure I stayed in their control. They assumed that I would do anything they wanted if they promised to give me back my body."

"Why didn't you?" Tarsem asked.

"Because I figured that they didn't have any intention of ever giving it back."

"But the Colonial Union could give you another body," Hado said. "They haven't. They're using you like this Equilibrium group did."

"They're growing me a new body as we speak," Daquin said. "It'll be ready soon. But Harry here asked me if I wouldn't mind being a part of the *Chandler*'s crew for a bit, especially for trips like these, where people might need convincing that Equilibrium is a thing and not just a convenient cover story for the Colonial Union."

"If this is real," Hado said.

"Get some scientists over here to test me if you like," Daquin said. "I like company."

"It still doesn't prove anything," Hado said, turning to Tarsem. "We're being asked to believe this unfortunate creature isn't being coerced into saying these reports are his. We can't believe that someone in his position can be expected to say anything but what his captors want him to."

"Captors," Daquin said, and the derision was hard to miss. "Seriously, who is this guy?"

"Representative Hado has a point," I said. "You're a brain in a box, Mr. Daquin. We have no assurance that you aren't being used."

"Do you want to tell them, Harry, or should I?" Daquin asked.

"For obvious reasons, you should," Harry said.

"General Gau, Councilor Sorvalh, you're aware that your director of intelligence tried to hack into the *Chandler*'s systems when we arrived, yes?" Daquin asked.

"We, we knew that," I said.

"Of course you did. You know what Director Oi found, right?"

"Oi said it was a picture of someone showing their posterior."

"Yup, that's called 'mooning,'" Daquin said. "I did that, Councilor. Not the mooning, for obvious reasons. But I put the picture where Director Oi would find it. I did that because I don't only pilot this ship, I *am* this ship. It is entirely and completely under my control. The *Chandler* has crew and they run operations—you can ask Captain Balla if you like, to confirm this—but ultimately they have only as much control over the ship as I allow them. Because this ship is me. And I choose to help. Without my cooperation, the only way the Colonial Union can control this ship is to destroy it. And I'd destroy it myself before that could happen."

"You still need sustenance, I assume," Tarsem said. "Your ship still needs energy. You have to rely on the Colonial Union for that."

"Do I?" Daquin said. "General, if I were to ask you for asylum right now, would you give it to me?"

"Yes," Tarsem said.

"And I assume you wouldn't let me starve."

"No,"

"Then you've just invalidated your own assertion."

"But you still need the Colonial Union to get your body back," Lowen said.

"To grow a new one, you mean."

"Yes."

"Ms. Lowen, there's a door to your left. When the ship was built, it was the captain's ready room. Go ahead and open it."

Lowen found the door and opened it. "Oh my god," she said. She opened the door fully so the rest of us could see.

Inside was a container with a human body in it.

"That's me," Daquin said. "Or will be me, anyway, once it's done growing and once I decide to put myself into it. Representative Hado, you can have your scientists check its DNA against the DNA in my brain here. It checks out. But the point is that no, the Colonial Union isn't holding my body hostage.

It's not holding *me* hostage. It's not coercing me. Now, you can still believe it or not, but at this point, if you don't believe me, it's not because we haven't made an effort to make it easy for you to believe."

"Mr. Daquin," I said.

"Yes, Councilor Sorvalh."

"You were the one piloting during the rescue of the diplomats."

"Yes, I was," Daquin said. "We have two other pilots, but I was the one at the helm for that."

"I know a pilot who called it an amazing piece of piloting, and wants to buy you several drinks to commemorate it."

"Tell your pilot friend I accept, in theory," Daquin said. "The actual drinking part will have to wait."

"Are you happy?" I asked Tarsem, when he and I were again alone in his office.

"Happy?" he said. "What an odd question."

"I mean did everything you plan for the day happen."

"All I planned for was to have Abumwe give her speech, and that wasn't even *my* plan," Tarsem said. "That was yours. So I suppose I should ask you if *you're* happy."

"Not yet," I said.

"Why not?" Tarsem said. "Abumwe's speech entirely disrupted the momentum Unli Hado and his partisans had in pushing a no confidence vote. The fact I assured Hado and Sca that I don't consider them traitors doesn't mean their reputations aren't irretrievably destroyed. Even if they stay on as representatives."

"I'm not going to pretend I didn't enjoy seeing Hado get crushed today," I said. "That vainglorious martinet deserved the thumping. But now we have the somewhat larger problem that both the Elpri and the Eyr have been smeared with the accusation of, if not treason, then treachery of the worst sort.

And you know they're not going to be the only nations who harbor members of this Equilibrium group. Vnac is sifting through the data right now."

"You're worried about what's going to come out in the sifting."

"No," I said. "I'm worried that you're going to get accused of using it to start picking off political opponents, including entire nations. As much as I liked seeing Hado shut down, it didn't help that the Elpri, of all people, are one of the two peoples called out by name in Abumwe's report. No matter if Vnac clears her entire report—no matter if all of it is unimpeachably true—there will still be those who will see it only as a chance for you to settle scores at a moment when you were vulnerable."

"You ordered Oi to release the data to avoid that."

"I ordered it to release the data so it didn't look like you were colluding with the Colonial Union," I said. "That problem is solved. The other problem remains."

"What do you suggest?"

"I think you need to address this directly and personally and on the floor of the Grand Assembly."

"And what would you have me say there?"

"What you said to Hado and Sca," I said. "Only writ larger. Encompassing nations, not diplomats."

"We're going to find traitors," Tarsem said.

"Yes, but they are people. Individuals."

"Individuals who might be able to persuade their governments to leave the Conclave."

"All the more reason to make it clear that the actions of a misguided few don't reflect on the people as a whole."

"You think this will work."

"I think it's better than encouraging our members to start accusing each other of undermining the Conclave. That road goes nowhere we want to go."

"How committed are you to this idea?" Tarsem asked.

"Presuming the Colonial Union isn't running a long con on us, which is a thing you've begged me to consider and so I shall, it's possible that entire member state governments *are* working to end the Conclave. We've had attempts before. We'd be allowing them to get away with it."

"No. We'd be offering them a way to step back from the abyss before we tumble into it."

"That's an optimistic way of looking at it."

"It's not optimistic at all. It's giving us more time to deal with the problem."

"And if we have no more time?"

"Then we deal with the problem now," I said. "But I think everyone is beginning to realize just how close the abyss is at the moment. Very few people actually want to go in."

"You are optimistic, then," Tarsem said. "Because at the moment I think there are still a few who think the abyss sounds like a very good idea."

"That's why I want you to convince them otherwise."

"I appreciate your faith in my abilities."

"It's not faith," I said. "It's trust."

PART FOUR

"Which news do you want first?" Vnac Oi asked me. I was in its office again, the first meeting of the sur.

"You have good news?" I asked.

"No," Oi said. "But some of the news is less objectively bad than the rest."

"Then by all means let us begin with that."

"We're done with the first pass of semantic and data mining of the Abumwe report," Oi said. "And we've cross-referenced with information we have in our own databases. The very short version is that the data are less problematic than the data in the Ocampo report."

" 'Less problematic.' "

"It means there are fewer obvious untruths compared to, and contradictions with, our own data set."

"So you're saying the Colonial Union, in a refreshing change of circumstances, is actually telling us the truth."

"I never said 'truth,' " Oi said. "I said there were fewer untruths that we can immediately see. And even if they are largely telling the truth, which is something we still have to ascertain, the truth in itself is not necessarily a positive thing. What they are telling the truth *about*—what information they are sharing with us—is just as relevant. When Abumwe shared this with us what I really wanted to know is what she *wasn't* sharing."

"I need to know whether you think this Equilibrium group exists and is the threat Abumwe says it is."

"Yes to the first, and inconclusive to the second. We need a couple more passes through the data to be sure. But here is the thing about that, Councilor."

"I am imagining this is where the less good news graduates into the bad news," I said.

"You are correct, because right now *it does not matter* whether the Abumwe information is true or not," Oi said. "The general is correct that the Colonial Union and Abumwe dropped a bomb into our lap—a bomb you suggest we let her set off, I will remind you—and now all the chatter I'm hearing is our members triangulating toward it or away from it. We've introduced chaos into the usual mix of ambition and venality we lovingly call the Grand Assembly. Before, we had two primary groups in the chamber: those generally drifting away from the Conclave and those generally supporting it. Right now my analysts have identified six distinct emerging philosophical groups. Some of these believe the Ocampo report and some believe the Abumwe, and then there are some who don't care about the truth value of either but merely whether they can be used as tools to settle political scores. The group that especially worries me at the moment is the one my analysts are calling the 'purgers.' You can guess what the purgers want to do."

"The general is addressing the Grand Assembly about this very problem."

"No doubt because of your advice."

"That sounds more accusatory than usual, Director."

"Apologies," Oi said. "I don't mean to imply it was bad advice. Just that you appear to have more influence over the general than usual recently."

"I don't believe that's true."

"If you say so. At the very least everyone else is too busy to notice."

"Do you think the general is worse off than he was before, politically?" I asked, changing the topic.

"No," Oi said. "Before Abumwe addressed the Grand Assembly, a large faction had targeted the general in order to push one of their own into power. Now that faction has fragmented and all the factions are fighting each other. So if your plan was to divert attention away from the general, it worked. Of course, now there are complications. What was best for the general in the short term is not, I think, the best for the Conclave in the long term. You do see that, Councilor."

"I do," I said. "We buy time where we may."

"You bought yourself time," Oi agreed. "I don't think it's of very good quality."

In my own office, just before the general's address, I regarded Ode Abumwe, and she me. "I believe we might be two of a kind," I said to her, finally. "Two people who believe in the usefulness of truth, despite the environments in which we work."

"I am glad you believe so, Councilor," Abumwe said, and waited for me to continue.

"You were blunt yesterday in our meeting after your presentation," I said. "I was hoping you might be again."

"As you wish," Abumwe said.

"What does the Colonial Union hope to gain by sharing the information you have with us?"

"We hope to avoid a war with the Conclave," Abumwe said.

"Yes," I said. "But what more than that?"

"I was given no other brief, either publicly or privately," Abumwe said. "We knew Ocampo and Equilibrium wanted to set each of us on the other for their own reasons. We knew it would end poorly for us, and that we would be obliged to make it end as poorly as possible for you as we could."

"Presenting us this information does not end the potential of conflict between us."

"No, of course not. But if conflict happens, it will be because of our own damn foolishness, and not anyone else's."

I smiled widely at this. Abumwe, a professional diplomat, did not flinch. "But you don't believe that your brief is the whole of the reason this information was given to us," I said.

"You're asking me for my opinion, Councilor."

"I am."

"No, I don't," she said.

"Will you offer me your thoughts as to some of the other reasons?"

"That would be irresponsible of me."

"Please."

"I would imagine we wanted what in fact happened," Abumwe said. "Using the information to destroy the comity of the Conclave and to force open the fissures that were already developing. You could destroy us, and even if we took you with us that would be of little comfort. Better if you destroyed yourselves without going through us first."

"And do you believe that's how it would happen?" I asked. "That members of the then-former Conclave, individually or severally, would conveniently forget it was your report that started us on the path to our destruction? Would forget Roanoke? Would forget all the other reasons we have to despise you?"

"What I believe is aside from what my responsibilities are to the Colonial Union."

"I understand that," I said. "But it's not what I asked."

"What I believe is that both our governments are in an impossible situation at the moment, Councilor," Abumwe said. "We've been pushed there by this Equilibrium group, yes. But Equilibrium could not by itself have gotten us to where both of us are now. We can blame this situation on Equilibrium, or on each other. But we are where we are because we put ourselves there. I don't know if there's any way for us to avoid what's coming. The best we can do is put it off and hope something else develops along the way, to save us from ourselves."

"Another thing we have in common, Ambassador."

"I don't doubt it, Councilor," Abumwe said. "The rumor is that the general is going to address the Grand Assembly today."

"He is."

"He's hoping to repair the damage my report created."

"That's some of it, yes."

"If I'd have been him—or you—I wouldn't have let me address the assembly."

"If we hadn't have had you do it, we would have different problems."

"They might have been better ones."

"It's debatable," I said.

"Do you think it will help anything? The general addressing the assembly today."

"Let's hope it does," I said. "For both our sakes."

"We are at a critical time in the history of the Conclave," Tarsem was saying, from the lectern at the focus of the Grand Assembly. And then he launched into many more words.

I was not paying attention to the particular words. From my vantage point behind and to the side of him, I was doing what I do best: I was counting heads. Looking at the ones who were nodding attentively at what he had to say. Looking at the ones which were registering skepticism, or anger, or fear.

If you think this is an easy task to do across four hundred species, some of which do not have heads which show appreciable emotion, or indeed, some which do not have what might properly be construed as "heads," I certainly invite you to try it.

"You need to be paying specific attention to Prulin Horteen," I said to Tarsem, directly before he began his speech. "She's the one that Oi has targeted as being the head of this emerging 'purger' faction. We need to cut them off before they get any larger."

"I know what she is up to," Tarsem said. "I spoke with Vnac."

"When?"

"Just before I was here. While you were speaking to Ambassador Abumwe. I do have meetings you aren't present for, you know."

"I don't advise those."

"I don't imagine you would." Tarsem smiled. "Don't worry, Hafte. This speech will resolve a number of issues. I'm confident of that."

"It could be a start, in any event."

"We've made a good thing here," Tarsem said. "The Conclave, I mean. You and I and everyone else in this assembly. It's been a life's work making it."

"It's indeed a wonderful thing," I said. "If we can keep it."

"I think we will," Tarsem said.

"Start by tamping down Prulin Horteen," I said. "And Unli Hado while you're at it."

I glanced over to where I knew Hado would be. There was substantial room around him; it appeared he was in bad odor after the Elpri had been accused by Abumwe of participating in Equilibrium. Not too far from him, however, was Prulin Horteen, who no doubt thought she was helping Tarsem by trying to put entire species on the Conclave's chopping block. I returned my attention to Tarsem, who as it happened was addressing that very issue.

". . . Director Oi and its analysts are even now sifting through the data of both competing reports to tell us what information is accurate, what isn't, and, importantly, what *isn't* being told to us. Until we have that full analysis and report from Oi's office, I cannot and *will not* speculate with regard to the loyalties of any of our member nations. Are there individuals within those nations who may mean the Conclave ill? Yes, of course. They will be found and they will be dealt with.

"But individuals are not precise mirrors of their nations. And regardless of which report you now place your faith in, the Ocampo report or the Abumwe report, the intention behind both is the same: the dissolution and destruction of the Conclave. A return to the violence and savagery between our nations that we all still remember. We cannot allow that to happen. *I* will not allow that to happen. We are not a hollow union. We all have chosen to take part in this best chance for peace.

"I repeat: We must not fall back into savagery. We are not a hollow union—"

Tarsem's lectern exploded.

I was not aware of it immediately. I was pushed backward by the blast and toward the ground. My physiology makes me or any Lalan difficult to topple. I fell nonetheless, stunned and deaf, and amazed that somehow I had found myself on the floor.

Then my mind snapped back into function, I screamed, and I dragged myself over to Tarsem.

He was torn apart but not dead yet. I grabbed him and held him as his eyes searched around, looking for something to focus on. Finally he found me.

He said nothing—I don't believe he could say anything at that point—but simply watched me looking at him, holding him in his last moments of life.

Then he stopped watching and left me.

As he did I became aware of the din and madness around me as representatives and their staffs climbed over each other trying to escape the Grand Assembly chamber. Then I became aware of Tarsem's security staff swarming over me and him, pulling me off of him and dragging the both of us away, me presumably to safety, and Tarsem to oblivion.

"You need to be examined by a physician," Oi said to me.

"I'm fine," I said.

"You're not fine. You're in shock and you're yelling because you can barely hear. And you are covered in blood, Councilor. Some of it might actually be yours."

We were in a secure room not far from the assembly chamber. I was surrounded by members of Tarsem's security detail, who were no longer his security detail because they had somehow fundamentally managed to fail at their task. The anger I felt at that fact was growing within me; I held it down and looked at the security officer closest to me.

"Go fetch me a physician," I said. "Preferably one familiar with Lalans."

The security officer looked up at me. "Councilor, perhaps it would be better if you went to the hospital itself, once we've secured the area."

"I don't recall asking you for your opinion," I said. "Do it. Now."

The security officer scuttled off. I returned my attention to Oi. "How did you miss this?" I asked.

"I don't have a good answer for you right now, Councilor," Oi said.

"No, I don't imagine you do. You don't have a good answer to how you could have missed someone planning to assassinate the general." I waved a bloody hand at the remaining security detail. "They don't have a good answer, I'm sure, how someone slipped past them to place a bomb at the lectern. No one has a good answer for who is in charge of the Conclave right now. We are all without good answers for anything that actually matters right at this very moment."

"What would you like me to do, Councilor?" Oi asked.

"I would like you to go back in time and to have done your goddamned job, Oi!" I said, and this time I was yelling not because I could not hear very well.

"When this is all over, if you want it, you will have my resignation on your desk," Oi said.

I laughed, bitterly. "My desk," I said.

"Yes, *your* desk," Oi replied, forcefully. "And you're wrong, Councilor. I don't have a good answer for you about who killed General Gau. But I have a good answer for who is in charge of the Conclave. It's you."

"That was Tarsem's job description, Oi. Not mine."

"With due respect to the moment and your grief, Councilor, the general is dead. The position is vacant. And it needs to be filled, immediately."

"And you don't think that's a thought that's not already occurred to several dozen representatives?"

"I know it has," Oi said. "I know that without even having to check with my analysts. And I know what an extended season of would-be General Gaus trying to claim his mantle would cost us."

"*You* take the job, then," I said. "You're better qualified for it."

"I'm not the right person for the job," Oi said. "No one would follow me."

"You have an entire directory of people who follow you."

"They follow the job, Councilor. I don't flatter myself that their loyalty extends to me."

"What makes you think it would extend to *me*, then?" I asked, and then waved again to the security detail. "Or their loyalty? Or anyone's?"

"Councilor, why do you think this security detail is *here*?" Oi asked. "This was General Gau's detail. It's yours now."

"I don't want the job."

"Think of who does. Think of who will, once it occurs to them that it's open."

"So you would have me take the job simply to avoid something worse."

"Yes," Oi said. "Although that would not be my main motivation."

"And what would be your main motivation?" I asked.

"To preserve the Conclave," Oi said. It motioned out, toward the Grand Assembly chamber. "Unli Hado wants the position for his own personal ambition, as would a dozen other representatives. Prulin Horteen would take it to settle scores, as would another dozen representatives. Ristin Lause, were it offered to her, and it wouldn't be, would take it out of the bureaucratic instinct to keep things running. None of them truly understand why the Conclave is more important than themselves or their immediate goal. In all three cases—in every case—it would end in ruin."

"It might buy time," I said.

"We have bought all the time we can buy, Councilor," Oi said. "The general has just paid for all of it. *There is no more time.* There are only the choices we have in front of us right now. You take control of the Conclave, or allow someone else to. One choice will preserve the union. The other won't."

"You have a lot of faith in me, Oi."

"I have absolutely no faith in you, Councilor," Oi said. "What I have is analysis. You don't think I haven't been modeling what would happen after the general left power, do you? Who would try to claim his position and what would happen from there?"

"No, I suppose that would be your job," I said. "Although I didn't expect to be part of that math."

"If anyone else said that I would call that false modesty," Oi said. "In your case it's not, I know. You've always been the one to walk behind, Councilor. But there is no one for you to walk behind anymore. The Conclave needs you to step forward."

I looked around the room, at the security detail there. All ready for something.

"I don't want the job," I repeated to Oi.

"I know," Oi said. "But with all due respect, Councilor, at the moment I don't care about what you *want*. I care about what you will *do*."

The security officer returned, a Lalan in tow.

"You're a medical doctor," I said.

"Yes," the Lalan said. "Dr. Omed Moor, ma'am."

"Well, Doctor?" I held out my arms. "Am I dead?"

"No, ma'am."

I put my arms down. "Then that's all the time I have for a checkup at the moment, I'm afraid. Thank you, Doctor." I turned from the bewildered doctor to Oi. "Does your analysis include you working on my behalf?"

"I serve at the pleasure of the leader of the Conclave," Oi said.

"And that's me."

"It has been since the moment of the general's death. All we have to do now is make it known."

"I have some people I need to see," I said. "And there are people you need to see too."

"I can guess who you want to see," Oi said.

"I'm sure you can."

"Do you still want my resignation?"

"If at the end of this sur I'm still in a position to accept it, no," I said. "And if I'm not, I'll assume it's because we're in the same airlock, waiting to be pushed out into space by whoever is."

"I question your right to call us here," Unli Hado said. "You are not General Gau. And the general did not leave instruction for passing on leadership of the Conclave to you. If anyone should be the leader of the Conclave now, it is Chancellor Lause."

Hado sat in the conference room next to Tarsem's public office, along with Lause, Prulin Horteen, Ohn Sca, and Oi.

"It's a fair point," I said, and turned to Lause. "Chancellor?"

"I'm leader of the Grand Assembly, not the leader of the Conclave," she said. "I neither want nor can accept that position."

"You're a coward," Hado said.

"No," Lause said. "But I'm not a fool, either. The Conclave has just lost its leader, Unli, and it's lost it to assassination. Are you so blinded by your own ambition that you don't realize that anyone claiming the general's title will look like the assassin's employer?"

Hado flung an arm at me. "And *she* won't?"

"No, I won't," I said. "Not if we come to terms now."

"I repeat: I question your right to call us here," Hado said.

"Oi," I said.

"Representative Hado, I have it on very excellent information that you are the one who authorized the assassination of General Gau," Oi said. "Evidence from the Abumwe report combined with my own agents' intelligence gathering lays it squarely at your door. Within the sur I expect that you will be arrested for treason and that a comprehensive report will show the Elpri government was providing logistical and material support not only for the assassination but for Equilibrium in general."

Hado stared, disbelieving. "That's a lie!"

"Don't protest too much, Hado," Horteen said.

Oi turned to her. "Prulin Horteen, I have evidence that you offered material support to Representative Hado for the assassination, and that your recent rhetoric about purging nations you deemed traitorous to the Conclave is a feint to draw attention from your own involvement."

"What?" Horteen said.

"Representative Sca, your government's collusion with Hado's assassination of the general and with Equilibrium in general is exhaustively documented as well," Oi said.

"I don't have any idea what you're talking about," Sca said.

"I do," Hado said, turning to me. "This is a beheading of anyone who is in a position to oppose you."

"No," I said. "It's a precautionary measure against a trio of representatives who are a material threat to the unity of the Conclave at the moment of her greatest instability. Any of the three of you could shatter the Conclave, by your own ambition, by your own greed, or by your own stupidity. We are not four serti past the assassination of our leader. The Grand Assembly is in chaos. The representatives are utterly terrified. And if Vnac Oi had the three of you arrested on charges of assassination and conspiracy, I could have you all on the other side of an airlock by the end of the sur and no one would do anything but congratulate me on my decisiveness. I might even get a commendation from the chancellor for it."

"Indeed you might," Lause said. It was instructive to watch the reaction of Hado, Sca, and Horteen to that comment.

"And when the evidence eventually shows that the accusation was a flat-out lie?" Hado asked. "Because it will. Both Ocampo's and Abumwe's reports are out there for everyone to see and compare."

"Representative Hado, I'm deeply insulted," Oi said. "You apparently have so little faith in my ability to manipulate data to tell precisely the story I want it to tell."

"Why are you telling us this?" Sca said. "If this was your plan, why didn't you just have us arrested?"

"I didn't say it *was* my plan," I said. "It was my rebuttal to Representative Hado's questioning of my right to call you all here. I trust I've made it clear that at the moment *right* is not the correct frame of reference. I have the *power* to call you here. As I have the power to condemn you to death. I hope we understand each other."

"You want to make an example of us, then," Hado said.

"What I want, Representative Hado, is to save the Conclave," I said. "And offer you three the chance to increase your power and influence while doing so."

"By throwing us out of an airlock?" Horteen said.

"I have a better idea," I said. "And it is precisely this simple. Representative Horteen, you and Representative Hado have significant power bases among assembly members. They don't overlap. You two are to come to Chancellor Lause and together declare that for the good of the Conclave you ask that I take on the leadership role of the Conclave. Representative Sca, you will second that proposal. Horteen and Hado will deliver their blocs for the vote, Lause will take care of the rest, and Oi will handle any stragglers. This will happen tomorrow, by mid-sur."

"And if it doesn't?" Hado asked.

"Then you three will have a meeting with an airlock," Oi said.

Hado glanced over at Oi and then turned back to me. "You didn't have to threaten us," he said. "You could have just asked."

"Representative Hado, we've been doing so well being bracingly honest with each other," I said. "Let's not ruin it now."

"General Gau would never have negotiated with us this way," Horteen said.

I glanced over at Hado for this. "Yes, he would have," Hado said, to Horteen. "He simply would have had Sorvalh here to cover for him."

"The general is no longer with us," I said.

"Pity," Hado said.

"It is," I said. "How ironic, Representative Hado, that it took you until this very moment to recognize his value."

"Do we have a deal?" Oi asked.

"Do we have a choice?" Hado replied.

"You said this would increase our power," Horteen said. "I haven't heard the part where that happens."

"This is how," I said. "After the present crisis is over, and the stability of the Conclave is no longer in question, I will announce the formation of a task force to create and establish a succession plan for the leader of the Conclave, so that we have no more crises like the one we are now conspiring to avoid today. I will name the three of you, with the chancellor, to head the task force, and give you free reign to create the process, with only one condition: that the next leader of the Conclave *must* come from the Grand Assembly."

"Interesting," Horteen said.

"I thought you might see it that way," I said. Already I could see both Horteen and Hado starting to think how they could use such a task force to their own advantage. "Please note that this process will be for *after* I retire."

"But you do plan to retire," Hado said.

"Yes. Not soon, to be clear. But soon enough."

"And in the meantime you will still have this threat over our heads," Sca said.

"No," I said. "The threat dies when the Grand Assembly elects me leader of the Conclave, tomorrow."

"But only then," Oi said.

"And who do you place the blame on then, I wonder?" Hado asked. "For the death of the general?"

I felt a pang in that moment, for my friend and against my own conscience, for having to use his death so opportunistically. "Let that be my concern for now, Representative Hado."

"As you wish, Councilor," he said, and stood to rise, as did the others. "But it's not 'councilor' anymore, is it? What do we call you now?"

"I'll let you decide," I said. "Tomorrow."

They exited, except for Oi. I slumped, exhausted.

"Well done," Oi said to me.

"It was a basic threatening," I said, weakly. "Nothing I haven't done before."

"Possibly higher stakes this time."

"Yes, possibly," I said. "Thank you for coaching Lause for me."

"It might interest you to know I didn't, really," Oi said. "When I met with her I just asked her if she would follow your lead. Do you know what she said?"

"I don't know."

"She said, 'For the Conclave, I will.' And there you have it."

"Do you believe her?"

"I think she knows stability is the key to her keeping her job."

"And the other three?" I asked. "Do you think they'll keep the deal?"

"I don't doubt it," Oi said. "One of the nice things about my line of work is that people who don't know much about it have an infinite capacity to believe that I can do anything, including fabricate incriminating evidence out of thin air."

"And don't you?"

"It's not *infinite*," Oi said. I smiled at this. "In any event they don't need to know that we were bluffing blind. And by the time they figure it out, it will be far too late. You have my assurance of that, Councilor."

"Thank you, Vnac," I said. "Now, would you send in our next two visitors."

Oi nodded and made its way to the antechamber, where the principals of my next meeting waited.

"Ambassador Abumwe, Ambassador Lowen," I said, as the two humans entered. "Thank you both for seeing me at such short notice."

"Councilor Sorvalh, please accept my condolences," Lowen said. "And the condolences of the governments I represent. This is a terrible day."

"Condolences from me and the Colonial Union as well," Abumwe said.

"Thank you both," I said, and motioned to the table. "Please sit."

They sat. Oi positioned itself in a corner, to observe. I stood, considering my two guests.

"Is everything all right, Councilor?" Lowen asked.

"Yes," I said, and smiled, slightly. "I apologize, ambassadors. I am trying to decide how to say what I have to say next."

"You told me earlier that you prize truthfulness," Abumwe said. "In spite of the environment in which we work. Perhaps at this moment truthfulness would be even more useful than usual."

"All right," I said. "Then here it is: By this time tomorrow I will be the ruler of the Conclave. The deal has already been made. It's not a role I would have asked for but it's one I need to take, for the stability of the Conclave."

"Understood," Abumwe said. Lowen nodded.

"One consequence of today's events is that the members of the Conclave will be looking to place blame for the assassination of General Gau. Time will eventually provide an answer but that won't stop the drive for a target in the short term. There are fundamentally two choices here: place blame internally, on a nation or nations within the Conclave, or place it externally."

"I can see where this is going," Abumwe said.

"You're not wrong, I imagine," I said. "But please let me finish. Understand, both of you, that at this very moment I have one priority: to keep the Conclave intact. There is nothing else that comes close to that goal. At this moment, this means I cannot allow internal doubt, internal accusation, or internal blame, *even if it is correct to do so.*"

"So you will blame us," Lowen said. "We humans."

"Yes," I said. "Officially."

"What does that mean?" Abumwe asked.

"It means that for the moment, the official response of the Conclave is to privilege the Ocampo report over your report. It means that we officially assume that the Colonial Union intends malicious action against the Conclave. It means that it is under suspicion with regard to the death of General Tarsem Gau. It means that although we will not declare that a state of war exists between our two governments, any future provocation from the Colonial Union will be met with the harshest appropriate response."

"It means you're using us as a scapegoat," Abumwe said.

"I'm not entirely familiar with that term but I can guess what it means. And yes."

"You understand that the Equilibrium group will use this as

an excuse to make attacks that appear to be from the Colonial Union."

"Yes, of course."

"Then you understand what my next concern will be," Abumwe said.

I nodded at Lowen. "Perhaps you wish to have further discussion on this topic privately. Ambassador Lowen does not need to be read in for this part."

"It's too late for that now, don't you think."

"All right," I said. "You know I have a back channel open to the Colonial Union. Director Oi here," I nodded to Vnac, "will be keeper of that channel. If the Colonial Union is genuinely interested in avoiding a war with us, Ambassador, then it will consider continuing the free sharing of information between us. It won't change the Conclave's official position on the Colonial Union for now. Unofficially it will help me keep the warmongers in the Grand Assembly in line. We understand each other, I trust."

"And what about Earth?" Lowen asked.

"I can't give the Colonial Union the slightest provocation or excuse for an attack," I said, turning to her. "Or allow any other group to use such as cover for attack. I am withdrawing our diplomats from Earth and expelling yours from Conclave headquarters. Existing agreements on trade and lend-lease ships will be followed to their precise letter and no more. Don't expect any further for the time being."

"That puts you in a bad position with us in respect to the Colonial Union," Lowen said. "Without your trade and material support, a number of our governments will start to look favorably at the CU again."

"I don't have any choice in the matter," I said. "Until things are settled I can't allow humanity to be a distraction to the Conclave." I turned to Abumwe. "With that said, let it be known that if the Colonial Union takes any hostile action against the

Earth, the Conclave will assume the Colonial Union is doing so in order to build up its military and colonial populations, with the intent of attacking the Conclave and setting up new colonies. I don't think I have to tell you what our response will be."

"We have no intention of attacking the Earth," Abumwe said.

"Attacking the Earth *again*," I said. "Our official point of view, Ambassador. For now."

"I can't say that I'm happy with this choice."

"I don't need you to be happy with it, Ambassador. I would like for you to understand why it's necessary."

Abumwe turned to Lowen. "And you? What's going to be the Earth's official position on Equilibrium?"

"I couldn't tell you," Lowen said. "We only just found out it existed. Or that you allege that it *does* exist. I'll take your information back to Earth with me, of course, and share it. You can expect a high amount of skepticism."

"I understand. But if I may ask, what do you think, Ambassador Lowen? Privately."

Lowen looked at me before continuing. "I would very much like to believe the Colonial Union had nothing to do with the destruction of Earth Station. I would very much like to believe that it means us no harm. But I don't know if we can *trust* the Colonial Union, Ambassador. As much as I would like to. I don't see it happening."

"Perhaps we'll find a way to earn it," Abumwe said.

"I know a way you can start," Lowen said.

"Tell me."

"My ship blew up," Lowen said. "And I've just been told that we can't stay here to wait for another one to arrive. I could use a ride home."

"The humans are off?" I asked Oi, as it came up to me. I was in the Lalan park. I was taking my last few minutes of peace in what was likely to be a very long time.

"A serti ago," it said. "The *Chandler* was rather crowded, as I understand it. They are going to Earth first to drop off Lowen and her team. Then I understand they are back to Phoenix Station."

"Understood."

"Not necessarily a very good idea to let them spend more time together," Oi said. "The two varieties of human. Our people have a hard enough time making a distinction between them."

"I'm not sure we had a choice," I said. "We needed them all away, sooner than later."

"We found it, by the way," Oi said. "The weapon that attacked the *Odhiambo*."

"What was it?"

"A very interesting new toy. A particle beam weapon, heavily cloaked in material that scatters electromagnetic radiation. We literally ran into it, otherwise we wouldn't have found it. The weapon had no particular manufacturing marks on it but my analysts guessed it might be human manufacture."

"The Colonial Union?"

"Or these Equilibrium people, borrowing their designs. We'll figure it out, but at the moment your guess is as good as mine. We figure either it was skipped in just before the *Odhiambo*, or it's been sitting out there for a while, waiting for a target."

"Are you looking for more of them?"

"We are now," Oi said. "You'll understand when I say they're hard to find. When you're elected leader you might authorize some more resources to the task."

"Indeed. And, how is the vote going?"

"It's going uneventfully," Oi said. "You will be elected leader of the Conclave in just a few ditu, I expect. It would have been done sooner but some of the representatives can't vote without making a speech."

"How hard did you have to work to change minds?"

"Not as hard as I might have in any other circumstance," Oi said. "People are still in shock about the general. They know who you were to him. Many of them are voting for you as a final way to honor him."

"That's a sentiment that would amuse Tarsem," I said.

"I'm sure," Oi said. "Not that I didn't have to threaten a couple of representatives, of course. But, again, fewer than I might have to otherwise."

"I'll need their names."

"You'll have them. Try not to have them killed."

"I'm more subtle than that."

"You'll have them killed later, you mean."

"I won't have them killed at all. Just their careers."

"When the vote is final they will want you to speak to the Grand Assembly."

"Of course," I said. "I'll be ready. Thank you, Oi. That will be all."

"One more thing," Oi said, and produced in its tendrils a paper envelope. "A letter."

"From whom?"

"From the general," it said. "He gave it to me in our last meeting. He asked me to hold it and to give it to you, after his speech. He told me I would know when to give it to you." It held it out to me. "I think it's all right to give it to you now."

I took the letter. "I assume you read it," I said.

"In fact that is the one piece of information on this entire asteroid that I have not read."

"Remarkable," I said, looking at the envelope. "How did *that* happen, I wonder."

"Simple. The general asked me not to." Oi nodded and departed.

I opened the envelope and read the letter inside.

Hello, Hafte.

First I will apologize. If you are reading this, you are now leader of the Conclave. I know it's not a position you wanted for yourself, and if you resent me a little for making you take it I understand. But also understand that I can't imagine that the next leader of the Conclave would be anyone but you. You have too long contented yourself to be the advisor and the councilor. It's not that I did not value your advice and counsel. But I always understood that your talents were not being used to their best extent, either by yourself or the Conclave. Now they will be. I hope you can forgive me for giving you that final push.

Not too long ago you and I sat in the Lalan park and you told me the story of Loomt Both and how he almost doomed the Lalans to extinction. You said to me that it was best for your people to have their pain early, to grow into their wisdom. I have come to believe the same is true for the Conclave. We had growing pains, rebellions, and loss. But none of these events have fixed the Conclave, changed it from a disparate collection of peoples into a single, galvanized nation. It needs something to be that catalyst.

If you are reading this, then you know what that catalyst was.

I set the letter down, trying to make sense of what I had just read. I looked around the park, and saw nothing but greenery, and a single young Lalan, mindlessly swimming in the pond. After a few moments I started reading again.

You were right. When the Conclave was an idea, and when it was growing, I was the right leader for it. But I'm not the right leader for it now. It needs someone else, someone with a cannier set of political skills. Someone like you. But neither can I simply step away and fade into the background. We both know there are those in the Grand Assembly who would have no intention of allowing me to pick my own successor. The process would be drawn out and messy and at the end of it I would be what you feared I would become—just another politician, who left the stage long after he should have.

Instead I choose to become something else: A symbol. A legend. A martyr to the Conclave. And, to be less precious about it, a bludgeon for you to pummel anyone who dares to get out of line, for a good long time now. I've given you a tool to build the founding myth of the Conclave—to set it on a path toward wisdom rather than dissolution. I trust that you will know how to do it. You would know how to do it better than I would.

Now, as to the matter of my death. I am reasonably certain that Vnac Oi has suspicions; it is very good at its job. I am also reasonably certain that it has no intention of delving too deeply into the mystery, or rather, will be content to pin it on some conveniently unprovable set of circumstances. This will leave you, and only you, to know the true nature of events. The only accounting of it is in this letter. What you do with this knowledge is entirely your choice. From my point of view there is no wrong answer. But I think you know what I would suggest you do. At least for now.

There is nothing left to say other than this: I wish I could be there to see you do what will come next. I cannot. Instead I will take comfort in knowing that you will be the one to finish our work. To set the Conclave's future in stone.

I wish you joy in the work, my dear Hafte.

Tarsem

I stared at the letter for a good long while, seeing the page but not reading the words.

Then slowly, deliberately, I tore the letter into pieces as small as I could make them and tossed them into the pond.

The paper drank in the water of the pond, turning to bits of pulp, and the ink on the individual torn shreds of letter spread and ran, obliterating any chance of legibility. After several moments there was nothing left of the letter but my memory of it.

"Madam Premier," Oi said, behind me.

I turned and saw it, along with Umman, my assistant.

" 'Madam Premier.' So that is my title now," I mused.

"It is, Madam Premier," Umman said.

"Your presence is requested in the Grand Assembly chamber," Oi said. "The Grand Assembly would acknowledge you as the Conclave's leader."

"I would be pleased to see it," I said.

"They have also asked if you would speak to them."

"If they wish."

"May I tell them what you will say?"

"Yes," I said. "You may tell them that I intend to say the following: The union is preserved."

CAN LONG ENDURE

To the production staff of Tor Books and at all my other publishers. Thank you for making me look good.

PART ONE

It was Tuesday, and we had to murder a revolution.

"It *is* Tuesday, yeah?" Terrell Lambert asked. There were four of us in the squad for this mission, and we waited, slowly circling, in a shuttle twenty-five klicks above the planet surface.

In one way, it was a reasonable question. Days fade into each other in the Colonial Defense Forces, especially when you're traveling from one mission to the next. One day is very much like another on a starship, there are no real "days off." Tracking days might make sense if you were waiting for your term of service to end, but recently we'd been made aware that our terms of service were likely to be extended indefinitely. This is what happens when your sole source of soldiers has been taken from you and you have no way to get any more anytime soon.

That being the case, tracking specific days didn't make a whole lot of sense. Was it Tuesday? It might be. Did it matter that it was Tuesday? Not as much as it might otherwise.

In another way it was a ridiculous question because every CDF soldier has a computer called a BrainPal in their head. The BrainPal is a marvelous piece of equipment that can tell you instantly what day it is, what time it is, what the ambient temperature around you is, and every single mission spec— along with, really, anything else you might want or need, information-wise.

Lambert knew exactly what day it was, or could know. He

wasn't asking as a point of information. He was making an existentialist point about the nature of a life in the Colonial Defense Forces. It's worth saying that it's doubtful that Lambert was specifically intending to bring attention to the existential nature of his question. That didn't mean it wasn't there.

Also, he asked because he was bored, waiting for our mission to begin. Boredom also happened a lot in the Colonial Defense Forces.

"Yeah, it's Tuesday," Sau Salcido replied. "Ask me how I know."

"Because of your BrainPal?" Ilse Powell asked.

"No. Because yesterday was Pizza Day in the *Tubingen* mess. Pizza Day is always Monday. Therefore: It's Tuesday."

"That messes me up," Lambert said.

"That it's Tuesday?" Salcido asked.

"No, that Monday is Pizza Day. Back on Earth I was a custodian at an elementary school. Pizza Day was always on Friday. The teachers used it to keep the kids in line. 'Behave yourself or you don't get pizza on Friday.' Having Monday be Pizza Day subverts the natural order of things."

"You know what's worse than that," Powell said. "That *Tubingen*'s mess serves tacos on Wednesday."

"When it should be on Tuesday," Salcido said.

"Right, 'Taco Tuesday.' It's *right there*."

"Well, only in English," Salcido pointed out. "If you speak Spanish, for example, it's *'martes de tacos,'* which isn't alliterative at all. I *think* it's *'martes de tacos.'* I could be messing up the translation."

"You could just check with your BrainPal," Lambert said.

"And you could have checked with your BrainPal about what day it is, so what's your point."

"At the school we always had tacos on Thursday," Lambert said, changing the subject.

"Why would you do that?" Powell asked.

"Why wouldn't you? It's still a day that starts with a 't.'"

"In English," Salcido interjected.

"In English," Lambert continued. "It's still alliterative."

"*Technically* it's alliterative," Powell said. "Functionally a 'th' sound and a hard 't' aren't alliterative at all."

"Sure they are."

" '*Thhhhhhhh,*' " Powell hissed. "It's nothing like 't.'"

"You're reaching," Lambert said.

"Help me out here," Powell said, to Salcido.

"She's got a point," Salcido said, to Lambert.

" 'Taco Thursday' still makes more sense than 'Pizza Monday,' " Lambert said.

"Only in English," Salcido said. "In Spanish it's *lunes*. So '*lunes de pizza.*' Which kind of makes sense."

"That doesn't make sense at all," Lambert said. "Not even a little bit."

"Sure it does," Salcido said. "There's that old song. 'When the moon hits your eye like a big pizza pie, that's amore.' '*Lunes*' comes from 'luna,' which is moon. So there you go."

"I have never once heard of this song," Powell said. "You just made it up. This is a thing you just made up to win an argument."

"Agreed," Lambert said.

"I did not."

"It's complete bullshit."

"No."

"Vote," Lambert said. His hand went up. So did Powell's. "The motion passes. It's bullshit."

"I said it was an old song," Salcido protested.

"Lieutenant," Lambert said, "you've never heard of this pizza moon song, have you?"

"I am not being drawn into your stupid argument," I said. "Or more accurately, *another* of your stupid arguments."

"The lieutenant has never heard of your pizza moon song

either," Lambert said to Salcido. "And she was a musician. She would know."

"There are a lot of different types of musicians," Salcido said, only a little defensively.

A notification pinged in my view. "They're done talking," I said, to my squad. "We're on. Forty-five seconds. Suit up." I grabbed my gear, which in this case included a nanobot pack, a drone, and my Empee rifle.

"When we get back to the *Tubingen* I'm going to find that song," Salcido said, grabbing his own gear. "I'm going to find it and I'm going to make all of you listen to it. You'll see. You'll *all* see."

"Masks," I said. I signaled my combat unitard to create a mask, covering my face. It crept up my head, obscuring my view until my BrainPal offered up a visual feed.

"What's for lunch today?" Lambert asked, through his Brain-Pal, because his mouth was now snugly covered, like everyone else's.

"Hamburgers," Salcido said. "Because it's Tuesday."

The shuttle door opened, exposing us to the frigid temperatures of the upper atmosphere of Franklin.

"Out you go," I said to the three. They jumped out of the shuttle without further prompting. I counted off thirty and then jumped out of the shuttle myself.

Franklin was close to the size and mass of the Earth, basically perfect for human life, and was one of the first few planets colonized, back in the early days of the Colonial Union. It was densely populated, with citizens whose ancestry ranged from first-wave North American colonists to recent refugees from the Indonesian civil war, most of them on the large, thin continent of Pennsylvania, which dominated the northern hemisphere. There were a number of provinces and sub-provinces, but New Philadelphia, the city above which I now found myself, was the home of the planet's global government.

The global government which was, in a matter of minutes, about to vote on a bill to declare independence from the Colonial Union.

My BrainPal alerted me to the location of the other three members of my squad, some thousands of meters below me. They had a different mission objective than I did, although we were all headed for the same place: the global capitol building, affectionately (or perhaps not so affectionately) called "the glass slipper." It was named so because the architect gave it a swooping, rising profile that vaguely resembled a shoe—*very* vaguely in my opinion—and because the building was clad in a transparent, glass-like material, designed, or so the architect said, to be a metaphor for the transparency of the Franklin government itself.

The primary entrance to the Franklin capitol was a large, open arch that led into a rotunda from which, if you looked up, you could see the shoes of the global representatives, because on the highest level of the "slipper" was the legislative chamber, which boasted a lovely, sloping roof and a transparent floor which looked down into the rotunda. It was my understanding that it wasn't until the construction that someone pointed out that the transparent floor meant visitors could look up and see the underwear (or not) of the legislators wearing open leg coverings like skirts and kilts, at which point piezoelectric opaquing elements were added to the floor at considerable additional expense. Someone also neglected to consider the fact that a large room whose walls were entirely composed of transparent elements might turn into something of a greenhouse during warmer months, leading to several early heat prostration events before the air-conditioning to the legislative chamber was improved.

Another thing no one had considered: that placing one's global legislative chamber at the very top of a transparent building might make it uniquely vulnerable to attack from above.

But then, with the exception of a single incursion by the Conclave right after the Colonial Union's attack on their fleet at Roanoke, Franklin, as one of the core planets of the Colonial Union, hadn't been meaningfully attacked by an alien species in decades. And by the Colonial Union itself, never. Why would it have been? It was a constituent part *of* the Colonial Union.

Until, possibly, today.

"We're down," Powell said to me. That meant that the three of them had landed and were heading toward the capitol rotunda, bristling with weapons and general menace. The idea was for them to draw the capitol security force—such as it was—to them, and to cause a lockdown of the legislative chamber, sealing all 751 representatives inside the room.

Which was where I was going.

I signaled to the *Tubingen*, the CDF ship on which I was stationed, that I was ready to begin. The *Tubingen* was currently floating directly above New Philadelphia. Normally Franklin's planetary sensors would have spotted the *Tubingen* after it had skipped in literally (and dangerously) close to the planet's upper atmosphere. The problem was that the planet's sensor apparatus—from its satellites to its ground stations—were designed, installed, and still largely operated by, the Colonial Union. If the Colonial Union doesn't want a ship to be seen, it won't be. Someone would have to be looking directly for it to see it. And why would they be looking directly for it if the sensors didn't say it was there?

The *Tubingen* acknowledged my hail and reported that it would begin in ten seconds, and that I should keep clear the beam. I agreed with this and acknowledged the warning. The capitol building was directly below me now. My BrainPal lit up a column that represented the incoming beam. If I were to wander into the path of the beam I might be uncomfortable just long enough for my brain to register the pain before I was turned into a floating pile of carbon dust. That was not on my schedule for the day. I kept myself well clear of its path.

A few seconds later my BrainPal visualized the high-energy beam, pulsing on and off faster than my eye could register, vaporizing a three-meter hole in the roof of the legislative chamber one micrometer at a time. The goal was to create the hole without shattering the roof or vaporizing the legislators directly below the beam. At this juncture of the mission we didn't want anyone dead.

Path cleared, I thought. *Time to make an impression.*

"Here we go," I said out loud, found the hole, and dove for it. I waited for the last few seconds to deploy my nanobots into a parachute form, braking with an abruptness that would have killed an unmodified human body. Fortunately, I don't have an unmodified human body.

As it was, I dropped through the hole with enough velocity to make an impression, and to make my combat unitard stiffen to protect me from the impact.

There was a thump, and a mess, and a general cry of confusion as I seemingly appeared from nowhere. I raised myself up from impact position, looked at the elderly gentleman stunned to see me, and smiled. I had landed on the speaker's podium, directly behind his desk, exactly where I had planned to. It's nice when a bit of political theater such as the one I was about to attempt starts out so well.

"Speaker Haryanto," I said, to the startled man. "A genuine pleasure to meet you. Excuse me for just one second." I reached behind me, took the drone off of my back, and activated it via my BrainPal. It whirred to life and rose directly above my head. While it was doing so, I looked down through the floor—the speaker was wearing pants and had opted to keep his podium transparent, though tinted—and saw Powell, Lambert, and Salcido, weapons up, drones deployed, cautiously being encroached on by capitol security. They weren't in any particular danger, or at least any that they couldn't handle.

That done, I unstrapped my Empee, placed it on the speaker's desk, and invited myself to the microphone, into which Speaker Haryanto had been intoning mere seconds earlier. I had my BrainPal pop up the notes I made earlier, because I knew I would have to give a speech.

"Speaker Haryanto, representatives of the Franklin global government, and all the citizens of Franklin who are watching this singular legislative event, at home or wherever you may be, greetings," I began. "I am Lieutenant Heather Lee of the Colonial Defense Forces. I do apologize for my abrupt and unscheduled entrance to your session today, but time was of the essence. I bring you a message from the Colonial Union.

"The Colonial Union knows that today—in fact, right now—this chamber has begun a vote to declare independence from the Colonial Union. We also know that this vote is hotly contested, and is likely to be very close. This is for good reason, as your independence would leave you vulnerable to the predations of any number of alien species who are even now watching, as we are, the result of your vote.

"Through standard channels the Colonial Union has made the government of Franklin aware that we are opposed to this vote. We feel it is dangerous not only to the people and government of Franklin, but also to the Colonial Union at large. We also maintain that such a vote is illegal and that Franklin may not, through legal means, separate itself from the Colonial Union. These points have proved to be unpersuasive to many of you, hence this vote that Speaker Haryanto was about to commence.

"You may believe that I have come here to stop this vote on behalf of the Colonial Union. I have not. The representatives of Franklin, or at least the minority required to bring this vote to the floor, have asked for this vote. The Colonial Union will allow it to proceed. What I am here to do is make you aware of the consequences of this action."

I paused for effect, just long enough to make them wonder about the consequences, and then began again. "During the lead up to this historic vote, some of you in this chamber—in a manner you believe fitting, given that the name of this colony is taken from the United States of America revolutionary figure Benjamin Franklin—have quoted the United States' Declaration of Independence, and specifically how you, like those revolutionaries who signed that document, would pledge your lives, your fortunes, and your sacred honors to your own independence.

"Very well."

I pointed to the drone hovering above my head. "As I have been speaking to you, this drone has identified and targeted every representative in this room, and has fed the information to a Colonial Union ship, which by now has trained high-energy particle weapons on each of you. As the Colonial Union has already declared that this vote is illegal, if and when you vote for independence, you will be offering up an act of treason to the Colonial Union. In doing so, you will lose your sacred honor.

"As you will be committing treason, the Colonial Union will freeze all your financial accounts, to restrict your ability, or the ability of others, to commit further treason with them. So you will lose your fortunes. And once you vote, confirming your treason, you will be summarily sentenced to death by the Colonial Union, with the sentence to be carried out immediately; as I said you are already tracked and targeted. So you will lose your life.

"Now, then," I said, turning back to Speaker Haryanto. "You may proceed with your vote."

"After you have threatened all of us with death?" Haryanto said, incredulously.

"Yes," I said. "Or more precisely, after the Colonial Union

agreed with the principles you have already set out—that this action was worth your life, fortune, and honor. What you may not have expected is that it would cost all these things as quickly as it will. But these are not the days of the American Revolution, and the Colonial Union is not the British Empire, an ocean and several months away. We are here now. It's time to find out who among you is willing to make the sacrifice for independence that you have declared you will make. Time to find out who means what they say, and who was simply posturing because you thought your posturing was consequence free—or at least, consequence free for *you*."

"But you won't give us our independence even if we vote for it!" someone yelled from the floor.

"Is this a *surprise* to you?" I asked. "Did you not think there would be a struggle to follow? Did you not believe the words you said? Or did you believe the repercussions of your actions would be shouldered by others—by the citizens who will be pressed into service to defend the so-called independence you wish to give them? The fellow citizens of Franklin who will die by the millions as other species claim this planet for their own when the Colonial Union is not here to defend it? Where did you think *you* would be when that happened? Why did you think *you* would not be asked to answer for your vote?

"No, my dear representatives of Franklin. You are being given an opportunity. You will be called to answer for your actions *before* any other citizen of Franklin. You will not evade this responsibility, as much as you may wish it. Your vote is being broadcast across this globe. You cannot hide now. You *will* not hide now. You will vote your conscience. And your fellow citizens will find out now whether you believe their so-called independence is worth *your* life."

"So, let's begin," I said, and nodded to Haryanto. "You first, speaker."

"We're off the clock now, yeah?" Lambert asked.

"Since we're on the shuttle back up to the *Tubingen*, I would say yes," Salcido said.

"Then let me question the usefulness of that last stunt of ours."

"I don't know," Powell said. "The declaration of independence was unanimously defeated, the entire planet of Franklin got to see its legislators revealed as cowards looking after their own skin, and *we* didn't die. I thought it was pretty successful."

"I didn't say it wasn't successful," Lambert said. "I said I question its usefulness."

"I don't see the difference," Salcido said.

"The success of the mission depends on whether we achieve our mission goals. We did that—like Ilse said we killed the vote, embarrassed the politicians, didn't get killed, and reminded the entire planet that the Colonial Union can come along and stomp them anytime it wants, so don't screw with us. Which wasn't explicitly in our mission parameters but was the subtext of the mission."

"Wow, 'subtext,'" Powell said. "For a former janitor you're using big words there, Terrell."

"This former janitor has a rhetoric degree, asshole," Lambert said, and Powell smiled at this. "He just learned he could make more money as a janitor than as an adjunct professor. So yes. Successful. Great. But did it address the root causes? Did it address the underlying issues that required us to have to take the mission in the first place?"

"One, probably not, and two, do we care?" Powell asked.

"We should care," Lambert said. "We should care because if we didn't, then one day we'll be back here dealing with this problem again."

"I don't know about that," Salcido said. "We stomped on that vote pretty hard."

"And we did it with a single fireteam," Powell said, and then pointed at me. "Plus the fact that the Colonial Union sent a mere lieutenant to deal with a vote of global consequence probably said something. No offense, Lieutenant."

"None taken," I said.

"The whole point of the mission was to shake their confidence and make them consider their action," Powell continued. "The Colonial Union was saying 'Look what we can do with four common soldiers, so think about what we could do with more—and think about what we're protecting you from.'"

"But it doesn't address root causes," Lambert said, again. "Look, the global legislature of an entire planet doesn't wake up one morning and decide to vote for independence just for the fun of it. There was a lot going on before that point. Things we don't know about because while it was all brewing, we were off doing other things."

"Right," Powell said. "And when the aftermath of this comes down, we'll also be off again, doing other things, so why are you worked up about it?"

"I'm not worked up about it," Lambert said. "I'm just asking if our so-called 'successful' mission actually helped."

"It helped the Franklins," Salcido said. "The ones who didn't want independence, anyway."

"Also the ones who didn't want to get shot for treason," Powell interjected.

"Them too," Salcido agreed.

"Right, but I'm not convinced it helped the Colonial Union," Lambert said. "The reasons the Franklins wanted independence, whatever they are, are still there. They haven't been addressed."

"Not our job," Powell said.

"No, it's not. I just wish whoever job it was had done it before we got there."

"If they had then we wouldn't have been there," Powell said.

"We would have been somewhere else and you would be trying to find deeper meaning about *that*."

"So you're saying the real problem is me," Lambert said.

"I'm not saying the real problem *isn't* you," Powell said. "Me, I'm just glad to get through the thing alive. Call me uncomplicated."

"Uncomplicated."

"Thank you. And you, Terrence, should stop overthinking the mission. Do it, get it done, go home. You'll be happier."

"I don't know about that," Lambert said.

"Fine, then I'll be happier, because I won't have to listen to you go on."

"You'll miss it when I'm gone."

"Maybe," Powell said. "I'm willing to find out."

"Found it!" Salcido said.

"Found what?" Lambert asked.

"That song. The song you said didn't exist."

"The pizza moon song?" Powell asked.

"Bullshit," Lambert said.

"Not bullshit!" Salcido exclaimed, triumphantly. "I'm putting it through the shuttle speakers now."

The cabin of the shuttle was filled a song about moons, pizza, drool, and pasta.

"This is a *terrible* song," Powell said, after a minute.

"It makes me hungry," Lambert said.

Salcido smiled. "The good news is, we'll be back in time for lunch."

PART TWO

Wednesday—not one immediately following the events of Franklin—and we were hunting a sniper.

"Just drop the building on him," Powell suggested, from behind our cover. She pointed to the apartment complex the rebel sniper had been using to take aim at the Kyoto security forces and the CDF that had been deployed to assist them. We were in Fushimi, the planet's third-largest city and the center of recent unrest.

"We can't," I said.

"Sure we can," Powell said. She pointed upward. "The *Tubingen* could level that entire building in six seconds. Pancake it into rubble. Sniper's dead, we're back on the ship in time for tacos."

"And then have the Kyotans pissed off at us because several hundred of their people are homeless, surrounding buildings are damaged or possibly destroyed, infrastructure compromised, plus a big pile of shattered apartment complex dead in the middle of the street," Lambert pointed out.

"You're doing that thing where you think you're thinking about long-term implications again, aren't you, Lambert."

"I'm pointing out flattening the building might be unsubtle and not the best course of action."

"I prefer to think of it as a Gordian knot type of solution," Powell said.

"The Gordian knot wasn't twelve stories high," Lambert countered. "With lots of people living in it."

There was a sharp crack and the whirr of masonry shearing off a building forty meters up the road. The Kyoto security officers who had been peeking their heads around it very quickly unpeeked.

"He should have hit them from that distance," Salcido said, unimpressed.

I motioned to the several dead Kyoto officers in the road in front of us. "He's accurate enough," I said. "Or she."

"He or she'd be a lot less accurate with several stories of apartment building falling on their heads," Powell said.

"We're not destroying the building," I said. "Get it out of your head."

"Well, what do you want to do then, boss?" Salcido said.

I craned up to look at the building again. It was your basic concrete block sort of apartment complex. The complex had several corner and near-corner apartments that the sniper could use as vantage points for the road we were on. The apartments were difficult to see into visually and heat scanning wasn't turning up anything; this sniper was using camo that made them difficult to spot across the whole electromagnetic spectrum. Or was wearing a nice insulating jacket.

"We could land a squad on the roof," Powell said. "Flush out the asshole."

"If I were the sniper I'd have wired the roof," I said.

"How much destructive power do you think this sniper has?"

"I'm willing to err on the side of caution, here."

"So he can blow up the building but we can't," Powell said. "Well, that's just perfect."

"The point is to have no one blow up the building," I said. "Suggest some other options, please."

"Track for movement," Salcido said. "Plug him the next time he takes a shot."

"This differs from what we've been doing how?" Lambert

said. "You can argue about whether this guy is a good shot, but he's at least pretty good at not being *seen* until he takes a shot. And unless our return shot is immediate, we're not going to hit him."

"But we *can* track the shot," I said. "I mean if the sniper takes a shot, our BrainPals can track its trajectory."

"As long as we're looking in the right place, sure, I guess," Salcido said.

"We'd still have to return fire almost instantly," Lambert said.

"Maybe," I said. "Or maybe not."

Lambert and Salcido looked at each other. "You're being cryptic, Lieutenant."

I looked at Salcido. "You're the resident Empee expert," I said.

"This is true," he said, and he was. He could tell you trivia about the CDF's standard rifle that you didn't know you didn't care about until he told it to you. "And?"

"The Empee builds its load on the fly out of nanobotic material."

"Right," Salcido said. "Keeps us from having to carry around six different types of weapons or ammo."

"Okay," I said. "I want to use the rocket launcher function, and I want to specify the payload of the rocket. Can I do that?"

"As long as the payload of the rocket is something that can be assembled almost instantly from the ammunition block, sure."

"Then I want you to make a payload of trackers," I said. "Tiny little trackers. The size of dust mites."

Salcido looked at me quizzically for a couple of seconds until the light went on. "Oh, okay. Got it."

"Can you do that?"

"Theoretically yes," Salcido said. "Practically, it would take me more time than we have to make an original design. I'm looking to see if there's anything on file that would work for our purposes."

"You have five minutes," I said.

"Of course, because any more time would make this too easy."

"I missed a step," Lambert said.

"I'm still for flattening the building," said Powell.

"Quiet," I said to Powell. And turned to Lambert. "We can track the shot but you said we'd have a problem accurately returning fire. And we don't want to blow up the building." I glanced back at Powell for this. "So rather than aiming *for* the sniper, we send a rocket filled with trackers into the apartment he's shooting out of."

"It busts open, covers the asshole with trackers, and then it doesn't matter where he goes, we know where he is," Powell said.

"Right," I said. "And we don't have to hit him head on, we just have to have him dusted."

"Found it!" Salcido said. "I've got something that should work. Building up a round now."

"So now all we have to do is wait for the next shot," Lambert said.

"We're not going to wait," I said. "We're going to draw his fire."

"How do you suggest we do that?"

I motioned to my combat unitard. "These should be good for one round."

"You're going to go out there and let the asshole take a shot at you," Lambert said.

"I didn't say it was going to be *me*," I replied.

"Well, I'm sure as shit not volunteering," Powell said.

"For once I'm with Ilse." Lambert jabbed a thumb at his squad mate.

"Sau?" I asked.

"You want me to build this Frankenstein rocket *and* take a slug to the head? Come on, boss. Cut me some slack here."

"I'm the officer here," I pointed out.

"And we're all super inspired by your leadership, Lieutenant," Powell said. "We'll be right behind you."

"Emphasis on 'behind,'" Lambert said.

I looked at the both of them. "When we get back to the ship we're going to have a little talk about military chain of command."

"We're looking forward to having that conversation if you survive, Lieutenant," Powell promised.

"We might have it with me on one side of an airlock and the three of you on the other."

"Seems fair," Lambert said.

"Locked and loaded," Salcido said, to me. "I'm already tracking the bots. Ready when you are."

"Fine," I said. I turned to Powell and Lambert. "You two make like you're laying down fire for me as I make my way up the road. With any luck that asshole will miss me when he takes his shot. Be watching the building for the shot. Sync with each other and with Sau so you can triangulate. It will give Sau a better target for the rocket. Sau, call it in and let them know what we're up to."

"Got it."

"We'll keep him busy," Lambert said. Powell nodded.

I had my combat unitard cover my face, loped out from behind cover, and started hoofing it up the street, Lambert and Powell's cover fire rattling behind me.

I made it about forty meters before I was hit by a truck.

Colonial Defense Forces combat unitards are amazing things. They look like something you'd wear if you were performing Swan Lake, but the fabric, designed with the Colonial Union's trademarked nanobotic trickery, protects its wearer better than anything short of a foot of steel. Probably better, since steel would fragment and spall and send shrapnel into your guts. The unitard doesn't do that. It stiffens on projectile impact and dissipates the energy it receives, up to a point. It's usually good for keeping your ass alive for a single direct hit of, say, a sniper's bullet.

But that doesn't mean you don't feel the hit.

I felt it just fine. Felt the stiffening of the unitard make it feel as if my ribs were cracking, and they might have been, felt my feet lift up off the road, felt my body fly backward through the air a few yards and then crumple into a heap as gravity took hold again.

All of which was according to plan. There was a reason I ran straight on into the sniper's sights. I wanted him to hit me center mass, where the unitard was best equipped to take the shot without killing me outright. If the sniper had been ambitious, he could have tried for a headshot, which I probably could have survived, but I wouldn't have been happy or mobile for several days afterward.

But Salcido was right. The sniper wasn't all that good. I figured—hoped might be the better word—that he'd go for the bigger, easier target. And he did.

Still hurt like hell.

I heard the *poomp* and hiss of Salcido's rocket fizzing toward the sniper's position, followed a few seconds later by a dull pop and the sound of glass shattering.

"Rocket hit," Salcido said, talking to me through my Brain-Pal. "You alive, Lieutenant?"

"It's debatable," I said. "You tracking?"

"Yeah. Sending the feed over the squad channel."

"That asshole still have a gun to my head?"

"No, he's on the move now."

I rolled and called up the squad feed and looked up at the building. The sniper was visible as a superimposed pattern of tiny dots, each representing a single, mite-size tracker. He was currently moving from one apartment to another.

"We going in after him?" Lambert asked.

"We don't have to," I said. "We just have to wait for him to position himself to take another shot. Then we take him."

"How are we going to get him to take another shot?"

"Easy," I said, and stood up.

"Your suit's not going to take another direct hit," Powell said.

"Then maybe the three of you should kill the shit out of him before he gets the chance to take another shot," I said.

"On it."

"Good." I stood there in the street, watching the pixelated sniper settle into another apartment, a floor below his previous one, and over the course of a couple of minutes, carefully position himself by a window to take another shot at me.

"Got you," I said.

The apartment building exploded.

More than a hundred meters away, I was knocked back by the crack of the pressure wave and then by the rush of heat and flying debris.

"What the *fuck* just happened?" I heard Salcido yell, followed by Powell and Lambert yelling at each other to get back. I rolled again, then looked up and saw a dirty wall of dust rolling toward me from the collapsing concrete. I ducked my head and held my breath despite my mouth being covered by my mask, and filtering my air for me.

After a minute the worst of the dust cleared and I stood up. There was a pile of rubble where the apartment building used to stand.

"Fuck," I said.

"Wasn't that what we *didn't* want?" I heard Lambert yell, via my ears rather than my BrainPal. I looked back and saw him, Powell, and Salcido walking up on me.

"It looks like what we wanted and what the higher-ups

wanted were two different things," Powell said. "I told you we should have just called it in. We could have saved ourselves some trouble."

"Shut up, Ilse," I said, and she shut up. I turned to Salcido. "Find out if there was anyone in the building besides the sniper."

"I'm pretty sure it was cleared out before we even got here."

"Make sure," I said. "If there are any civilians in there, we start digging them out."

"You've got to be kidding me," Lambert said. I turned to him to snap his head off for complaining about rescuing civilians, but he held his hand up. "Not about that," he said. "Look at your feed. That goddamn sniper is still alive."

I looked back at the building—or more accurately, at the pile of rubble. Near the periphery of the rubble, under about a meter of concrete, our sniper was trying to push a pile of concrete and rebar off of him.

"Come on," I said.

We reached the spot where the sniper was buried. Salcido trained his Empee on where the sniper's head would be while Powell and Lambert and I pulled chunks of building away from the hidden shooter. After a minute, I pried off a final slab, clearing a shot for Salcido.

"Jesus," he said.

Our sniper was fifteen standard years old at best and she was covered in blood from where the fallen concrete had creased her skull. I glanced through the rubble as best I could and saw her left arm pinned and her right leg going off in a direction it shouldn't.

"Get away from me," she said, and her voice told me that at least one of her lungs had collapsed.

"We can get you out of there," I said.

"Don't want your help, green."

I was confused by this until I figured out she meant me, with my green skin. I looked back at Salcido and his Empee. "Put that down and help us." He looked doubtful but did as he was told. I turned back to the sniper. "We're not going to hurt you," I said.

"You brought a building down on me," she wheezed.

"That wasn't our intent," I said. I skipped over the part where our intent was to shoot her in the head the moment she gave us a chance. "We'll get you out."

"No."

"You don't want to die here," I said.

"I do," she said. "This is where I lived. I lived here. And you destroyed it. Like you destroy everything."

"How are we doing?" I asked, not taking my eyes off the girl.

"Almost there," Powell said. Then she sent a message to me through her BrainPal. *The chunk of concrete on her leg is the only thing keeping her from bleeding out,* she said. *If we move it, she dies. She's dying anyway.*

"Okay," I said. *Call in for a medic,* I said through the BrainPal.

Why? Powell asked. *You're being awfully nice to someone who was just trying to kill you and who we were just trying to kill. She doesn't even want our help. You should just let her die.*

I gave you an order, I said. Powell visibly shrugged.

"We're going to call for a medic," I said, to the sniper.

"I don't want a medic," she said, and her eyes closed. "I don't want you. Why don't you leave. This isn't your planet. It's ours. We don't want you here. *Leave.* Just leave."

"It's not that simple," I said.

The girl didn't say anything. About a minute later she was dead.

"Well?" Lambert asked. He, Powell, and Salcido were waiting for me outside the security offices in Fushimi, where I had gone for a discussion—to use the word euphemistically—of the sniper incident.

"I talked to Colonel Maxwell," I said, naming the head of the CDF joint mission in Fushimi. "She tells me that it was the Kyotans who requested we drop the apartment building."

"Why would they want that? I thought we were working on the assumption they *didn't* want that. Thus, all the sneaking up and trying not to destroy it on our part."

"The apartment block was apparently the local headquarters of the rebellion. Or more accurately, the local headquarters of the rebellion was in the apartment block."

"So the building was chock full of agitators," Powell said.

"Maxwell didn't break down the ratio of agitators to normal humans," I said. "And I didn't get the impression from her that the Kyotan government much cared. They wanted to send a message."

"How many other people did we kill getting out the message?" Lambert asked.

"None," Salcido said, and looked at me. "Sorry, you asked me to find that out and I didn't tell you because we got busy with other things. The Kyotan security forces did a sweep of the building a week ago and pulled everybody out. Block questioning and intimidation. That's what started this whole set of riots we're helping put down."

"So if they weren't all rebels before, they probably are now," Powell said.

"You wanted to drop the building," Lambert reminded her.

"The building got dropped," Powell reminded him. "Although Lambert's right. If they were just going to drop the building, why the hell *did* they send us in?"

"They sent us in before someone in the Kyoto security upper ranks remembered a CDF ship could level a building in a single shot, apparently," I said.

"We could have been killed."

"I guess they decided we were safe."

"*That's* reassuring," Powell said.

"At least it wasn't our idea," Lambert said. "That girl hated us enough. And if she hated us, she had to have learned it from someone else."

"It wasn't our idea, but one of our ships did the honors," I said. "I don't think that distinction would matter much to her or to anyone else. We're on the hook for this as much as the Kyoto government."

"Did you get anything on the sniper?" Salcido asked me.

"Rana Armijo. Sixteen standard. Parents apparently in deep with the rebellion. No sign of them. Either they're gone or the Kyotans already have them."

"So she becomes a martyr for the rebellion," Lambert said. "The government rounds up everyone in her apartment block, she stays behind, starts taking out security officers, and is so successful they have to drop the building on her head. It's a good story."

"It won't do *her* much good," Powell said.

"That's how it's supposed to work for martyrs."

"So what now?" Salcido asked.

"We're done here," I said. "There's ongoing rebel action in Sakyo and Yamashina, but the *Tubingen* has other orders. It's someone else's problem now."

"It was already someone else's problem," Lambert said. "Then we made it ours, too."

"Don't start, Lambert," Powell said. "It's especially tiring today."

"If it's tiring for you, think how it feels to them."

PART THREE

A Thursday this time, and we're called upon to manage a protest.

"I'm not going to lie, I'm *really* curious to see these things in action," Lambert said, as the hurricane funnels were set up around the Colonial Union administrative building in Kyiv.

The administrative building itself was a skyscraper deposited in the center of a hectare of land in the downtown district. The entire hectare was a flat plaza, featureless except for a single piece of abstract sculpture. That sculpture was currently populated by several protesters, as was a large chunk of the plaza. The skyscraper was ringed by Kyiv policemen and CDF soldiers and hastily assembled metal barriers.

The protesters had not taken it into their heads to try to rush the skyscraper, but it was early in the day yet. Rather than wait for the inevitable, and the inevitable casualties to both protester and security forces, the Colonial Union had decided to employ the latest in less than lethal protest management: the hurricane funnel. One was being placed directly in front of my squad.

"It looks like an Alp horn," Powell said, as it was placed and started expanding out and up.

"Alpenhorn," I said. I was a musician in my past life.

"That's what I said," Powell replied, and then turned to Salcido. "You're the weapon nerd here. Explain this."

Salcido pointed up, at the very long tube snaking up to the

sky, now about two hundred feet up. "Air gets sucked into the thing from up there. It gets drawn down and accelerated as it goes. It hits the curve, gets an extra push, and out it goes that way." He waved in the general direction of the protesters. "We set a perimeter length, and anytime one of them tries to get past it, the funnel ramps up a breeze and blows them down."

"Which should be fun to see," Lambert said. "Although these things are awfully inefficient, if we're talking *real* crowd control. It's like we're daring them to try to cross that line."

"They're not supposed to be efficient," I said. "They're supposed to send a message."

"What message? 'We'll huff and we'll puff and we'll blow your protest down'?"

"More like 'We don't even have to shoot you to render your protest utterly pointless.'"

"We seem to be sending a lot of messages recently," Lambert noted. "I'm not sure the message we're sending is the message they're receiving."

"The message this time will be a blast of wind that could knock over a house," Salcido said. "It'll get received."

"And we're not worried about getting sucked out into the rioters," Powell said. "Because that would be bad."

Salcido pointed upward again. "That's why collection happens up there," he said. "Plus there's some airflow mitigation happening on this side of the thing."

"All right," Powell said.

"Just . . ."

"What? Just *what*?"

"Don't get *too* close to the thing when it's running."

Powell looked sourly at Salcido. "You're fucking with me, aren't you."

"Yes. Yes I am. Fucking with you. You're right, by all means, stand close to the thing when it goes off. Nothing bad will happen to you at *all*."

"Lieutenant, I may have to shoot Sau."

"Both of you, knock it off," I said. I was watching the technicians finishing setting the thing up, which mostly consisted of them watching it, because like most things involving the Colonial Defense Forces, it was designed to operate with minimal assistance from humans, who were without exception the moving part most likely to fail. Left and right of where we were, other hurricane funnels were also unpacking themselves while technicians stood by. In all there were twenty-four of the things, circling the building.

When they were all set up the chief technician nodded to me; I nodded back and took control of the three funnels closest to me. I set the perimeter to thirty meters, which was ten meters further out than where the closest protesters were standing. I was pinged by the other seven CDF squads manning the other funnel stations, all of which I was commanding, letting me know they were online and also set at thirty meters. I stepped out in front of the funnels so the protesters could see me. They started jeering immediately, which was fine.

"Attention protesters," I said, and my voice was amplified mightily by the funnel directly behind me, too loud for anyone to ignore. As close as I was to the thing I might have been deafened if I hadn't already had my BrainPal dial down my hearing for a minute. "I am Colonial Defense Forces Lieutenant Heather Lee. In one minute, I will be establishing a protest perimeter of thirty yards entirely around this building. Your voluntary cooperation with this goal would be greatly appreciated."

This received the response that I entirely expected it would.

"Suit yourself," I said, and stepped back behind the funnel. "Turn down your ears," I instructed my squad. Then I turned to the commander of the Kyiv police and nodded to him; he yelled at all his officers to fall back behind the funnels. They did, taking the metal barriers with them. A cheer went up from the crowd and it started to surge forward. I turned on the funnels.

The output from the funnels went from zero to fifty kilometers per hour in about three seconds. The crowd, sensing a challenge, pressed forward with more determination. In another three seconds the funnels were blasting at a hundred klicks per hour; in another five seconds at one hundred and thirty. At one hundred and thirty kilometers an hour, the funnels also emitted a horrendous, eardrum-crushing note designed to encourage crowd dispersal. I turned my hearing up a little to listen.

It was a very low E.

Did I mention these things are REALLY LOUD? sent Salcido, over the squad's BrainPal channel.

The crowd was pushed back despite their best efforts. Some of them flung bottles and other objects toward the funnels and were surprised when they shifted course right back at them. Apparently you don't have to understand physics to protest.

When the last of the protesters were pushed back to the thirty-meter line the funnels ramped their output down to thirty kilometers an hour, and the low E dissipated. The crowd muttered and shouted, angry. The Kyiv police, no longer needed, filed into the administration building, where they went to the roof and were airlifted out.

And so it went. Over the next hour, occasionally one or two of the protesters would try to see if they could sprint to the barricade before the funnels could push them back. The answer: No.

"That kind of looks like fun, actually," Lambert said, as the latest protester blew back across the plaza. His speaking voice was augmented in my ear by his BrainPal signal.

"Don't be so sure." Powell pointed to a streak of red on the plaza, where the protester's head had connected with the concrete.

"Well, I don't want to do *that*, obviously," Lambert said. "The rest of it might be fun."

"Hey, boss," Salcido said, and pointed out into the crowd. "Something's up."

I looked out. In the distance the crowd was parting as a motor vehicle made its way up toward the front. I identified it with my BrainPal as a heavy truck of local manufacture, without the trailer that usually accompanied these types of haulers. As it moved closer to the front, the crowd started chanting and hollering.

"Why the hell didn't the police stop that thing all the way at the back?" Lambert asked.

"We sent them home," I said.

"We sent the ones up *here* home," Lambert said. "I find it hard to believe at least *some* of the Kyiv police aren't still on duty."

"Sau," I said. "Are these things going to stop that?"

"The funnels?"

"Yeah."

"Lieutenant, these babies can blast out wind up to three hundred kilometers per hour," Salcido said. "They won't just stop the truck. They'll pick it up and toss it."

"Right back into the crowd," Lambert noted.

"There is that," Salcido agreed. "That is, the part of the crowd that is not *also* tossed straight up into the air, along with anything else that isn't nailed down, and probably some stuff that is." He pointed down the plaza at the sculpture. "If these things go top speed, I wouldn't count on that staying put."

"Maybe these things weren't such a great idea after all," Lambert said.

The truck, at the front of the crowd now, started blinking its lights, as if to threaten us. The crowd cheered.

"Standard electric engine for something that size, if it's not modified," Salcido said. He'd pulled up the same manufacturer ID I had. "It's gonna take it a couple of seconds to get up to ramming speed."

The driver of the truck let loose on his horn, issuing a blast almost as loud as the funnels.

"This will be interesting," Lambert said.

The wheels of the truck squealed as the driver floored it.

"Powell," I said and sent at the same time.

The front of the truck blossomed into flame as Powell's rocket shoved itself into the truck's engine compartment and erupted, shattering the truck's battery banks and puffing out the hood with an explosive *crump*. The spinning wheels, robbed of momentum before they could completely grip, lurched forward slightly and then stopped, barely moving a few meters. The driver of the truck bailed out of the cab and took off running, one of many protesters who decided they'd had enough for the day.

A few still stood near the truck, uncertain of what they should be doing next. Powell shoved another rocket into the truck, this time into the empty cab. It went up like the proverbial Roman candle. More protesters decided it was time to go home.

"Thank you, Powell," I said.

"Took you long enough to ask," she said, cradling her Empee.

"Those things aren't exactly a long-term solution, now, are they?" Lambert asked. He nodded to the hurricane funnels, now five stories below us. The four of us were in a conference room that had been turned over as a rest area for the CDF recruited for guard work.

"It's local midnight and that crowd out there's not going anywhere," Powell said. "I think the funnels might be a feature for a while."

"It's going to make going to work difficult for the Colonial Union folks who work in this building."

"Maybe they'll all telecommute," Salcido said.

Lambert looked back out at the crowd. "Yeah. I would."

"How much longer are we here?" Powell asked me.

"The technicians are training the Kyiv police on operating the things," I said. "So a couple more days."

"And then what? Off to the next planet to squash another protest or stomp on another building?"

"You wanted to stomp that building in Kyoto," Lambert reminded Powell.

"I didn't say otherwise," Powell said, turning to Lambert. "I didn't mind putting a rocket through that truck today, either. The alternatives might have involved me getting hurt or killed. So, fine." She turned back to me. "But this wasn't the gig I signed up for."

"Technically speaking, you didn't know what the gig was when you signed up for it," Salcido said. "None of us did. All we knew was we were getting off the planet Earth."

"Sau can play lawyer all he wants, but you know what I mean, Lieutenant," Powell said.

"Ilse's right," Lambert said. "This is our third mission in a row where we're trying to keep a lid on people rebelling against the Colonial Union."

"These sort of missions have always been part of the deal," I said. "Before you three came on I and the *Tubingen* were called on to squash an uprising on Zhong Guo. Some people there got it in their head that they wanted an alliance with Earth."

"Did they tell the Earth about that?" Salcido asked.

"Don't think they did," I said, and then motioned out the window, to the protest. "My point is that *this* is, in fact, our mission. Part of it, anyway."

"Okay, but three in a row," Lambert said.

"What about it?"

"Has that happened before, in your experience? Ever?"

"No."

"And you've been in the CDF how long, now? Six years?"

"Seven," I said. "And three months."

"Not that you're counting," Powell said.

"If you don't you lose track," I said. I turned back to Lambert. "All right, yes, it's unusual."

"And that doesn't bother you?" Lambert asked. "Wait—I phrased that poorly. I mean to say, you don't find it troublesome? Because when Ilse here, our current queen of the 'who gives a shit' line of thinking, is starting to get tired of our act, there might be a problem."

"I didn't say I was tired of it," Powell said. "I said it's not what I signed up for."

"There's a distinction in your brain between the two," Lambert said.

"Yeah, there is," Powell said. "I'm not *tired* of this. I can do this shit in my sleep. But I don't see it as *my* job. My job is shooting the hell out of aliens who are trying to kill us."

"Amen to *that*," Salcido said.

"What we're doing here, I mean, really, who gives a shit?" Powell said. She waved out the window. "These people are protesting. So what? Let them protest. They want to break up with the Colonial Union, let them."

"When the other species come down to scrape them off the planet, then *your* job would get harder," I pointed out.

"No it wouldn't, because they're not part of the Colonial Union anymore. Fuck 'em."

"I don't think I've ever told you how much, and in a twisted way, I assure you, I admire your commitment to amorality," Lambert said.

"It's not amoral," Powell said. "If they're part of the Colonial Union, I'll defend them. That's my job. If they want to go their own way, fine. I don't see it as my job to stop them. But I also won't stop the aliens from shoving them into a pot if they do, either."

"Maybe that's what we need," Salcido said. "One of these planets to go it alone and get the hell kicked out of them. That would bring the rest of them back into line."

"But that's the problem, isn't it?" Lambert said. "It's not just one of them. Not just one planet. It's a bunch of them, all at the same time."

"It's that thing," Salcido said. "That group. Equilibrium. Showing up and doing that data dump."

"What about it?" Powell asked.

"Well, it makes sense. All of these planets with people getting worked up all of a sudden."

"They're not getting worked up *all of a sudden*," Lambert said. "That rebellion in Kyoto was long-cooking. And the lieutenant here made the point about putting down a rebellion a year ago, on . . . where?"

"Zhong Guo," I said.

"Thank you. Maybe that Equilibrium thing is crystallizing action now, but whatever it's tapping into has been there already for years."

"Then the Colonial Union should have been preparing for this for years," Powell said, bored now with this conversation. "But it didn't, and now we and everyone else on the *Tubingen* are shuttling from one stupid internal crisis to the next. It's stupid and it's a waste."

"No, it makes sense," Lambert said.

"You figure? How's that."

"We're not attached to this place. We're not attached to Kyoto. We weren't attached to Franklin. We're not attached to any of the colonies because we originally came from Earth. So it's not difficult for us to come in and stomp around if we have to."

"We're handing off the work here to the Kyiv police," Salcido pointed out.

"Right, after we handled the hard part. That's our job. Handling the hard parts."

"But you just said that this isn't a long-term solution," Salcido said, waving out to the funnels. "In which case the hard part is still here, which means we'll be back. Or someone like us."

"Yeah, funny, I remember talking about not addressing root causes a couple of weeks ago, and got shouted down with 'who cares' and a song about pizza."

"It was a great song."

"If you say so."

"All I'm saying is that what we're doing now is increasingly full of bullshit," Powell said, bringing the discussion around. "If this is what we're doing now, fine. So be it. But I'd rather be shooting aliens. I think everyone else would too."

"She's not wrong," Salcido said, to me.

"No, she's not," Lambert agreed.

"I know," I said.

PART FOUR

Friday.

"Root causes," Lambert was saying. "You all kept mocking me for talking about them and now look where we are. Another colony planet. Another uprising. Except this time the planet's already declared independence."

The shuttle rocked on the way through Khartoum's atmosphere. This time it was not only the four of us but my entire platoon, as it was on Rus. We weren't doing protest suppression this time. This time we were making a surgical strike on Khartoum's prime minister, who had declared the planet independent, encouraged mobs to occupy Colonial Union buildings, and then hidden himself, with a circle of advisors, in an undisclosed location, presumably because he knew that the Colonial Union wasn't going to be particularly happy with him.

Indeed it wasn't. It wasn't happy with him, or in fact any of his party's leadership, all of which had endorsed the independence—without, it should be noted, actually presenting it to the entire parliament for ratification.

"They learned from Franklin," Lambert continued. "This time they knew not to give us a chance to respond first."

"Which makes their independence illegal," Salcido noted. He was sitting next to Lambert.

"It was always going to be illegal," Lambert said. "By which I mean there was no possible way the Colonial Union would accept the legality of their independence. So there was no reason for them to put it up to a vote."

"But now it's also illegal by their own system of government."

"No, because the prime minister had his cabinet approve a declaration of emergency powers and dissolved the current government," Lambert said. "All legal as can be."

"For what little good it's going to do him," Powell said. She was down a bit from Lambert and Salcido, on the other side of the shuttle, as was I.

"Oh, now, Ilse, he'll be *fine*," Salcido said. "He's in an *undisclosed location*."

"Which we're on our way to right now. Another high-altitude drop and destroy."

"We need to get Prime Minister Okada alive," I reminded Powell.

"High-altitude drop, snatch, and *then* destroy," Powell corrected.

"Which begs the question of how we know where this undisclosed location is," Lambert said, to me.

"Okada's had nanotransmitters in his blood since he became prime minister," I said.

"I assume he doesn't know that."

"Probably not."

"How did they get there, if you don't mind me asking?"

"No idea," I said. "If I had to guess, I imagine at some point or another he had a meal at the Colonial Union compound, and they were slipped to him then."

"And we wonder why the Colonial Union isn't looked on with great enthusiasm," Lambert said.

Powell rolled her eyes. "Here we go."

"You can snark at me all you want, Ilse," Lambert said, and then disappeared as a hole in the shuttle appeared behind him and he was sucked out into Khartoum's upper atmosphere, along with Salcido and the soldiers on either side of them. My combat suit, sensing pressure drop and shuttle damage, immediately snuck its mask over my head and started drawing oxygen out of what remained of the air in the shuttle cabin. Simultaneously as platoon leader I was patched into the shuttle's systems, which told me what I already knew: The shuttle had been hit and was no longer in full control of its descent.

I fought down the urge to panic and focused on damage assessment. The pilot was trying to keep the shuttle from tumbling, fighting with the now damaged controls. Four soldiers out the growing hole in the side of the shuttle. Five others dead or mortally injured, another five seriously injured but alive. Fifteen uninjured and me.

The shuttle was declaring it was being tracked; whoever hit us wasn't done.

I connected to the shuttle and authorized the shuttle doors to open. *Everybody out now,* I said, through the platoon Brain-Pal feed. My simulated voice made me sound more calm than I was.

We were all already suited up to jump out of the shuttle. We were just doing it earlier now.

By fireteams. Let's go.

The remainder of the platoon started out the doors. Powell stayed back with me, yelling at stragglers. The pilot kept the shuttle steady as possible. Powell and I got out of the door just before some sort of kinetic round tore the shuttle apart. I did a quick ping on the pilot's uniform's system feed. There was nothing there.

Lieutenant, Powell sent. She was falling about one hundred meters away from me and sent to me via tightbeam. *Look down.*

I looked down and saw flickering beams shooting up into the evening sky. They weren't going all the way up into the atmosphere; they were terminating on points below me.

They were hitting my soldiers. Killing them.

Full camo chaos dive, I sent over the platoon channel, to

everyone still alive. Then I ordered my suit to seal me in, went dark on communication, and made myself as close to a hole in the atmosphere as I could. The suit's camo function would hide me visually and would do what it could to scatter any electromagnetic waves that would be sweeping over me, trying to bounce back to a receiver set on targeting me. My suit was also making subtle movements and sending out extensions to move me around randomly, changing my speed and direction of descent, almost making it harder to target me. Every platoon member who heard my order was now doing the same.

Chaos diving could kill an unmodified human with the jerks and turns. My suit stiffened up at the neck and other joints to minimize the potential injury. It didn't mean I didn't feel my insides strain. But it wasn't meant to be comfortable. It was meant to keep you alive.

One other thing: The electromagnetic-scattering camouflage effectively makes you blind. You fall, relying on the data your suit polled before you turned it on to allow it to track where you were and how far you had fallen, factoring in all the shifts in direction and descent speed and feeding that into your Brain-Pal. The camo was designed to give me a visual feed again one klick up—just enough time to assess and plan a final descent path.

Unless there was an error, in which case I would see the ground just before I smacked straight into it. Or I might never see the ground at all. There would just be a sudden thump.

Also: I wouldn't know if one of those beams had found me until it started frying me.

The point is that you don't do a full camo chaos dive unless you absolutely have to. But that's where we were at the moment. Me and every other soldier in the platoon.

It also meant that when we landed, we would be scattered all across the countryside, coms quiet to avoid detection. In our briefing I had given the platoon an alternative extraction point in case something went wrong, but having the shuttle shot out from under us so far up and then performing a chaos dive meant that the remainder of the platoon was likely to be scattered over an area a hundred klicks to a side. When we landed, we were going to be alone, and hunted.

I had several minutes to contemplate all of this as I fell.

I also had several minutes to think about what had happened. Simply put, there should have been no way for the shuttle to have been shot out of Khartoum's upper atmosphere. Khartoum had defenses like any Colonial Union planet would, to prevent alien species from attempting an attack. But as they had been on Franklin and every other planet we'd visited recently, these defenses were built and run by the Colonial Union itself. Even if these installations had been overrun by Khartoum's citizens and abandoned by their CU operators, anyone trying to operate them would have been locked out by a nested set of security measures. Unless the CU operators had gone over to the other side—possible but not likely—those were someone else's beams.

Another wrinkle: The *Tubingen* should have been tracking the shuttle's descent and alerting us to, and defending us from, any ground-based attacks. If it hadn't, it would have been because it was otherwise occupied. Which is to say, that it was being attacked, either from the surface of the planet or above it. In either case, also not from the Colonial Union.

If this was correct, then it meant a couple of things. It meant that whatever was happening on Khartoum, it wasn't just about the planet's independence—the planet had aligned itself with enemies of the Colonial Union. And then it laid a trap for us. Not for the *Tubingen* itself—whoever was doing this didn't know which among the Colonial Dense Forces ships were going to respond. The *Tubingen*, its shuttle, and my platoon were all incidental in this. No, the trap was for the Colonial Union itself.

But why, and for what purpose?

My visual feed kicked on and I was a klick above the ground. In the distance were lights which suggested some form of civilization. Directly below me was dark, hilly, and full of vegetation. I waited as long as possible and deployed breaking nanobots, which spread out widely to catch the air. I landed hard and rolled and then stayed on my back for a moment, catching my breath and looking up at the sky. It was local night and the darkness of the vegetation combined with my Colonial Union-designed eyes meant I could see the stars in all their local constellations. I sighted several and, with local time and date, calculated my position.

I checked with my BrainPal to see if there was any signal from the *Tubingen*. I didn't want to try to signal them, in case anyone was listening, but if they were sending to us they might have information we survivors could use.

Nothing. That wasn't good.

I stood up, visual camo still on, and walked to where I could again see the lights in the distance. I applied the visual to the data for ground maps I had in my BrainPal for the mission. I checked that against the position of the stars in the sky. I was in the foothills above the suburbs of Omdurman, Khartoum's capital city. I was forty-five klicks southeast of the city's capital district, thirty-eight klicks south of the "undisclosed location" where I knew the prime minister to be, and twenty-three klicks southwest of the secondary extraction point where I hoped any survivors of my platoon were now heading.

I wasn't interested in any of those at the moment. Instead I called up my visual cache of the last hour and tracked back to a visual of one of the beams targeting a soldier of mine, and started using the visual information, along with my descent data, to track back the location of whatever was creating that beam.

Sixteen klicks due almost directly north, also in the foothills, near an abandoned reservoir.

"Got you," I said, bumped up my low-light visual acuity as much as possible to avoid falling into a hole, and started jogging toward the target. As I did I had my BrainPal play me music, so I would be distracted from thinking about Lambert, or Salcido, or Powell, or any other members of my platoon.

I would think about them later. I would grieve them later. Right now I needed to find out who shot them down.

Six klicks from the target, something knocked me off my feet and threw me to the ground. I immediately pushed off and rolled, confused because I had my visual camo on, and because whatever hit me and tossed me to the ground was nowhere to be seen. I had been shoved by a ghost.

Lieutenant.

It took me a second to realize that the voice I heard was through my BrainPal, not my ears.

Directly in front of you, the voice said. *Tightbeam me. I don't know if we're still being tracked.*

Powell? I said, via tightbeam, incredulous.

Yes, she said. She sent me visual permissions on her suit, which allowed my BrainPal to model where her body would be. She was indeed a meter directly in front of me. I tightbeamed her similar permissions.

Sorry about tackling you, she said.

How did you do that? I asked. *I mean, how did you know that I was there?*

Are you listening to music?

I was, I said. *So?*

You were singing as you ran.

Jesus, I said.

You didn't know?

No. But I'm not surprised. When I was a musician they had to turn off my microphone at gigs because I would sing along. I can play any stringed instrument you can name, but I can't sing worth a damn.

I noticed that much, Powell said, and I smiled despite myself. Powell motioned back, to the southeast. *I came down that direction and started heading this way and began hearing you a couple of klicks back. I waited until I was sure it was you.*

You could have tightbeamed me instead of tackling me.

It seemed safer this way. If you were on the ground there was less chance of you grabbing your Empee and spraying the brush out of surprise.

Point. Why are you headed this way, though? The secondary extraction point is not this way.

No. But the assholes who shot us down are.

I smiled again. *It does not at all surprise me to hear you say that.*

Of course it doesn't. Just as I'm not surprised to find you on the way there.

No, I suppose not.

Shall we go?

Yes, I said. We both stood up.

Just to be clear, I plan to kill the shit out of every single one of them we find, Powell said.

We may want one or two for questioning, I said.

Your call. You better point out which ones you want ahead of time.

I will. Also, Ilse?

Yes, Lieutenant?

What was your job back on Earth? I've always been curious.

I taught eighth-grade math in Tallahassee.

Huh, I said. *That's not what I expected.*

Are you kidding? Powell said back. *You try teaching algebra to a bunch of little shitheads for thirty-eight years straight. The way I figure it I've got about another decade before my rage from that gets entirely burned up.*

Whatever works. Ready?

Yes I am, Powell said. *I've got some anger to work out. And not just from teaching.*

———

Well, this is definitely not good, Powell said to me.

The two of us, still in full camo, lay two hundred meters out from a large concrete slab, itself on the edge of a disused reservoir. On the slab were two missile launchers, an electromagnetic mass driver, and two beam weapons. One of the launchers was missing two of its missiles, and next to it two specialists had hauled over new weapons to load onto it. The specialists were not human.

Fucking Rraey, Powell said, naming the species. *What are they doing here?*

Shooting down our shuttles, I said.

But why? How did they even get onto this planet?

I think they were invited.

By the prime minister? I'm going to shoot him twice now.

We still need to bring him in alive, I said.

I didn't say I was going to kill him, Powell replied. *Just that I was going to shoot him twice.*

Let's focus on what we're doing here first.

All right, Powell said. *How do you want to do this?*

I looked again at the slab. Each of the weapon platforms had its own set of technicians and operators, which amounted to four Rraey each. Each of the platforms also had its own power source, the largest being attached to the mass driver, which had to pull some serious energy into its electromagnets. The platforms were spaced haphazardly, as if they were hastily installed and meant to be equally hastily removed. And indeed toward the back of the platform were a set of trucks large enough to pack up the platforms and drive them away. There was a fifth truck as well, smaller than the rest, out of the top of which sprouted various communications receivers. Inside of it were several Rraey, visible through windows. Command and communications. Finally, two Rraey with rifles walked the perimeter of the slab. Security, such as it was.

I see about twenty-four Rraey, I said, to Powell.

I check your math, she said.

I want at least a couple alive.

Fine. Anyone in particular?

Let's keep the C&C staff breathing for now.

You're the boss.

You take the security and the trucks, and knock out the C&C power.

Some of them will still have handhelds.

Don't give them time to use them.

You said you wanted them unharmed.

I said I wanted them breathing.

Oh, okay, Powell said. *That makes things easier.*

I'll take the weapons crews.

That's a lot.

I have a plan.

Yeah? What is it?

Watch this, I said, set my Empee for a particle beam, and shot into one of the missiles the weapons crew was trying to install into the launcher. I aimed not for the payload, but the fuel.

It went up like holiday fireworks, taking the launcher, its missiles, its crew, and the crews of the adjoining platforms with it. Everything on the slab crumpled, including any Rraey unfortunate enough to be outside when the missile platform went up. It was a good thing we still had our masks on; they protected our ears from the blast.

"I thought you might do that," Powell said out loud, breaking cover and standing up.

"You're not worried about them seeing you?" I asked.

"Lieutenant, at this point I *want* them to see me coming," she said, and stalked off, Empee up.

I smiled, stayed crouched, and waited for any of the Rraey on the slab to start moving again. From time to time one would start to move away. I stopped them from continuing to do so.

There was a soft thudding sound; Powell had taken out the

command truck's power source. I saw her stalk across the slab, toward the truck, shooting truck drivers as she went. Behind her, one of the Rraey truck drivers had grabbed a weapon and was maneuvering around its truck to get a shot. I dealt with it.

You missed one, I sent to her.

I knew he was there, she sent back. *I knew you were there too.*

A Rraey appeared out the door of the command truck's cabin. Powell shot it in the leg; it went down squawking.

Keep a couple alive, I said.

That depends on them, Powell sent back. She reached the truck, grabbed the squawking Rraey, and pushed it in front of her as she went through the cabin door.

Things were quiet, at least from my point of view, for a couple of minutes afterward.

I left a couple alive, Powell said, after those couple of minutes had passed. *But you might want to hurry.*

I hurried down.

The inside of the command truck was a mess. There were three dead Rraey in it, including the one Powell had shot in the leg. Two more Rraey were at the back of the cabin, keening. From what little I knew of Rraey physiology, they were both sporting broken limbs. Powell had stripped them of their personal electronics; the rest of the cabin's electronics were down. Light in the cabin consisted of a couple of small emergency lights.

"Any trouble?" I asked Powell as she entered.

"No," she said. "They're not very good at close quarters."

"Well, that's something," I said.

Powell nodded and pointed to one of the survivors. "I think that's the one in charge," she said. "At least that's the one everyone tried to keep me from getting at."

I went over to the Rraey, who was looking up at me. I accessed my BrainPal, which had translation modules for the couple hundred species we humans had encountered the most often; the Rraey were in there. Their language contained sounds that we can't make, but the BrainPal would pick words that suited our mouths and throats. I'd tell the BrainPal what I wanted to say and it would offer me a suitable translation.

"Are you in charge here?" I asked the Rraey Powell had pointed out to me.

"I will not answer your questions," the Rraey said to me, in its language, which my BrainPal translated for me.

"I could break something else," Powell said. She was listening in.

"Torture isn't useful to get information," I said.

"I didn't say anything about getting information."

I looked back to her. "Give me a minute here, please," I said. Powell snorted.

I turned back to the Rraey. "You are hurt," I said, in its language. "Let us help you get better."

"We're hurt because of that animal over there," the Rraey said, jerking its head to Powell.

"You are hurt because you attacked us," I said. "You cannot attack us and expect nothing to happen in return."

The creature said nothing to this.

"You are here on a planet you should not be," I said. "Helping humans, which you should not do. You need to tell me why."

"I will not."

"We can help you. We will help you and your soldier here," I said, pointing to the other injured Rraey. "You will not survive if you do not get help."

"I will gladly die."

"But will you ask this soldier to die too?" I said. "Have you asked this soldier what it wants?"

"You're doing that thing where you're trying to be nice to someone you were just trying to kill," Powell said. "It doesn't work, because they remember you were trying to kill them five minutes ago."

"Ilse."

"I'm just pointing this out. Someone needs to say it."

I ignored her and turned back to the Rraey. "I am Lieutenant Heather Lee of the Colonial Defense Forces," I said. "I promise you that from this point forward you will not be harmed. It's a promise whether you help me or not. But if you help me, then I may say to my superiors that you have been useful. And they will treat you better."

"We know how you treat your prisoners," the Rraey said.

"And we know how you treat yours," I said. "We can change things now."

"Kill me and get it over with," the Rraey said.

"I don't want to die," said the other Rraey.

The first Rraey squawked something at his underling, which my BrainPal translated as "[Silence/You are making a shameful utterance]."

"You won't," I said, turning my attention to it. "Help me, soldier. Help me and you will live. I promise you."

"I am Specialist Ketrin Se Lau," it said. It motioned with its head to the other Rraey. "This is Commander Frui Ko Tvann. We are here on behalf of Equilibrium. We are here because the government of Khartoum has struck a deal with us."

"What's the deal?"

"Protection," it said. "Once the Colonial Union falls, Equilibrium will protect it from species who will try to raid or take over."

"In exchange for what?"

Commander Tvann squawked again and tried to strike Lau. Powell crossed the distance between the two and held her Empee on Tvann.

"In exchange for what?" I repeated.

"You won't kill us," Lau asked. "You promise."

"Yes, I promise. Neither of you."

"You won't torture us."

"We won't. We're going to help you. I promise, Specialist Lau."

"Protection in exchange for laying a trap," Lau said. "For luring you here."

"That doesn't make sense," Powell said. "The Colonial Union only sent one ship. Even if the *Tubingen* is destroyed we'll just send more. A lot more. This uprising will fail and then we'll go after the Rraey for helping them."

"Unless there's more to it," I said, and turned back to Lau. "What else is there?"

"I don't know," Lau said. "I'm a specialist. They only told me what I had to know for my part."

I turned to Tvann. "And I don't expect you want to fill me in." Tvann turned its head from me.

"So we have a dead end here," Powell said.

"No," I said, and then cut off as the *Tubingen* opened a feed, searching for us. It had been attacked and damaged but had survived and with the help of another ship had destroyed the two ships attacking it. It was now asking for status reports.

"Well, at least we're not entirely screwed," Powell said.

"Call it in," I said to her. "Let them know we need immediate medical evac for two Rraey prisoners of war. Tell them I've promised they won't be further harmed."

"That's going to go over well."

"Just do it."

"Anything else?"

"Tell them to send another shuttle for the two of us. We have another mission to finish."

On the way back, our shuttle was diverted from the *Tubingen* to the other Colonial Union ship.

"I haven't heard of the *Chandler* before," Powell said.

"It's a State Department ship, not a CDF ship," I said.

"A State Department ship with a fully operational offensive weapons system."

"Times have changed," I said.

"These constraints are hurting my arms," said Masahiko Okada, the now-former prime minister of Khartoum. It's possible that he might still be considered the prime minister by some, but from a practical matter his days in charge of things were now over. "I'm very uncomfortable."

"And several of my friends are dead," Powell said, to Okada. "So maybe you should think you're getting the better end of the deal and shut up."

Okada turned to me. "If you don't think people will know about how you're treating me—"

"Let me throw him out," Powell said, to me.

Okada turned back to Powell. "What?"

"Let me throw him out," Powell repeated to me. "This shit-bucket is the reason Lambert and Salcido are dead. Not to mention everyone else in the platoon."

"Not everyone else is dead," I reminded her. "Gould and DeConnick survived, too."

"Gould and DeConnick are both in critical condition," Powell said. "They *might* survive. And if they don't that leaves just you and me. Out of an entire fucking platoon." She jabbed a finger at Okada. "I think that rates him getting a space walk without a suit."

I turned to Okada. "Your thoughts, Mr. Prime Minister?"

"It's the Colonial Union that instigated this rebellion, not the government of Khartoum," Okada began.

"Oh, that is *it*," Powell interrupted, and stood up. "Time for you to breathe some vacuum, motherfucker." Okada visibly shrunk away from Powell.

I held up a hand. Powell stopped advancing on Okada. "New plan," I said. I pointed to Okada. "You don't say another single word until after we dock with the *Chandler*"—I glanced back to Powell—"and you don't toss him into space."

Okada said nothing more, even after we had landed and some of the *Chandler*'s crew took him away.

"He seems quiet," the *Chandler* crew member who approached me said, nodding over to Okada. Unlike all the others, he was green, which meant he was CDF.

"He was sufficiently motivated," I said.

"It appears so," he said. "Now, then. Do you remember me, Lieutenant Lee?"

"I do, Lieutenant Wilson," I said. I motioned to Powell. "This is my sergeant, Ilse Powell."

"Sergeant," Wilson said, and turned his attention back to me. "I'm glad you remember me. I'm supposed to debrief you and catch you up with things."

"What we'd really like to do is get back to the *Tubingen*," I said.

"Well," Wilson said. "About that."

"What is it?"

"Maybe we should find someplace to sit down and chat."

"Maybe you should just tell me right now because otherwise I might punch you, Wilson."

He smiled. "You definitely haven't changed. All right, here it is: The *Tubingen* survived the attack on her, but 'survive' is a relative term. She's essentially dead in orbit. She might have been entirely destroyed but we managed to get here in time and help her fight off the ships attacking her."

"And how did you do that?" I asked. "Arrive in the nick of time."

"We had a hunch," Wilson said, "and that's all I can say about that right now, here, out in the open in a shuttle bay."

"Hmmmm."

"My point is that if you really want to head back to the *Tubingen* you may after we're done debriefing. But you won't be staying there. At best you'll have time to collect any personal belongings that weren't destroyed in the battle before the *John Henry* and other ships arrive to take you and all the other survivors of the *Tubingen* back to Phoenix Station for reassignment. You might as well stay here. We can have your effects brought to you."

"How many people died in the attack on the *Tubingen*?" Powell asked.

"Two hundred fifteen dead, another several dozen injured. That's not counting your platoon. Sorry about that. We've retrieved them, by the way."

"Where are they?" I asked.

"They're in one of the mess coolers at the moment."

"I'd like to see them."

"I don't recommend that. It's not very dignified. How they are being stored, I mean."

"I don't care."

"I'll have it arranged, then."

"I also want to know about the two Rraey I sent back."

"They're in our brig, and receiving medical attention, inasmuch as we can give it to them," Wilson said. "Their injuries were substantial but thankfully not terribly complicated. Mostly broken bones, which we could set and tend. Which one of you did that, by the way?"

"That would be me," Powell said.

"You're fun," Wilson said.

"You should see me on the second date."

Wilson smiled at this and turned his attention back to me. "We received your instruction that they were not to be further harmed. That was not a problem because we had no intention of doing so. You do understand we will need to question them."

"You can question them without harming them," I said.

"Yes we can," Wilson said. "I just want you to be clear that the questioning is likely to be aggressive, even if it's not physical. Particularly of Commander Tvann, who is interesting to us for other reasons than just his involvement here."

"Who's going to do the questioning?"

"Well, here it's going to be me."

"Commander Tvann doesn't seem very forthcoming."

"Don't worry, I think I can get him to talk without breaking anything else in his body. I've worked with Rraey before. Trust me."

"All right. Thank you," I said. I nodded in the direction of where Okada went. "What's going to happen with him?"

"Him, I'm not going to make too many promises about," Wilson said. "He's managed to perform a neat little trick. Not only has he betrayed the Colonial Union, he's also betrayed his own rebellion."

"How do you mean?"

"I mean that there were ten Colonial Union planets that were supposed to announce their independence from the CU simultaneously, and that Khartoum was one of them. But Khartoum jumped the gun, announced early, and then lured the *Tubingen* into a trap."

"Why would they do that?"

"That's what we need to find out," Wilson said. "What he tells us is going to make a difference in how the Colonial Union as a whole deals with these rebellious planets."

"Do you think he'll talk?" Powell asked.

"By the time we get done with him, getting him to talk won't be the problem. It'll be getting him to shut up. Now, are you ready for the formal debriefing?"

"Actually, I would like to see my soldiers first," I said.

"All right," Wilson said.

I found Lambert waist high in a stack of dead bodies near the back of the mess cooler. Salcido I found two stacks over, closer to the floor. They did not bear close observation.

"Lambert was right, you know," Powell said. She was with me in the cooler. Wilson had walked us to the cooler, opened it, and then waited outside. The cooler had been cleared of shelves and the contents they usually stored; the latter were either restocked in a different cooler or being fed to the survivors of the *Tubingen*, who were in the mess itself, unhappily crowded together.

At least they weren't crowded together in here.

"What was he right about?" I asked.

"Root causes," Powell said.

"You of all people," I said, almost smiling.

"I didn't ever say he was wrong. I said 'who cares.'"

"But now you do care."

"I care more than I used to. What are we doing here, Lieutenant? We're running around putting out fires. And fine, we're the fire brigade. Our job is putting out the fires. Not worrying about how they got started, just putting them out. But at some point even the fire brigade has to start asking who is starting all these fires, and why it's being left to us to continually put them out."

"Lambert would be laughing his head off to hear you say that."

"If he were here to laugh his head off, I wouldn't be saying it. He'd be saying it. Again." Powell motioned to where Salcido was. "And Sau would be geeking out over some point of trivia. And I would be sniping at both of them, and you would be playing referee. And we would all be one happy family again, instead of the two of us looking at the two of them in a meat locker."

"You've lost friends before," I said.

"Of course I have," Powell said. "And so have you. It doesn't make it any easier when it happens."

We were silent for a moment.

"I have a speech running through my head," I finally said, to Powell.

"One you were going to make?" Powell asked.

"No. One someone else made, that I've been thinking a lot about the last few weeks, when we've been running around putting out fires."

"Which one is it?"

"It's the Gettysburg Address. Abraham Lincoln. You remember it?"

Powell smirked. "I lived in America and taught in a junior high. I remember it."

"It's something like three hundred words long, and it wasn't even well received when Lincoln gave it. The part I'm thinking about is where he says 'Now we are engaged in a great civil war, testing whether that nation, or any nation so conceived and so dedicated, can long endure.'"

Powell nodded. "You think we're in a civil war right now."

"I don't know what we're in right now," I said. "It doesn't feel like a real war. It's too strung out. Too diffuse. It's not battlefield after battlefield. It's skirmish after skirmish."

"Let me clear it up for you," Powell said. "It's a civil war. We lost the Earth. The Colonial Union only has so long before it has to turn to all the colonies to support it with the things it used to get for free from the Earth. The colonies are asking if what they get from the Colonial Union is worth the cost, and worth the cost of having the Colonial Union keep running things. Sounds like the answer for at least some of them is no. And it seems like now they think the arm the Colonial Union was using to shield them is now up against their throat. So they're trying to get out before the whole thing falls down around them."

"They're not doing a good job of it," I said.

"They don't have to do a good job of it for it to be a civil war. And they're *not* doing a good job of it so far." Powell motioned around her. "But it looks like they're learning. And it looks like they're getting allies with this Equilibrium group."

"I don't think Equilibrium, whoever they are, are doing this out of the goodness of their own heart."

"You're not wrong about that, but it doesn't matter from the point of view of this being a civil war. If they don't think the Colonial Union has their interests at heart, then it's a case of 'the enemy of my enemy is my friend.'"

"That's not a very smart strategy."

"Smart has nothing to do with this. We could go around and around like this for hours, Lieutenant."

"What do you think?" I said.

"About what?"

"About the Colonial Union," I said. "About it controlling these planets. About how it responds to things like this." I waved my hand around the room. "About all of *this*."

Powell looked vaguely surprised. "The Colonial Union's a fascistic shit show, boss. I knew that much from the first day I set foot on one of their boats to get away from Earth. Are you kidding? They control trade. They control communications. They don't let the colonies protect themselves and they don't let them do anything that doesn't go through the Colonial Union itself. And let's not forget everything they've done to Earth. They've been doing it for centuries. Shit, Lieutenant. I'm not surprised we have a civil war on our hands right now. I'm surprised it didn't happen *sooner*."

"And yet here we are," I said. "You and me, in their uniform."

"We didn't want to die old," Powell said. "I was seventy-five and I spent most of my whole life in Florida and I had bone cancer and never did the things I wanted to do and it was eating me up. You think I'm an asshole now, you should have seen me just before I left Earth. You would have pushed me off a building just on principle, and you wouldn't have been wrong to do it."

"Well, all right," I said. "We didn't know coming out here what we'd be getting ourselves into."

"No, we didn't."

"But now you *do* know," I said. "And if you knew then what you knew now, would you still do it?"

"Yes," Powell said. "I still don't want to die old."

"But you just said the Colonial Union is a fascistic shit show."

"It is, and right now it's the only way we survive," Powell said. "Look around. Look at the planets we've been on. Look at all the species out there we've had to fight. Do you really think any of these planets and the people on them won't get carved up the first minute the Colonial Union disappears? They've never fought before. Not on the scale they would need to. They have no military infrastructure on the scale they'd have to have. And they would have no time to ramp any of that up. The Colonial Union is a monster, but the colonies are fucking baby deer in a forest full of predators."

"Then how does any of that change?"

"Got me, boss, I just work here. What I do know is that it *is* going to change. It has to change because we don't have the Earth anymore. The mechanics of the Colonial Union, what it was founded on, just don't work anymore. It changes or we all die. And I'm doing my part to keep it together until then. The alternative is grim."

"I suppose it might be," I said.

"What about you? Would you do it again, Lieutenant?"

"I don't know," I said. "I didn't want to die old, you're right." I reached out and touched Lambert's cold arm. "But there are worse ways to go."

"He went mid-pontification," Powell said. "I'm pretty sure that's how he would have wanted to go."

I laughed at that. "Fair enough," I said. "I think my point is that I get it now. I get that there are worse things than to have lived a life and have most of it behind you. I wouldn't be afraid of that anymore, I think."

"Maybe. It's easy to say that now that you look twenty years old and will live for another sixty even if you left the CDF today."

"Again, a fair point."

"This is why I told Lambert to stop going on about it, you know," Powell said. "All the thinking about the steps beyond what we were directly doing. It never makes you happy. It never solves anything for you, right now."

I smiled. "And yet you were the one to bring it up, here, now."

"Yes, well." Powell grimaced. "Think of it as a tribute. To our departed friend. I'll never do it again."

I motioned to Salcido. "And him?"

"Shit, I don't know," Powell said. "Maybe listen to that stupid pizza moon song again. Or think about what day it is in the mess. Which is complete bullshit, by the way. You can get pizza and tacos and hamburgers any day you want. It's just which entrée they push out in front."

"I know," I said. "But that wasn't the point of the conversation, was it."

"No," Powell said. "No, it wasn't."

PART FIVE

Why are we even here? Powell said to me, through her BrainPal. We and the rest of our platoon on the *Uppsala* were policing a protest on Erie, in the city of Galway. The protest was entirely peaceful. All the protesters were doing, all anyone was doing, as far as I could see, was lying down. Everywhere. There were at least 100,000 of them. She was thirty yards away from me, part of a defensive line in front of the Colonial Union offices.

We're protecting Colonial Union property, I sent back.

What are they going to do, lay on it?

I seem to remember you recently complaining about people thinking too much about our missions, I said.

This seems like something the local police can handle.

Indeed, I said, and pointed at a woman lying about two meters from me, in a police uniform. *There's the chief of police. You can talk to her about it.*

Even from thirty yards away I could hear Powell's snort of derision.

The problem with Erie was not that the population had tried to declare its independence, or tried to burn down the Colonial Union local headquarters, or had invited less than entirely altruistic alien species to attack Colonial ships and soldiers. The problem was that Erie had gone on strike.

Not entirely on strike; the planet was still feeding itself and clothing itself and taking care of its own internal needs. But it had decided that, for now, it was no longer in the export business. This presented a problem for the Colonial Union because the Colonial Union bought a substantial amount from Erie, and Erie, as one of the earliest colonies, had one of the most developed export economies in the whole Colonial Union.

The Colonial Union trade representative for Erie had asked what the problem was. No problem, Erie (or more accurately its governor for trade) said. We've decided to get out of the export business.

The Colonial Union trade representative pointed out that doing so would trash Erie's economy. Erie's governor for trade noted that its economists said that the change would be difficult but weatherable as long as everyone made certain sacrifices.

The Colonial Union trade representative offered to raise the amount it offered for goods. Erie's governor for trade politely declined.

The Colonial Union trade representative hinted that not doing business with them was tantamount to treason. Erie's governor for trade asked what particular Colonial Union statute covered enforced, involuntary trade.

The Colonial Union trade representative then made a crack about the entire planet lying down on the job.

This is stupid, Powell said.

As stupid as the Colonial Union trade representative? I asked.

Close, Powell replied. *We're wasting our time here, boss. We're not stopping anything, or saving anyone, or doing any good. We're just walking around a bunch of people lying down, waving our Empees around like assholes.*

They could spring up and attack us all.

Lieutenant, I've got a guy two meters from me who is fucking snoring.

I smiled at this. *What do you suggest we do, Ilse?* I asked.

I have no idea. I'm open to suggestion.

Okay, try this one on, I said, dropped my Empee, and walked out into the crowd.

What are you doing? Powell asked.

Leaving, I said. I began to navigate around the prone bodies so I wouldn't step on any.

Where to?

I have no idea.

I don't think we're allowed to do that, boss. I think the technical term for what you're doing is "desertion."

They can shoot me if they want.

They might!

Ilse, I said, stopped, and looked back. *I've been doing this for seven years. You know as well as I do that they're not going to let me stop. They've stopped rotating us out because there are no more of us coming in. But I can't do this anymore. I'm done.* I turned and started walking again.

They will definitely shoot you.

They might, I agreed, echoing her earlier words. I made my way through the plaza and down to one of the side streets. I turned and looked back at Powell.

It's not like they won't know where you are, she said to me. *You have a computer in your brain. It tracks your every movement. Hell, I'm pretty sure it can track your every thought.*

I know.

They'll come get you.

They probably will.

Don't say I didn't warn you.

I won't.

What will you do?

I used to be a pretty good musician, I said. *I think I'd like to do that again. For a while, anyway.*

You're nuts, Lieutenant. I want it out there on the record that I said that.

Duly noted. Want to join me?

Hell, no, Powell said. *We can't all be deserters. And anyway there's a lieutenant position opening up. I think I'm in line for a promotion.*

I grinned. *Good-bye, Ilse,* I said.

Good-bye, Heather, she said, and then she waved.

I turned the corner and a building hid her from my view.

I walked down the street, found another street that looked interesting, and started walking down it into the first day of another life.

I think it was a Saturday.

TO STAND OR FALL

■

To the Committee and attendees of Swancon 40, in Perth, Australia, where this novella—and book—was completed. Hey, didn't I say I would do this?

There's a saying: "May you live in interesting times."

To begin, it's a curse. "Interesting" in this case uniformly means "Oh god, death is raining down upon us and we shall all perish wailing and possibly on fire." If someone wanted to say something nice to you, they wouldn't tell you to live in "interesting" times. They would say something like, "I wish you eternal happiness" or "May you have peace" or "Live long and prosper" and so on. They wouldn't say "Live in interesting times." If someone is telling you to live in interesting times, they are basically telling you they want you to die horribly, and to suffer terribly before you do.

Seriously, they are not your friend. This is a tip I am giving you for free.

Second, the curse is almost always ascribed to the Chinese, which is a flat-out lie. As far as anyone can tell it appeared in English first but was ascribed to the Chinese, probably due to a combination of casual racism and because someone wanted to be a shithole of a human being but didn't want it to be marked down against them personally. A sort of "Hey, I'm not saying this, those terrible Chinese are saying it, I'm just telling you what they said" maneuver.

So not only are they not your friend, they may be also a bigot and passive-aggressive.

That said, the Chinese do have a saying from which it is

alleged that the bigoted passive-aggressive curse may have been derived: "宁为太平犬, 莫做乱世人," which, roughly translated, means "It's better to be a dog in peace, than a man in war." Which is a maxim which is neither bigoted nor passive-aggressive, and about which I find a lot to agree with.

The point is this: My name is Lieutenant Harry Wilson. I've been a man in war for a very long time now. I think it would be preferable to be a dog in peace. I've been working toward that for a while.

My problem is, I live in interesting times.

My most recent interesting time began when the *Chandler*, the ship on which I was stationed, skipped into the Khartoum system and promptly blew up the first two other ships it saw.

They had it coming. The two ships were attacking the *Tubingen*, a Colonial Defense Forces ship which had been called into the system to quell a rebellion against the Colonial Union, instigated by Khartoum's prime minister, who really should have known better. But apparently he didn't, and in came the *Tubingen*, which sent a platoon of soldiers to the planet to escort the prime minister off the planet. Which is when these other two ships skipped in and started using the *Tubingen* for target practice. I imagine they expected that they would be able to finish the job, unmolested. They were not prepared to have the *Chandler* come at them out of the sun.

In reality we had done no such thing, of course. We had just skipped into the space above Khartoum slightly closer in toward the planet's star than those two ships, and the *Tubingen*, which they were busy attacking. And the fact that we were, from their perspective, hidden in the disk of Khartoum's star did not give the *Chandler* any special advantage. The ships' systems would have detected us no later. What gave us an advantage was that they were not expecting us at all. When we showed up, they were giving all their attention to destroying the *Tubingen*, firing missiles at close range to shatter the ship at its weak points, to end the lives of everyone on the ship and throw the entire Colonial Union into disarray.

But coming out of the sun was a nice poetic touch.

We had launched our own missiles before our particle beams touched the ships' missiles, detonating all of them before they could smash into the *Tubingen*. Our missiles jammed themselves into the hulls of the enemy ships, targeted to disrupt power systems and weapons. We didn't worry about the crews. We knew there wouldn't be any, except for a single pilot.

From our point of view the battle was over before it began. The enemy ships, only lightly armored, went up like fireworks. We hailed the *Tubingen* by standard coms and by BrainPal networking, to assess the damage.

It was significant. The ship was a loss; it would barely have time to evacuate its crew before its life-support systems collapsed. We started making room on the *Chandler* and sent skip drones back to Phoenix Station for rescue ships and crews.

Reports trickled in from the surface of Khartoum. The platoon from the *Tubingen*, tasked to bring the planet's prime minister into custody, had been shot out of the sky from ground-based defenses. The soldiers who had leapt from the shuttle to escape its destruction had been picked off by the same defense.

Only two soldiers had escaped unharmed, but between them they destroyed the defense installation, staffed with Rraey soldiers aligned with Equilibrium, the group who had wreaked so much havoc on the Colonial Union and the Conclave. They captured two of the Rraey from the ground installation, including the commander. Then they finished their original mission and brought back the prime minister of Khartoum.

Someone was going to have to interrogate them all.

For the two Rraey, that someone was me.

I entered the room where the Rraey prisoner of war had been waiting for me. The Rraey had not been shackled but a shock collar had been placed around his neck. Any motion quicker than a very casual and deliberate movement would generate a jolt, and the faster the movement, the more powerful the jolt.

The Rraey did not move very much.

He sat in a chair very badly designed for his physiology, but no better chair was to be had. It was positioned at a table. On the opposite side of the table stood another chair. I sat in the chair, reached out, and placed a speaker on the table.

"Commander Tvann," I said, and my words were translated by the speaker. "My name is Harry Wilson. I am a lieutenant in the Colonial Defense Forces. I would like to speak to you, if you don't mind. You may answer in your own language. My BrainPal will translate for me."

"You humans," Tvann said, after a moment. "The way you speak. As if you are asking for permission when you are making demands."

"You could choose not to speak to me," I said.

Tvann motioned to the collar around his neck. "I do not think that would go very well for me."

"A fair point." I pushed up from the chair and walked over to Tvann, who did not flinch. "If you will permit me, I will remove your collar."

"Why would you do that?"

"As a token of good faith," I said. "And also, so if you choose not to speak to me, you will not have to fear punishment."

Tvann craned his neck to allow me access to his collar. I removed it, unlocking it via a command from his BrainPal. I set the collar on the table and then returned to my seat.

"Now, where were we?" I said. "That's right. I wanted to speak to you."

"Lieutenant . . ." Tvann trailed off.

"Wilson."

"Thank you. Lieutenant, I—may I be candid with you?"

"I hope you will."

"While I do not wish to suggest I do not appreciate you removing this instrument of torture from my neck, allow me to note that the act is hollow. And not only hollow, it is, in fact, disingenuous."

"How so, Commander?"

Tvann motioned around him. "You have removed the shock collar. But I am still here, in your ship. I have no doubt that on the other side of this door is another CDF solider, like yourself, with a weapon or another implement of torture. There is no escape for me and no assurance that aside from this immediate moment, I will not be punished or even killed for not speaking with you."

I smiled. "You are correct that there is someone on the other side of this door, Commander. It's not another CDF soldier, however. It's just my friend Hart Schmidt, who is a diplomat, not a killer or a torturer. He's on the other side of the door primarily because he's running a recording device—an unnecessary thing, as I am also recording this conversation with my BrainPal."

"You're not worried about me trying to kill you and escaping," Tvann said.

"Not really, no," I said. "I mean, I *am* a CDF soldier. You may know from your own experience that we are genetically engineered to be faster and stronger than unmodified humans. With all due respect to your own prowess, Commander, if you attempted to kill me you would be in for a fight."

"And if I did kill you?"

"Well, the door is locked," I said. "Which kind of puts a damper on your whole escape plan."

Tvann did the Rraey equivalent of a laugh. "So you're not afraid of me."

"No," I said. "But I don't want you to be afraid of me, either."

"I'm not," Tvann said. "The rest of your species, I am afraid of. And of what might happen to me if I don't speak to you now."

"Commander, allow me to be as candid with you as you have been with me."

"All right, Lieutenant."

"You are a prisoner of the Colonial Defense Forces. You are, in point of fact, a prisoner of war. You were captured having taken up arms against us. You, either directly or by the orders you gave, killed many of our soldiers. I will not torture you, nor will I kill you, nor will you be tortured or killed while you are on this ship. But you have to know that the rest of your life is going to be spent with us," I motioned around, "and in a room not much larger than this one."

"You are not inspiring me to be forthcoming, Lieutenant."

"I can understand that, but I'm not finished," I said. "As I said, the rest of your life is very likely to be as our prisoner, in a room about this size. But there is another option."

"Talk to you."

"Yes," I agreed. "Talk to me. Tell me everything you know about Equilibrium and its plans. Tell me how you got ten human colonies to agree to rebel against the Colonial Union. Tell me what the endgame is for your organization. Tell me all of it, start to finish, and leave nothing out."

"In return for what?"

"In return for your freedom."

"Oh, Lieutenant," Tvann said. "You can't possibly expect me to believe it's within your power to offer that."

"It's not. As you've implicitly noted, I'm just a lieutenant. But this offer doesn't come from me. It comes from the highest levels of both the Colonial Defense Forces and the Colonial Union's civilian government. Disclose everything, and when this is all over—whatever this is, whenever it's over—you'll be handed over to the Rraey government. What they do to you is another kettle of fish, assuming that they have something to do with Equilibrium at all. That said, if you're especially forthcoming, we can make an effort to have it seem like we didn't know what an excellent intelligence asset you were. That we thought you were just some common military commander."

"But I am," Tvann said. "The scope of my orders were limited, and focused on this mission."

I nodded. "We were pretty sure you were going to try that," I said. "And who could blame you? There's no percentage for you letting on any more than you had to. But we know something you don't think we know, Commander."

"What is that, Lieutenant?"

"Commander, does this ship seem familiar to you in any way?"

"No," Tvann said. "Why should it?"

"No reason," I said. "Except for the small detail that you've been on it before."

"I don't believe so."

"Oh, believe it," I said, and then looked up toward the ceiling. "Rafe, have you been listening in?"

"You know I have," said a new voice, from the speaker. A translation, in a slightly different voice to differentiate it from my translation, followed almost immediately afterward.

"Okay, good," I said, and looked back to Tvann. "Commander Tvann, I would like to introduce you to Rafe Daquin, our pilot. Or more accurately, I would like to reintroduce you, as the two of you have met before."

"I don't understand," Tvann said.

"You don't remember me?" Daquin said. "I'm hurt, Commander. Because I remember *you* very well. I remember you threatening to blow my ship out of the sky. I remember you shooting my captain and first officer. I remember you talking with Secretary Ocampo about the best way to murder my entire crew. Yes, Commander. I have a whole heap of memories with you in them."

Tvann said nothing to this.

"Ah," I said. "See. Now you're remembering after all. This is the *Chandler*, Commander. The ship you took. And the ship you lost. Well, maybe not you *specifically*, but Equilibrium. We know you were on it. And we know you're not just some field commander. No, sir. You're a key member of the Equilibrium military. And your presence on Khartoum, leading the forces that shot our people out of the sky, isn't just luck of the assignment draw. You're here for a reason."

"How is it that you're here?" Tvann asked me.

"How do you mean?"

"Your ship thwarted the attack on the CDF ship that responded to the Khartoum rebellion," Tvann said. "How did you know? How did you get here to stop it?"

"We had inside intelligence."

"From whom?"

"From whom do you think?" I said.

"I'll give you a hint," Daquin said. "It's the guy I stole from you when I made a break for it."

"Secretary Ocampo has been very forthcoming," I said. "When Khartoum declared its independence, he suggested to us that there was a good chance that there might be a trap laid for any ship that responded. The *Chandler* happened to be near skip distance—and the Colonial Union didn't want to inflame things by sending a large contingent of CDF ships—so we got the call."

"Thanks for grafting those weapons systems back onto the ship," Daquin said. "They came in handy."

"Secretary Ocampo," Tvann said. "No doubt *forthcoming* because you've put his brain into an isolation chamber."

"You're not really going to go there, are you?" Daquin said.

"Because I have news for you, pal. You don't have much high ground to stand on with that one."

"If you have Ocampo you don't need me," Tvann said, to me. "Ocampo has far more operational knowledge than I ever did. He was a primary architect of our plans."

"We know," I said. "We have all his records. The thing is, we also know *you* know we have all his records. You have to have assumed that once Rafe absconded with the secretary. Which means Equilibrium can't use them anymore. You have a new game plan, one that's being carried out on an accelerated schedule. Ocampo can make educated guesses. But we need more than educated guesses at this point."

"I'm captured," Tvann said. "They'll know to change their plans."

"You're not captured," I said. "You're dead. At least that's what they'll think. You and every other Rraey, obliterated beyond identification, and *before* identification. And you died completing your objective of luring the Colonial Union into a trap—and making it look like Khartoum was responsible for the attack. That was a nice touch, by the way."

Tvann was silent again.

"That's our communication plan—everything that's coming out of us is pinning it on the Khartoum government. So as far as Equilibrium knows, it's still game on for the latest plan. We'd like you to tell us the plan."

"And if I refuse?"

"Then you better get used to walls," Daquin said.

"Rafe, why don't you sign out for a bit," I said.

Daquin signed out.

"You're not the first Rraey I've ever met," I said, to Tvann, after Daquin had departed.

"I'm sure you've killed many in your time," Tvann said.

"That's not what I meant," I said. "I mean that I knew another

Rraey as a person. A scientist named Cainen Suen Su. He, like you, was captured by us. I was assigned to him."

"To guard him?"

"No, to assist him. We worked on several projects together with him as the lead and me following his direction."

"He was a traitor, then."

"I don't know that he would disagree with you," I said. "He was aware that in helping us, his knowledge could be used against the Rraey. Nevertheless he did help, and in the course of time, he also became a friend. He was one of the most remarkable people I've ever met. I was honored to have known him."

"What happened to him?"

"He died."

"How?"

"A soldier, who was also his friend, killed him at his request."

"Why did he ask to die?"

"Because he was dying anyway," I said. "We'd introduced a poison into his blood and the daily antidote he was given was increasingly less effective. He asked his friend to end his suffering."

"The suffering you had imposed on him in the first place."

"Yes."

"Lieutenant, if there is a point to this discussion of yours, I'm afraid it has entirely escaped me."

"Cainen was an enemy who became a friend," I said. "And despite the terrible thing we had done to him—and yes, it was terrible—he still chose to find friendship among us. I've never forgotten that."

"I do not think we will be friends, I'm afraid."

"I'm not asking for that, Commander," I said. "My point in telling you this is to let you know that, at the very least, I don't see you merely as an enemy."

"You will understand, Lieutenant, if I'm not convinced that this fact does anything for me at all."

"Of course." I stood up. "Just understand that it can. If you want it to. In the meantime, give consideration to what I've asked for. Let me know when you're ready to talk." I started for the door.

"Aren't you going to put that back on me?" Tvann said, pointing to the shock collar on the table.

"You can put it back on if you want," I said. "But I wouldn't if I were you." I opened the door, leaving Tvann to stare at the collar on the table.

"Are you going to kill us?" Specialist Ketrin Se Lau asked me. The two of us were in the same room I had previously been in with Tvann. The room had been reset. Lau was not wearing the shock collar; he'd never been given one.

"Lieutenant Lee promised you that we wouldn't, if her report to me is accurate," I said.

"That was her. You are someone new."

"Do you think we're going to kill you, Ketrin?" I asked.

"Humans aren't well known for being kind to their enemies," Lau said.

"No, I suppose not," I admitted. "No, Specialist Lau. We're not planning to kill you, or Commander Tvann." I watched as relief spilled over the Rraey's body. "In fact, what we're hoping to do, after all of this is done, is return you to your government."

"When?"

"I'm not going to lie to you, it's going to be a while," I said. "We have to get to the end of this current conflict. In the meantime you're going to be our guest."

"You mean prisoner."

"Well, yes," I said. "But within that framework, there's a lot of latitude for how you are treated."

"I don't know anything important," Lau said. "I'm a specialist. I was only told specific things about my own job."

"We know that you don't know anything above your pay grade," I said. "We don't expect you to know the secret plans of Equilibrium."

"Then what can I tell you that I didn't already tell your Lieutenant Lee?"

"I'm interested not so much in what you know as I am in what you've heard. Rumors and speculation and things like that. We're both soldiers, Ketrin. Although we're different species I think we probably share one thing in common: Our jobs are boring most of the time, so we spend a lot of time bullshitting with our friends. I'm interested in the bullshit."

"I don't know that word, but I think I know what it means."

" 'Bullshit'? Yes, I think you probably do. I'm also interested in you, Ketrin."

"How so?"

"Your experience with Equilibrium," I said. "Beginning with the very simple question of: How did you get involved with them in the first place?"

"That's your fault," Lau said. "Humans, not you specifically. Our wars with you went poorly for us, particularly after the Obin, who had been our allies, turned on us. When that happened we lost planets and lost power, and our military shrank. Many former soldiers were out of work. I was one of them."

"There are other lines of work."

"Lieutenant, when we lost planets, we had an influx of people to our remaining worlds. There were no jobs to be had. You and the Obin didn't just shrink our military. You killed our economy. I'm originally from a colony planet named Fuigh. We don't have that planet anymore. I was relocated to Bulni. Jobs there mostly went to native Bulnians."

"Got it."

"So when I was approached by a former commander of mine about Equilibrium, I didn't spend any time thinking about it. I was being offered a job and a chance to use my skills. The pay was excellent. And I got to leave Bulni, which I hated."

"I understand that."

"If you are planning to attack any planet of ours, let me suggest Bulni first."

I grinned. "It's not on our agenda at the moment, but I'll keep it in mind. How long have you been with the Equilibrium?"

"I don't know your time measurements."

"Tell me in your years, I'll make the adjustments."

"About six years, then."

"Which is about five of ours. Which is a long time."

"It was steady work."

"Right," I said. "My point is that we only started learning about Equilibrium very recently. It's a long time for your organization to be flying under our radar."

"Maybe you're not very good at intelligence."

"That might be it," I allowed. "But I like to think there's something more to it than that."

Specialist Lau did the Rraey equivalent of a shrug. "The organization was always small and focused and decentralized until very recently. For the first couple of years I didn't even know there was a larger organization. I only worked with my team."

"So you thought you were a mercenary."

"Yes."

"Being a mercenary didn't bother you."

"I liked being able to eat. And like I said I didn't have very many other options."

"So you thought you were a mercenary, but then you found out about the rest of Equilibrium."

"Yes."

"No thoughts about your team suddenly being made part of a larger organization."

"Not really," Lau said. "Mercenary companies are like any other company. Sometimes they work with other companies. Sometimes they merge with them. I was being paid on time and working with the same group of people, so it was all the same to me."

"And what about the philosophical aims of the Equilibrium? What did you think about them?"

"I was fine with them. I'm still fine with them. Lieutenant, the Colonial Union is our enemy, and the Conclave won't allow us to colonize, even on the planets we lost and want to retake. The two of you have made life very difficult for us. I don't mind returning the favor."

"All right."

"But you have to understand that at the level I work at, we don't really get into the philosophy of the organization. Do you, sir? Do you spend a lot of time thinking about the ethics and philosophy of the Colonial Union and what it does?"

"Actually, I do," I said, and smiled. "But overthinking things is a hobby of mine. I'm the first to admit I'm weird."

"My job was to manage communications," Lau said. "I spent most of my time thinking about my immediate tasks and the people I was working with. I'm not a great thinker, Lieutenant."

"This mission," I said. "It was with the same group you've been with since the beginning."

"No. The team I was part of was mostly wiped out when the *Chandler* attacked Equilibrium headquarters. I survived because I had been temporarily assigned to another team to train some new recruits. After that attack I stayed with that team, which Commander Tvann led. That's the team you obliterated."

"I'm sorry for the loss of your friends."

"Thank you. It's kind of you to say, even if I doubt you're entirely sincere."

"I have to say you're more forthcoming than Commander Tvann has been."

"I have a lot fewer secrets to keep," Lau said. "And I don't want to die."

"I know Tvann was not happy with you that you were willing to talk with us. That he tried to attack you to shut you up."

"Like I said, he has more secrets to keep than I do."

"I suspect he's unhappy with the level of loyalty you're showing."

Lau barked out a Rraey laugh at this. "You said it yourself, Lieutenant. I'm a mercenary. I have been since the moment Equilibrium hired me. Equilibrium pays well, but right now I can't spend a single coin of what they pay me. You, on the other hand, can kill me. I value my life more than all the money in the world."

"That's a very practical point of view, Ketrin."

"I was hoping you might appreciate it, Lieutenant."

"I do, very much. And I think you'll find that my superiors will appreciate it too."

"I was hoping that you would say that. Remember, there's only so much I know. I won't withhold anything but there are limits to my knowledge."

"Like I said, I'm interested in other things from you than I am from Commander Tvann. I think you'll be very useful."

"Then let's get to work," Lau said. "I do have one request for the moment."

"What is it?"

"Lunch."

"Do you know who I am?" Masahiko Okada asked, with just the right amount of outrage to his voice. The same room again, but a slightly different cast of characters. Okada was sitting at the table. I was standing against the wall near the door. The question was not directed at me but at the person sitting directly across from him.

"You're Masahiko Okada," said Ode Abumwe, Colonial Union ambassador, and also my boss.

"Precisely," Okada said. "And you know my position."

"Yes I do," Abumwe said. "You're a Colonial Union prisoner of war."

"I'm prime minister of Khartoum!" Okada said, voice shaking.

"No," Abumwe said. "No, you are not. You may have been, but that was before you acted in open rebellion against the Colonial Union. That was before you ordered ships to attack a Colonial Defense Forces vessel. That was before you ordered ground-based weapons to blast individual CDF soldiers out of the sky. Whatever you were before, Mr. Okada, right now you are a traitor, and a murderer, and a prisoner of war. Nothing more than that."

"I don't know what you're talking about," Okada said. "We declared independence from the Colonial Union, that's all."

"You declared independence from the Colonial Union and then hid in a secret location," Abumwe said. "Which surely suggests you knew the Colonial Union would respond to your independence and would send forces to retrieve you. And when we did, we were attacked. Not by Khartoumians, Mr. Okada. By others entirely."

"*I* didn't authorize any attack."

Abumwe sighed audibly at this.

"I want to speak to Secretary of State Galeano. When she finds out what you and your Colonial Defense Force stooges have done to me, you'll be lucky just to be fired."

"Mr. Okada."

"*Prime Minister* Okada."

"Mr. Okada," Abumwe repeated, and I could see the mottled rage rising up Okada's neck and face, "you appear to be under the impression that by sheer force of personality, you will change your circumstances at the moment. That you will, by issuing demands in that stentorian campaign voice of yours, cow me to your will. You misunderstand my role here, Mr. Okada. I am not the one keeping you from returning to your previous, exalted status. I am the one that is keeping you from being turned into a floating brain in a transparent column of nutrient broth."

The mottled flush of Okada's cheeks disappeared, followed by something rather paler. "Excuse me?" he said.

"You heard me, Mr. Okada," Abumwe said. "You declared your planet independent of the Colonial Union, which was enough to have you labeled a traitor. For that alone you would be looking at the rest of your life in a Colonial Union prison, if they didn't simply decide to execute you. But then you also attacked Colonial Defense forces. And the CDF doesn't forgive the deaths of its people. It especially won't forgive them when it's clear that you, the prime minister of an entire planet, planned and coordinated the attack with enemies of the Colonial Union.

"The CDF won't kill you for that, Mr. Okada. What they will do is strip your brain out of your head and let it lie in isolation— horrible, endless isolation—until you tell them every single thing you know. And then when you're done, you'll be sent back into that endless isolation."

Okada's eyes flickered up to me. I stared back at him, impassive. I knew what my role in the room was, which was to be the silent avatar of every horrible thing the Colonial Defense Forces would do to Okada. It would be an inappropriate time for me to note my own personal objection to the brain removal tactic, which I found frankly criminal.

"The *only* reason you haven't already been prepared for this operation is because I, as a courtesy owed to your former station," Abumwe continued. "Tell me everything you know, now. No hesitation, no omission, no lies. Start with your deal with Equilibrium. Share it all, and you will stay you. Or don't."

"I didn't authorize that attack," Okada began.

Abumwe shoved up from her seat, a look of genuine disgust on her face.

"Wait!" Okada held up a hand, imploringly. Abumwe paused. "We had a deal with Equilibrium, yes. But it was only for defense if and only if the Colonial Union attacked Khartoum itself. A major attack. A single CDF ship in orbit wouldn't have triggered it."

"But you hid yourself," I said. "You and your cabinet."

"We're not *stupid*," Okada spat at me. "We knew you would come for us. We hid to delay you finding us, and to keep you from destroying infrastructure and creating civilian casualties when you went looking for us." He turned back to Abumwe. "We always knew we were going to be captured. We knew you would send a single ship for us, because we all know how the Colonial Union like to imply that it only takes a single ship to deal with any internal problem. We *wanted* to be captured. Our plan was civil disobedience. To act as an inspiration for the other colony worlds who were planning to declare their independence as well."

"Civil disobedience doesn't usually include calling in outside forces to act as muscle," I said.

"It's one thing for me and my cabinet to participate in civil disobedience," Okada said. "It's another thing to leave three hundred sixty million people defenseless against the Colonial Union. Our deal with Equilibrium was defense and deterrence, not aggression."

"And yet they attacked anyway," Abumwe said, sitting down again.

"Not on my orders," Okada said. "The first I knew of it was

when your soldiers blasted their way into our bunker and dragged me out."

Abumwe looked at me. I shrugged.

"I am telling the truth!" Okada protested. "I don't want my brain in a goddamned tube, all right? I was misled by Equilibrium. By Commander Tvann. He told me his role was deterrence only. Encouraged us to declare independence before the other colonies to set the example—and to make them aware that Equilibrium would protect them like it was protecting us. To encourage every colony to break free of the Colonial Union."

"So why did Commander Tvann do it?" Abumwe asked. "Why did he attack?"

"Why don't you ask him?"

"We have and we will again. But right now I'm asking you. Speculate."

Okada laughed bitterly. "Obviously because whatever plans Equilibrium has, they deviate substantially from our own. What they are, I cannot even begin to tell you. All I know, Ambassador, is that I was used. I was used. My government was used. My planet was used. And now all of us are going to pay for it."

Abumwe stood up again, less dramatically this time.

"What's going to happen now?" Okada asked.

"We'll make sure you stay intact," Abumwe said.

"That's not what I meant. I meant, what's going to happen to Khartoum? What is the Colonial Union going to do to my planet? To my people?"

"I don't know, Minister Okada," Abumwe said. I wondered if he noticed that she gave him his honorific the one time he gave thought to those he was supposed to represent, and not just himself.

"We don't have a lot of time," Abumwe said to her current brain trust, which at the moment was Hillary Drollet, her assistant;

Neva Balla, the captain of the *Chandler*; my friend Hart Schmidt; and me. All of us were crammed into that same small room. "It won't be long before Equilibrium discovers that their attack has failed."

"I don't think it did," I said.

"How do you figure?" Balla said, to me. "The *Tubingen* isn't entirely destroyed. The two ships attacking it were. The Rraey attack on our soldiers was likewise countered and the Rraey eliminated, except for our two prisoners. And Khartoum isn't independent. If anything it's just signed up for more direct Colonial Union oversight. There are twenty CDF ships on the way here now to make that point."

I pointed at her for emphasis. "But, see, that's the victory condition."

"Explain yourself, Lieutenant," Abumwe said to me.

"What does Equilibrium want?" I asked the room. "It wants to destabilize and destroy the Colonial Union. And the Conclave, too, but let's focus on us for a minute."

"Right," Balla said. "And they *failed*. Khartoum is still in the Colonial Union. It didn't destroy the Colonial Union."

"It's not just destroy. It's also *destabilize*," I said. "The CDF is sending ships not just to deal with the *Tubingen*'s survivors, but to exert control over a rebellious planet. You said twenty ships, Captain."

"That's right."

"When was the last time the Colonial Union committed that number of CDF ships to a colonial world that wasn't directly under attack by another species?"

"You're the one with the computer in your head," Balla said. "You tell us."

"It hasn't happened in over a century," I said.

"We've never had the level of uprisings we're seeing now," Hart said, to me. He looked around the room. "Harry and I talked to Lieutenant Lee, who led that *Tubingen* platoon to get the prime minister. She said that all of her previous recent missions were either stopping rebellions on Colonial Union planets or containing them if they'd already begun. That's new. That's different."

"This goes to my point," I said. "The Colonial Union is already destabilizing. Bringing in twenty ships won't help."

"I don't know about that," Balla said. "I think no one on Khartoum is going to start anything anytime soon."

"But the audience here isn't just Khartoum," Abumwe said, to Balla, and then looked at me. "That's what you're going to say next, isn't it."

"Yes," I said. "Because it's not. We know that Khartoum was one of ten colony worlds that were going to jointly announce their independence. Equilibrium got them to jump the gun for its own purposes. I think part of that purpose was to invoke an outsized military response on our part."

"But that would just intimidate the other colonies," Balla said.

"Or anger them," Hart said.

"Or inspire them to stick to their guns, as it were," I said.

" 'Stick to their guns' is a curious phrase to use," Balla said. "Because they don't have any. The Colonial Union has all the weaponry on its side. Whether they're inspired or angry or both, the colonies can't miss the Colonial Union's message that the party's over."

I glanced over to Abumwe.

"Unless Equilibrium has been talking to these other colonies as well," she said.

"Right," I said. "Equilibrium is small so it has to maximize its impact. It has to go for gestures that make a splash. It's something they learned from us."

"How so?" Abumwe asked.

"Like when we fought the Conclave over Roanoke," I said. "It's four hundred alien races, all with their own military reach.

We couldn't possibly take them on ship-to-ship. So when we wanted to destroy it, we lured them into a trap we devised, destroyed their grand fleet by subterfuge, and waited for the fallout to take down the Conclave."

"There is the minor detail that the plan didn't work," Balla said. "The Conclave survived."

"But the Conclave wasn't the same after that," I pointed out. "Before Roanoke, the Conclave was this dauntingly large force that was impossible to fight. After Roanoke, there was an open rebellion and there was the first assassination attempt on General Gau, their leader. Those tensions never went away, and Gau was in fact later assassinated. We were there for it. You can lay out a path from Roanoke to Gau's death. The Conclave today is what the Colonial Union made it. Which also means in some way the Colonial Union helped create the conditions that make Equilibrium possible."

"And now Equilibrium is shaping the Colonial Union," Abumwe said.

"It's certainly making the effort, yes."

"There is some irony to that."

I nodded at this. "And the thing we have to remember is that it's doing it for its own purposes." I pointed in the direction of the very small room in which we were currently keeping Khartoum's prime minister. "Okada and his government got sold a bill of goods by Equilibrium, which attacked us. But it's not Equilibrium who is being punished, it's Khartoum."

"When you lay down with dogs, you get fleas," Hart said.

"Yes. I'm not defending Okada's act. He and the planet wouldn't be in the position they are today if he and his government hadn't let Equilibrium through the door. But Equilibrium got what it wanted out of the exchange. More Colonial Union oversight means more resentment of the Colonial Union, not just here, but everywhere that finds out about it."

"The Colonial Union holds a virtual monopoly on information," Balla said.

"It did," I agreed. "It doesn't anymore. And, leaving aside the general philosophical issue with a single source bottlenecking every bit of communication for its own purposes, that presents its own problems."

"Like Equilibrium creating its own version of events here on Khartoum and presenting it to the other colonies," Abumwe said.

"Right again," I said. "Which goes back again to my point about Equilibrium maximizing its efforts. It doesn't take a lot for them to leverage mistrust of the Colonial Union into the appearance of being a fair dealer to the colonial worlds." I pointed to Abumwe. "You said we don't have much time. I think it's more correct to say that we're already out of time. Equilibrium is almost certainly already out there selling its version of events, and when it shows a feed of all our ships floating above the surface of Khartoum, that's just going to act as confirmation to the rebellious colonies."

"How do we know about the rebellious colonies?" Balla asked.

"The Colonial Union is not entirely without friends on the colony worlds," Abumwe said. "Or in their governments. We have had people feeding us information for a while now."

"And we never did anything on it? We let it get to this point?"

"With the politics of the colony worlds the Colonial Union prefers to do things as quietly as possible, until they can't be handled quietly anymore." Abumwe shrugged. "It worked before, for decades. The Colonial Union is resistant to change. And at the top there's the belief that things can still be managed quietly. That we will be able to control the actions of the colonies."

"That's not working out very well at this point, Ambassador," Balla said.

"No, it isn't," Abumwe agreed.

"And we knew nothing about Equilibrium's involvement."

"Remember that one of the prime movers of Equilibrium turned out to be a highly placed member of our State Department," I said, to Balla. "It's entirely possible that what we thought we knew about the independence movements on the colony worlds was based on highly edited information. And once Ocampo was retaken, Equilibrium would naturally change tactics. That would be my guess, anyway."

Balla turned to me. "Have you always had this sort of paranoid mind?"

I smiled. "Captain, the problem is not that I'm paranoid. The problem is that the universe keeps justifying my paranoia."

Abumwe turned her attention back to me. "So, your analysis, paranoid or otherwise, is that this encounter was a success for Equilibrium."

"Yes," I said. "It wasn't perfect; I think they would have liked to have destroyed the *Tubingen*, killed everyone aboard, made it look like the Khartoumian government was entirely responsible for it all, and have us none the wiser for it. But as it is, they'll be able to sell their version to people who are receptive to hear it. Equilibrium's been working on a strategy of making us look deceptive and dissembling for a while now. It works because we are, in fact, deceptive and dissembling."

"What's their next step, then?" Hart asked.

"I think that may be the lieutenant's point," Abumwe said. "They don't have to have a next step. They just have to wait for us to do what we always do, the way we always do it."

I nodded. "Why do the work to destabilize us when we'll do it for ourselves."

"But there still has to be a *point* to it," Balla said, to Abumwe. She turned to me. "Look, Lieutenant, I understand that you are deeply enthusiastic about this convoluted web of actions that you're spinning. I'm not going to say that it's wrong. But Equilibrium isn't doing this just for the fun of it. They're not nihil-ists. There has to be a point. There has to be a plan. This has to *lead* to something."

"It leads to the end of all things," I said. "Or less dramati-cally, to either or both the Colonial Union and the Conclave frac-turing, and the return of every species in our local slice of space being constantly at war with each other."

"I still don't know why anyone would want that," Hart said.

"Because it worked really well for some people," I said. "Let's not lie, Hart. It worked really well for us. For humans. And more specifically for the Colonial Union. A system of govern-ment, stable for centuries, predicated on killing the shit out of everyone else and taking their land. That's practically the mo-dus operandi of every successful human civilization to date. No wonder some of us wanted to return to it, even at the risk of destroying the Colonial Union itself. Because if we got back, we'd be meaner than ever before."

"Unless we weren't, and were just wiped out instead."

"Well, there is that. You can't make an omelet without break-ing eggs, but you also have to make sure that what's inside the egg makes it to the pan."

"I . . . don't know what that means," Hart said.

"It means destroying the Colonial Union isn't a trivial act for the survival of the human race," I said. "We might not have time to think up something new before we're wiped out."

"That's what I said," Hart pointed out. "More compactly."

"Whether or not it leads to the end of all things is not my concern right now," Balla said. "My concern is the next *specific* thing that Equilibrium is going to do, or wants to have happen."

"I think it's something to do with the planets that are plan-ning to announce their independence," I said.

"I agree," Abumwe said.

"Okay, that's great," Balla said. "What, exactly?"

"I don't know," I said.

"Isn't that why you questioned those Rraey and the prime minister? To find those things out?"

"We found out a lot," I said. "Just not that."

"Maybe you should try again."

"You might be right," I said. "Specifically, I want to try another pass at Commander Tvann."

"You going to still try to be his friend?" Abumwe asked. "I don't see that being a very effective tactic."

"The point of the first session wasn't to make him my friend. It was to make him not fear me."

"And what do you plan to do now?" Balla asked.

"I'm going to introduce him to something he actually *might* fear," I said.

"I don't know what these are," Commander Tvann said, when I handed him a printout. We were back in the same room. I was beginning to get tired of the room, to be entirely honest about it.

"That's a printout of targets the Colonial Defense Forces are planning to hit sometime very soon," I said.

Tvann handed it back. "I don't read your language, and I'm not sure why you would want to show me confidential information in any event."

"Because in a way you were the inspiration for the list," I said, and handed him another printout. "Here, this one might be more readable for you."

Tvann took the list and read it. He read it a second time. Then he set the printout on the table between us.

"I don't understand," he said to me.

"It's simple enough," I said. "You are Rraey. The Equilibrium crew who you commanded were all Rraey. The crew which you commanded, which took the *Chandler* and killed its crew, were Rraey. The base from which Equilibrium operated until Rafe shot it up and rendered it unusable was formerly a Rraey military base, until your species abandoned it and the system it was in. You are seeing a pattern here, I trust."

"It's a false pattern."

"It could be," I admitted. "However, the top brass of the Colonial Defense Force doesn't think so. They're pretty well convinced at this point that the Rraey—your government—is actively involved with Equilibrium. It's not the only one, to be sure. We have enough evidence of that. But time and again we see Rraey participation in ways we don't see other species participating. It is, shall we say, statistically significant."

"You and the Conclave drove millions of us out of work and out of our homes," Tvann said. "Of course you will see lots of us involved in Equilibrium."

I smiled. "It might interest you to know that's the very rationale Specialist Lau gave for joining up. And I'm not saying it's wrong. I am saying it's not an argument that's going to convince the CDF that your government isn't offering material assistance to Equilibrium."

I pointed to the printout. "So the CDF has decided to act. Equilibrium is difficult to find—it's designed to be that way, I know—so we've decided to stop looking and to go straight to the source, as it were. Those are the first-wave targets we're going to hit on the Rraey worlds. Mostly military and industrial sites, as you can see, but also shipping and processing sites. The plan is to make it more difficult for you to equip and assist Equilibrium."

"You'll also destroy our infrastructure and cause millions to starve."

"Our analysts agree with the first. Not so much to the second. That will happen with the second wave of targets, however, if Equilibrium keeps up its attacks."

"If Equilibrium keeps hitting you after your first set of targets, then it should be obvious that the Rraey are not equipping us."

"Like I said, we know the Rraey aren't the only ones chipping in with Equilibrium. But we think it's the primary one. And aside from the value of snapping off that primary supply line, we think it sends a fine warning to everyone else: You may be using Equilibrium to destroy the Colonial Union, but we're still strong enough to take you down with us."

"When will you do this?"

"The thinking is there's no reason to wait," I said. "The operation is in motion as we speak. In fact, some of the ships that were being tasked here at Khartoum are being reassigned to this. It's become the CDF's top priority now."

"It's genocide."

"I think you might be surprised at how little you and I differ in this opinion, Commander Tvann. But I have to tell you that I'm not the one you need to make that argument to. This is a discussion that's taking place far above either of our heads."

"No," Tvann said. "You wouldn't have come to me with this if there was nothing you wanted from me."

"I do have something I want from you," I agreed. "I want you to tell me Equilibrium's strategy for Khartoum and the other colonies. Tell me and convince me that this is something we can better direct our attention to than that list of targets." I pointed to the printout again. "You have no reason to trust me but I will make you this promise regardless: Help me convince them and I will do everything I can to shift their focus."

"What can you do?" Tvann said. "You're a lieutenant."

"I am," I said. "But I am an unusually well-placed lieutenant."

Tvann was silent, and, I suspect, skeptical.

"Commander," I said. "Let me be clear. The Colonial Defense Forces has made a decision. It's going to hit something, and it's going to hit something hard. And what it's going to hit is whatever is directly in front of it. Right now, that's the Rraey planets. You know that the CDF is weaker than it used to be. But the Rraey are weaker even than that, and when the CDF hits your people, it's going to knock them back as close to the Stone Age as possible. A lot of your people are going to suffer. The only way this doesn't happen—the *only* way, Commander—is if we have something else to hit instead. Give me something else they can hit. Help me, Commander."

An hour later I emerged from the room. Hart was waiting for me, along with a pair of CDF soldiers waiting to escort Tvann back to the brig.

"You got everything you needed?" he asked.

"What, you weren't out here recording?"

"After you mocked me for it the last time I decided there were other things I could be doing with my time."

"Yes, I think I got everything I needed." I nodded to the soldiers, who entered the room. I motioned to Hart to walk with me.

"He didn't catch on."

"That I was bluffing about the Rraey targets? No. I sold it well enough. It helps that it was exactly the sort of thing the CDF would do."

"So now what?"

"So now we go tell Abumwe," I said. "And then, I suspect, we head back to Phoenix Station and tell a whole bunch of other people. And then maybe find a hole to hide in."

"Why? I thought Tvann told you what Equilibrium is planning."

"He did," I said.

"Well? And?"

I stopped and turned to look at my friend. "And if everything he told me is true, Hart, then we're all kind of magnificently fucked."

I started walking again. Hart stayed stationary, staring at me as I walked away.

PART TWO

"The organization known as Equilibrium is dedicated to bringing about the end of the Colonial Union," Ambassador Abumwe said. "We know this. But we should be aware that the end of the Colonial Union is not the only goal of Equilibrium—indeed it's not the primary goal. The primary goal is the dissolution of the Conclave, the largest single government this part of space has ever seen. To this end, Equilibrium is using the Colonial Union as a tool, and not just the Colonial Union, but Earth as well."

Abumwe was speaking from the well of one of the State Department lecture theaters at Phoenix Station. This particular theater could easily seat a couple hundred people, but at the moment held just four: Abumwe in the well, me sitting off to the side, and Colonels Abel Rigney and Liz Egan front row center, facing Abumwe.

Egan's formal title was Colonial Defense Forces liaison to the Colonial Union's Department of State, but in the aftermath of Assistant Secretary Ocampo's betrayal of the CU, she had stepped into the role of ad hoc number two at State, someone trusted by both the secretary of state and the CDF brass. The closer entwining of those two entities should have filled any rational person with a sense of foreboding, but at the moment no one seemed to blink. This was in itself a commentary of the state the Colonial Union was in at the moment.

Colonel Abel Rigney, I think, didn't have an actual title. He was just That Guy in the CDF: the one that went everywhere, saw everything, advised everyone, and was privy to it all. Honestly, if you wanted to cripple the CDF—and by extension the Colonial Union—all you would have to do is put a bullet into his temple. I suspect entire chunks of the Colonial Union government would simply stop working because no one would know who to talk to without Rigney acting as intermediary.

Officially, Egan and Rigney were mid-level apparatchiks at best. Unofficially, they were the people you talked to when a thing needed to be done, whatever thing it was.

We had a thing that needed to be done.

"You're saying that what happened at Khartoum is not meant to be a direct attack on the Colonial Union," Egan said, to Abumwe.

"No, of course it was a direct attack," Abumwe replied, in the straight-ahead, blunt manner that if you were not smart, you would think was profoundly nondiplomatic. "The act served its own short-term goal in that regard. But its true value to Equilibrium is long term—what it allows the organization to build towards for its ultimate goal: the destruction of the Conclave."

"Walk us through it, Ambassador," Rigney said.

"At Khartoum, we secured a high-value prisoner, a Commander Tvann of Equilibrium." A very slight smile crossed Abumwe's face. "The best way to describe him is as the Equilibrium equivalent of *you*, Colonel Rigney. Someone who is very well connected and often at the center of Equilibrium plans."

"All right."

The ambassador nodded in my direction. "During interrogation, Lieutenant Wilson here got Tvann to reveal Equilibrium's most recent plan, which begins with the attack on the *Tubingen* above Khartoum."

Colonels Rigney and Egan looked over to me. "'Interrogation,' Lieutenant?" Egan said to me.

I understood the implication. "The information was not secured under torture or duress," I said. "I used misdirection and false information to convince him that it was in his interest to cooperate."

"What false information?"

"I told him we were going to obliterate every major Rraey city and industrial site on four different planets because we believe the Rraey are the primary movers behind Equilibrium."

"Are they?"

"I don't have the data to speculate," I said. "If you were asking me to go with my gut, I'd say the Rraey government offers clandestine logistical support that's difficult to prove. Certainly the Rraey wouldn't mind if we were out of the way. Even if they are offering support, however, going after the Rraey at this point won't make a difference in the immediate plans of Equilibrium. Equilibrium is and should be our primary concern at the moment."

Egan nodded and looked back to Abumwe. "Continue," she said.

"Khartoum is one of ten colonies who conspired to declare independence from the Colonial Union. The plan was to do it simultaneously and in doing so give the Colonial Union too many targets against which to effectively retaliate. The longer it took us to respond to the event, the more colonial worlds would be inspired to also declare independence. The idea here is that dissolution of the Colonial Union would succeed in part because the CU would lack the resources to deal with the mass exodus.

"However, Colonel Tvann convinced the government of Khartoum to announce its independence early, arguing that it could act as the catalyst for the dissolution of the Colonial Union alone, and that Equilibrium would effectively serve as Khartoum's defense forces. That would benefit both Khartoum and Equilibrium, which wanted to be seen as an ally to the newly independent colonies."

"That didn't work out," Rigney said, dryly.

"No," Abumwe agreed. "In fact, Equilibrium's true plan was to attack any CDF ship which responded—which it did with the *Tubingen*. The attack, whether it was seen by the Colonial Union as directed by Khartoum or by Equilibrium, would result in a massive response by the CDF—which it did. We sent twenty ships to Khartoum.

"Equilibrium did this for the specific purpose of massively militarizing the Colonial Union response to our planets declaring independence. The next planet or planets which declare will not receive a visit from a single CDF ship as they would have done before. Instead the CDF will send a fleet to any planet, with the specific intent of overwhelming any independence movement from the beginning." Abumwe stopped for a second and looked at Egan and Rigney curiously. "Is this Equilibrium assessment accurate?"

The two colonels looked uncomfortable. "It might be," Rigney said, eventually.

Abumwe nodded. "Equilibrium, through its own strategy of misdirection and false information—and its campaign to establish the Colonial Union as an unreliable source of truthful information, aided by the fact that the Colonial Union is, in fact, deeply censorious of news between colonies—plans to encourage the nine remaining planets in the original independence scheme to stick to their plan and jointly announce. It will promise logistical and defense support, which it has no real intention of providing except for its own purposes, as it did over Khartoum. This will happen as soon as practicably possible. And of course the CDF will respond."

"And then what?" Egan asked.

"Once the Colonial Union is fully occupied with this independence movement and has committed a substantial amount of its military force and intelligence capabilities to quash it, Equilibrium attacks."

"Attacks the fleets over the rebellious colony planets?"

Rigney said. "That's just stupid, Ambassador. Equilibrium can be effective with sneak attacks but their ships and armaments can't stand up to a prolonged battle."

"They won't be attacking our fleets," Abumwe said. "They will be attacking the Earth."

"What?" Egan said. She pushed forward in her seat, now intensely interested.

Abumwe glanced over to me and nodded. I connected my BrainPal to the theater's presentation system and popped up a visual of Earth, and above it, several dozen starships, not to scale.

"Equilibrium acquires ships by pirating them," Abumwe said. "The Colonial Union has lost dozens over the years. The Conclave and its constituent states have lost even more." She pointed into the graphic. "What you see here is a representation of all the Conclave-affiliated ships that we know have been taken and have not, as yet, been destroyed in battle. There are ninety-four shown here and we have to assume our estimate is low.

"According to Commander Tvann, the Equilibrium plan is to skip these ships into Earth space, destroy the planet's defense, communication, and scientific satellites, and then target hundreds of major population areas with nuclear warheads."

"*Nuclear* warheads," Rigney said.

"Where the hell are they getting nukes?" Egan said. "Who still uses them?"

"Tvann indicated that many of them came from the stores of planets now aligned with the Conclave," Abumwe said. "The Conclave doesn't allow their use as weapons, so they're supposed to be dismantled and the fissionable material disposed of. It was a trivial matter for Equilibrium to insert itself into that process and come away with warheads and fissionable material."

"How many are we talking about?" Rigney said. "Warheads, I mean."

Abumwe looked at me. "Tvann didn't know all the specifics," I said. "The ones he seemed to consider standard yield would be the equivalent to three hundred kilotons. He said there were several hundred of those."

"Jesus Christ."

"They could do the same damage without nuclear weapons," Egan said. "At this point in weapons technology, using nuclear weapons is only a step up from using the longbow."

"The *point* is to use the nuclear weapons," Abumwe said. "Not just for the immediate devastation, but for everything else that follows."

"When the Romans defeated Carthage, they salted the ground there so nothing could live or grow there anymore," I said. "This is the same concept, writ large."

"Equilibrium would be slitting their throat by doing this," Rigney said.

"If you can find their throats to slit them," I pointed out.

"I think we would be *motivated*, Lieutenant."

"Colonel, you're missing the important thing here," Abumwe said.

"And what is that, Ambassador?" Egan asked.

Abumwe gestured up toward the image floating there. "That every one of the ships tasked to the attack is originally from the Conclave. *We* are meant to believe this is an attack not by Equilibrium, but by the Conclave. We're meant to believe the Conclave has decided that the only way to deal with humanity—to deal with the Colonial Union—is to destroy the source of its soldiers and colonists once and for all, so we can never get it back, either by force or negotiation. This is meant to be the earnest of the Conclave's intent to wipe us from the universe forever."

Rigney nodded. "Yes, all right."

"We would blame the Conclave, refuse its denials, assume it was behind Equilibrium all along," Egan said. "We'd go to war with the Conclave. And we'd be defeated."

"Inevitably, yes," Abumwe said. "We are far too small to take it on directly. And even if all the colony worlds stopped fighting us for independence—or we crushed all their attempts at independence—it would still take us time to fully convert to the colonies being the well from which we draw our soldiers. And meanwhile elements of the Conclave would be agitating for our destruction, because whether the Conclave attacked us or not, we would now be a clear and present danger to it."

"We'd lose in a fight with the Conclave," I said. "But that doesn't mean the Conclave would win."

Abumwe nodded. "It wouldn't simply be about us attacking the Conclave. It would be the internal stresses the Conclave would face in being obliged to obliterate us permanently. It goes against every reason the Conclave was founded in the first place. It would be antithetical to the goals of General Gau."

"Not to mention that of the Conclave's current leader, Hafte Sorvalh," I said. "And she would be criticized relentlessly if she refused to deal with us. And no matter how capable she is—and she's very capable—she's not General Gau. She won't be able to keep the Conclave together through her own sheer force of will like the general could. It will fracture and die."

"Which is Equilibrium's ultimate goal," Egan said.

"Yes," Abumwe said. "Again, our destruction is part of its plan, too. But we are mostly incidental. We are the lever Equilibrium will use to destroy the Conclave. Everything the organization has ever done, including the destruction of Earth Station, has been part of the drive toward that goal."

"I don't know how I feel about the complete destruction of the Colonial Union being a *side benefit*," Rigney said.

"It should make you angry," Abumwe said. "It makes me angry."

"You don't look notably angry," Rigney observed.

"Colonel Rigney, I'm furious," Abumwe said. "I also recognize that there are more important things for me to be and do than just be furious."

"Ambassador, a question," Egan said.

"Yes, Colonel."

Egan pointed to the graphic. "We know Equilibrium's plan now. We know that it plans to use our colonies and our standard responses against us. We know it plans to frame the Conclave for the attack on Earth. We know its game, its strategy, and its tactics. Isn't this now a trap we can easily step out of?"

Abumwe looked over to me. "There are other complications," I said. "Tvann suggested to me that if it became clear the Khartoum strategy failed or that we had thwarted their plans with the other nine planets or informed the Conclave of the subterfuge, that Equilibrium may simply attack Earth anyway."

"For what purpose?" Egan said.

"Equilibrium doesn't appear to be fussy," I said. "It'll take half a loaf if it can't get a full one. What I mean by that is right now its optimal plan is to distract the Colonial Union, destroy the Earth, frame the Conclave, and let us destroy each other. But if Equilibrium has to take credit for nuking Earth instead, it will. Because it knows that an obviously weakened Colonial Union, an obviously weakened human race, will still force the Conclave's hand."

"You have to appreciate just how many Conclave species hate humans," Abumwe said. "They hated us before what we did at Roanoke. They hate us even more after it. And some of them blame us for the assassination of General Gau."

"We had nothing to do with that," Rigney said.

"But we were there when it happened," Abumwe said. "We and humans from Earth. That's enough for many of them."

"So you're saying that Equilibrium is perfectly fine going with a 'Plan B,'" Egan said, bringing the topic back around.

"We're *already* on Plan B," I said. "Plan B went into effect the moment Rafe Daquin stole the *Chandler* and brought back Secretary Ocampo. This is closer to Plan K. Equilibrium has been very good at improvisation, Colonel. It knows its limits in terms of scale and makes them advantages. Taking credit for killing Earth is not the primary goal but it has its own advantages. It means that it has done something no other entity, no other power has ever dared to do: destroyed the planet that gave the Colonial Union its power. If Equilibrium plays its cards right, it could profit immensely from taking credit for killing Earth. It could gain new members and funding. It could become a legitimate power in itself. It could step out of the shadows it lives in now."

"No matter what, the Earth is fucked," Rigney said. "Excuse the language, but that's the gist of what I'm hearing from you."

I looked over to Abumwe. "There is another option."

"Tell us," Egan said.

"Before I do, a question for the two of you," Abumwe said. "Are we agreed that the goal here is survival, not a win?"

"I don't understand the question," Egan said.

"I don't believe that, Colonel," Abumwe said, and stared fixedly at Egan. "I think you know very well what I mean. We four in this room can indulge in the luxury of being utterly honest with each other. So we don't have to pretend that we don't know that the Colonial Union, as it exists now, is headed for collapse. If we're not destroyed by Equilibrium or the Conclave, we'll tear ourselves apart. It's already happening.

"We don't have to pretend that we don't know the structure and organization of the Colonial Union itself is unsupportable as it's currently constructed. We don't have to pretend that there's any way we get the Earth back into the role it played for us before. We don't have to pretend that we are not staring our extinction in the face. We don't have to pretend that any petty victories or side goals are important right now. What matters is that we agree that what we do here now is for the survival of *us*, of humanity. Not the Colonial Union as it is now. But of our species. We four have to agree to this, or there is simply no point in continuing this meeting."

Egan and Rigney looked at each other. "We agree," Egan said.

"And this agreement will be supported how?" Abumwe said. "If we are agreed that we are talking about survival, are we also agreed that we do what it takes to allow survival to happen?"

"Ambassador Abumwe," Rigney said. "Tell us your plan. We'll tell you how we can make it happen."

"Very well," Abumwe said.

"Thank you for attending this meeting," Abumwe said, to the representatives of the nine colonies who were planning, in what they believed to be secret, to announce their independence.

"'Attend,' hell," said Harilal Dwivedi, the representative from Huckleberry. "We were just about dragged out of our beds and forced to be here." Several of the other representatives nodded in agreement.

"I do apologize," Abumwe said. "Unfortunately time is of the essence. I am Ambassador Ode Abumwe."

"Why are we here, Ambassador?" asked Neida Calderon, of Umbria.

"Representative Calderon, if you would look around at who else is here among you, I think you will have a good idea why you are here."

The low-level muttering and complaining cut off abruptly. Abumwe was now very definitely the focus of all their attention.

"Yes, we know," Abumwe said.

"Of course you know," Dwivedi spat. He was clearly of the "when cornered, attack" school of rhetoric. "You have the prime minister of Khartoum in custody. I can't imagine what you've done to him."

Abumwe nodded to me. I went to a side door in the State Department conference room we were in and opened it. "Come on in," I said.

Masahiko Okada walked out and sat down at the table with the representatives. They stared at him like he had three heads.

"Any more surprises, Ambassador Abumwe?" Calderon asked, after she stopped staring at Okada.

"In the interest of saving us all time, allow me to be brief," Abumwe said.

"Please do," Calderon said.

"Each of your worlds is planning to jointly announce your independence from the Colonial Union. The fact that each of you is in this room right now should indicate our awareness of your plans. We are also aware that each of your governments has been in discussion, either individually or severally, with an entity called Equilibrium, which has shared information with you and has, we believe, offered each of you protection against the Colonial Union when you declare your independence."

Dwivedi opened his mouth to speak; Abumwe hit him with a hard stare. "This is not the moment to offer up excuses or rationalizations either for your desire for your independence or your fraternization with Equilibrium. We don't have time for it, and quite bluntly at the moment we don't care."

Dwivedi closed his mouth, clearly annoyed.

"Equilibrium has been deceiving each of your governments," Abumwe continued, and motioned to Okada. "In a moment Minister Okada here will detail to you how Equilibrium deceived him and his government and attacked a Colonial Defense Forces ship with the intent to pin the blame—and the punishment—on Khartoum and its government, for the purpose of galvanizing your governments into action. Not for your purposes, representatives. Not for the freedom you believe you seek. But for its own agenda, of which your planets and their fates are mere stepping-stones.

"With that in mind, the Colonial Union is making a request of each of you."

"Let me guess," Calderon said. "You don't want us to declare our independence from the Colonial Union."

Abumwe smiled one of her very rare smiles. "In fact, Representative Calderon, we very much want you to."

Calderon looked uncertain for a moment and glanced around at the other representatives, who were equally confounded. "I don't understand," she said, finally.

"We want you to declare independence," Abumwe said again.

"You *want* us to leave the Colonial Union," Dwivedi said.

"No."

"But you just said you want us to declare our independence."

"Yes," Abumwe said, and held up her hand before Dwivedi could complain further. "We do not want you to leave the Colonial Union. It is dangerous for each of us. But we ask each of you to follow through with your plan to declare independence. We need for Equilibrium to believe that your planets are going to go through with the plan you've already arranged."

"And why is that?" Calderon asked.

"I can't tell you," Abumwe said. "Quite obviously your governments are not secure. We can't tell you everything."

"And what will happen when we declare independence?"

"The Colonial Union, quite predictably, will overreact and fill your sky with ships in order to intimidate you."

"I'm failing to see the benefit to any of us in this plan," Calderon said, wryly. She had, for whatever reason, assumed the leadership role for the assembled representatives.

"We want you to declare independence but not become independent," Abumwe said. "We will respond with the appearance of force, not force itself."

"You're asking us to believe that the CDF won't crush us flat."

"If we wanted to do that we wouldn't need to have this meeting," Abumwe pointed out. "No. I'm offering you a way out of that eventuality. Make no mistake, Representatives. Any attempt to leave the Colonial Union will be met with force. We cannot afford to have your planets leave the union, and at the risk of sounding patronizing, we are absolutely certain you don't appreciate the danger you are putting yourself into." Abumwe motioned to Okada again. "Minister Okada here can speak to this from experience."

"You want us to trust you. You might understand why it's difficult for us to do that."

"I'm not asking for your trust," Abumwe said. "I'm making you an offer."

"There's not much you can offer us, Ambassador, if you're already denying us our freedom."

"Representative Calderon, let me suggest that it's not freedom that you are looking for."

"It's not."

"No."

"What is it, then?"

"It's control," Abumwe said. "Which is what I am offering you."

"Explain," Calderon said, after a moment.

"You are all representatives to the Colonial Union government," Abumwe said. "I don't need to tell you how little that actually means in terms of how the Colonial Union is administered and its relationship to your home planets. At best you are responsible for the most minor of tasks. At worst you are ignored entirely."

She stopped to let her comment take root. There were nods among the representatives.

"That is going to change. It has to change. The Colonial Union will need to rely on the colony worlds more than ever, including for soldiers, which it has never done before. It can no longer rule from the top down. Bluntly, it will need the consent of the governed. It will need to be ruled by the governed. It will need to be ruled by you."

There was dead silence for a moment. Then:

"You're *joking*," Dwivedi said.

"No," Abumwe said, looking at Calderon rather than the Huckleberry representative. "It's been agreed to in principle. At the top. What we need now is a group of representatives willing to do the work to create a system that reflects the reality of our situation with the Conclave and others, along with a truly representative government."

"You want us to draft a constitution," Calderon said, only a little incredulously.

"Yes."

"In exchange for this little act of subterfuge with our declarations of independence."

"Yes," Abumwe said.

"It's that important."

"Yes."

"We're going to need to consult with our governments," Dwivedi said.

"No," Abumwe said, and looked around. "I need to be clear about this. *There is no time*. We already know that you plan to announce your independence in as little as a couple of weeks. We need that timetable to continue. We need everything to run as if it's already been decided. There can be no pause, no hint that anything has changed. You are your colony's representative. Represent. Your decision here now will commit your planet and we will hold it to your decision. And one other thing: This decision must be unanimous. Either you are all in or none of you are."

"You're expecting us to create a viable system of interplanetary representative government right now," Calderon said.

This got the faintest of smiles from Abumwe. "No. Details will wait. But you have to commit now."

"How much time are you giving us?"

"You'll have tonight," Abumwe said. "I'll be here to answer what questions I can. Okada is here to tell you about Khartoum's experience with Equilibrium. It's eleven P.M. now. By eight, I will either need your unanimous agreement or your refusal."

"And if we refuse?"

"Then you refuse and everything becomes much harder and much more dangerous. For everyone," Abumwe said. "I'm going to leave you for a few moments. I will be back to answer questions presently." She walked out the side door I had brought Okada in from. I followed her.

"That was inspiring," I said.

"Of all the things I need at the moment, Wilson, your sarcasm is not one of them," she said.

"It's only partly sarcasm," I said. "Do you think they'll commit?"

"I believe Calderon is convinced. I think she might be able to convince others."

"And do you think the Colonial Union is actually going to agree to the changes you've just committed it to?"

"That's Rigney and Egan's department," Abumwe said. "But none of us would be here if we didn't already see the writing on the wall."

"True enough," I said.

"I need you to call in Hart Schmidt," Abumwe said. "I need him to take your place in the room. I will brief him on everything."

"All right," I said. "What are you going to have me do?"

"I have two things I need you to do," Abumwe said. "First, I need you to talk to Ocampo."

"What about?"

"The whereabouts of Equilibrium. They fled from their base

but that hasn't stopped them from continuing their operations. We need to know where they are now."

"He might not know," I said.

"And he might. You need to ask him."

"You're the boss," I said. "What's the other thing?"

"I need you to go to Earth."

"Interesting," I said. "You know they don't like us, right? As in, if one of our spaceships shows up above the planet, they're likely to shoot it out of the sky. Not to mention it'll take me several days to get there, with no reasonable expectation of getting back, once they shoot my ship out of the sky."

"I expect you to solve all of these problems before you leave."

"I admire your confidence in me."

"Then don't disappoint me, Wilson."

Tyson Ocampo and I stood on a beach, watching the waves roll in and the seagulls circle overhead.

"It's beautiful here," Ocampo said, to me.

"I thought you might like it," I replied.

"Which beach is this?"

"Cottesloe Beach. It's near Perth, Australia."

"Ah," Ocampo said. "I've never been."

"Well, it's on Earth, so that's understandable," I said.

"Have you ever been?"

"Once," I said. "I went to Perth on business and had a free day. Took the train over to it and spent the day watching the waves and drinking beer."

Ocampo smiled. "We're watching the waves, at least," he said.

"Sorry about the lack of beer."

"Lieutenant, when you're not here, the simulation I see is of a small, square cell. It has three books in it, the titles of which rotate after I read them. I don't get to choose the titles. There's a single small screen on which is ported just enough entertainment material that I do not go entirely mad. Once a day they make a track appear so that I can give myself the appearance of physical exercise. My only visitor—aside from the occasional Colonial Union interrogator—is a chatbot which is not quite well programmed enough to give the appearance of being a person, and only serves to remind me that I am, well and truly, alone in my brain. Trust me. This beach is enough."

I had nothing to say to that, so we continued watching the simulated waves of simulated Cottesloe Beach tumble onto the simulated shore, while the simulated birds reeled in the sky.

"I assume this is a reward," Ocampo said. "For our last session."

"As it turns out, you were entirely correct that a trap was being laid for the CDF ship at Khartoum," I said. "My ship got to skip distance in a dangerously short time—we nearly overloaded the engines—and skipped directly into the attack. That was lucky timing."

"The CDF didn't send one of the ships it has on standby."

"With all due respect, Secretary Ocampo, you're a confirmed traitor, and you have a history of leading ships to their doom. They would not send their own ship, but they didn't mind if we played Russian roulette with ours."

"I'm glad you trust me, Lieutenant."

"I trust that you have nothing left to lose, Secretary."

"That's not quite the same thing, is it."

"No," I said. "It's not. Sorry about that."

Ocampo smiled again, and ran a toe into the sand of the beach. This simulation was about as perfect as I could make it, and from a programming point of view was in fact a bit of a marvel. The simulation was only detailed to the degree of Ocampo's attention. Any part of the beach he wasn't looking at was a low-resolution map. Any part of the sand that wasn't directly under his toes was an undifferentiated texture mat.

The beach existed as a bubble of perception around a man who himself existed as a brain in a jar.

"Did you make this beach for me?" Ocampo said. "As a reward?"

"It's not a reward," I said. "I just thought you might like it."

"I do."

"And I confess I didn't make it for you," I said. "Rafe Daquin had a birthday recently. I modeled it for him."

"You still haven't given him a body?" Ocampo asked.

"His new body is ready," I said. "And he can move into it any time he likes. Right now, he's decided to stay with the *Chandler* and pilot it from the inside. He's really very good at it now. He's done some amazing things."

"I wonder how he would feel if he knew you'd given a gift you made for him to the man who caused his brain to be taken out of his body in the first place."

"Actually he was the one who suggested I do it. He told me to tell you he remembers how lonely it was, and is, to be a brain in a jar. He hoped this might give you some peace."

"That was very kind of him."

"It was," I agreed. I conveniently left out the part where Daquin told me that if I wanted I could program in a great white shark that tore Ocampo's simulated body to pieces. It would not be convenient to the current situation. Rafe might have forgiven, in his fashion, but he had not forgotten.

"Lieutenant," Ocampo said. "As much as I appreciate a trip to the beach, I'm not under the impression that you're here because you and I are friends."

"I need a little more information from you, Secretary. About Equilibrium."

"Of course."

"Will you give it?"

Ocampo didn't answer this. Instead he stepped forward onto the beach, into the water that rushed up to surround his feet and make them sink just a little into the sand. Despite myself I smiled at this; it really was a good simulation that I had thrown together.

"I've been thinking about why it was I became part of Equilibrium," Ocampo said. He looked back at me as he said this and grinned. "Don't worry, Lieutenant, I'm not going to try to make this a monologue of disillusioned nobility that you will have to politely nod through. At this point I can admit that much of the reason I did was ambition and megalomania. That is what it is. But there was another part of it, too. The belief that the Colonial Union, however it had gotten that way, was antithetical to the survival of our species. That every other species we know had come to associate humanity with duplicity, savagery, ambitious cunning, and danger. That this is all that we would ever be to them."

"To be fair, none of the rest of them are exactly angels," I said.

"True enough," Ocampo said. "Although the response to that is how much of that is them dealing with us. The Conclave brought together four hundred species of spacefaring beings into a single government. We can barely get any to tolerate us. It does suggest the problem is not them, but us, the Colonial Union."

I opened my mouth to respond; Ocampo held up a hand. "It's not the right time to debate this, I know. My point is this, Lieutenant. For whatever reasons, I aligned myself with Equilibrium; independent of that, the problem of the Colonial Union remains. It's toxic to itself. It's toxic to humanity. And it's toxic to our survival in this universe. I'm going to help you if I can, Wilson. At this point there is no reason not to. But you have to understand that unless something happens to the Colonial Union—something big, something substantive—then all we're doing here is kicking the can just a little further down the road. The problem will still exist. The longer we wait the worse it gets. And it's already almost as bad as it can get."

"I understand," I said.

"All right. Then ask your question."

"After Daquin attacked Equilibrium headquarters the organization pulled out from there."

"Yes. The location was no longer secure, obviously."

"We need to know where its new headquarters is."

"I don't know," Ocampo said. "And if I did know definitively, they wouldn't use it, because they would have assumed that you would have extracted the location from me."

"Then I would like a guess, please."

"Equilibrium is a relatively small organization but the emphasis here is 'relatively.' It can operate from a single base but that base has to be relatively large and also recently abandoned, so that its systems can be brought back up to operational capacity quickly. It needs to be in a planetary system that's either friendly to the Equilibrium cause, or recently abandoned, or not heavily monitored outside of core worlds."

"That should cut down on the number of available military bases," I said. "At least that's something."

"You're limiting yourself," Ocampo said.

"How?"

"You're thinking like a soldier, and not an opportunistic scavenger, which is what Equilibrium is. Or still is, for the moment."

"So not just military bases," I said. "Any sort of base with the requisite infrastructure."

"Yes."

"And not just of species obviously aligned with Equilibrium."

"Right. They would know you'd already be looking at those. They'd want something that's in the Colonial Union's blind spot."

I considered this for a minute.

And then I had a really truly stupendously far-fetched idea. My computer simulation must have accurately replicated my eureka moment, because Ocampo smiled at me. "I think someone may have thought of something."

"I need to go," I said, to Ocampo. "Secretary, you need to excuse me."

"Of course," he said. "Not that I could make you stay, mind you."

"I can leave this simulation running," I said.

"Thank you," he said. "I would like that. They won't keep it running for more than a couple of minutes after you leave. But I will enjoy it until then."

"I could ask them to let it run longer."

"You can ask," Ocampo said. "It won't make a difference."

"I'm sorry," I said, and despite everything Ocampo had done, I was.

Ocampo shrugged. "This is how it is," he said. "And I can't say that for all I've done I don't deserve it. Still, let me put a thought in your head, Lieutenant. If that idea in your head pans out, and all your plans for it succeed, then ask a thing for me."

"What is it?" I asked. I was concerned he would ask for a new body, which I knew the Colonial Union would never ever give him.

He anticipated that thought. "I'm not going to ask you to ask them for a new body. They won't do that. Institutional forgiveness never goes that far. But I have a place, on Phoenix. Had it, anyway. A small summer cabin up in the mountains, by a small lake. It's on a hundred acres of forest and meadow. I bought it ten years ago with the idea that it would be a place for me to think and write. I never did, because who ever does? Eventually I thought about it as a foolish investment. I thought about selling it but I never did. I guess I lived in hope I'd eventually make use of it. And now I never will. I won't ever see that cabin again. Really see it."

He looked back out, away from the beach, into an Indian Ocean that didn't exist.

"If it all works out, Lieutenant, and you get what you want out of this whole adventure, then use your influence to get me that cabin, here, in simulation. I know that I'll never be out in the real world. But if the simulation is good enough, maybe I can live with that. And these days I have nothing to do now but think. Finally, I would use the cabin for what I bought it for. A version of it, anyway. Say you'll do that for me, Lieutenant Wilson. I would appreciate it more than you can possibly know."

"Sedna," I said.

Colonel Rigney, who was in the small conference room with Egan, Abumwe, and Hart Schmidt, frowned at me. "You're trying to get me to use my BrainPal to look something up," he said.

"Sedna is a dwarf planet in Earth's system," I said. "More accurately, it's a dwarf planet just outside of Earth's system, at the inner edge of its Oort cloud. It's about three times further out from the sun than Neptune."

"All right," Rigney said. "What about it?"

"Ocampo said he didn't know where Equilibrium's new base was, but that they would likely take a base, military or otherwise, that was recently abandoned. And also one that we wouldn't think to look for. One that's in our blind spot."

I used my BrainPal to turn on the wall monitor in the conference room. The image of a small reddish planet popped up. "Sedna," I repeated. "It had one of the Colonial Union's oldest maintained science bases. We used it for deep field astronomy and for planetary science; Sedna's in a good place to observe Earth's entire system and the orbital dynamics therein."

"I've never heard of it," Egan said.

"The last couple of decades it's been largely dormant," I said. "It's had a basically caretaker staff of three or four scientists on a month-on, month-off basis, mostly to monitor some very long-term observations undertaken there, and to run the maintenance robots." I popped up a map of the base on the monitor.

"But the relevant thing here is that during its heyday, over a century ago, the base was far more active. At its peak of activity there were more than a thousand people there."

"How do you know about it?" Hart Schmidt asked me.

"Well, and I'm not proud of this, back in the day I worked in the CDF's research and development arm, and there was a staff member I thought was a real asshole," I said. "I had him transferred there."

"Nice," Rigney said.

"He wasn't the only asshole in that scenario, I realize that now," I allowed.

Egan pointed to the base map. "We don't have a caretaker staff there anymore?"

"No," I said. "After Earth broke off formal ties with the Colonial Union in the wake of the Perry incident"—and here I allowed myself a small smile at the idea of my old friend precipitating the greatest political crisis the Colonial Union ever had—"we abandoned the base. Partly for political reasons, since we didn't want the Earth to feel like we were lurking on their frontier. Partly because of economics."

"So, a large, recently abandoned base, dead square in our blind spot," Rigney said.

"Yes," I said. "It's not the only large, recently abandoned base that the Colonial Union or the CDF has, or that's out there generally. I'll create a list of sites we should survey. But if I were going to lay my money down on a site, it would be this one. We should check that out right away. Discreetly, obviously."

"Well, are you busy?"

"Yes, he is," Abumwe said. "I have another immediate task for him. I need him on Earth, right away."

Rigney turned to Abumwe. "And you were going to tell us about this when, exactly?"

"I just told you," Abumwe said. "Prior to this I have been

babysitting nine representatives, getting them to agree to our terms."

"How is that going?" Egan asked.

"As well as can be expected. The representative from Huckleberry is complaining, but the representative from Huckleberry is a complainer. The others see the opportunity here and are working on him. We'll have an agreement on time."

"Good."

"And you will need agreement on your end, Colonel."

Egan and Rigney looked at each other. "It's in process," Egan said.

"That doesn't sound as optimistic as I would like."

"It will get done. Right now the question is how messy it will have to be."

"I'd still like to talk about Lieutenant Wilson going to Earth," Rigney said. "We can't send a ship there. Not now."

"I have a solution to that," I said. "Well, sort of."

"Sort of," Rigney said.

"It involves a bit of technology that we sort of abandoned a few years ago."

"Abandoned why?"

"When we used it there was a slight tendency to . . . explode."

"Explode?" Hart said.

"Well, 'explode' maybe isn't the most accurate term. What *actually* happens is much more interesting."

As I floated over the surface of the planet Earth, a thought came to me: *One day I'd like to visit this planet without having to toss myself down its atmosphere.*

The small wire-frame sled I was currently sitting in was the size of a small buggy and entirely open to space; only my combat suit and a small supply of oxygen kept the vacuum of space from eating me whole. Behind me in the buggy was an experimental skip drive, one designed to take advantage of the relative flatness of space at the Lagrange points of two massive objects, say, a star and its planet, or a planet and its moon. The good news is that the theory behind this new type of skip drive checked out, which meant that, if this new drive was reliable, it could revolutionize how space travel happened.

The bad news was that despite our best efforts, it was only 98 percent reliable for masses under five tons, and the failure rate went up in chartable curve from there. For a ship the size of a standard Colonial frigate, the success rate dropped to a very unsettling seven percent. When the drive failed, the ship exploded. And when I say "exploded" I mean "interacted catastrophically with the topography of space/time in ways we're not entirely able to explain," but "explode" gets the gist of it, particularly with regard to what would happen to a human caught in it.

We could never fix it, and the Colonial Union and the Colonial Defense Forces had a strange aversion to having their ships potentially explode ninety-three times out of a hundred. Eventually the research was abandoned.

But there were still the small, very light vehicles we created with the prototype engines attached to them, currently stored in a warehouse module of Phoenix Station. They would be the perfect way for me to get to Earth both in a hurry—because I would only have to travel as far as the nearest Lagrange point—and undetected, because the sled was very small and could skip very close to the atmosphere of the planet. It was, in short, perfect for the mission.

As long as I didn't explode.

I did not explode.

Which, frankly, was a relief. It meant the hard part of my trip was over. Now all I had to do was let gravity do its work and just fall to the ground.

I unlatched myself from the sled and pushed off, getting

distance from it. Its fate would be to burn up in the upper atmosphere. I did not want to be there when it went.

My own trip through the atmosphere was thankfully uneventful. My nanobotic shield held perfectly well, the turbulence was mostly tolerable, and my descent through the lower reaches of the atmosphere was smartly managed by my parachute, which landed me, light as a feather, in a small park on the Virginia-side banks of the Potomac River, outside of Washington, D.C. As the nanobots that comprised my parachute disassociated into dust, I reflected on the fact that I had become a little jaded about falling to the surface of a planet from space.

This is my life now, I thought. I accessed my BrainPal to confirm the local time, which was 3:20 A.M. on a Sunday, and to confirm that I had landed near where I wanted to be: Alexandria, Virginia, in the USA.

"Wow," someone said, and I looked around. There was an older man, lying on a bench. He was either homeless or just liked sleeping in the park.

"Hello," I said.

"You just fell from the sky," he said.

"Brother, you don't know the half of it," I replied.

I came across who I was looking for several hours later, having brunch at an Alexandria restaurant, not too far from her home, which I did not visit even though I knew where it was, because, come on, that's rude.

She was sitting by herself on the restaurant patio, at a two-seater table near the patio's sidewalk railing. She had a Bloody Mary in one hand and a pencil in the other. The former she was drinking; the latter she was applying to a crossword puzzle. She was wearing a hat to block the sun and sunglasses, I suspect, to avoid eye contact with creeps.

I walked up and glanced down at the crossword puzzle. "Thirty-two down is 'paprika,'" I said.

"I knew that," she said, not looking up at me. "But thanks anyway, random annoying dude. Also, if you think butting into my crossword puzzle is a good way to hit on me, you should probably just keep walking. In fact, you should just keep walking anyway."

"That's a fine 'hello' to someone who's saved your life," I said. "Twice."

She looked up. Her mouth dropped open. Her Bloody Mary slipped out of her hand and hit the ground.

"Shit!" she said, flustered, at the spilled drink.

"That's better," I said. "Hello, Danielle."

Danielle Lowen, of the United States State Department, stood up as a waiter came to pick up her spilled drink. She looked me over. "It's really you," she said.

"Yes it is."

She looked me over again. "You're not *green*," she said.

I smiled. "I thought it might make me stick out."

"It's throwing me," she said. "Now that I see you without it I recognize how disgustingly young you look. I hate you."

"I assure you it's only temporary."

"Will you be trying purple next?"

"I think I'll stick with the classics."

The waiter had finished cleaning up the spilled drink and broken glass and ducked away. Danielle looked at me. "Well? Are you going to sit down or are we going to keep standing here awkwardly?"

"I'm waiting for an invitation," I said. "When we left off, I was told to keep walking."

Danielle grinned. "Harry Wilson, will you have brunch with me?"

"I would be delighted," I said, and stepped over the railing. When I did Danielle came over to me and gave me a fierce hug, and a peck on the cheek.

"Jesus, it's good to see you," she said.

"Thank you," I said. We both took our seats.

"Now tell me why you're here," she said, after we sat down.

"You don't think it's just to see you?" I asked.

"As much as I would like to, no," she said. "It's not like you live down the road." She frowned for a moment. "How *did* you get here, anyway?"

"It's classified."

"I'm close enough to stab you with a fork."

"I used a very small experimental craft."

"A flying saucer."

"More like a space dune buggy."

"A 'space dune buggy' doesn't sound very safe."

"It's perfectly safe, ninety-eight percent of the time."

"Where did you park it?"

"I didn't. It burned up in the upper atmosphere and I did a jump the rest of the way down."

"You and your jumps, Harry. There are easier ways to visit the planet Earth."

"At the moment there's really not," I said. "At least not for me."

The waiter returned with a new Bloody Mary for Danielle, and she ordered for the both of us. "I hope that's all right," she said, of the ordering.

"You know this place better than I do."

"So you dropped in. Tell me why."

"I need you to get me in to speak to the U.S. secretary of state."

"You need to speak to my dad."

"Well, what I really need to do is speak to the entire United Nations," I said. "But for the very short term I will settle for your father, yes."

"You couldn't send a note?"

"This isn't really something I could have put into a note."

"Try it now."

"All right," I said. " 'Dear Danielle Lowen: How are you? I am fine. The group that destroyed Earth Station and made it look like the Colonial Union did it is now planning to nuke the surface of your planet until it glows, and frame the Conclave for it. Hope you are well. Looking forward to rescuing you in space again soon. Your friend, Harry Wilson.' "

Danielle was quiet for a moment. "All right, you have a point," she said, finally.

"Thank you."

"That's accurate?" she asked. "The part about Equilibrium planning to use nuclear weapons against the Earth."

"Yes," I said. "I have all the documents and data with me." I tapped my temple to indicate my BrainPal. "The information is not yet one hundred percent confirmed but it comes from sources we can verify."

"Why does Equilibrium want to do that?"

"You're going to hate the reason, I assure you."

"Of course I'm going to hate it. There's no good reason to nuke an entire planet."

"It's not really about Earth," I said. "Equilibrium is pitting the Colonial Union and the Conclave against each other in the hope they'll destroy each other."

"I thought they had a different plan for that. One that didn't involve the Earth."

"They did, but then we found out about it. So they changed their plans to include you."

"They'll kill billions here just to make the two of you fight up there."

"That's about right."

Danielle glowered. "This is a fucked-up universe we live in, Harry."

"I've been telling you that for as long as I've known you."

"Yes, but before this I could still believe you might be *wrong* about it."

"Sorry."

"It's not your fault," Danielle said. "It might be the Colonial Union's fault. In fact, I'm pretty sure it is, if you go back far enough."

"You're not entirely wrong."

"No, I'm not. The Colonial Union—"

I held up a hand. Danielle paused. "You know you lecture me about the Colonial Union every time I see you," I said. "And every time I see you I tell you that you and I don't really disagree. If it's okay with you, I'd be fine with just having this bit of our interaction tabled as read, so we can move on to other things."

Danielle looked at me sourly. "I *like* ranting about the Colonial Union."

"I'm sorry," I said. "By all means please continue."

"It's too late for that," she said. "The moment's gone."

Our food arrived.

"Now I'm not hungry," Danielle said.

"It's difficult to keep an appetite in the face of global nuclear extinction," I said. I carved into a waffle.

"You don't seem to be having a problem," Danielle observed, dryly. "But then it's not your planet."

"It certainly is my planet," I said. "I'm from Indiana."

"But not recently."

"Recently enough, I assure you," I said. I took a bite of waffle, chewed it, and swallowed it. "The reason I can eat is because I have a plan."

"You have a plan."

"That's why I'm here."

"And you thought up this plan on your own, did you."

"No, Ambassador Abumwe thought it up," I said. "Most of it. I helped in the margins."

"Don't take this the wrong way—"

"This is gonna be good," I said, and took a drink of my orange juice.

"—but the fact it's Abumwe who thought up this plan is more reassuring than if you thought it up."

"Yes, I know," I said. "She's a grown-up."

"Yes," Danielle said. "Whereas you look like my kid brother."

"Despite the fact I'm older than you and Abumwe combined."

"Scratch that. You look like my kid brother's distractingly hot college roommate. And please stop telling me you're old enough to be my grandfather. The cognitive dissonance really ruins it for me."

I grinned. "You seem to be processing the end of days pretty well," I said.

"Do I?" Danielle said. "Yes, well. Rest assured that the moment the flirty banter stops I'm going to be well and truly losing my shit, Harry."

"Don't," I said. "Remember, we have a plan from a responsible grown-up."

"And what does this plan entail, Harry?"

"Several small things, and one very big thing," I said.

"And what's that?"

"The Earth trusting the Colonial Union."

"To do what?"

"To save you."

"Ah," Danielle said. "I can already tell you *that's* going to be a tough sell."

"And now you know why I'm here instead of sending you a note. And why I'm talking to you first."

"Harry," Danielle cautioned. "Just because we like each other as people doesn't mean that my father or anyone else will listen to you."

"Of course not," I said. "But us liking each other, and me saving your life twice, is enough to get my foot in the door. And then the plan will take over."

"It better be a good plan, Harry."

"It is. I promise."

"What else are you going to need besides us trusting you?"

"One of your ships," I said. "And, if you're not too busy, you."

"Why me?"

"Because we're going to go talk to Hafte Sorvalh, the head of the Conclave. You've been head of a mission to the Conclave very recently. If we get an agreement down here, we have things to talk about to her up there."

"The Conclave's officially not talking to you right now."

"Yes, I know. We have a plan."

"Abumwe again?"

"Yes."

"All right," Danielle said, and got out her PDA.

"What are you doing?"

"I'm calling Dad."

"Let me finish brunch first."

"I thought this was a matter of some urgency, Harry."

"It is," I said. "But I fell from the sky today. I could use a couple of waffles."

PART THREE

"Well, and here we are again," Hafte Sorvalh said, to the three of us. "And how completely unsurprising this seems to me."

Sorvalh's audience consisted of Ambassador Abumwe, Ambassador Lowen, and me, as their joint underling for the meeting. Sorvalh had her own underling with her, if one could genuinely call Vnac Oi, the head of intelligence for all of the Conclave, an underling. Sorvalh and the ambassadors were sitting; Oi and I, standing. I was doing a lot of standing in meetings recently.

We five were in her private study at Conclave headquarters. On the other side of the door, literally and figuratively, were ambassadorial staff and experts and advisors, from Earth, from the Colonial Union, and from the Conclave. If one was quiet, one could feel their combined howling frustration at not being in the room at the moment.

"May I be honest with you?" Lowen asked Sorvalh. I noted that I found it difficult to think of her as "Danielle" when she was on the job. Not because she materially changed her personality when she was working, but simply out of respect for her position.

"Ambassador, I believe the point of this current discussion is to be honest with each other, is it not?" Sorvalh asked.

"I assumed that there would be more of us in the room for this discussion."

Sorvalh smiled one of her absolutely-terrifying-to-humans

smiles. "I believe each of our staffs thought the same thing, Ambassador," she said. "But I have always found that there's an inverse relationship between the number of people in a room and the amount of useful work that can be done. Now that I am the person in charge of things, I find it even more so. Do you not?"

"No," Lowen said. "I think you're right, by and large."

"Of course I am. And, Madams Ambassador, I believe that the reason we are here is to have a *definitively* useful meeting, are we not?"

"It is to be hoped," Abumwe said.

"Precisely," Sorvalh said. "So, no, Ambassador. I believe we have precisely the correct number of people in the room."

"Yes, Premier Sorvalh," Lowen said.

"Then let's not waste any more time." Sorvalh turned her attention to Abumwe. "You may begin, Ambassador."

"Premier Sorvalh, Equilibrium intends to attack the Earth with nuclear weapons and make it appear to the Colonial Union that it is the Conclave that initiated the attack."

"Yes," Sorvalh said. "Vnac Oi here gave me a précis of the report you prepared for us. I assume you are going to ask us for our help in thwarting the attack, seeing that we are meant to be blamed for it."

"No, Premier," Abumwe said. "We want the attack to proceed."

Sorvalh reared back slightly at this, looked over to Lowen, and then back at Abumwe. "Well!" she said, after a moment. "This is certainly a bold and unexpected strategy. I'm fascinated to learn how this will be beneficial to any of us, not least the poor irradiated citizens of Earth."

"Lieutenant," Abumwe said to me.

"We want the attack to proceed because we need to draw out Equilibrium," I said. "The group is small, driven, and has been difficult for us—any of us—to locate and attack. The one successful attack against the group as a whole was by Rafe Daquin, when he escaped from their control. But other than that they've been very good at working in the shadows."

"Yes they have," Oi said. "We've purged known Equilibrium operatives, as I'm sure both Earth and the Colonial Union have." Abumwe and Lowen both nodded here. "But at this point they don't appear to need any additional operational intelligence to continue their plans."

"Or they simply have new allies," Abumwe said.

"Either way your man is correct." Oi motioned at me with a tendril.

"We found their new base," Abumwe said.

"Where?" asked Oi.

"On Sedna," I said. "A dwarf planet on the edge of Earth's solar system. We confirmed it just before Ambassador Abumwe's ship skipped here."

"Then this conversation should be about how you've wiped them out already," Sorvalh said.

"It's more complicated than that," Abumwe said.

"We know where their new base is, but their fleet—the fleet with which they intend to wipe out Earth—isn't there," I said. "They're showing cautiousness."

"So even if the Colonial Union destroyed the base, Earth would still be vulnerable to attack," Lowen said.

"That's why we need the attack to proceed," Abumwe said. "Draw out the ships over Earth, and simultaneously destroy Equilibrium at their base. Leave nowhere for either element to go."

"I'm still not clear how this involves the Conclave," Sorvalh said.

"We can't do both," I said. "Equilibrium will only act if it's confident the Colonial Union has no way to respond to their attack on Earth. We need to commit a substantial portion of our CDF fleet to give the appearance we're threatening the nine planets declaring their independence. We need to be seen taking ships away from the skip drive line, to make it look like it would take days for our ships to respond to an attack on Earth. We also have to have enough ships to immediately respond to Equilibrium's attack, hidden where it would not think to look for them. We need to be sure we have enough ships to keep even a single nuke from making it to the Earth's atmosphere. That means generously overestimating the number of ships we need."

"So you'll need the Conclave to attack the Equilibrium base," Oi said.

"Yes," Abumwe said. "And we want you to allow us to hide a fleet in Conclave space, at skip distance, so we can respond immediately to the Equilibrium attack on Earth. We don't believe Equilibrium will look for our fleet in your space."

"That means trusting you not to attack whatever system we'd put you in," Oi said.

"You don't have to trust us," Abumwe said. "Put whatever protections you like on us. Just give us a place to park our fleet."

"And you?" Sorvalh turned her attention to Lowen. "It's still the general consensus on your planet that the Colonial Union engineered the attack on Earth Station and killed thousands, including much of your global diplomatic corps. You're telling me that the Earth trusts *them*"—she flicked a hand to encompass Abumwe and me—"to protect *you* from annihilation."

"It wasn't an easy sale, no," Lowen admitted. "This is where the Conclave comes in again. Our assent for this plan is contingent on your acceptance. If you don't trust the Colonial Union, we don't trust it."

"And what then?" Sorvalh asked. "What if I don't, in fact, trust it?"

"Then we give you everything we have on the attack," Abumwe said. "We give it to you and pray that, despite your recent actions, you are willing to protect the Earth. You did before. Your predecessor General Gau did, at the very least."

"We wouldn't do that out of the goodness of our souls," Sorvalh said. "If we intervened to the benefit of the Earth, you can assume that we would no longer be dissuaded from pulling it into our sphere of influence. So, Ambassador, you're asking me to believe that the Colonial Union could accept that. And even accept possibly in time allowing the Earth to join the Conclave."

"The Colonial Union accepts at this point that the Earth is lost to us," Abumwe said, nodding at Lowen. "We have told as much to the governments on Earth that will still speak to us. It will no longer be the captive source of our soldiers and colonists. We are now beginning to make the changes that will allow us to survive in this new reality. That being the case, we no longer factor the Earth's participation, voluntary or otherwise, into our plans. We do not want to see it as part of the Conclave. But better the Earth is in the Conclave than destroyed. It is humanity's home, Premier."

Sorvalh nodded and turned to Oi. "Your analysis, please."

"This is a lot, Premier," Oi said. "And from a people we have no historical reason to trust. At all."

"I understand that," Sorvalh said. "For the moment, treat the information given as accurate."

"Then leaving aside the moral issue of leaving a planet open to a genocidal attack, there's very little upside here for the Conclave," Oi said. "Both the Earth and the Colonial Union need something from us but offer no benefit to us outside the destruction of Equilibrium, which we could now attack ourselves and cripple operationally. They need us but we don't need them. And bluntly, there are hundreds of our member species who would be happy to be rid of either or both. There's still no way politically that we could bring Earth into the Conclave without tearing it apart."

"You're saying we shouldn't be involved," Sorvalh said.

" 'Should' is a relative term," Oi said. "Remember that I am leaving aside the moral dimension of this for the moment. What I am saying is that if we *do* get involved, there is almost no upside to it for us."

"Except, perhaps, the gratitude of the two houses of humanity," Sorvalh said.

Oi snorted at this. "With no offense to our human friends here, Premier, I wouldn't set any great store in the gratitude of humanity."

"Too true," Sorvalh agreed.

"So you won't help us," Abumwe said.

"No, I won't," Sorvalh said. "Not without obvious benefit for me. For the Conclave."

"What do you want?" Lowen asked.

"What do I want?" Sorvalh repeated to Lowen, and leaned in toward the human ambassadors, accentuating just how large a creature she was relative to our species, and also, how exasperated. "I want to not have to think of you, Ambassador Lowen! Or of you, Ambassador Abumwe! Or of humanity. At all. Can you understand this, Madams Ambassador? Do you understand how truly tiring your people are? How much of my *time* has gone into dealing with humans?"

Sorvalh threw up her hands. "Do you realize that I have seen the two of you—and *you*, Lieutenant Wilson—more in the past two of your years than I have seen the representatives of most of the Conclave's constituent members? Do you know how much of my predecessor's time was taken up with you? If I could magically wish humanity away, I would do it. Instantly."

"It's a fair call," I said. Abumwe turned to look at me, incredulously, and I was reminded that not too long ago, she could hardly stand me. It might be we were about to be headed back down that road.

Sorvalh noticed. "Don't glare at the lieutenant, Ambassador.

"He's perfectly correct, and I think you know it. It is a fair call. Humanity is more trouble than it's worth. However."

Here the reluctance in Sorvalh's voice was palpable. "I cannot magically wish humanity away. I am stuck with you, both of you. And you with us. So. Here is what I want in order to help you."

Sorvalh pointed to Abumwe. "From the Colonial Union, I want a comprehensive nonaggression treaty with full diplomatic trade relations. Meaning no more of these nonsense back channels and saber rattling. Once we eradicate Equilibrium, we can jointly reveal everything we knew about it, end all speculation, and make the argument that a great deal of *our* recent hostility was manufactured by them. I can use that to push the treaty through the Grand Assembly, and you can use it to convince whoever it is you need to as well."

"You're asking me to sell the Conclave an ally," Abumwe said.

"Not at all. I don't think either of our governments is ready for that. I'm merely asking to no longer so actively and intentionally be at each other's throats."

Sorvalh turned to Lowen. "Likewise, a nonaggression pact and full diplomatic and trade relations with Earth."

"I don't see how we can be aggressive toward the Conclave," Lowen said.

"You can't," Sorvalh agreed. "But it's not for the Conclave's protection. It's for yours. From us."

"I understand."

"Good," Sorvalh said. "Finally, the same nonaggression pact and full diplomatic and trade relations between Earth and the Colonial Union. Because while for now I don't want you two merging back together, you entirely separated will always be a danger to the Conclave. For better or worse, for all our sakes, this division of humanity has to come to an end."

"It's a three-way stalemate," Oi observed.

"It's perfect," I said.

"It might be," Sorvalh said. "Thus are we all bound to each other in a mutual agreement to leave each other alone, while still keeping open actual lines of communication and commerce."

"It's a nice thought, Premier," Oi said. "There's just one problem."

"Everyone who is not in this room," Abumwe said.

"Yes," Oi agreed. "You said, Premier, that the more people involved, the longer things will take. This set of agreements will involve *everyone*. You're never going to get such a treaty through the Grand Assembly. And I doubt that Ambassador Abumwe will get sign-off from her people. And as for Ambassador Lowen, well. Earth doesn't even have a functional global government. She literally can't make an agreement that the entire planet will abide. This won't get done."

"Fine," Sorvalh said. "Then we don't let anyone outside this room have a vote."

"They won't like that," Oi said.

"Your head of intelligence is understating the case," I added.

"I don't care," Sorvalh said. "Everyone in this room understands this is a thing that should be done. We are all agreed to this. Yes?"

Abumwe and Lowen nodded.

"Then let's call it done," Sorvalh said.

"It's an imperial action," Oi warned.

"No," I said. "It's an opportunistic one." I turned to Lowen. "The Louisiana Purchase."

"You're speaking gibberish," Lowen said.

"Go with me here," I said, and looked at Sorvalh. "Back on Earth, a long time ago, a U.S. president named Thomas Jefferson was offered a deal on territory that would more than double the size of his country. The Louisiana Purchase. Technically speaking, he wasn't empowered to accept the deal—the

U.S. Constitution was ambiguous about whether the president could authorize the purchase. But he did it anyway. Because it doubled the size of the country, and then what was Congress going to do? Give it back?"

"We're not buying land, Lieutenant," Abumwe pointed out.

"No, but you're buying something else: peace," I said. "And you're buying it by mutually acting against Equilibrium, which exists to bring the end of the Conclave and the Colonial Union, and is planning immediate harm to Earth, with immediate consequences for the Conclave and the Colonial Union. So don't wait. Premier Sorvalh is right. Agree to terms here and now and present it as a fait accompli. Then get everyone busy with punching Equilibrium in the throat. We stand or fall together on this one. I prefer to stand."

"By the time it's all done, it's too late to go back," Oi said. "There's a new normal."

"It's not a bad idea."

"It's a *terrible* idea," Oi said. "It just has the advantage of being better than the other option."

"Is that your assessment as my head of intelligence?" Sorvalh asked Oi.

"My assessment as your head of intelligence is that the Colonial Union has consistently shown itself to be the greatest single threat to the Conclave, and Earth isn't much better," Oi said. "If you have an opportunity to take them out of your equation, then do it. If it means presenting this as a done deal that isn't able to be taken back, do it. You'll get pushback and criticism for it. But you may still have the goodwill of the Grand Assembly for holding the Conclave together."

"Oi, will this work?"

"You're the premier of the Conclave, madam," Oi said. "If you want to make this work, it will. When you can tell them about it, mind you. We need to destroy Equilibrium first. For *that* to work, it will need to be as covert as possible."

Sorvalh nodded and turned to Abumwe. "Can you agree to this?"

Abumwe nodded. "Yes."

"Can you make it *stick*?"

"I will tell them they have no other option but to make it stick."

"And you, Ambassador Lowen?" Sorvalh asked.

"You're asking me if I can accept a deal that saves my planet from nuclear annihilation," Lowen said. "I'm pretty sure I can sell it."

"Don't sell it," I said. "Present it as sold."

"Agreed," Oi said, and pointed to the door. "When we walk out of here it's done."

"Yes?" Sorvalh asked.

"Yes," Abumwe said.

"Yes," Lowen said.

Sorvalh smiled, and it was terrifying, and glorious. "And so we learn how simple it is to change the history of the universe," Sorvalh said. "All you need is for every other thing to have gone so horribly wrong first."

She stood, with Abumwe and Lowen following her example almost immediately. "Come, Madams Ambassador. Let us announce our new era of peace together. Let us dare anyone to take it from us. And then, let us go to war together. For the first, and hopefully last, time."

Two weeks later, on October second, using the standard calendar of the Colonial Union, and at roughly three in the afternoon, the Colonial Union received official notice from nine of its colony worlds that they were declaring themselves independent from the union. Each of these planets was independent of the others but declared immediate diplomatic relations with each other and offered the same to the Colonial Union.

In times past the Colonial Union might have sent a single

ship per planet to deal with the uprising; when a planet has no real defenses against you that you yourself did not create, you didn't have to make that much of an effort. But since the *Tubingen* event over Khartoum, it was evident that there had to be a change in strategy, and in the Colonial Union's response to rebellion. Especially to a rebellion that involved multiple planets simultaneously.

The skies above the rebellious worlds added new constellations as a flood of CDF ships flowed into their space. Each rebellious planet received no fewer than a hundred ships—a piece of psychological warfare designed to cow and intimidate those trying for their freedom.

They would not be cowed. They shouted their defiance and dared the Colonial Union to do its worst.

This went on in a seemingly intractable manner. There was no clear end to the stalemate. The planets demanded the Colonial Union and the CDF withdraw from their skies. The Colonial Union replied that they would not. The large majority of the human military fleet was now permanently stationed above the worlds that it used to protect.

On October 21, a ship appeared in the skies above Earth, a trading ship registered to a world of the Conclave. It was the *Hooh Issa Tun*, and it had disappeared almost a year before. In a moment, the *Hooh Issa Tun* was no longer alone as another ship of Conclave ancestry appeared, and another, and another. A student of recent history would recognize the staggered appearance as a bit of theater. The late General Tarsem Gau, when he was the head of the Conclave, would do the same thing when his grand fleet appeared over the sky of an unauthorized colony. The Conclave would then give the colony the choice of being evacuated or destroyed.

The Earth would not have the same choice. The fleet would follow the same dynamic as Gau's fleet, waiting until the very last ship arrived, waiting until the audience below could register its immensity, before launching its weapons to destroy those watching below.

Which meant that timing was going to be a tricky thing indeed.

The satellites the Colonial Union placed in orbit around the Earth registered the *Hooh Issa Tun* the second it arrived in Earth space. The data was shot at the speed of light to a brace of very special skip drones located at the L4 Lagrangian point in the Earth-moon system, each carrying the prototype skip drive designed to work at those gravitationally flat spots in space.

Three of the drones skipped immediately. One of them arrived at its destination as a topographically interesting shower of metal shards. The other two arrived intact.

And in a space outside the solar system that housed Premier Hafte Sorvalh's home world of Lalah, two fleets readied their final preparations for attack.

The first fleet was a small one: ten ships, specifically selected by Vnac Oi. The second one was substantially larger. Two hundred CDF ships waited—had waited—for battle.

Back at Earth, the influx of ships had stopped at one hundred eight, a number ever so slightly higher than either the Colonial Union's or Conclave's estimates of the fleet. Their first action would be to begin disabling the Earth's network of satellites. This would take it several minutes.

The satellites marked the position of each of the fleet's ships above the Earth and shot that information to the waiting skip drones. Three of them immediately skipped. This time all three made it.

Inside the CDF ships, each of them was receiving a list of their primary, secondary, and tertiary targets. This transfer of information, and the acknowledgment thereof, took on average ten seconds.

Twenty seconds after that, every single CDF ship simultaneously skipped into Earth space.

Including the *Chandler*. Who alone among the fleet did not have targets. Its job was to observe. On the *Chandler* were Ode Abumwe, Colonels Egan and Rigney, and Vnac Oi of the Conclave. And me.

From Nava Balla's bridge we watched as CDF ships appeared less than a kilometer from their primary target ships and surgically attacked with particle beams and other relatively low-carnage armament, pinpointing propulsion, navigation, and weapons systems.

"Put the comms on speaker, please," Abumwe asked Balla, who nodded and did Abumwe's bidding.

The air was a cacophony of CDF ships reporting back, confirming their attacks were successful. In less than two minutes, the entire Equilibrium fleet had been disabled.

Disabled, not destroyed.

"Are you ready?" Abumwe asked Rafe Daquin.

"You know I am," Daquin responded.

Abumwe smiled at this. "Then begin."

"Pilots of the attacking ships," Daquin said, and his words were broadcast to each of the ships we had disabled. When we could make a reasonable guess as to the identity and species of the pilot of the ship, we automatically translated Daquin's words into their language. Otherwise we relied on the ships having translation software. "My name is Rafe Daquin. The pilot of the *Chandler*. I am like you. My ship was attacked and taken by an organization I learned was called Equilibrium. Equilibrium killed my crew and singled me out as a pilot. They took my body from me and forced me, like you, to pilot my ship alone and to do their bidding.

"We know that you have been forced into this attack. We know that you were offered a terrible bargain for your complicity: death if you refused and the promise of your bodies returned if you accepted. You should know Equilibrium never intended to return you to your bodies. To them you are disposable. You were always disposable. After this attack you would have been killed and your ships destroyed in order to preserve their goals and their anonymity.

"You may not have been made fully aware of the scope of your mission. It was to attack this planet, the planet Earth, with nuclear weapons. Those weapons would have obliterated life there and the lingering aftereffects would have made the planet uninhabitable. We, who are human, and for whom this is our home world, could not allow that to happen. We have stopped you from carrying out your mission.

"We have attacked your ships. We could have easily destroyed them, and you. We choose not to do this. We have not destroyed your ships. We have not destroyed you. We did not because we know you did not have a choice. We know because I did not have a choice when I was in the same position as you.

"We are giving you a choice now. The choice is this: Surrender your ships now, and we will care for you, protect you, return you to the Conclave, alive and intact, so you may go home, be with your families, and god willing, be given new bodies to live your lives.

"Some of you may already be trying to repair your ship systems to carry out your mission. If you do, we will have to stop you. If we have to stop you, we may have to destroy you. The weapons you carry have too much death in them. We can't allow the launch of a single one.

"I am like you. I am still like you. I have stayed this way because I was waiting for a moment like this. So you would know, you would truly know, that you are not alone and that you are not without a choice. That you don't have to kill in order to live. That your life can be returned to you, and all you have to do is spare the innocent people that an organization who has enslaved you wants you to kill.

"I am Rafe Daquin. I am like you. I live and I am no one's

slave. I am here to ask you to surrender now. Surrender and live. Surrender and let others live. Tell me what you will do."

And then we waited.

For close to a minute there was dead silence on the comms. And then.

"I am Chugli Ahgo, pilot of the *Frenner Reel*. I surrender to you, Rafe Daquin."

"Iey Iey Noh. Pilot of *Chundawoot*. I surrender."

"Lopinigannui Assunderwannaon of the *Lhutstun*. Holy shit, human. Get me the fuck out of this thing."

"I am Tunder Spenn. I pilot the *Hooh Issa Tun*. I want to see my family. I want to go home."

I helped Rafe write that. I just want that out there.

One hundred four of the pilots surrendered their ships. Two sabotaged their internal systems after attack and before Rafe sent his message, committing suicide, I guess from fear of what would happen if they were captured—or from fear of what Equilibrium would do to them if they were captured. One pilot had what could best be described as a psychotic break and was unable to surrender or indeed do much of anything else. We took the pilot out of the control loop of its ship before it could hurt itself or anyone else.

One pilot refused to surrender, managed to repair his weapons systems, and tried to launch his nukes. His ship was destroyed before the nukes were out of their tubes.

"You're going to get credit for this," Oi said to Abumwe, as the surrender notices came in. "You've spared the lives of pilots of dozens of Conclave species. They'll remember it. It was smart."

"It was his idea," Abumwe said, pointing to me.

"Then it was smart of you," Oi said.

"Thank you," I said. "But I didn't suggest it to be smart."

Oi dipped its tendrils in acknowledgment.

As the surrender notices came in we received the first news from the Conclave attack on Equilibrium's base on Sedna. The Conclave chose not to wipe out the Equilibrium members it found there. Instead it disabled the base's life support and communication systems and destroyed any ship or vehicle capable of getting anyone in the base out of it.

Then the commander of the mission gave those inside the base a choice: surrender, or not so slowly freeze to death.

Most chose not to freeze.

In the coming weeks and months the scope of Equilibrium was revealed, its agents named, and its ability to wreak havoc on the Conclave, the Colonial Union, or Earth negated. In the end it was difficult to believe that Equilibrium could have ever presented a threat at all. But then it never would have, had the Colonial Union, the Conclave, and Earth not been so determined to be a threat to themselves.

"Interesting times we live in," Danielle Lowen said to me. She and I were at the Thomas Jefferson Memorial, in Washington, D.C. Hart Schmidt was with us, on his first trip to Earth—the surface of it, at least. He was determined to be the most touristy tourist who had ever touristed, and was presently snapping pictures of the statue of Jefferson from every conceivable angle. It was late March, and the cherry blossoms were beginning to bloom.

"You know there's a curse about living in interesting times," I said to her. "It's attributed to the Chinese."

"That's a myth, you know," Danielle said. "The Chinese never said anything that foolish."

I smiled at this. "Ode says hello, incidentally," I said. Ode Abumwe, who had retired from active diplomatic duty to take on a new role: primary architect of the new constitution that the Colonial Union was creating with its colonies.

"How goes the nation building?" Danielle asked.

"When I last talked to her about it she said it was an immense pain in her ass, but there was just no other alternative. Her deal with you and Sorvalh, ironically enough, served to force the Colonial Union to accept her deal with the rebellious colonies. They couldn't accept a fait accompli agreement with the Earth and Conclave and not accept one from their own colonies. I think that's why she was appointed to run the discussions. The higher-ups wanted to punish her."

"The irony being that they're making her the mother of the new Colonial Union. She's going to be remembered forever for that."

"If she can get a deal."

"This is Ode Abumwe, Harry," Danielle said. "As if she's not going to get a deal."

We watched Hart take his photos.

"I can't help but notice you're still not green," Danielle said to me. "I thought this natural skin tone thing was just supposed to be a summer look for you."

"I've been busy," I said.

"We've all been busy."

"All right, fine," I said. "I also missed being this particular tone of me."

"Is this indicative of anything? Subconsciously or otherwise?"

"Probably not."

"Right."

"Fine," I said. "I might be thinking of retiring."

"Hanging up the superbody and aging like a normal, decent human should?"

"Maybe," I said. "This is only an idle thought."

"If nothing else, you can't say that the Colonial Union didn't get its money out of you, Harry."

"No, I suppose not," I said.

"If you did retire, where would you go? What would you do?"

"I haven't thought that far out."

"I have an opening on my staff," Danielle said.

"I don't want to work for you, Dani."

"I'm a terrific boss, and I'll brutally sabotage the career of any underling who says different."

"You should use that as a recruiting statement."

"What makes you think I don't?"

I smiled at this. Hart was now photographing the bits of the Declaration of Independence carved into the walls of the monument.

"Seriously, Harry," Danielle said, after a minute. "Come back to Earth."

"Why?"

"You know why," she said. "And you can now."

"Maybe I will," I said.

"*Maybe.*"

"Don't rush me. I've got a lot to work out."

"All right," Danielle said. "Just don't take too long."

"Fair enough," I said, and took her hand.

"Interesting times we live in," Danielle repeated. "That's not meant to be a curse. I like interesting. I like it now, anyway."

"So do I," I said. She squeezed my hand.

"This place is great!" Hart said, coming up to the both of us.

"Glad you like it," I said.

"I really do," he said. He looked at the both of us, excited. "So. What's next?"

AN ALTERNATE
"THE LIFE OF THE MIND"
Deleted and Alternate Scenes

Introduction

The End of All Things took me longer to write than most of my books do, in part because I had a number of false starts. These false starts weren't bad—in my opinion—and they were useful in helping me figure out what was best for the book; for example, determining which point-of-view characters I wanted to have, whether the story should be in first or third person, and so on. But at the same time it's annoying to write a bunch of stuff and then go *Yeaaaaah, that's not it.* So it goes.

Through various false starts and diversions, I ended up writing nearly 40,000 words—almost an entire short novel!—of material that I didn't directly use. Some of it was recast and repurposed in different directions, and a lot of it was simply left to the side. The thing is when I throw something out of a book, I don't just delete it. I put it into an "excise file" and keep it just in case it'll come in handy later.

Like now: I've taken various bits from the excise file and with them have crafted a first chapter of an alternate version of *The Life of the Mind*, the first novella of *The End of All Things*. This version (roughly) covers the same events, with (roughly) the same characters, but with a substantially different narrative direction.

In an alternate universe, an alternate version of me went ahead with this version, and *The End of All Things* ended up being a rather different book. Which would be cool. I'd like to meet up with that John Scalzi and trade books.

Please note: This version of the story is noncanonical and

mildly spoilery for the version that is, in fact, canonical. While you don't have to read the official version of *The Life of the Mind* to read this (or to enjoy it), I recommend that you do to fully appreciate the compare and contrast.

Also, this version ends on a bit of a cliff-hanger. Which will never be resolved. Sorry about that.

Enjoy!

—JS

The *Robert Anton* skipped into the Inhe system, near a small asteroid that in the not too recent past had served as a Rraey space station and repair dock. The Rraey had officially abandoned it, along with a substantial number of other territories, after a series of military political setbacks, contracting back to the species' core planets and systems. "Officially abandoned" did not mean it was not in use, however.

Control, sent Giovanni Carranza, pilot and captain of the *Robert Anton. This is the* Robert Anton, *requesting docking assistance.*

"Copy, *Robert Anton,*" said an artificially generated voice, the standard voice of Control. "You're some distance away. Can you maneuver any closer to base?"

Negative, Carranza said. *Engines are dead. Maneuvering jets are dead. Both died on the other side of the skip.*

"How did you get to skip distance?"

Inertia, Carranza said. *Burned the engines as long as I could before I had to take them offline. Saved enough energy to run the skip drive. It was a very slow trip.*

"Copy that," Control said. "Your status otherwise, please."

The Anton is heavily damaged, Carranza said. *Hull compromised, weapons systems partially destroyed. Communications work, obviously, but outside sensors are dead. I knew I skipped from timing alone. If anyone other than me were on the ship, they'd be long dead. We're a mess.*

"Did you complete your mission?"

There was a hesitation. *Yes*, Carranza said. *The mission was completed. It wasn't pretty but it got done.*

"It's going to take us some time to get you back to dock," Control said. "We'd like to start analysis of your mission as soon as possible. Please send along your mission logs and recordings, as well as your damage report."

Sending, Carranza said.

"Thank you," Control said.

The Anton *took a beating. I'm not sure it's repairable at this point.*

"I'm looking at your damage report now. You may be right about that."

What does that mean for me?

"You don't need to worry about that right now."

You and I agreed that if this mission was successful that I would be done, Carranza said.

"I'm well aware of our agreement," Control replied.

I don't want the state of the Anton *held against me.*

"We asked you to complete the mission," Control said. "You did what we asked you to do."

I know it's been harder for you to get more ships. To get more pilots.

Control didn't say anything to this.

I would like my body back, Carranza said. *I would like to go home.*

"Don't worry," Control said. "We'll take care of you."

Thank you, Carranza said, and then died as Control signaled the release of a neurotoxin into his brain. The effect was instantaneous; Carranza had felt relief that his wishes would be granted and then he felt nothing at all.

The person behind Control waited until it received the signal that Carranza's brain was past any attempt at revival—not long at all—and then ordered tugs to bring the *Anton* into dock and crews to take what was salvageable from the ship before reducing it to scrap.

Carranza had been correct that it was harder to get ships recently, but the *Anton*'s useful days were done. As were Carranza's. Pilots were also hard to come by. But their usefulness was limited by their ability to believe they would ever be free. There would be no way for Carranza to believe that after today.

A waste.

But fortunately, a replacement was on the way.

"The time has come for treasonous ideas," said Otha Durham, from his lectern.

An amused murmur rippled through the corps of Colonial Union diplomats, assembled in one of the State Department's conference theaters. Durham, undersecretary of state for the Colonial Union, and speaking to the crowd on the occasion of an otherwise-standard assembly to award a medal to one of their number, smiled along with them.

"I know what you're thinking," he said, and then assumed the part of a bored diplomat in his audience. "Oh, God, there Durham goes again, pretending to have big thoughts and presenting them with *such drama*." He smiled again as laughs emerged from his audience, and held up his hands as if to acknowledge an affectionate criticism. "Fair call. Fair call. I don't think it's any secret that I've made dramatic statements a calling card of my career. But work with me for a minute here."

Durham looked out over his audience, becoming serious. "For decades—scratch that, for centuries—the Colonial Union has been charged with the role of keeping humanity safe and secure in our universe. A universe which was and continues to be hostile to the idea that humans exist within it. Ever since we have made our presence known in space, other species and other powers have sought to remove us—to eradicate us. And if we know anything about humanity it is this: We don't go down without a fight.

"And so we have fought. Humanity has fought, for centuries, to earn and keep our place in the universe. The Colonial Union and the Colonial Defense Forces has fought that fight for our species, for centuries."

Durham shrugged, acknowledging the fact of centuries of near-constant warfare. "So be it," he said. "But where does that leave us, the diplomatic corps of the Colonial Union? We have existed all this time, alongside the Colonial Defense Forces, but as an afterthought, an also-ran—because not only was the idea that diplomacy with the alien races we encountered might be a useful tool ridiculed, it was indeed considered very nearly a treasonous thought.

"How can we seriously think diplomacy could work when time and time again the other species out here with us attacked us, killed our colonists, and claimed the planets and systems we had claimed for our own? In this light, how could diplomacy be seen as anything other than an abdication of responsibility for the species? How could it be anything other than treason?"

Durham looked out at the diplomats assembled before him, quiet now.

"Diplomacy as treason. Reaching out with an open hand instead of a fist, treason. The idea that intelligences that evolved on different worlds, in different ways and in different environments, might yet still find a common ground, treason. If you consider all these things almost fundamentally a betrayal of humanity, it makes sense that in the end, all you have left is the war. The fight. The struggle that leads to ruin, for one or both species."

And here Durham smiled. "But this is the thing," he said, and then motioned to the diplomats attending his words. "We know better. We have always known better. The Colonial Defense Force's battle for us is often necessary, and sometimes inevitable. But when the opportunity comes for the open hand rather than the fist that, too, is often necessary.

"And now, also inevitable. The Colonial Union has long—has too long—relied on the planet Earth to provide it with the soldiers the Colonial Defense Forces needs to fight our battles and enforce our will. But we no longer have that option. Colonel John Perry's appearance in Earth's skies with the Conclave trade delegation put our relationship with the Earth on hold; the destruction of Earth Station, the planet's sole egress into space, destroyed it."

Durham looked directly at Ambassador Ode Abumwe, sitting in the front row of his audience with her team, nodding to her in recognition of her presence on Earth Station when it was destroyed. Abumwe nodded back.

"The Earth wrongly blames us for its destruction, but right or wrong, we can't go back to what was before," Durham continued. "Now the Colonial Union will need to find soldiers from its own colonies, from its own planetary populations—a transition that will take time, and is already causing no small amount of unrest in the Colonial Union's previously peaceable ranks.

"And in the meantime, the formerly *treasonous* idea of diplomacy becomes the Colonial Union's primary tool. To make allies. To buy time. To secure our place in the universe, not with a weapon, but with reason. Diplomacy is now the primary resource by which the Colonial Union, and by extension humanity, keeps its place. What was treason has now become a treasure."

"Which, clearly and obviously, brings us to Ambassador Ode Abumwe," Durham said, lightly. Once again, laughter rippled through the assembled diplomats. Durham motioned for Abumwe to rise and to stand next to him at the lectern. She did so. Durham's assistant Renea Tam also approached the lectern, wooden box in hand.

"Ambassador Abumwe, over the last year you and your team have found yourself at the center of a number of diplomatic storms," Durham said, turning to her. "When you could, you triumphed. When you could not triumph, you were able to at least find a silver lining to some of the Colonial Union's darkest clouds. We have asked a lot of you, and of your people. None of you have disappointed us. Time and again you've impressed us with your determination and your resourcefulness. Also, the fact that one of your team saved the daughter of the United States secretary of state from the destruction of Earth Station was no small feat." Another ripple of laugher. "The initiative your team shows flows from the top. It is your leadership that set the example, for them and for all of us.

"The Colonial Union owes much to you and your team in these difficult times," Durham said, and nodded to Tam, who opened the wooden box, revealing a medal and a framed document. "As a symbol of the regard of both the Colonial Union Department of State, and the secretary herself, it is my absolute pleasure to present you with the Distinguished Honor Award, for your exceptional and outstanding service." He lifted the medal with its ribbon out of the box and placed it around Abumwe's neck. The assembled diplomats applauded and Abumwe's team leapt to their feet and cheered. Abumwe offered up one of her rare smiles to them.

Durham held up a hand to silence the audience. "On a personal note," he said, and turned to Abumwe, "Ambassador, I have known you since you first arrived at the State Department. You were an intern and I was on my first posting, and that was"—here Durham intentionally mumbled a number—"years ago. Even then you were a smart, perceptive, driven, and serious person. The first three of these I would never fault. They have taken you far. But I still believe that you are sometimes more serious than you absolutely need to be." He nodded to Tam again, who set down the medal box and reached into her suit jacket to offer a small object to Durham, who took it. "And so in addition to the Distinguished Honor Award, as a token of personal esteem, my dear friend Ode, I offer you this." He presented the object to Abumwe, who took it. It was a funny-shaped rubber doll.

"What do I do with this?" Abumwe said.

"Squeeze it," Durham said.

Abumwe did so. Its eyes popped out and it offered up a squeaky chuckle. The diplomats laughed.

"Thank you, Otha," Abumwe said. "I don't know what to say."

"On the contrary, I think you know *exactly* what to say," Durham said. "You're just too diplomatic to say it."

Durham spent an hour at the after-ceremony reception meeting and greeting with Abumwe's team, and in particular making the acquaintance of Hart Schmidt and Harry Wilson, the two members of Abumwe's team who escaped Earth Station as it was literally disintegrating around them.

"I don't imagine that's something you want to relive much," Durham said to Schmidt, after he had been introduced to him and one of his friend's friends, whose name vaporized from Durham's mind almost instantly after the introductions were made.

"Well, I was actually unconscious for the worst of it, sir," Schmidt said, and nodded to Wilson. "Harry is the one who can tell you what it was really like."

"And what was it really like?" Durham asked Wilson, turning to him.

"Completely terrifying," Wilson said, and everyone laughed. "Or it would have been, if I hadn't been actively distracted by trying to stay alive on a trip through the Earth's atmosphere. Which was also terrifying."

"That's right, you skydived from Earth Station down to the planet."

"Yes, sir."

"Which means you're the one who saved the U.S. secretary of state's daughter."

"Danielle Lowen," Harry said. "I did. She's a diplomat in her own right as well."

"Yes, of course," Durham said. "But the fact that she was the secretary's daughter is one reason why the United States, if no one else on Earth, will still speak to us. So thank you for that."

"Just doing my job," Harry said.

"I hope we gave you a medal for that."

"You did," Harry said. "The CDF gave me one, too. I'm all medaled up."

"Very good," Durham said. "Now let me buy you a drink to go with them."

Wilson smiled. "I knew I liked this posting."

Shortly thereafter Durham excused himself and exited the reception area, to find Renea Tam and his luggage, ported by a State Department employee pushing a cart.

"I don't think you need that many clothes," Tam said, looking at the cart. "You're going on vacation, not moving away."

"My vacation is three weeks long," Durham said. "I want to spend very little of that time doing laundry."

"You're staying at an embassy," Tam said. "They have *staff* there. Who would do your laundry."

"In the future I will set forth with a single change of clothes in a duffel bag," Durham said. "But as my shuttle to the *Chandler* is leaving in forty minutes, this time I'll just have to manage."

Tam grinned at this, and the three of them headed toward the shuttle to the *Chandler*. Durham took his leave of his assistant at the shuttle door and took a seat on it, across from the only other passenger, a young man with dark hair.

"I liked your speech today," the young man said, after the shuttle had departed from Phoenix Station and was making its way to the *Chandler*.

Durham, who had been resting with his eyes closed, cracked them open and glanced at the speaker, looking him over. "You look familiar."

"You were introduced to me earlier today," the young man said. "Don't worry, I don't expect you to remember. I expect you shook a lot of hands today."

"You're in the diplomatic corps?" Durham asked.

"No," the young man said. "But a friend of mine is. Hart Schmidt."

"One of Abumwe's people."

"Yes. He and I went to school together. Well, he was about three years ahead of me. But our dads were friends, so I got to know him. When he found out I was going to be on Phoenix Station on my way to the *Chandler*, he invited me to the ceremony. I was in the back for most of it. I'm Rafe Daquin." He reached over and held out a hand.

Durham took it. "You're crew on the *Chandler*, then," he said.

"Yes," Daquin said. "I'm a pilot."

"That's not a bad job."

"Thank you," Daquin said. "I get to travel and see the universe. I expect you get to do the same as a diplomat."

"Not as much as I used to," Durham said. "I'm a bureaucrat now. The most I get to see of the universe these days is my desk."

"Why are you traveling now?"

"Vacation," Durham said. "I'm going to Huckleberry, to see friends and do some hiking."

"Why travel on the *Chandler*, if you don't mind me asking?" Daquin said. "We're a cargo ship. I'd think you'd just have one of your diplomatic ships take you."

"Borrowing a diplomatic corps ship to taxi me to my vacation spot would be looked on as misappropriation of resources, I think," Durham said, smiling. "And also there were none going my way when I needed it. Anyway the secretary encourages us to support private enterprise." He closed his eyes again, hoping Daquin would pick up the hint.

He didn't. "Do you really think diplomacy is treason?" Daquin asked. "That the Colonial Union sees it that way, I mean."

Durham kept his eyes closed. "I may have been exaggerating for effect," he said. "But it's certainly true that given a choice, the Colonial Union would rather shoot than talk. It's gotten us in trouble."

"You know about the disappearing ships?" Daquin asked.

Durham cracked his eyes open again at this. "Disappearing ships," he said.

"More civilian ships are going missing over the last couple of years," Daquin said. "Cargo ships, mostly. Ships like the *Chandler*."

"There's always been piracy," Durham said. "That's one of the reasons why the Colonial Defense Forces were formed. That and other intelligent species trying to kill us."

"Right, but pirates usually go for cargo," Daquin said. "They don't make ships disappear."

"What do you think it is?" Durham asked. "What are the rumors?"

Daquin shrugged. "If you ask me, it's got to do with us losing the Earth. Other species know we've started rationing our military to deal with major problems, so they're starting to pick off trade ships to weaken the Colonial Union's infrastructure."

"Seems a long way to go about it," Durham said.

"Every little bit counts."

"This doesn't make you afraid?" Durham asked. "You're a pilot on a cargo ship. Presumably you're a target."

Daquin smiled. "I have to eat."

"That's a very practical way of looking at one's potential fears," Durham said.

"That, and I've been through some close scrapes before,"

Daquin said. "I should have been dead a couple of times already because of ship failures and accidents. I've survived."

"Have you," Durham said. "Why do you think that is?"

"I don't know," Daquin said. "I think I may just be luckier than most people." This time it was Daquin who closed his eyes and put his head back to rest. Durham watched him for a few moments before doing the same.

Three days out from Phoenix Station and less than one day prior to the skip to Huckleberry, Durham asked for and received a private audience with *Chandler*'s captain, Eliza Perez.

"What is this about?" Perez asked. The two of them were in her stateroom, which, like everything else on the *Chandler,* was cramped. "If you're going to complain about the accommodations, as you can see, you are traveling with the same appointments as the captain."

"The accommodations are fine, of course," Durham said. "Captain Perez, I have something to confess to you. I came onto your ship under false pretenses." He had his PDA in his hand. He activated it and handed it to Perez. "I booked passage on the *Chandler* with the story that I am headed for vacation on Huckleberry. In fact, I am going somewhere else entirely."

Perez took the PDA and looked at what was on the screen. "What is this?" she said.

"It's an official request from the State Department for you to take me to a destination I will give you once you give me back my PDA," Durham said. "It's a secure and official request, which is why I'm showing it to you on my PDA rather than just transferring the document to your own PDA. It's awkward to do it that way but this way you know the orders aren't forged."

"You just said 'orders,' " Perez said. "That's substantially different than a request."

"Officially it's a request, which you are able to refuse," Durham said. "Unofficially we both know it's not in your interest to refuse it."

"Where would I be taking you?"

"To a system that has nothing at all of interest in it, which makes it a good place to have a secret meeting."

"A secret meeting with whom?"

"That I can't tell you."

"Then I can't let you borrow my ship."

"That's not wise."

"Sending the *Chandler* to a destination far off our schedule for 'secret meetings' isn't *wise*, either," Perez said. "You either tell me what you're asking me to do, or it won't get done."

"And if I tell you?"

"Then it still might not get done," Perez said. "Because I still have to make a decision. But there is a difference between 'won't' and 'might.' So you don't have a choice."

"I'm meeting with representatives of the Conclave to—informally—discuss an alliance with them."

"Seriously," Perez said, after a moment. "An organization of four hundred alien species, most of whom tried to murder us, and you want to make friends with them."

Durham sighed. "Captain Perez, I don't think I actually have to tell you that the Colonial Union is in a deep well of shit at the moment," he said. "The cargo ships that whoever it is are picking off are just the start. Sooner or later someone is going to go after an established colony. Sooner or later someone is going to go after the Colonial Union itself. We're vulnerable and becoming more so every day. All they'll have to do is wait until we're weak enough to be attacked."

"And we think joining the Conclave is going to fix this."

"Not *joining*," Durham said. "An alliance. A mutual defense against aggression pact."

"This after the Colonial Union tried to destroy the Conclave,"

Perez said, and noted Durham's expression. "Yes, we all know about that. About the incident at Roanoke. I run a trade ship, Mr. Durham. You can keep news away from the official channels if you like but trade ships have their own lines of communication. We travel. We talk. We know."

"Then you know why the meetings have to be secret for the time being," Durham said. "If this round succeeds then we can do something more public. If it doesn't then it will never have happened. Another reason, incidentally, to have the *Chandler* take me to the meeting, and not one of the State Department's ships."

"There is a small matter of the cargo we're carrying," Perez said. "Gaalfruit and other highly perishable products. We timed our travel to arrive at Huckleberry just before the gaalfruit ripens. If we arrive even a few days late we can't sell it. Insurance won't cover the loss if we can't tell why the cargo didn't arrive in time."

"Obviously the Colonial Union Department of State will purchase your cargo."

"All of it."

"Yes, and before you ask, yes, at fair market value," Durham said.

"It's not just about the cargo," Perez said. "We have relationships with distributors. We are supposed to pick up new cargo as well. Also agricultural products. Also highly perishable. If we're not there when we're supposed to be, they lose out and we damage that relationship."

"State will cover it all."

"That's going to cost a lot of money."

"Yes, well," Durham said, and smiled. "The Colonial Union actually creates the money in question, so I don't think covering your expenses and expectations will be a problem."

Perez was silent for a moment.

"Is there anything else you would like?" Durham asked.

"Would you like me to promise to wash and wax the *Chandler* after I am done using it?"

"I don't like this," Perez said.

"I can understand that," Durham said. "I do apologize for presenting it to you this way. I am under orders. You can, at least, understand why secrecy is actually important for this mission."

"Do you think it's going to work?" Perez asked. "The mission, I mean."

"I think if it doesn't, you should probably spend all the money you're going to make off this trip," Durham said. "And spend it as quickly as you can."

The first thought that came to Rafe Daquin as he bubbled up uneasily into consciousness was, *I can't feel my legs.*

The second thought he had, after another moment, was, *I can't feel my anything.*

Rafe sunk back into unconsciousness after that, falling through a blackness of indeterminate length and depth.

Rafe was dreaming and knew he was dreaming, because this was one of those dreams where he stood still and everything moved around him.

He started on the bridge of the *Chandler,* beginning his first day as an apprentice pilot, after six months at navigation and a year in the ranks of the engineers before that. The *Chandler's* chief of pilots was not entirely pleased to find Rafe in her charge. Rafe had been dumped into her lap by Captain Walden, and he knew that Lieutenant Skidmore thought Walden had been bribed by Rafe's family to accelerate him through the ranks. And, well, she had; Rafe's father told him as much the last time the *Chandler* was at Phoenix Station. In Rafe's dream he was experiencing Skidmore's thinned lips and otherwise carefully neutral demeanor for the first time.

Rafe's response in the dream was the same as it was in life: outward careful politeness and attentiveness, inward lack of concern because the fix was already in, and he was going to be a pilot whether Skidmore liked it or not. She hadn't liked it. She left the *Chandler* not too long after. This occasioned Rafe's promotion to assistant pilot, right on schedule, which was to say, ahead of schedule and ahead of others.

A blink-shift and he was in the headmaster's office at Tangipahopa Hall, waiting for either his mother or father to arrive. This time it was for punching one of the sixth-form students in the head; other times it would have been for infiltrating the dining hall at 3 A.M., stealing one of the custodial carts for a joyride, or taking money to change grades for other students (and then not doing it, which prompted one of his unsatisfied customers to complain). Rafe was hoping it would be his father, who graded transgressions on a curve, as opposed to his mother, who emphatically did not. Rafe's eventual graduation from Tangipahopa required his father agreeing to speak at the graduation ceremony, and his mother funding a science lab.

Another blink and it was the day after Rafe's graduation from University of Metairie, with an ordinary degree in engineering, earned less by lack of ability than by overall lack of attendance and interest. His mother was telling him she wouldn't sign off on the release of his trust fund, which customarily was given to the Daquin children on completion of their degree. Rafe pointed this out; his mother noted that "customary" was not the same as "obligatory," and then stood there daring him to argue the point with her, she who regularly argued cases before the Phoenix High Court.

Rafe did not take the challenge. He instead looked to his father, whose face was carefully blank. He was not stupid enough to argue with Colette Daquin either. Nor could he do anything on his ow the rules of the Daquin Family Corporation and Trust, if they were living, had to sign off on any trust disbursements prior to thirty-five years old (standard). Colette Daquin wanted her slacker child to get a job that would fill in the large and obvious blanks in his education, *not* with the family business. Jean-Michel Daquin suggested the Colonial merchant space fleet. An old supper club acquaintance would find an opening on one of his ships.

A final shift and Rafe was not standing anymore. He was running through the corridors of the *Chandler,* slower than he wanted, trying to avoid whoever it was who had taken the ship, and failing as two of the raiders stepped out of the T intersection ahead of him. Rafe skidded on his heels and turned, falling over his legs in the process. He righted himself and prepared to sprint away and was knocked off his feet for good by a shot to the back of the head.

In the dream as in real life Rafe could feel the shot strike his skin, impact against the bone of his skull, and begin to burrow through into his brain. In the dream as in real life Rafe felt the cold shock of certainty that this was the moment he was going to die, and the thought that rocketed through his brain before there was nothing else at all:

Unfair.

"All right, I give up," Colonel Abel Rigney said, looking into the glass-walled State Department conference room at the two unsmiling men sitting there. "Who are they?"

Colonel Liz Egan pointed, using the index finger on the hand holding her coffee cup. "The humorless one on the left is Alastair Schmidt," she said. "He's Phoenix's minister of trade and transport. The humorless one on the right is Jean-Michel Daquin. He's the CEO and chairman of Ballard-Daquin, which is one of the largest shipping companies on the planet."

"That's great," Rigney said. "And we're meeting with them, why, precisely?"

"Because Secretary Galeano told me to," Egan said.

"Let me rephrase," Rigney said. "Why am *I* meeting with them?"

"Because they want to talk about merchant ships being pirated and what we're doing about it, and if memory serves, that's something you know about."

"Fine, but why do they care?" Rigney asked. "Phoenix's Minister of Trade and Transport doesn't have any jurisdiction over interplanetary or interstellar trade."

"He has jurisdiction over the spaceports."

"Right, but his interests stop right around the stratosphere. Piracy is a problem, but it's not his problem. There's not enough of it to have an impact on his planet's trade." Rigney pointed to Jean-Michel Daquin. "Is it his ships getting pirated?"

Egan shook her head. "Ballard-Daquin is planetside only."

"I'm back to my original question," Rigney said. "My second original question, I mean. The one about why are we meeting them."

"You didn't let me finish," Egan said, very calmly, which is how Rigney knew he was close to being taken to the woodshed.

"Sorry about that," Rigney said.

Egan nodded and pointed to Daquin. "His son Rafe is a pilot on the *Chandler*, which is a merchant ship that went missing a week ago."

"Missing as in overtaken by pirates and late to its next destination, or *missing* missing?" Rigney asked.

"You tell me," Egan said. "That's actually *your* department, Abel."

Rigney grunted and quickly accessed his BrainPal for the latest on the *Chandler*. "We sent a skip drone out when it was two days late to Erie," he said, reading. "It's the new policy after Earth Station went down."

"And?"

"And nothing," Rigney said. "It wasn't where it should have been pre-skip, and there's no evidence of it being destroyed. We have nothing."

"So it's missing missing," Egan said.

"Looks like."

"And now you know why Daquin is here."

"How do you want to play this?" Rigney said.

"How I wanted to play it before this conversation," Egan said. "I want you to talk to them about what the CDF is doing about piracy. Make it informative, sympathetic, and conversational."

"You might be better with the sympathetic part," Rigney said. "You're the one who ran a media empire back on Earth."

Egan shook her head. "I was CEO," she said. "You don't become CEO by being sympathetic. I had PR people for that."

"So that's my job here?" Rigney asked. "PR flack?"

"Yes, it is," Egan said. "Any problems with that?"

"I guess not," Rigney said. "And you wouldn't care if I did."

"I would care," Egan said. "Later."

"That's comforting," Rigney said.

Egan nodded and motioned toward the two men waiting in the room. "The way I see it is that between the two of us we can answer their questions and convince them we are on top of things, and then shuffle them off as close to happy and satisfied as we can. Which will make my boss happy. Which will make me happy. And then I will owe you a favor. Which should make *you* happy."

"So, a never-ending circle of happiness, is what you're saying."

"I never said 'never-ending,'" Egan said. "There's no point in overpromising. Just a little happiness. Take what you can get, these days. Come on."

Egan and Rigney entered the conference room, introduced themselves to Schmidt and Daquin, and sat down across the table from the two men.

"Minister Schmidt, I have the honor of being acquainted with your son Hart," Egan said.

"Do you, now," Schmidt said. "He hasn't mentioned you, I'm afraid."

"I'm better acquainted with his boss, Ambassador Abumwe."

"Ah," Schmidt said. "Late of the unpleasantness at Earth Station."

"Yes," Egan said. "We were pleased that her entire team, including Hart, survived the attack."

Schmidt nodded.

Your turn, Egan sent to Rigney, through her BrainPal. *Informative. Conversational. Sympathetic.*

"Mr. Daquin," Rigney said. "I want you to know that prior to this meeting I accessed the latest information about the *Chandler*. I know you must be anxious—"

"One hundred sixty-five million metric revenue tonnes," Daquin said, interrupting Rigney.

"Excuse me?" Rigney said, taken off balance by the interruption.

"My company ships one hundred sixty million metric revenue tonnes of cargo through Phoenix Home Port to Phoenix Station, and to the ships that berth here," Daquin said. "That's close to ninety percent of the shipping that runs through Phoenix Home Port to this space station of yours."

"I did not know that," Rigney said, not sure where this was leading but not wanting to ask directly.

"I understand my telling you this fact must appear random," Daquin said. "But I need you to understand that figure because it will offer gravity to what I tell you next."

"All right," Rigney said, and glanced over to Egan, who was not returning his glance.

"You know about the *Chandler*, and my son," Daquin said.

"Yes," Rigney said. "I was just about—"

"You were just about to tell me nothing," Daquin said,

interrupting again and silencing Rigney once more. "I'm not a stupid man, Colonel Rigney, nor am I without resources, which include Minister Schmidt here. I'm well aware you currently have no idea what happened to *Chandler* or any of its crew. Please do me the courtesy of not trying to placate me with your vapidity."

"Mr. Daquin," Egan said, interjecting herself into the conversation, which Rigney assumed meant that he was being benched. "Perhaps it's best if you come right out with whatever it is you came here to say."

"What I have to say is simple. I control ninety percent of all the cargo that comes up and through Phoenix Station," Daquin said. "Ninety percent of the food. Ninety percent of essential materials. Ninety percent of everything that makes your space station"—Daquin emphasized these two words—"habitable and the place from which the Colonial Union runs its little empire of planets. If I don't know within a week the certain fate of the *Chandler* and its crew, shipping to Phoenix Station stops."

This was met with silence all around. Then Egan turned to Schmidt. "This is unacceptable."

"I agree," Schmidt said. "And I told Jean-Michel that very thing before we came up here."

"But you still brought him here to make this ultimatum," Egan said.

"I did," Schmidt said. "Which should in itself tell you the lack of options I had, as minister of trade and transport, in dealing with this."

"Perhaps it was not advisable to let one company handle the vast majority of shipping to Phoenix Station," Egan said.

Schmidt smiled thinly at this. "I would agree, Colonel Egan," he said. "But if you're looking to blame the Phoenix government, you're going to need to look at the Colonial Union contracts first. You're the ones who have given Ballard-Daquin control of your shipping, not us."

"We can't guarantee that we will have any information," Rigney said, to Daquin. "We're not being lazy about this, Mr. Daquin. But if a ship or its wreckage"—Rigney regretted the phrasing almost immediately, but there was nothing to be done for it at the moment—"is not found immediately, the task of finding it becomes exponentially more difficult."

"This is your problem," Daquin said.

"Yes, it is," Rigney said. "But if you are going to put us on the hook for this problem, you need to understand its scope. What you are asking may well be impossible in the timeframe you're asking for."

"Mr. Daquin," Egan said. Daquin turned his attention to her. "Allow me to be entirely frank with you."

"All right," Daquin said.

"I sympathize with your concern for the *Chandler* and her crew, and your son," Egan said. Rigney noted wryly that it was Egan, after all, who ended up deploying the *sympathy* card. "But you are mistaken if you think that attempting to hold Phoenix Station's shipping hostage is going to work. For one thing, the shipping we get from Phoenix can be replaced by other colonies. For another, the damage you'll cause Phoenix's export economy will be immense." Egan pointed to Schmidt. "Whether Minister Schmidt here wants to tell this to you or not, he and his government will be quickly obliged to nationalize your company. And no matter what, you'd find yourself in court for violating your contracts with the Colonial Union. It's also entirely possible, because Phoenix Station is the seat of the Colonial Union government, that your attempt to starve it out of existence will be looked on as treason. I don't think I need to tell you that the Colonial Union is not notably forgiving of that."

Daquin smiled. "Thank you, Colonel Egan," he said. "I know a little of your history. I know you were a CEO on Earth. It's clear we speak the same language. So allow me to offer you the compliment of being equally blunt with you. Your threat of replacing Phoenix shipping with shipping from other colonies is empty. The Colonial Union is *weak*, Colonel Egan. You've lost the Earth and you're not getting it back. You're running out of soldiers and the colonies know that when that happens you're going to start preying on them to fill the Colonial Defense Force ranks. That makes them all nervous, makes them all finally question whether the Colonial Union has come to the end of its usefulness.

"You start ordering shipping from other colonies for Phoenix Station, they're going to want to know why. And when they find out that it's because Phoenix is starving you from below, some of them are going to realize how weak you are right now and decide it's better to break away now than wait until you've bled them all a little more. You know that. I know that. You don't dare show all the other colonies how weak you truly are."

"A pretty speech that conveniently forgets that your company will be nationalized before that can happen," Egan said.

"Schmidt," Daquin said.

"The Phoenix government won't nationalize Ballard-Daquin," he said, to Egan. "Right now we're a coalition government. That coalition is both unpopular and unstable. As bad as Daquin shutting down exports would be, attempting to nationalize the company would be worse. It would fracture the government. The current government would rather be unpopular and in power than unpopular and out of it."

"The issue could be forced," Egan said.

"The Colonial Union could force the issue," Schmidt agreed. "But that is a solution that is worse than the problem, Colonel Egan, Colonel Rigney." He motioned to Daquin with a slight nod of his head. "Right now you just have one citizen of Phoenix irrationally angry with you. If you force the issue, you'll have a billion quite rationally angry with you. And that anger will be certain to spread. Jean-Michel is right: The Colonial

Union is weak at the moment. You don't want to advertise the fact."

"You have a week," Daquin said.

"Even if we could accept your demands, a week is not nearly enough time," Rigney said.

"I don't care what you think is nearly enough time," Daquin said.

"It's not about what I *think*," Rigney said, more testily than he intended. That, at least, seemed to cut Daquin off. "It's about the limitations of travel and communication. We don't live in a science fictional universe, Mr. Daquin. We can't just zap messages instantaneously from one part of space to another. We have to use skip drones and ships that have to travel to where space is flat before they can leave a star system. Even if we were to start an intensive search and investigation *today*, the fact of how travel works means we have almost no chance of getting you information in a week. Hell, we are *already* searching for the *Chandler*. We *still* would be lucky to get you information in a week."

"I'm not moved," Daquin said.

"I understand that," Rigney said. "But this, at least, isn't something that can be negotiated. If you are only giving us a week, you might as well make your power play now, because we *will* fail you. But if this is actually about your son, Mr. Daquin, then you're going to give us the time to do our job. And our job is what you want us to do: find the *Chandler*."

"How much time," Daquin said.

"Four weeks."

"Two weeks."

"No, Mr. Daquin," Rigney said. "Four weeks. You know shipping and you know what you can do with your company. I know our ships and what they can do. I'm not bargaining with you. I'm telling you the time we need to do this. Take it or don't."

370 | John Scalzi

Daquin looked over to Schmidt and to Egan, and then turned back to Rigney. "Four weeks," he said, and then stood up and walked out of the room.

"You know this is going to end badly for him," Egan said to Schmidt after he'd gone.

"If all that happens is that it ends badly for him, I will be profoundly grateful," Schmidt said, and stood himself. "My problem is that I don't see any way that it doesn't end badly for all the rest of us." He turned to Rigney. "At least you've given me a little more time to prepare. I should thank you for that, but I don't think it's going to matter." Schmidt excused himself and left.

"Well, this was a fun little meeting," Rigney said to Egan, when they were alone.

"You going to be able to find this ship in four weeks?" Egan asked.

"I'm going to try," Rigney said.

"Don't try," Egan said. "Do it. Otherwise in a month we'll all be eating each other alive."

"Literally," Rigney said.

"Having that happen literally would be the worst-case scenario," Egan said.

Acknowledgments

It's been my custom in my book acknowledgments to give a shout-out to the people at Tor who have worked on the book in order to bring it to you, my editor, Patrick Nielsen Hayden, first among them. This time, I want to even more directly acknowledge them, because this time I was a particularly troublesome author—I blew deadlines that I should not have and thus made them go into high-speed mode on their end to get the book out on time. Note I said "high-speed" mode and not "panic" mode—they're too good at their jobs to panic.

So: to Patrick, to Miriam Weinberg, to Christina MacDonald (copy editor), Rafal Gibek (production editor), Karl Gold (production manager), Heather Saunders (designer), Nathan Weaver (managing editor), Megan Hein (assistant to the managing editor), Caitlin Buckley (digital managing editor), and Natalie Eilbert (senior QA associate), thank you, thank you, and again, thank you. I'm sorry you had to deal with me being a problem. I will try very hard not to be a problem to you in the future. And if I am, you can punch me (uh, like, on the arm. Not too hard, please). A shout-out to Tor UK and the folks there for their work on this as well, to Steve Feldberg and everyone at Audible, and, heck, to everyone at all of my publishers, everywhere.

Seriously: Thank you, everyone, who worked on this book with me. People like to rant about getting "the middleman" out of book production, and I wonder if they realize just how much the "middlemen"—the folks who do *everything else* but write the words in the book—add to their enjoyment of the work they read. I know, and I am grateful for the work and care.

Additional thanks to John Harris for his continuing and amazing artistic representations of the Old Man's War universe, and to Irene Gallo, Tor's art director, for her care and appreciation of the visual side of these books, and Peter Lutjen for his design. And to Alexis Saarela and Patty Garcia, who handle my publicity.

Many thanks to my literary agents, Ethan Ellenberg and Bibi Lewis, for selling me in this and many other languages. Thanks also to Joel Gotler, my film/TV agent, with whom I always enjoy taking a meeting.

My wife, Kristine, is the first reader of everything I do and is the person I most trust in the world to call me on my crap as a writer. If you enjoy the book, the credit goes to her (if you don't, it's my fault). I give her thanks and as always my everlasting love.

My wife is my first reader, but I am deeply fortunate that she is not the only one. This is the sixth book in the Old Man's War universe; as I write this it's been ten years since *Old Man's War* was first released. The reason we have gotten this far into it is that so many of you, all over the world, started with it and kept reading. When I think about it, I am amazed. There is so much I owe to each of you, personally and professionally. Thank you so much.

—John Scalzi
April 6, 2015